Dying to
Have Her

Heather Graham

Dying to Have Her

WHEELER
PUBLISHING, INC.
ROCKLAND, MA

★ AN AMERICAN COMPANY ★

Published in Large Print by arrangement with New American Library, a
division of Penguin Putnam Inc., in the United States and Canada.

Wheeler Large Print Book Series.

Set in 16 pt Plantin.

Library of Congress Cataloging-in-Publication Data

Graham, Heather.
    Dying to have her / Heather Graham.
        p. (large print) cm.(Wheeler large print book series)
    ISBN 1-58724-085-8 (hardcover)
    1. Private investigators—California—Los Angeles—Fiction. 2. Tele-
vision actors and actresses—Fiction. 3. Los Angeles (Calif.)—Fiction.
4. Soap operas—Fiction. 5. Large type books. I. Title. II. Series

[PS3557.R198 D95 2001]
813'.54—dc21   2001026359
                                                              CIP

Dedicated to some wonderful Californians who have made their great state a special place to me: Meryl Sawyer, Red and family, Kat and Larry Martin (even though they've moved!), Mark and Jo Lichtman, and William Fabrizio. Also, to some great stores, including Duck Soup and Dark Delicacies. And to the Orange County RWA, with admiration and thanks.

Also, to Lily Zeledon and Laura Perez, with tremendous thanks for their enthusiasm.

ACKNOWLEDGMENTS

Special thanks to Lance Taubold and Rich Devin, who have shared their casting and acting experiences in the field of daytime drama with me. Again, a deep note of thanks to Greg Marx. Any mistakes and misconceptions are my own. Also, once more, to the incredible Janet Leigh, whose beauty and grace inspired the first book, and therefore, the second.

Thanks, also, to the patient officers of the L.A. County police who were willing to answer so many questions.

Chapter 1

Jane Dunne entered the dressing room and paused, vaguely aware that even her pose on the threshold was dramatic. She was a dramatic person, and she did everything with a flair— whether or not she had an audience. At the moment, her curiosity and careful perusal were natural.

She was using another woman's dressing room. For now. But maybe not for long.

There were flowers on her dressing table. A wonderful, extravagant display. A dozen red roses in the center were surrounded by pinks and yellows, then encompassed by magnificent flowers in a shade of magenta unlike any she had ever seen before.

Yes, she had come a long way.

She had gone to the right parties, pulled the right strings, played the right games. Not to mention the fact that she did have talent. It had taken her a while. She wasn't exactly a spring chicken anymore, and this was a young town. But she was on the rise.

She had a nice spot in a major movie about

1

to open, plus a choice role on what might very well soon be *the* most popular soap on the air, even if it was temporary.

She swept into the room and sat.

There was a note on the dressing table by the flowers. She ignored it at first, certain that it was some gushing memo from the producers, directors, or even her fellow actors. Sitting before the mirror, she fluffed out her hair, studied her reflection with total objectivity—and nodded slowly, approving what she saw. Two tons of thick, platinum blond hair. Enhanced by Bobby at the Tahi Salon, to be sure, but then...what *was* life without a bit of enhancement and drama? Her eyes were her best feature. Huge and blue—no, violet. Her smile deepened. It felt good to be where she was.

She smiled, leaned forward, still gazing deeply into the mirror, and said softly, "Life has just begun. I'm gonna live forever. Yeah, baby. I am gonna live forever."

She sat back again, glancing at her watch. She inhaled on a deep breath, closed her eyes, and opened them. Her gaze fell on the note. Perhaps she'd better open it.

She slipped open the envelope and quickly read the words.

Roses are red
And blood makes you dead.
Violets are blue
Baby, death you are due!

She threw the note down in anger, alarmed to realize that she was shaking, and reached into her purse for a cigarette. She'd tried to quit smoking. Hell, you couldn't smoke anywhere in California anymore. Bad for your own health, secondhand smoke, killing the neighbors and all that. Frankly, she'd tried to quit because she'd seen what wrinkles years of smoking eventually caused. But then, she'd smoked to begin with to keep from eating.

Right now she wanted a cigarette, and so she lit one with her monogrammed lighter.

She wasn't supposed to be smoking here. No ashtray in Miss Connolly's dressing room. She rose anxiously and found coffee cups and saucers on a ledge. She brought a saucer to the dressing table, stared at her reflection again, and then at the note.

"Ass!" she hissed. She tossed back her hair. "I'm going to live forever. And you'll be sorry as hell, you fool!"

She squashed out the cigarette, refusing to need it. Using her monogrammed lighter, she set fire to the note and watched as it burned over the saucer. *Most* of it. She realized the saucer was slightly wet, and part of the paper had stuck to it. Someone, probably that mousy little Jinx, had just washed it.

"Burn, dammit," she muttered. She started to lift the paper, but a tap on her door made her jump. Unnerved, she snapped out her words in a voice far too loud for poise. "Come in!"

3

A small blonde poked her head in. She was carrying a makeup bag that seemed to be bigger than she was. "Miss Dunne—"

"You again? What are you doing here?"

"Martha, Miss Dunne. I'm your assigned makeup person—"

"The hell you are!" Jane snapped. "When I started three weeks ago, I was promised Gilby Sayres, a personal makeup man."

Martha retreated into herself, like a turtle. "I'm sorry. Jim Novac told me this morning that I was still working with you."

"Jim Novac is the director. I was promised by the producers—" She broke off, wondering why she was making such a big deal out of this, arguing with this...*nothing* of a girl. No, it was a big deal. She had to establish her star status once and for all.

"Miss Dunne," Martha began again, "I am so sorry—"

"No, baby, don't you be sorry. But someone will be."

Jane swept out of the dressing room. She was tall, thin and elegant, and one thing she had learned to do over the years was *sweep*. She stormed onto the soundstage.

An assistant director was blocking stand-ins where she and Serena McCormack would soon be filming their first scene together. Lighting technicians were raising the long horizontal poles that held the overhead lights. The setting was an Italian restaurant where the characters were to have an argument. Full of self-righteous anger, Jane strode onto

4

the set, staring at the befuddled little nobodies standing in for the real talent.

"Where's Novac?" she barked. "You all heard me. Where's Jim Novac?"

The assistant director—a kid who looked like he could hardly be out of high school—spoke quickly to the stand-ins. "Thank you, we're through for now."

"Hey! I'm talking to you!" Jane persisted.

The stand-ins fled from the set. The sandy-haired kid spoke to her politely. "I'll find Mr. Novac."

She watched him scurry away. She looked around the set, feeling the heat from the overhead lights. A lighting tech on a huge A-frame ladder was staring down at her. "You! What are you looking at?" she demanded.

He didn't answer, but slid down the ladder, exiting the set.

"Jane, there you are!"

Serena McCormack was striding toward her now. Serena, with her beautiful turquoise eyes and thick mane of auburn hair, ready smile, and easy sway. Her words seemed sincere. Her elocution was perfect, her voice melodious. Jane hated her, but of course Serena didn't know that. It wasn't personal. Serena was simply in her way. Always at ease. Loved by the press. Adored by directors. Enough to make you want to throw up.

"Um, hello, Serena."

"What's the matter?" Serena asked.

"These people don't stand by their agreements!" Jane said angrily.

Jim Novac, with the sandy-haired assistant at his side, came out onto the set. An attractive man nearing middle age, he didn't seem to see her at first, though surely the assistant had told him she wanted to see him. Consulting a clipboard, he walked across the set, stopping at a table not far from where she stood.

"Fresh flowers, guys," he told his assistant. "Did I ask for withered flowers, day-old flowers? No, I do not think so. Do you know the meaning of *fresh*? Now—"

"Mr. Novac!" She was distressed to realize that she had to snap out his name to draw his attention.

"Jane?" He turned, looking at her expectantly, a warm smile on his face. "Good, you're right in place. Now—"

"I'm not in place! I'm not going on until we have things straightened out."

"Oh?" He folded his arms over his chest. "What things?"

Makeup people, set people, camera people, the prop peons—all were watching them. She had to play this carefully. She walked around the table to him. She noticed that there was a mark on the floor, indicating Serena's first blocked position.

Smoothly, calmly, with determination, she put her hands on her hips. She was vaguely aware of a light creaking sound above her head, but, set on her purpose, she ignored it.

"Three weeks ago I was promised my own makeup man, Novac." She purposely left out the *Mister*. "Promised. Do you know the meaning of *promised*?"

She saw his face redden. "Your makeup man wasn't in the budget."

She plucked one of *yesterday*'s roses from the vase on the table and waved it beneath his nose. "Maybe fresh flowers weren't in the budget. I have some in my room. From the producers." Well, that was a lie, but how would he know? "The producers. Who made a promise to me. Do you want to know another word used frequently with *promise*? It's *contract*. A contract is one of those things that helps see to it that people who make promises keep them."

She saw Jim's Adam's apple bob.

Suddenly the creaking noise grew louder. She looked up.

The lights appeared to be moving. The entire light pole was dropping. She heard a noise—a whir, a gasp, a collective gasp from everyone watching. The lights were coming down—fast.

A scream rose to her throat. It never left her lips.

A huge spotlight landed directly on her. It struck her on the head and scraped down her cheek, knocking her to the wood stage floor. She was aware of blinding pain. She stared up to the rafters, seeing double. Then her vision started fading. She knew that she was bleeding. The pain was so sharp...and then she felt her limbs growing numb.

She was aware only of the visions... So

much light. So bright. Blinding her. Then...the light was fading. All vision nearly gone.

I'm going to live forever! her heart cried out in panic.

No. Nobody lived forever.

Someone on the set screamed at last. She was only vaguely aware of the sound.

Fade to black.

Her fingers, which had clutched the rose, uncurled. It fell free from her hand. Yesterday's rose.

Nobody lived forever.

Chapter 2

Serena McCormack never came to work expecting the ordinary. The people with whom she worked were just simply too...artistic. Or one might say eccentric. The term *crazy* might work just as well.

But this morning the totally unexpected, the tragic, had occurred.

They were all shell-shocked. A member of their cast had just died in a horrible, bizarre accident. The paramedics had come, and with little hope except for a faint pulse, Jane Dunne had been rushed off to the hospital, where she had been pronounced dead on arrival.

Serena had stood there and watched it all. She'd been frozen in place at the shattering sound as the lights had fallen. Like everyone else, she had rushed to Jane, struggled to free the woman. The paramedics had responded within a matter of minutes, but it had seemed like eons.

Now the police were the only ones remaining. First had come a pair of uniformed officers, who tried to maintain the remaining integrity of an accident scene that crew members had already compromised in their efforts to reach Jane. Then a plainclothes detective named George Olsen arrived, taking charge. With him came a photographer and a forensics team, bagging and labeling bits and pieces and lights and equipment. Olsen listened gravely to the lighting technicians explain that this couldn't have happened, that they were good, they were thorough when they mounted the lights. They had safety systems in place, and they always double-tied electrical cords and support wires. Olsen actually was calming and reassuring to the crew, telling them that they would get to the bottom of the incident. The restaurant set was roped off with yellow crime tape, and though Jane had died in the ambulance and not on the floor, a chalk mark had been drawn to show where she fell. The photographers took pictures of the area from every angle. The forensics team picked up every tiny piece of the spotlight they could find, carefully handling it all with their gloved hands, and then duly marking each of the plastic bags.

"Routine," they had all been assured. They

were all being questioned again, one by one, alone. This was shocking to them, but it was business as usual to the police.

"Jane Dunne. Dead, on her first day of work." It was Kelly Trent, seated with Serena just outside the office of producer Joe Penny—a space now taken over by the police—who spoke. Kelly played Serena's younger sister on the set. Five-seven, slim, sweet, with wide eyes and a look of innocence, she was the middle sister. Serena herself had deep auburn hair, Kelly's was a shade lighter, and Jennifer Connolly—whose maternity leave had brought Jane Dunne to the set—was a strawberry blonde, an inch taller than Kelly, an inch shorter than she. They'd been perfectly cast as sisters. All three had been with *Valentine Valley* since the show's first day, and though they were constantly at odds on the show, they were close friends off the set. The cast had supposedly been an assembly of "beautiful people." As the oldest sister, and the oldest of the three cast members, Serena was usually the one to reassure the other two. She was the take-charge sister. But right now she was feeling awfully unnerved herself. It didn't help that everyone had been so concerned for her because she had been so close to Jane when the light fell.

"It's so sad," Serena said. That sounded lame. Was that the best that she could come up with?

"Poetic justice!" snorted someone nearby. Startled, Serena turned to see Allona Sainge, one of the writers on the show. She was being as outspoken as usual. Allona was a striking African American woman with skin a stunning shade of copper and eyes that were almost yellow, gorgeous cat eyes. Allona was often frustrated because plot lines seldom had much to do with reality. She was still astonished when the producers would ask her opinion and then come up with ideas that totally disregarded everything she'd said.

Allona let out a sigh as she saw the way Serena looked at her. "Oh, I am sorry," she said. "That did sound awful, didn't it? But what a bitch she was."

"Allona!" Kelly whispered. "She's dead!"

"That's why I say that it was poetic justice. The spotlight *didn't* hit Serena—and it might have. That is what scares me most—*you* were on that set. This could have happened to you. I'm sorry, but you would have been a real loss to both humanity and the show. Jane Dunne...all right, I'm sorry she's dead. It's tragic. But she was scratching and scrounging her way up the ladder, wanting a rewrite on every scene so she could take center stage. She meant to get in so tight that Jennifer wouldn't be wanted back after her maternity leave."

"Allona, I'm glad that you're grateful it wasn't me, but God is going to strike you down. What you're saying is terrible," Serena said.

"Serena, you're too kind. God has spoken— He struck down Jane Dunne."

"It was a freak accident," Kelly said. "That's all."

"It was the hand of God," Allona muttered.

"The police aren't acting much like it was the hand of God," Kelly said. "Look, here comes poor Jinx. She's nearly in tears."

Serena's assistant was emerging from the door to Joe's office, where they were doing the interviews.

Jinx had come on the show about six months ago, and now Serena wondered what she had ever done without her. She helped Jennifer Connolly out, too, since she and Serena had always received the most fan mail and gifts. Even though Jennifer was on leave, her mail continued to pour in. Jinx was charged with the responsibility of responding.

A tiny person with huge blue eyes and sable hair, she was young, adorable, slim—and painfully shy.

"Jinx!" Serena jumped up. She always felt like the Jolly Green Giant next to Jinx, towering over her assistant's five-foot-two-inch frame. "Are you okay?"

"I think so," Jinx muttered. "I'm so confused. When they finished with me, I wasn't even sure that I was there, sitting in the office anymore. Oh, my God, Serena, it's just so horrible..."

"Yes, of course, it really is horrible," Serena said. "But you're done now. Go on home. Go relax, try to forget about it."

"There's so much mail... I'll take it with me," Jinx said.

"Don't you dare. Go home, go to the movies,

do something that will take your mind off this. The rest of us will be leaving when we're done. They're closing the set. Don't you dare work, do you hear me?"

Jinx was almost smiling. "Thanks. But if you need me for anything—"

"I'm going to go home; the show will wait, and the mail will wait. We'll make it all up when this is over—"

She broke off when she spied Jay Braden coming down the hallway. Dark-eyed, tall, and sleek, he was the actor who portrayed Randy Rock, muscled hunk and estranged husband of Jennifer's character on the show. Seeing him these days still gave her a start. Last year he'd had sandy blond hair. Because his character had gone through an almost-twin plot twist a few months back, he'd gone back to his own deep brown color. He looked good that way, she thought.

She thought that he had already been questioned.

"Jay, did they call you back?" she asked.

He shook his head. "I was about to head out. I heard you wound up at the tail end of the questioning since that cute lady cop had checked your hair and head for glass again. They should let you go. I mean, you were right there..."

"I'm all right. Really." Was she? She would never forget the look on Jane's face. Never forget the way her eyes had closed, the light fading from them. She'd still had a pulse, but standing there, watching as the paramedics worked, she had known that the pulse would fade, just as the light had faded from Jane's eyes.

"Jinxy, you okay?" Jay asked softly.

Jinx nodded. "Of course." She didn't look or sound all right.

Serena met Jay's questioning gaze. "Why don't you see Jinx home, Jay?"

"No, no, I don't want to be any trouble," Jinx protested.

But over her head Jay nodded at Serena. "Jinx, it's no trouble whatsoever. Let's get some fresh air, eh?"

"All right. Thanks. Maybe I am a little too shaky to drive. My car will be all right in the studio lot."

"Okay, let's go," Jay said.

Jinx flashed a weak smile at Kelly and Allona, and moved past them.

Watching Jinx and Jay leave, Allona let out a long sigh. "You do need kids," she said, studying Serena with a sage appraisal. "The maternal instinct is all over you. Poor little Jinx, hell. I promise you, the writers won't be getting any breaks for emotional adjustment. We'll be up for days. We have to totally redo all the scripts."

"They're not going to hire a replacement for Jane?" Kelly asked.

"The producers closeted themselves right away and the answer to that is no. We want to show our care and compassion to the world," Allona said.

"Miss McCormack?"

At the sound of her name, she nearly jumped

out of her seat. George Olsen was calling her in. He was a pleasant-looking man with large jowls, short-cropped white hair, and a coffee stain on his blue tie. He was probably good at his job, she thought. His voice was so carefully modulated, his expression so benign, that talking to him seemed like talking to a grandparent.

"Watch it," Allona warned softly. "He looks like Santa Claus, but I'm betting he knows how to go right for the jugular. Look how Jinx came out of that office!"

"Be strong," Kelly told her. "She's right. Think of Jinx."

"Jinx is shy and young. I'm not shy, and—well, I'm not young either," Serena murmured.

"Hey, we're talking about the queen of daytime television," Allona told Kelly. "She'll put those cops in their places."

Serena made a face at her and entered the office.

The detective offered his hand. "I know how upset you must be, Miss McCormack, but of course, as you already know, we have to question everyone about this tragic circumstance."

"Of course."

He was silent for a minute, smiling. "Do you wear contacts, Miss McCormack?"

"What? No. Why?"

"Nothing." He shook his head and smiled ruefully. "I admit I'm not a soap fan, but my wife is. She loves this show. Still, in person, Miss McCormack, you do have the most

15

extraordinary eyes. Aqua. Like the Caribbean Sea."

"Thanks. Thanks very much."

"And they're real?"

"They're not contacts. And they don't dye eye color yet, even in Hollywood."

He laughed, but she wondered if it was a real laugh. Did he start off with compliments to set people at ease? Yet she wasn't really nervous. A woman was dead. Tragically. An accident. And they were all shocked, emotionally drained and horrified. This was an inquiry to find out exactly what had happened. They had started with the lighting and set personnel, and they were being thorough, questioning anyone who had anything to do with the case. She would do whatever she could.

"Please, come in all the way and sit down, Miss McCormack."

He sat behind Joe's desk. She took the seat in front of it. She'd taken that same chair many times before, but never to face anyone other than Joe.

"She hadn't been here very long," Olsen said, shaking his head. His jowls wiggled.

"We're all in—total disbelief."

"Naturally." He leaned forward. "You were close when the light fell, Miss McCormack?"

She couldn't help shuddering. "Yes."

"Tell me how you came to be on the set."

"I was in the scene."

"But you hadn't started taping. Did you talk with Jane Dunne before the accident?"

"I said hello…but she was trying to get a point across to Jim Novac, our director."

"You hadn't seen her earlier this morning?"

"No. Actually, I'd tried to. I'd left my dressing room and headed for Jen's—well, Jane's room, since Jennifer's on maternity leave. But she wasn't there."

"Why?"

"Pardon?"

"Why were you going to see Miss Dunne?"

"Oh, well…she was new here, and I was going to walk on set with her and chat a bit before we started taping."

"But Miss Dunne had left?"

"Yes. She…like I said, she wanted to talk to Jim," Serena murmured.

Olsen sat back, watching her. "You've been with the show a long time—right, Miss McCormack?"

"About five years. Since it began."

"Um, so the show is near and dear to your heart?"

Serena felt the faintest twinge of guilt. Yes, she loved the show, but she'd also just done a screen test for a disaster movie that was sure to be a summer blockbuster. She'd done the shoot for a friend, not really planning ahead. If she got the role, and took it, she would either have to leave *Valentine Valley* or arrange for a very long leave of absence. She hadn't told anyone at the show, except for Jennifer.

"The show is near and dear to your heart?" Olsen repeated, shaggy brows furrowing.

"Very."

"And it's my understanding that Jennifer Connolly is one of your best friends."

"Absolutely true."

"Hm."

She leaned forward. "Excuse me. What is that 'hm' for?"

"Oh, just that Miss Dunne was a threat to your friend."

"A threat?" Serena stood up. "A threat? No, there was no way that any other actress would be a threat to Jennifer. Jen asked for time off to be with her baby; it's as simple as that. The producers love her, the director loves her, the cast loves her, and what is most important, sir, the audience loves her."

"Miss McCormack, please, please, sit!" Olsen said, apparently distressed. "There's been a terrible accident. I have to ask these questions."

"Fine. Let me try to answer you. Jennifer's place here is totally secure. This is a soap, and we have lots of room for errant daughters and wild, wicked women appearing from the past. Jane was asked onto the show, and she was wanted here, and none of us was in the least worried about our jobs. I went to see her as a friendly gesture—"

"Did you see anything unusual in the dressing room when you tried to find her?"

"No. Unless..." She paused, frowning.

"Unless?"

"Oh, nothing, really. Except that Jennifer doesn't smoke. Jane must have been more nervous about the role than she was letting on.

There are no ashtrays in the room. Jane had taken a saucer to use as an ashtray. And apparently she had burned a piece of paper. There was a charred scrap of something in the saucer along with the ashes. I'm not sure what that could possibly mean, but..."

"I'm assuming you checked that out?" Olsen said.

He was talking to someone behind Serena, a man seated on the couch at the far end of the room. She hadn't really looked at him. As the man stood up, her heart almost caught in her throat. It couldn't be.

Liam.

Liam Murphy, with whom she'd had a passionate affair before he'd walked out her door, never to return.

But it wasn't Liam. This man was tall, broad-shouldered, and well muscled, which had first made her think of Liam. He had thick, dark hair that made him a perfect barbarian type. She knew this detective. He had worked with Liam. He'd asked her out for coffee when she'd split up with Liam. She'd gone—admittedly, to stay close to Liam. She'd known it was wrong. But they'd had coffee one day, she'd seen a movie with him, and then they'd had dinner. That evening she'd told him the truth, that she just wasn't ready for another relationship.

Bill Hutchens was a nice man, attractive, serious, and capable of being very charming—and understanding. She wished she could have felt something for him. The chemistry just

19

hadn't been there, and he'd wanted more than she had to give. Still, they had remained friends. He liked being a cop, but he liked shows, movies, and actors as well. She had gotten him a walk-on in a Viking movie once, and he had helped her with a parking ticket.

"Bill!"

"Hi, Serena."

"Well, I see you two know each other," Olsen said.

"Old friends," Bill told him.

"Well, good. Bill is going to be in charge of the investigation here, Miss McCormack. So you call on him if you need to."

"Terrific," Serena said. Maybe it would be. Bill would understand that there wasn't a cast member on the soap who had felt even remotely threatened by Jane Dunne.

"Did you find the saucer and the charred paper?" Olsen asked.

Bill shook his head, watching Serena worriedly. "No."

"Are you sure of what you saw, Miss McCormack?" Olsen asked. "Maybe..." He lifted his hands.

"I'm sure of what I saw, because Jennifer doesn't smoke."

"Maybe someone removed it, not wanting anyone to speak badly of her now that...now that she can't defend herself," Bill suggested.

"And you looked thoroughly through the dressing room?" Olsen inquired. "You're sure you didn't miss it?"

The look that Bill gave his superior was

20

eloquent. Of course, he hadn't missed such a thing. He'd been a cop for more than ten years. He knew his business.

"Well..." Olsen murmured.

"Shall I sit back down, or were you finished with me, Lieutenant Olsen?" Serena inquired. She suddenly wanted to escape. This was really terrible. She had watched a woman die, and she did feel shaky, and she wanted to go home and be alone.

"Just one more thing, Miss McCormack."

"Yes?"

"You were so close to that light."

"What do you mean?"

"Weren't you supposed to be in that spot?"

"I...I think my marker was near where the light fell, yes."

Olsen nodded, as if he knew something she didn't.

"Lieutenant—"

"Don't you see, Serena?" he interrupted, leaning forward. "It could have been you beneath that light. Is there a reason anyone would want to kill you, Miss McCormack?" Olsen asked.

"What?" she asked, startled.

"Is there a reason anyone would want to kill you?"

"No. Emphatically no."

"They say you can be rather feisty."

"You'd have to arrest half of Hollywood if that was a crime."

"Miss McCormack—" Olsen began.

"I have no intention of leaving town."

"Of course not," Olsen said. He actually smiled. "But you should be careful as well, don't you think?"

"I'm always careful." She locked her doors, she had an alarm, she drove into her driveway backward so that she could escape if someone got in the house.

Olsen riffled through some notes on the desk. "Miss McCormack...your brother-in-law works on the set, right?"

"No, not really. My sister, Melinda, and her husband, Jeffrey, both have degrees in ancient history. Jeff specializes in Egyptology. He has been contracted as a consultant from time to time."

"Time to time has been lately—right?"

She nodded. "My character on the show is into archaeology. She's been to Cairo on a dig and brought back a number of artifacts. When she gets angry—or when she's afraid she's going to be caught in some evil deed or another—she heads back to Egypt." Serena offered him a small smile, reminding him that this was a soap opera they were talking about—entertainment loved by many, but not TLC or the Discovery Channel.

"Your brother-in-law was in this morning, right?" Olsen persisted.

She sighed. "Yes. Joe Penny had Jeff in to talk about some props he's acquiring. We're going to have an accident occur on a dig. But Jeff was gone before the lights fell. Look, Jeff isn't a real cast or crew member. He and Melinda are academics. They're not really

'Hollywood' types at all. They've been married nearly twenty-five years, and their major interest in life is their twins." She stopped, aware that she was defending him. "Lieutenant, what does this have to do with anything?"

"I like being thorough, that's all. This is L.A., and I see lots of things go down." He waved a hand in the air. "Like today. So you tell me, what do you think, Miss McCormack?"

"Think?" She arched a brow. "Frankly, I'm not thinking. I'm feeling. My heart bleeds for Miss Dunne, and in all honesty, even though I'm feeling really terrible and a lot of pain for a life lost, I thank God that it wasn't I. I thank Him sincerely for my life."

"I was just thinking that maybe you should have some protection."

Serena frowned. "A light fell, Lieutenant. No one was..."

Olsen leaned forward. "How often do lights just fall?" he asked.

"Well..." She'd never seen a light just fall before, but it wasn't impossible. "This was an accident," she said. "No one was..."

"Homicides often look like accidents," Olsen said. "Union people work here. Experts—who know how to work with lights. The investigation will take some time. I hope you're right, though, that it was merely a tragic accident." He stood. "Just take good care of yourself, Miss McCormack. Okay?"

"Sir, it's a promise."

He smiled. "A pleasure to meet you, Miss

McCormack. Oh, I may call you into the station soon for a formal deposition."

She nodded.

"Great eyes, Miss McCormack."

"Thanks."

She was dismissed. She hadn't seen Bill leaving, much less coming back into the room, but he had done so. He had apparently been assigned to see her out.

He squeezed her arm as he walked her through the door. "A lot more than great eyes, Serena," he told her. That was Bill—trying to be nice, trying to make her feel better. A nice, even-tempered guy. Why hadn't she been able to fall for him? In life, not even chemistry seemed fair. She had to go for the uncompromising macho man who gave no quarter.

"Thanks," she said softly. "Bill—"

"Hey, that was from a friend. Who hoped to be more, but I'm still glad to be a friend. A friend who's worried about you. Please—"

"Hey!" she murmured. She studied his handsome, too serious face, then gave him a kiss on the cheek. "I'll be very careful."

He nodded, ready to call in the next person. "Ms. Allona Sainge?"

Allona rose. "Here—right here," she said to Bill. Then, "Santa Claus—or jugular chewer?" she whispered to Serena.

"Hm. Mostly Mr. Claus. Honestly. But watch out for vein chomping, anyway."

Allona grimaced. "See you later, baby."

Serena nodded and watched as Allona elegantly sashayed into the office.

"I guess I'm last," Kelly said with a shiver.

Serena paused to squeeze her hand. "Want me to wait around?"

"Good heavens, no. Go home. This place is giving me the creeps today. Honestly, I just want to go home myself, sink into a hot tub, and have a big, big drink."

Serena nodded. She felt like doing absolutely the same.

It was going to be a very hot bath—and a very, very big drink.

Later, Olsen sat looking at his notes. He was done with the first round of questioning. Bill sat in front of him.

"Tragic accident?" Bill inquired. "Or..."

"We won't know anything until forensics finishes with the rigging," Olsen reminded him. "Accident. Yeah, it could have been. Such bizarre things do happen. But still..." He scratched his forehead. "You know what sticks in my craw? It's that Serena McCormack saw something in the deceased's dressing room that wasn't there when you went back to check."

Bill leaned forward. "Maybe she didn't really see anything. Maybe she was upset."

Olsen shook his head. "You've been a good cop for a long time, Bill. But I've been a cop much longer. There was no reason for her to be upset when she went by Jane Dunne's dressing room. She saw something."

"Lieutenant, I searched that room after we

first arrived. There was no ash-filled saucer in the room, no note."

"Right. But time passed between the accident and when we arrived." He tapped his pencil on the desk, thinking. "And what about that producer's idea?" He looked back at his sheet. "Joe Penny. He thinks Serena McCormack needs some protection." He shrugged. "He's right. There's a possibility that she was the intended victim. Jane Dunne was standing on a tape marking what should have been Serena McCormack's position."

"We don't know that there was an intended victim." Bill hesitated. "Pearson from forensics said there are no obvious marks that would indicate tampering on any of the lighting remnants they've gathered."

Olsen pursed his lips. "There's not enough there to warrant police protection. But if Penny wanted to hire someone on his own..."

"Serena's a friend," Bill said with quiet vehemence. "I will do my absolute best with whatever resources we have—"

Olsen let out a snort. "Hell, no, we don't have the manpower to guard her, even if it was an attempt on her." He looked up at Bill with a shrewd grin. "Look, this is a soap, a highly rated soap, in Hollywood, California. We'll tell Penny to hire a P.I. Then give Liam Murphy a call."

Bill hesitated. "Liam Murphy?"

"Is there a problem?"

"There might be some bad blood there."

"Why?"

"He and Serena McCormack dated for a

while. If you're trying to throw Liam some work, that's great, but—"

"I'm not throwing anyone anything," Olsen said irritably. "From what I understand, he's had more work than he did as a cop since he's gone out on his own. Liam is the best man I know for the job. He knows this place, and these people—especially after the past trouble here." He paused as a thought came to him. "Didn't you date Miss McCormack?"

"Dinners…a few casual dates. Then we became friends," Bill said.

Olsen grunted. "Then you have a current relationship, even if it's friendship. I'm not taking you off the case because of that."

"Serena and I had coffee once, dinner once, and saw one movie. Serena and Liam…" Bill was lost for a moment, then he shrugged. "They *dated*. It was different."

"He won't be taking her to a high school prom."

"No, of course not."

"This may be a tricky case, Bill. It looks like an accident; it might have been a murder. If Penny wants to be extra careful about the talent, it couldn't hurt."

Bill lifted his hands in resignation. "Yeah, all right."

"I need to see both of the producers. Penny and Larkin. Get them in here for me."

"Sir, you've spoken with them both—"

Olsen glared at Bill. "And get hold of Liam. We want to try very hard to keep whatever happened here down to just one…accident."

Chapter 3

Liam took one last look in the hatch of his black Jeep, marking off the contents. Fishing poles, skis, food boxes, tools, Miller Lite, and—the one major change in this trip's packing—a few packs of Seagram's wine coolers. Staring at them, he felt the slightest twinge of unease. He loved the wilderness, a rushing stream, the mountains. California was a great state, filled with boundless natural wonders.

All his life, he had been fond of the wilderness. All his life, he had been fond of women. He'd just never tried to mix the two before.

He liked being alone, with the natural world around him, though he didn't always go alone. Once or twice a year he met Charlie Eagle, a member of the Nez Perce tribe, and they fished, hunted, drank too much beer and shot up tin cans together, discussing the fate of the world. As yet they hadn't managed to do too much about it.

Today, though, he'd be taking off with Sharon. Twenty-eight, platinum blond, long-legged—and the toughest little tomboy he'd ever met. She was studying ancient man, and she had visited a number of sites that had been found recently, proving there had been settlements in North America long before what had been previously believed. They'd met when, in the pursuit of a missing person, he'd found human remains in the desert. The remains were those of a murder victim, but as an L.A. medical examiner and his team of experts discovered, the poor fellow had been beheaded before the time of written history on the continent. As it happened, his story had been recorded in a nearby cave drawing, found after the discovery of the body had created an academic frenzy. Sharon and Liam had hit it off right away, which had been nice, since he'd still been lying awake far too often at night, recalling what almost was—and then wasn't—with Serena McCormack.

He should have known better, from the beginning. Serena's world wasn't real, and his was far too much so. She had been the most incredible woman he had ever seen. Coming close to her had been like throwing gas on a fire, truly explosive. And falling out with her had been the same.

He slammed the hatchback with far greater vigor than necessary. He told himself that he was going to go and have a good time. He walked back into the house, sliding his fingers through his hair. He was supposed to call Sharon and tell her when he was leaving. He strode into the kitchen and reached into the fridge. Sparse, he thought, surveying the contents. He selected a large bottle of orange juice, shook two aspirin out of a container, and downed them, drinking the juice right out of the bottle. Then he headed for the living room.

His place was small, a fine old house in Laurel Valley, carved into a canyon. Cowhide in front of the hearth, dark leather sofa and chairs. There was a lot of stonework in the house, and some paneling. A large elk head was flanked by a gazelle and a deer—not animals that he had killed but trophies that were in the house when he bought it from an attorney, who told him that the heads had been there when he had bought the place as well. So, they stayed. They were kind of like friends.

There were a few pictures on the mantel. One was from his stint in the service, another from when he graduated from the police academy. In another he stood with Conar Markham, who was as avid a diver as he was himself. They had been involved with diving for the force at that time.

Conar had gone on to acting; Liam had stayed with the police. He had liked his work. Curious, though, even to himself, that soon after the Hitchcock killings, which had involved the cast and crew of *Valentine Valley* last year, he had suddenly decided to leave the force. Maybe it had even been Serena. He had wanted to change his life, to branch out on his own as a private investigator. It was interesting work. He refused cases that had to do with wives spying on their husbands or vice versa. Most of what he took on were missing persons cases.

Of course, a few of them had turned out to be wives—or husbands—who had gone off with their lovers. And in a few cases he had been too late. Two had involved kidnapping victims who had been killed almost immediately after being abducted. The best he had been able to give the families was closure, and that was hell. It was, even after all these years, heart-wrenching to tell someone that a loved one wasn't coming back. But on the positive side, he'd twice found the victims of kidnappings: a woman buried alive in a coffin behind her abductor's home and a child tied up in a closet. That had felt good, damned good. Rewarding.

He glanced at the phone on the small table between the couch and one of the leather chairs. He didn't pick it up to call Sharon. He would do so, soon. He couldn't help but think about the last time he'd been about to take off on a good wilderness trek. Just before he left, he'd been called to take on a case. Well, he wasn't a cop anymore. His time was his own.

To his amazement, the phone rang as he stared at it.

Let the machine pick it up! he commanded himself.

He forced himself to remain still. Probably just Sharon, calling him. The machine picked up. He heard his own voice. Then he was surprised to hear the voice of Bill Hutchens, an old coworker.

"Liam, pick up if you're around. The boss has asked that I call you and twist your arm. Liam, pick up, pick up..."

Let it go! he told himself. But it seemed that his hand reached out of its own volition, and his fingers wound around the receiver.

"Yeah, Bill, it's me. What's up?"

31

"Accident on the set of *Valentine Valley*."

Despite himself, Liam felt his heart thud against his chest. "Serena?" he inquired.

"Serena's fine. But that Jane Dunne who was just hired...dead. Falling spotlight."

"And it was an accident?"

"Olsen wanted me to call you. The producer, Joe Penny, seems afraid that we might wind up with a higher body count."

"More lighting equipment is going to fall?" Liam murmured skeptically.

"Serena was on the set at the same time. Penny wants you watching her."

"Me?" Liam said incredulously.

"With great subtlety, if you will. This hasn't been discussed with the lady in question yet."

"You want me to play bodyguard to a woman who doesn't know she has a body-guard?"

"Something like that—for the moment. Olsen wants to talk to you, then he'll explain it to her. She'll know the score soon enough. Hey, not my idea. Olsen wanted you called in."

"No. I'm taking off to the lodge. With a date."

"Charlie Eagle is a date?"

"Bill, you asshole, you've been in Hollywood too long. No, I have a date with the woman I'm seeing now."

Bill whistled softly. "The blonde I saw you with at the Italian restaurant the other night?"

"That's the one. So—no. Tell Olsen thanks, but I can't take the job."

"I'm supposed to twist your arm."

"Twist it. The answer will still be 'Fuck, no.'"

"You can name your terms."

"The department can't afford me. You can't begin to imagine the terms I'd demand."

"The department won't be paying—the show is picking up the tab. And this is Hollywood. They give millions of dollars here to assholes who can't even act but can attract teenage kids. They'll pay you what you ask—the lady is a major investment to them."

Liam's fingers tightened around the receiver. No, he wasn't doing it.

Yes, he was.

Dammit, no.

He'd been the one to actually walk away, but she'd been the one with the ability to change things—well, at least that was the way he saw it. Serena had her own opinions. He'd closed the door; he'd made himself walk away. There hadn't been a way to close the door in his mind, though, so there had still been those nights, lying awake. He could picture her, always, in his mind's eye. No one in the world had hair like hers, deep, dark auburn, richer than a fire at sunset. And her eyes...like a turquoise sea. And her shape, tall, statuesque.

"No."

"Liam, you have to."

"No. I'd want way too much money. I'd want..." He thought for a moment, then named an outrageous sum.

"Well, I'm going to be gumshoeing it for a fraction of that," Bill told him wryly. "Shit. I should have left the department. Olsen could have called me in for half of that. But

I told you—the producers are paying. Serena is their biggie now, especially with Jennifer Markham off the set."

"I still say no."

"What if something does happen to her, something you might have prevented?"

Liam sat on the couch, his grip on the receiver so tight it might snap.

Hell, he had been the one to walk away.

Yeah, physically.

Because she just hadn't really been with him. He'd been involved to the neck; she'd been involved to her own convenience. Best to back away before he became another casualty along the path of Serena McCormack's spectacular rise to world-wide domination.

And still...

If something were to happen to her that he could have prevented...

"Where does Olsen want to brief me?"

"Down at the station."

"At the station? What about the set?"

"The set is closed down today and tomorrow. They'll reopen after the funeral and the weekend. For now, Olsen wants to see you at the station."

"All right, I'll go to the station. But I need to see the set. As soon as possible."

"That can be arranged right after you see Olsen. Who, by the way, has already informed Captain Rigger that he's trying to bring you in."

Captain Rigger. Liam shook his head. The captain had managed the homicide unit as long as he had been with the force. Liam had first met him when he'd been a rebellious teen and the bodies of a friend and his entire family had been found in their house, which had caught fire. Liam had been the one to see the flames and call 911; Rigger had been the detective who tracked down the mother's boyfriend when it was discovered that the wife and children hadn't been murdered by the father, who was found with a bullet in his head, a gun by his hand. Forensics had proved that the father had been dead far longer than the mother and children.

He had met up with Rigger again later when he was diving for the police. Rigger had been impressed with his work and brought him into the regular force. At that time, he'd had no interest in college. Rigger had, over the first years, subtly made him see the benefits to going to night school and taking the time to get a degree in criminology. Eventually, Rigger had brought him off the streets to homicide.

He owed Rigger. And Olsen.

"Dammit, Liam, you there?"

"Yeah, I'm here. All right, you can tell Olsen I'll be there in a couple of hours."

"Thanks. I mean it—thanks."

Bill rang off. Liam set down the receiver. "Shit!" he swore. "Shit!"

He sat on his couch for several minutes, tight as a bowstring. Then he remembered what he was supposed to be doing that day. He picked up the phone and called Sharon.

She answered with her usual endless cheer.

"Are you coming for me?" she asked. "Hey, if you're sorry that you asked a date along—"

"I'm not sorry that I asked you. But I need to take a rain check. Something has come up."

"Oh?"

"A case. It involves a lot of old friends. I'm really, honestly, sorry. Do you understand?"

"Sure."

"There's been a death at a television studio."

"*Valentine Valley*?"

"How did you know that?" he inquired.

"When I met you, I knew you'd worked on the last case that involved *Valentine Valley*. And Serena McCormack," Sharon said.

"Serena wasn't really involved in that case."

"You dated her for a while, right?"

"Yeah, I did. It began and ended, Sharon."

"I'm sorry," she said quickly. "I didn't mean that the way it sounded."

"Thanks," he said.

"What's happened?" she asked.

"A spotlight fell. An actress was killed."

"Not Serena McCormack?" Was her voice *hopeful*?

His fingers again tightened around the receiver. He forced himself to ease his grip. He was going to break the damned thing.

"No. Jane Dunne."

"Jane Dunne...oh, yeah, I think I saw something on the news about her being a hot property right now and joining the cast. She's dead? She died on the set?"

"An accident, except that... I don't really know all the particulars yet."

He could almost see her shiver. "That show is jinxed."

"It's the highest-rated daytime serial out there."

"You're a P.I. now, not a cop."

"But I have friends who are calling in favors. The show is important to a lot of people."

"Yeah, I'm sure. And it will be more so now. People love to stop and watch the blood at the scene of an accident."

"I'll make this up to you," he said.

"You will. And I'll make it up to you. Remember that if the queen of daytime starts getting nasty. Call me when you can. I'm going to go unpack."

"Thanks for understanding."

"Oh, sure. Maybe I'll head out on the dig that's going on with some folks from UCLA. They'll still let me in on it, I'm sure."

"Great."

"I'll let you know what I'm up to—just in case you do need me. Or want to see me."

"Thanks. You're easy to want to see, Sharon." Those were words he could say and mean completely. He cared about her. Just not the way he should. Pity he couldn't explain.

There was this other woman, once. Perfect and beautiful, but so far from the concept of commitment that there was nowhere left to go. She was into entertainment; he'd spent some time as that entertainment. She dangled men from her career. He

37

hadn't been able to dangle any longer. It was over. Really over.

He stared at the fireplace and started swearing again. Then he got up and paced.

So much for being his own man.

"Thank God you're home! Are you all right?"

It wasn't going to be a peaceful evening, Serena thought. Melinda was asking a rhetorical question. She had barely gotten home and kicked off her shoes before she'd heard the knock at her door, checked through the peephole, and seen her sister.

Melinda's first action was to throw her arms around Serena and hug her tightly enough to break bones. Serena hugged Melinda back, naturally grateful that her sister was so concerned, but both annoyed and unnerved that everyone seemed to feel she had escaped a fate intended for her.

"I'm fine, Melinda." She withdrew from her sister's embrace, realizing that Melinda was very agitated. Melinda passed through the small marble entry and went straight through to the rear of the house, where she stopped by the sliding glass doors that led out to the pool. She stared out at the pool and patio, shaking her head.

"She's dead," Melinda said. She was trembling.

"It was a terrible accident."

"They're sure that's all there was to it?" Melinda queried, her back to Serena.

Serena paused, surprised by her sister's worried tone. Melinda was five years her senior, and though Serena resembled her sister physically, they were nothing at all alike. Melinda had been a brilliant student; Serena had been good herself in school, but nothing to compare with her sister. She had been far too interested in dance classes, then guitar lessons, mime lessons. She had always known that she wanted to act. She had done theater work through high school and college, and then started landing commercials and guest spots on sitcoms, did movie work, then a stint on an old soap, and finally she'd gotten the chance to be a main character on *Valentine Valley*. Melinda had gone on to college, then graduate school, then to get her Ph.D. on the pottery of the ancient Etruscans.

She had married another serious brain, Jeffrey Guelph, and the two of them had lived in academic bliss ever since. They traveled the world—the remote world. They were familiar with dozens of Third World countries and were the only people she knew well who were fluent in Swahili. Serena had been amazed when Joe Penny, at a barbecue at her house one day, had hired Jeff to be a soap opera consultant. Until that time, Serena was quite certain that Melinda and Jeff were basically unaware that there was such a thing as network television.

After three weeks of working with Jane Dunne, Jeff had come to know her, but why was Melinda so upset?

"Melinda, naturally there's an investigation."

"Naturally." Her sister's back was still to her. "Oh, my God, this is so horrible."

"Melinda, it's upsetting...but I wasn't aware that you knew Jane so well."

"I knew her enough to know that she...she was a horrible person."

Serena walked over to where Melinda was standing and forced her sister to look at her. Melinda did so at last, her blue-green eyes, so much like Serena's own, glittering with tears.

"Melinda, did she do something to you?" Serena asked, baffled. Here was Melinda, close to shedding tears, while basically saying that she had despised Jane.

"No, but I... Serena, I did! I hated her. I only saw her a few times, at Joe's 'get acquainted' parties, but she was rude and obnoxious. To me, at least. It's just that she's dead! I'm all right, really."

"Hey, Melinda," Serena said softly. "It's tragic, but you didn't have anything to do with it. A lot of people—" She hesitated, then spoke the truth. "Apparently, a lot of people hated her. Your hating her isn't the reason that she died."

"I hope not."

"What?"

"Nothing, nothing. Oh, Serena!" Melinda threw her arms around her, hugging her tightly again. "I'm so glad *you're* okay."

Those words were heartfelt, and again Serena was grateful. They were close, as close as it was possible for sisters to be when they were so unlike each other. Melinda had spent

40

years sniffing at her acting career, merely tolerating what she considered to be a life with no true vocation. When Serena had been younger, acting in plays, Melinda would shake her head, but she would also be in the audience for any show Serena ever did.

"I'm okay. I'm really just fine."

Melinda drew away, smiling. "I'm sorry. I'm being an idiot, huh?"

"Melinda, I'd worry about you if you *weren't* upset about a woman dying!"

"Oh, Serena, now I feel really terrible. It's more than that. I'm worried because of Jeff. And he wasn't home...and he'd been to the studio..."

"Melinda, you have no reason to worry about Jeff. He left the studio early—before this happened. And he's a consultant, not a stagehand, and certainly not with the lighting crew."

"I know, it's just that..."

"Melinda, it's just what?"

Melinda inhaled, looking at her as if she was ready to burst into tears again.

"Melinda?"

"I don't know... I'm not really sure. She was so mean to me every time we met. Well, maybe not mean—she just ignored me, totally, as if I were dust to be shuffled under the carpet. She was rude to Jeff...but then there was something else there..."

"She was a flirt, Melinda. A high-powered flirt."

"She was more than that. She used men. She

drew them in...like a spider drawing victims into a web to be consumed when the time was right. But I am sorry she's dead. Do you believe that, Serena?"

"Of course, I do."

"And Jeff...he has his faults, but...it had to have been an accident. Serena, maybe you should leave the show. Maybe they're too careless."

Serena sighed, rubbing her temples. Her sister sounded almost hopeful. "No, Melinda. I've worked with all the people at *Valentine Valley* for years. And I'm under contract anyway. I can't just quit."

"Your life is more important than a contract."

"Yes, I believe that wholeheartedly. But I don't believe that I was an intended victim, or that lightning—or stage lights—strikes twice in the same place."

Melinda walked away from her. "So you really think it was an accident?" she asked, pausing by the small bar setup that could be opened to accommodate the patio as well. To Serena's surprise, her sister, who never drank, poured herself a scotch.

"Melinda, I don't know," Serena said slowly, thinking about the saucer ashtray that had disappeared but determined not to say anything about it to Melinda, partly because she'd been told not to mention it and partly because her sister was so upset.

The doorbell rang, causing them both to jump. The glass of scotch jiggled dangerously in Melinda's hand.

"It's the doorbell. Just the doorbell," Serena said.

She walked back through the foyer to the door. It was her brother-in-law. Tall and very thin, he had fine features, as lean as his wiry frame. Now his sandy blond hair with its distinguished touch of gray was all but standing on end, as if he'd threaded his fingers through it a hundred times. Serena and Jeff had always gotten along—except that he, like her sister, seemed to feel that she had wasted her life in frivolous pursuits.

"Jeff," she said. "Come in."

"Melinda is here?"

It was obvious, Serena thought. Her sister's minivan was in the driveway.

"Yes."

He entered the foyer. Melinda had turned. They seemed to stare at each other for a long moment, then Melinda cried out and rushed to him. It was like a scene out of a movie.

"Jeff..." Melinda said, looking up at him.

"Let's go home. Together."

Melinda nodded, eyeing her husband of so many years as if she didn't want to let him go. "You heard?" she said.

"Of course. I've been down to the station."

"The police station?"

"Of course."

"Jeff—"

"Melinda, I'm really tired. Let's get home."

"Jeff, she was a horrible person. Horrible."

"She didn't deserve to die that way," Jeff said.

Melinda appeared to be relieved at his words. "My car—" she began awkwardly.

"If you want," Serena suggested, "come pick it up on Sunday. We'll all have dinner together here, and you can drive both cars home then."

Melinda stiffened. "You're going to invite all the soap people?"

"No, just us. How's that?"

"Sure, that sounds good," Jeff said. "Thanks, short stuff." He sounded gruff. The "short stuff" was a joke. She had been in high school when he started dating her sister. She had since shot up to be an inch taller than Melinda. "You sure you don't have plans?"

"Yes, I have plans for you two to come over on Sunday."

"Great." Jeff looked at Melinda again, took her hand, and started out the door. At the last minute, Melinda turned and gave Serena a fierce hug once again.

"I love you," Melinda told her sister.

"I love you, too," Serena said.

"I'm always here, if you need me."

"Hey, I'm here, too. You know that. If you're upset, alone, if you just want to talk—"

"We're going to be back on Sunday!" Jeff said. "No one is leaving town or anything."

"Or dying," Melinda murmured. Again she hugged her sister, then the two were gone.

Chapter 4

That night Serena found herself double-checking her already locked door.

She'd spent some time with a script and some time picking up around the house. At last she realized that she had just been trying to find things to do. She was definitely on edge.

In the refrigerator, she found a bottle of Chablis. She poured a large glass, though not getting quite as carried away as Melinda had earlier. She went and stood by the windows that looked onto the patio. Images from the day kept sweeping through her mind. An awful day. And then...her sister.

Had Melinda behaved strangely, or was it just that everything seemed strange today?

She shivered, looking out, and stepped back from the windows. She loved her pool and patio area, and it was surrounded by a high privacy fence. She suddenly felt uneasy, though, as if standing in the light, she might be seen by anyone.

She pulled the heavy drapes and realized that she was feeling...*scared.*

Silly! The house is all locked up.

She remembered the way Melinda had greeted Jeff, running into his arms. Together, they had seemed so much stronger.

She was envious. She wished that...

No, don't think about him. He was an ass...

But still, color flooded her cheeks, and she couldn't help but remember how great it had been to be with him. *Go ahead—be angry and righteous, you're entitled!* And yet she remembered the way he had taken her home that first time, and how he had come in, and how, suddenly, clothes had been strewn everywhere and she had felt the heat of his flesh.

She had known almost nothing about him at the time; nothing about his family, if he had a family, what he did in his spare time, how he liked his coffee. The living room drapes had even been wide open. He had looked through her house because she'd been nervous about the Hitchcock killings, and he'd said that the house was secure and she shouldn't be worried, and the next thing she knew, he touched her, and she had been on fire...and then his hands...and his lips moving over her flesh, and then his question: Hey, are you...all right with this? And her answer, oh, my God, yes...and then feeling him, the extent of his arousal, pressing intimately against her bare flesh. All right? Yes, she was about to die...

She had never done anything like that before. Never. Her natural inclination was to refrain from sex unless a relationship was entirely *right*. That was probably why she had married Andy. But Liam wouldn't know that, or believe that, because the magazines had a tendency to make a handshake with any man in Hollywood or beyond into a tempestuous affair.

He was the best sex you ever had! an unwanted voice told her.

Not that much to compare to, no matter what

the rags say! she protested. Andy didn't really count. He was really always making love to himself.

"More wine!" she murmured aloud and headed back to the kitchen.

"Lots more wine," she said.

Then, after still another glass, she told the refrigerator, "He was an ass!"

A damned good-looking ass, with his dark eyes and hair, built like a brick wall, tight and tan and rugged. And convinced he was right, and patronizing, and annoying, and...

He had walked out.

Because of her schedule. When he was a cop, being called in continually. Being a cop mattered, he said. His emergencies were always crucial. She was just an actress. It was all pretense.

She lifted her glass to the refrigerator. "To put it crudely, fuck him! And if he were ever to walk back into my life, I'd tell him exactly that!"

Still, the whole thing today had been more than sad and horrible and a tragic loss of life. It had been...bizarre.

She was never afraid at home alone. Her neighbors were private people, but great folks. There was little crime here. Now she could hear every rustle of a branch or tree outside. Or at least she thought she could. There was a breeze tonight. A light breeze. Yet to her, the night suddenly seemed to be moaning. And each rustle outside sounded like footsteps...

"No!" she declared out loud.

She switched the TV on. Loud. So much for sounds beyond. The doors were locked, the windows all had alarm wires. No one could get in.

But despite the charming sitcom on the television and the wine she was drinking—and all the logic she forced through her mind—she found herself returning to the front of the house and peeking out the drapes. Nothing. A car rode by.

It was a black-and-white police cruiser. *See? Relax. It's a great neighborhood,* she told herself.

But that night, she had an awful nightmare. She was looking down at Jane Dunne. Jane's eyes were still open. Jane was dead, but she spoke to Serena. *It should have been you!* Jane's gaze stayed fixed on her. The red rose slipped through her fingers.

On the ride to her pleasant ranch house not more than a mile from Serena's home, Melinda Guelph was quiet, sitting close to Jeff, holding his hand as he drove his crimson Volvo, staring straight ahead at the road.

When they reached their house, the home where they'd lived for twenty-some years together, where they had raised their two boys, shared interests, been a family, they held each other close inside the foyer for a very long time.

She offered to cook. Neither of them was hungry.

He wanted a long shower. She took a hot bath.

And so it wasn't until late that Melinda brought up the issue of what had happened.

"Frankly, I'm worried. I still don't understand. The police called you in to the station?" she queried.

"Yep. Caught me on the cell phone, right when I was buying some new tools."

"Why did they call you?"

"I was on the set before it happened," Jeff explained. He sounded very casual. "They wanted to know if I had seen anything strange, if I had been around the lighting or the set for any reason, or her dressing room."

"And?" she asked softly.

He stared at her in the darkened shadows of their bedroom, frowning. "And what?"

"Were you near any of those places?"

He looked at the ceiling. "I was with the writers. I barely passed through the set—and no, I was nowhere near any of the dressing rooms."

"And did you see anything—strange?"

"Nothing. Nothing at all. I told you, I was nowhere near any of the dressing rooms."

"Why—why did you come for me at Serena's?" she asked, her voice a whisper.

"You weren't home," he said flatly, "and I was sure that you'd heard about what had happened by now. I knew you'd be upset."

She was silent.

"Dammit, I love you, Melinda," he said, and despite the words he spoke, his voice was angry.

"Yes, of course. I love you, too," she said. But she made no move to touch him. She didn't even look his way.

He reached out to touch her. She shrugged his hand off her shoulder and turned her back on him.

"Melinda—"

"I'm tired, Jeff. Really, really tired."

She felt him draw away. She didn't know when he finally slept. She only knew that she lay awake hour after hour after hour.

It was late when Liam got down to the station. He stopped to say hello to Morna Daily, the duty officer manning the front desk. Before he could exchange more than a few pleasantries, Olsen appeared and led him past a habitual prostitute who waved a friendly greeting and a drugged-out teen throwing a tantrum about who his daddy was and what was going to happen to the cops. It was prime time—for television and for the crazies at a metro police station.

Joe Penny was already seated in a chair in front of Olsen's desk. Liam shook hands with Joe, who looked exhausted. Olsen shut the door and began a quick briefing on what had happened. When he was done, Liam stared at his old friend. "Let me get this straight—a spotlight fell, in full view of at least a dozen people?"

"Yeah. In full view of a lot of people," George said.

"Why are you so convinced that it might be something other than an accident?"

Olsen hesitated, then shook his head with a rueful smile. He inclined his head toward Joe Penny.

"I want to be cautious," Joe said. "In all my years in television, I've never seen a light fall on a set like that."

Olsen riffled through his notes. "The two fellows responsible for lighting are Emilio Garcia and Dayton Riley. They're both union, and both have been with the show since it began. Between them, they have thirty-five years of experience. Both of them swear that every light is checked and double-checked when it's mounted. The lighting cords are also tied in a safety knot."

Liam admitted it did sound suspicious.

"Both Emilio and Dayton swear that their routine never changes," Joe Penny said. "Although, frankly, it's hard to believe that this is anything other than a bizarre accident."

Joe sounded sincere. He was a man Liam had come to know during the investigation into the Hitchcock killings, which had taken place more than a year ago now. Joe had been among the suspects, so Liam had done some serious looking into the man's life. He was a womanizer, beyond a doubt. He was fifty-something with ash-blond—almost platinum—hair, a tightly muscled body, and a dignified look. He was doing his best to age gracefully, but Hollywood was a young town. Joe meant to survive. He had definitely been somewhat touched up. His surgeon had done an excellent job.

"There's something else that's bothering you," Liam said, eyeing the lieutenant, with whom he'd worked closely for years. No matter how far police science progressed, the old adage still applied: Sometimes a cop's best tool is his gut feeling. Liam realized there was also something that George hadn't yet told him.

"Serena McCormack reported seeing an ashtray in the dressing room—no, a saucer used as an ashtray. She thought that she saw a half-burned piece of paper in the saucer. We'd looked in the dressing room before we interviewed her, and I sent Bill Hutchens back to look again after she made the statement. No such saucer or piece of burned paper was there, and no one else saw it, or mentioned it."

Liam set his hands on the desk. "Maybe someone hid it, knowing that Jennifer would be upset about people smoking in her dressing room."

"Maybe. Maybe it's nothing. I just don't like a dangling thread like that." He cast a sidelong glance at Joe Penny. "In any case, Joe here is convinced that he should err on the side of caution. Serena McCormack is important to *Valentine Valley*. Hell, the whole soap-following, magazine-buying, television-watching population of America loves that evil woman."

"You'll take the job?" Joe asked.

"You know what I've asked for, right?" Liam said.

"Yeah, highway robbery. They should lock you up," Joe said.

Liam grinned. "Take it or leave it."

"If you'll do it, you're hired."

Olsen cleared his throat. "Hutchens seems to think that you and Serena had some kind of a volatile past. I know the kind of work you do. You're professional to a fault. But if you think that a disagreement between you two is going to hamper your work in any way—"

"It won't," Liam said flatly. "I have one question, though."

"Shoot."

"What if Serena says no way to a bodyguard?"

"We won't let her," Joe told him.

"Last I heard, it's a free country."

"It's an expensive free country, especially in California," Joe said gruffly. "Andy and I are convinced that we've a lot more at stake than what we're paying you. And hell, we both know you, like you, the cast knows you...you won't have much of a problem from that end."

You don't really know Serena, Liam thought.

"Just one other small detail," Liam said, leaning forward and staring hard at Joe.

"Go on," Joe told him.

"If it wasn't an accident, then someone on that set was behind the death."

"Obviously," Olsen said.

"When do I see the set?"

"Now," Olsen told him. "Right now. And as to watching out for Miss McCormack..."

"Don't worry," Liam said. "I'm on it."

"Subtly, right?" Joe said anxiously.

Liam shook his head. "No way."

"But she hasn't been told yet—" Joe protested.

"Okay, Joe. I'll give you the weekend to tell her. She won't know I'm anywhere near. But after that...if you haven't told her, I sure as hell will."

Chapter 5

The funeral was huge. When Serena arrived, it was already under way.

Despite her best intentions, she had run late. She had called a taxi, knowing there would be a shortage of parking. During the drive from her hilly, forested neighborhood in the residential area of Glenwood, she watched the landscape changes in the town she loved so much, coming from winding, quiet heights down to the commercial bustle along Van Ness.

St. Brendan's was already crowded when she arrived, with police holding back the throngs who couldn't fit into the church. She was stopped herself, and though she didn't think that the young officer who halted her mad dash down the street had ever watched a soap opera in his life, he studied her and at last seemed to believe she was who she said she was, an actress in the daytime serial *Valentine Valley*, a coworker and friend of the deceased.

Friend. She had said the word *friend*.

She wasn't too certain about the last herself. She'd thought about Jane a lot in the few days between her death and the funeral. She had known her better than some of the staff, but she still hadn't known her very well. Jane had only come on the set as a new character when Jennifer's baby had been born. She had been pleasant enough during her appearances for discussions with the producers—pleasant enough to Serena. On the set, though, she'd been very demanding, a prima donna. Andy complained that they were looking at an "attitude problem" right from the get-go.

St. Brendan's looked spectacular. Jane's ornate coffin was down by the altar. The priest was already conducting the service. The smell of the candles and flowers mingled with that of expensive perfumes. Serena stood still for several seconds, trying to get her bearings. Her long view gave way to the backs of men's well-groomed heads, some long, loose female hair, and a variety of hats in all colors, shapes, and sizes.

She sneezed.

"Serena!"

Her name was hissed softly as an arm reached for her.

Jennifer Connolly—no, she kept forgetting. Her friend had married and taken her husband's name—Jennifer *Markham*. She had slipped from the *Valentine Valley* pew to grab Serena up like a lost puppy and pull her into the fold. Gratefully, she followed, whispering an "Excuse me!" each time they stepped past someone to reach the middle where Jennifer had been sitting.

She knew that people had turned to watch her arrive. Who was she? How important? What was she wearing?

There were press people everywhere.

Lord, but Jane would have loved this, she thought.

Jennifer sat to her left, with her husband, Conar, at her side. He nodded to Serena, a small, welcoming grin before he turned back to the priest and his handsome face sobered in reflection of the occasion.

Turning slightly, Serena saw that the row behind her was filled with crew members from *Valentine Valley*. Lighting, makeup, set design. Allona was with the crew; she arched a brow with a shrug, indicating that it had been suggested that she come. Jinx sat next to Allona. Thorne McKay, from makeup, was next to Jinx. She gave them all a weak smile.

When she turned to face the front again, Serena realized that she had squeezed past Joe Penny and Andy Larkin. Though Joe was the main producer on the show, Andy held titles as both producer and actor. Andy was also her ex-husband. On the show—and in real life.

Watching him, she realized that she did still feel a fondness for Andy—she always would. He was tall and good-looking and usually very pleasant. She had once thought that he really loved her, that he couldn't bear to stop looking at her anytime they were out, especially at the beach. She had been so flattered, so certain that he really cared for her, that he had eyes for no one else but her.

Then she had realized one day that he was studying his own image in the reflection of her sunglasses, and bit by bit, she had begun to realize that the man on the surface was the only man there was. He was still her friend. She loved him like...a brother. A spoiled, willful brother. Or perhaps the child she didn't have—and had thought that she had wanted with him.

Andy looked her way, smiled, squeezed her hand. She felt guilty. In his way, Andy was a really good guy. He still wanted to get remarried. He brought it up now and then. *Hey, Serena, want a cup of coffee? Hey—how about getting married again? Man, it would be so good for the show's ratings!*

"You okay?" he asked quietly.

"Yes, of course. In fact..."

"In fact?"

"I'm feeling a bit guilty," she admitted. "I barely knew her."

"Well none of us knew her that well. She was just starting with us. But...well, it was terrible," Andy said. He waved a hand in the air and spoke softly. "An act of God."

An act of God! She had heard that term so many times now. But the police had been crawling over the set since the event, so she had heard.

Seated in the pew behind Andy, with others

in the cast and crew of *Valentine Valley*, Jay Braden sniffed loudly. It was, in fact, Serena decided, a snort.

"An act of a merciful God!" he muttered.

"Jay!" Kelly, seated next to him, chastised him swiftly. Serena was surprised; she had seldom heard Jay make such snide comments.

"She's dead!" Jennifer whispered to Jay. "Don't be terrible."

"I'm not being terrible. I'm being honest. You guys should never have hired her!" Jay continued, tapping Andy on the shoulder. His voice seemed loud; Serena prayed that it hadn't carried.

"Hey! This is a funeral, for God's sake!" Serena reminded him.

"She was on a roll. She seemed a good choice at the time," Andy said dolefully, still looking forward.

Silence fell over them, and Serena heard the funerary liturgy of the priest, smelled the death-room smell of too many lilies, and breathed in the smoke from the candles that filled the church.

Dust to dust. Ashes to ashes.

There was a brief eulogy, given by an old acting teacher. That surprised Serena. If she had been the one killed in an accident, her sister would have spoken for her—or Jennifer. Or even one of these guys. They might have been crude, but their words would have had some emotion in them.

Soon the service ended. They all stood up and started filing out to the center aisle.

"A great funeral. Jane would have loved this! Will you look at the crowd!" Joe said.

"Hey," Andy murmured, "everyone loves a good funeral."

"Everyone loves a good wedding, gentlemen," Jennifer cut in. "Will you people please behave!"

"Of course, Jennifer, of course. You're so right," Andy said and immediately fell into a semblance of gravity and dignity.

"What on earth is this going to do to our plot line?" Jim Novac said as they were walking out.

"We're not changing anything," Andy said. "Much."

"That's not what I heard," Serena said, kicking herself. This was a funeral. And here she was, getting drawn into the conversation. "Allona said on the phone last night that she was going crazy rewriting everything—"

"Every scene that had Jane in it," Jim murmured.

"Our big deal is love and *death* by Valentine's Day. The other soaps will be pointing fingers at us, saying, 'Death—they really mean it over there!'" Serena pointed out.

"Maybe we should change things," Andy said.

"We can't!" Joe Penny insisted suddenly. "All of our teasers are out already in the soap magazines, the women's magazines, and newspapers. We have Valentine's Day contests going on—*Who's the Killer? Who's the Lover? It All Comes to Light on Valentine Valley!*"

"*Who's the victim* has already happened," Serena said dryly.

"She isn't a *victim*. There was an accident. A very sad accident," Andy told her. His voice was full of the proper pathos. *He doesn't mean a word of it!* she thought. *The three of them! They're all just worried about how a death was going to affect their livelihood!*

Accident. They were all saying *accident*. It was what she believed herself, right?

"We have to just live the way we want to live," Jim said. "There was Jane, torturing herself to quit smoking so she wouldn't die of lung cancer. And there she is, dead from a spotlight. I quit smoking myself. She was a bitch, but I wish I could have rushed her one last cigarette."

"She had her one last cigarette," Serena said.

She was startled when they all turned to stare at her. A flush touched her cheeks. Olsen had told her not to mention the note.

She wouldn't mention the note—or scrap of burned paper—she had seen. "She was smoking before she went on the set. Using a saucer for an ashtray. She did have her last cigarette, Jim."

He nodded gravely, as if that meant a lot.

They came out to the walk that surrounded the church and ambled around to the parking lot behind it. Others also headed to their cars, talking all the while. Serena overheard the usual comments.

"What a tragedy!" came from a lovely young woman.

"Um. Cuts down on the competition, though, eh?" That from a jaded dame in a wide-brimmed hat.

"Think someone did her in?" queried an older man.

"Whatever for?" asked the woman.

"To cut down on the competition?" the young woman suggested.

"For pure meanness!" the man said.

The woman laughed softly. "A mercy killing—for the rest of the cast?" she said, and they moved on.

Standing alone, away from the others for a moment, Serena felt a real and terrible sadness for the woman who had lost her life. Where were Jane's real friends? Did playing in the world of pretend too much mean that she didn't have any friends who were *real*?

Too many people let the struggle to be on top become the entire focus of their lives.

"Somebody did her in, you can bet. Murder. And someone on that set did it!"

She jumped as she heard the words, spoken in a hiss. She spun around to see who had spoken.

No one seemed to be really near her, although dozens of people stood in clusters, not at all far away.

One word ricocheted in her mind.

Murder.

She saw Conar Markham. Realizing that she had stopped walking with the group, he and Jennifer had come back for her. "What's wrong, Serena?"

Leave it to Conar. He was studying her with both curiosity and real concern. She smiled. She was lucky. She did have real friends. She shook off the unease that had gripped her. She wasn't about to tell Conar that she had felt a sudden panic.

"Nothing. I was just—feeling sorry for Jane. Not even so much for the fact that she died, but...I can't help wondering about her *life*."

"I know," he said softly.

She smiled. "How's the baby?"

He started to answer her, but someone tapped him on the arm. It was one of the funeral attendants. Conar was a tall man, and he lowered his head as the funeral home employee spoke to him in a whisper.

Conar then said, "I'm a pallbearer."

"What?" Jennifer said, puzzled.

Conar shrugged. Jane had had no real friends! They were calling on the cast and crew of the soap to bear her coffin, Serena thought.

"Oh, of course," Jennifer said.

"Ride with Serena?" Conar said.

"We'll be with Andy," Serena said quickly.

Conar nodded and left them. Andy, coming up, sniffed. "Serena, I'm a pallbearer. Doug will drive you, all right?" Doug Henson was the head writer on the show. Handsome to a fault, gay, funny, talented, self-mocking, and as irreverent as Allona was cynical. Serena loved him.

Serena looked at Jennifer. "Of course."

"Well," Serena said, then smiled at Jennifer and repeated the question she had earlier put to Conar. "How's the baby?"

She was referring to three-month-old Ian, who was home with Jennifer's mother.

"He's wonderful. Wonderful! I love every minute with him. You should see him smile. He's going to be a heartbreaker. He looks just like Conar, except his eyes are bluer, just like mine. But his hair is dark, and he has so much of it." Jennifer's eyes lit up when she talked about the baby. She came alive in a way Serena had never seen before. "And you should see the way he watches and listens to everything—" She broke off suddenly, flushing. "Okay, I'm gushing. You just wait. You'll see what it's like," Jennifer told her.

"Jen, you can gush to me anytime you like, you know that. I adore the little angel. I just wish he were mine."

"You'll have your own."

"Not if I get much older," Serena commented, looking around and assessing the display of the funeral once again. Um, but people were dressed. They milled about and chatted in the sunshine. The young and beautiful sidled up to the old and powerful. Lunch dates were made. Photographers snapped pictures with a fury. Lights flared, even in the sunlight of the beautiful, powdery blue day.

Jennifer grabbed Serena's arm, swinging her around to oblige a photographer. "*L.A. Times,*" she whispered.

"This is a funeral," Serena reminded her, smiling for the camera, then remembering it was a somber occasion.

"Thanks!" the photographer said.

"Certainly," Jennifer told him.

He nodded and moved on. There was a B-movie queen ahead of them on the sidewalk. Other photographers were beginning to gather.

"You know, this *is* a funeral," Serena repeated.

"Um. But we aren't rich and famous enough to be nasty when that decent fellow from the *L.A. Times* is giving us a photo op."

Serena groaned. "Jennifer! That does not sound like you. And I'm willing to bet that the diva up ahead never met Jane Dunne."

"Well, you know, it's sad but true: a funeral does remain a photo op," Jennifer said with a shrug of her shoulders.

Doug Henson stepped up between them. He really was incredibly good looking. Everyone assumed he should want to be an actor, but he loathed acting, loved writing. And though he mocked his soap writing himself, he was excellent at it. Still he longed to do his own great American novel. He kissed Serena's cheek. "A funeral for a bitch. The goddamned Wicked Witch of the West, and that's not gossip but a major consensus. And you're not old."

"What?" Serena said.

He grinned. "Couldn't help but eavesdrop."

"You've been eavesdropping for a long time!"

"Trying to reach you. I even got stopped by the paparazzi on this one. I'm your designated driver, you know. And besides," he said to Serena, suddenly indignant, "I've been around you charming ladies often enough.

I know you wouldn't dream of shopping for any important occasion without my advice. Now that should include a husband, and you're quite right, I haven't seen Mister Perfect around yet myself. Not for you, anyway."

"Well, thanks. I wouldn't want to snag Mr. Wrong again."

"You almost had Mr. Right," Doug told her.

She felt a strange warmth seize her; her tongue felt suddenly dry. She knew to whom he was referring.

"No, he wasn't Mr. Right at all."

"He sure as hell looked damned good."

"Looks are deceiving, and I don't want to discuss this."

Doug decided to back off. He grinned and leaned down to whisper in her ear. "If you want, and you're free this weekend, we can have lunch on Sunset and watch the men go by."

She didn't answer him right away. His comments had made her feel unnerved, opened a wound that was just beginning to heal. *Yes, I'd thought that he was Mr. Right, too!* she might have said. And she still felt that same hurt and loss when she thought about...him.

Her almost Mr. Right.

She wasn't going to allow him to torture her mind and soul. Especially now.

"Please?" Doug said hopefully. "It would be fun. We haven't done it in a long time."

His endearing look was sincere. She couldn't help but smile and laugh. "I don't know. You're too good looking. You always get a guy, and I don't."

He winked at her. "We're looking for different things in a fellow, remember?"

Serena slipped her arm through Doug's. "We'll have lunch this weekend because I love you to death and we haven't had lunch together in a while, how's that?"

"Maybe I'll come, and bring the baby," Jennifer suggested.

"I would love to have you, but we're going on a hunt!" Doug told her. "A man-hunt. Men don't coo-coo over babies the way that women do."

"We're not going on a man hunt. Jen, you're coming to lunch," Serena said.

Doug sniffed. "We'll attract nothing but women with Serena's own nesting instinct," he said with a sigh. "But if that's the way you want it..."

"Doug, you cannot pick up good men by watching people go by on Sunset," Serena said.

"Speak for yourself, my poor dear sweet!" Doug told her.

Doug caught her arm, hurrying her along again until they reached his car. It was a brand-new sporty Mercedes in metallic silver. Once in the driver's seat, he revved the engine, and a smile lit his face, as if he were in heaven, just listening. "God, I love that sound. Just hearing it... I almost feel as if I just had some great sex."

"Luxuriate in the afterglow later, Doug," Jennifer commanded dryly. "We're at a funeral. Going to a grave-site. Remember?"

Doug cast Jennifer a hurt look. Serena

patted his knee. He revved the car again and drove off.

They arrived at the burial ground to another crowd. The famed old Hollywood cemetery was as mobbed as the church had been. The fabled graves of the stars of yesteryear were rudely trampled as the attendees crushed forward for close spots around the new grave. Serena would have hung back, but Jennifer caught her arm. "Look. The guys have saved us places."

They wedged forward. Cameras were flashing. News trucks, reporters, broadcasters, cameramen were everywhere. NBC, ABC, CBS, and cable.

"She would have loved this! Loved it, adored the attention!" Andy raved, whispering as Serena, Jennifer, and Doug found their places.

"Just spectacular!" Joe Penny said. He pinched Serena suddenly. "Can you cry?" She stared at him indignantly. "Then look remorseful, please. The cameras are right on us now."

The priest began the grave-side service. Serena noted vaguely that even he was a good-looking man, tall, handsomely tanned, with a fine speaking voice. It was Hollywood. Maybe he had come out here to be a movie star—and decided on the cloth instead. She winced, ready to kick herself. When had she gotten so jaded?

She wasn't aware when the service came to an end. Close to the coffin, she was handed a rose to toss down upon it. She did so and walked away, feeling Doug's escorting hand upon her elbow. They were followed by the others in their party.

"Miss McCormack!"

As her name was called, she turned around. At first she thought it was the man from the funeral home. Then she realized that it was just someone who looked similar to him.

"Yes?"

He handed her a flower. A beautiful red rose in full bloom.

"I...I set a flower upon the grave," she said.

Something almost like a smile touched his face. "No, this one is for you. From a fan. It would be a kindness if you would take it."

"A fan?"

"Someone shy, I think. But someone who very much wants you to know that...you're watched. Please...as I said, it's from a fan."

She nodded. "Yes, of course. Thank you very much."

She took the rose and turned away with Doug once again.

An odd chill suddenly seeped through her.

"See? You are adored, my lovely diva of the daytime!" Doug teased.

But Serena wasn't really listening. Being in the cemetery had made her uneasy, as if she were being watched.

She turned back, looking through the crowd for the nondescript man who had given her the rose.

She curled her fingers more tightly around the stem of the flower she carried.

"Hey, careful!" Doug warned her.

She looked down. She hadn't felt the thorn digging into her flesh. Her hand was bleeding. Doug pulled a handkerchief from his suit pocket and quickly blotted the wound.

"It's all right," she said quickly. "Just a prick."

"Man, it's bleeding like a son of a gun," Doug said.

"It's all right."

"Let me help you get the blood off, at least. You'll ruin that great outfit."

She barely heard him. Her eyes were still searching through the crowd for the messenger. He was gone. Gone as if he had never been.

All that remained was the rose, held in her bloody hand.

A rose. Just a rose.

Liam had kept his distance from the *Valentine Valley* people at the funeral. At the cemetery he'd found a large oak where he could lean back and watch. As he saw the man give Serena the rose, he was troubled. Why? It was a rose, a pretty gift for a beautiful woman. But he saw the troubled expression on her face.

He left his tree, hurrying across the cemetery. The place wasn't that big. It was set in the middle of studios and offices, and visited daily by all manner of tourists. The man who had given Serena the rose had headed toward the mausoleums. Liam followed him in that direction.

He entered the first memorial courtyard. No one. He entered the second, cursing himself for not moving quickly enough. He entered the third, and the fourth, then looked up in the last of them. A wall had crumbled. There was a fair space for a man to have slipped through—and into the stream of the city.

It was just a rose, he reminded himself, *from a fan.* Someone taking the opportunity of the funeral to get close to Serena McCormack.

Walking back across the cemetery, he made sure that he could still see the *Valentine Valley* group. Serena was getting into Doug Henson's car. Doug was talking to Conar; they were probably discussing somewhere to go for a cup of coffee.

Liam headed for the hearse and the three tuxedo-clad men from the funeral home who were closing it up. "Hey, do you guys have a fellow working for you who is ash-blond, about five-ten, late twenties, and in a tux?"

The apparent head of the group responded. "No, sorry, we're the only ones from the funeral home at this site. You looking for a friend?"

"Not exactly. Did you notice anyone fitting that description take off around here?"

"I'm afraid not. But there were hundreds of people here. Lots of fans, you know. We tried to maintain a certain decorum, but...maybe someone wore a tux to look like a mortuary employee in order to rub elbows with some of the elite. This place was a zoo; anyone could have been here, you know."

"Thanks for the help."

He turned quickly and hurried to his car, aware that Doug Henson had slid into the driver's seat of his vehicle.

Moving into traffic, keeping the group in sight, he told himself again that it had been a rose, just a rose. Serena had legions of fans.

Still, the rose incident bothered him, and he knew why.

Olsen had shown him the set. The police markings had shown him where the body of Jane Dunne had fallen, the way her arm had been extended.... And right where her hand would have been there was a single red rose.

When it was all over, the killer stood at the gravesite. In darkness and shadow, the killer was just a silhouette, standing before a grave, head bowed, as if in mourning.

Hands...the killer stretched them out. There was no blood on those hands. No way to see the weapons of a killer. Who would have thought that it could actually work? Well, almost work. Still, these were now the hands of a killer.

The cops were suspicious, but they knew *nothing. It would be harder now. Yet better. Now* she *would be afraid.*

Serena had seen the note. She was suspicious. Soon she would be scared.

The killer would watch.

And wait...

Chapter 6

The set seemed strange on Friday morning when Liam arrived.

It was his second trip to the studio. Yesterday, Olsen and Joe Penny had accompanied him. He had seen the crime tape and the markings. He also met up with Bill Hutchens for a drink. They'd never been partners, but they'd always worked well together. He wanted to make sure that Bill was okay with him on the case.

"As long as *you're* okay with it," Bill told him.

"Why wouldn't I be?"

"Serena."

"That's been over."

Bill shrugged. "Hey, you know, I took her out for coffee and stuff after. That was some heavy 'over' between you two. But, hey, actresses, huh? They live in a different world."

"So it seems," he assured Bill. They went over a few notes Bill had taken. He learned nothing new, except that he became convinced that if it had been a murder and not an accident, it was definitely an inside job. And a peculiar one at that. No matter how you fooled with equipment, it would be hard to know exactly when it would fall.

Today Liam was meeting with Emilio Garcia and Dayton Riley, the lighting technicians. Emilio started out not surly but weary. "I can't tell you how many times we've been through this all with the police," he told Liam.

Liam had met him briefly before, and he liked the man. A big fellow with dark hair and a dark moustache, he looked like the Frito Bandito.

"I know that," Liam told him. "And I know that you and Dayton are longtime pros. That's why this is such a mystery."

"Mystery, hell!" Dayton Riley said. He was the opposite of Emilio Garcia—thin as a beanpole, barely thirty, with carrot-red hair and a face full of freckles. "I'm telling you, Emilio and I are never careless. I could almost swear I watched Emilio on the ladder tightening the clamp on that light."

"Hey, I know, guys. Joe Penny told me that you have never had so much as an exploding lightbulb before."

They both seemed mollified.

"Since I can change a fuse and a lightbulb and that's about it, would you mind explaining some of the setup here? I need to understand what happened," Liam continued.

"If you look up," Emilio said, "you'll see that we have a ceiling light grid that supports suspended equipment. It's common in smaller studios like this—especially where we have a number of permanent sets. Lamps, or lights, are clipped, clamped, or slung. As you can see, it's a tubular, lattice structure. See there—at the far ends of each side? Those are the power outlets, fitted right into the workings. There were two Fresnel spotlights on the piece of grid that went down." He sighed. "Heavy lights. They were focused on the action at the front table. The light beams had softened edges, making the light blend well with the dimmer lamps that lit the background of the set."

"How could the light come down?" Liam asked.

"It shouldn't have," Dayton said. "The grid is permanent, fitted together. If the Fresnel spotlights were properly clamped, their weight could never have dislodged the fittings."

"But it did?" Liam said softly.

Emilio shook his head. "The way I see it," he said quietly, "a clamp had to have been loosened."

"Unless someone had messed with it," Dayton said. "Not us. I'm telling you, we're more thorough here than you can imagine."

During the whole conversation Liam had been watching them closely, sizing them up. They both seemed genuinely distressed.

Dayton said, "This could have meant our jobs. Or God knows we could still be charged with something. Manslaughter through negligence or something like that."

"The detective, Hutchens, thinks it was an accident," Emilio said, shaking his head.

"Well, I guess it's kind of hard for him to figure that someone would tamper with lighting equipment. I mean, the studio was open, right?"

"Yeah, but...this is usually a closed set," Dayton said.

"Tell me, who was down here, on the set, when the two of you left that morning?" Liam asked.

Dayton looked at Emilio bleakly. Then he looked at Liam.

"No one," he said.

"What time was it?" Liam asked.

Dayton looked at Emilio again. "Seven-fifteen, seven-thirty?" he suggested.

"About that."

Seven-fifteen, seven-thirty. According to Jim Novac, the first scene had been slotted for taping at nine. More than an hour for someone to slip in...

"You've got to find out what happened," Emilio said earnestly. "Please. I know that Detective Hutchens is doing his job the way he sees best, but..." He paused, lifting his hands. "What he sees is an accident."

"I promise, I won't stop until we know the truth—whatever the truth may be," Liam assured them.

Standing by the side of the set, Liam looked down at the tape where Jane Dunne had fallen. He could still see the marker tape that had delineated the actors' positions. And even from this distance, he could clearly see the name marked on the tape closest to the position of the body.

Serena McCormack.

"That one...now there's a good-looking guy," Doug said.

It was Saturday, a perfect day, though it seemed strange that they could be sitting at a cafe so casually, just people-watching, after the week that had passed. But Serena had always enjoyed Doug, and she couldn't stay in her house forever. Allona had come, too, though Jennifer had begged off—the baby had an ear infection.

As Doug spoke, taking the "man-hunting" part of their luncheon seriously, he didn't point. He inclined his head, looking across the expanse of the sidewalk.

Serena adjusted her sunglasses, looking over the man in question. He was tall, with a head full of sable hair very cleanly cut, and nicely dressed in casual khakis and a print shirt.

"Yes, very good-looking," Serena agreed. She studied the man from a distance. He was wearing dark sunglasses—common in Hollywood. He wore them well, but they absorbed his eyes. There seemed to be something vaguely familiar about him, but she wasn't sure what. She shrugged to herself. Handsome, clean-cut, attractive. Tanned, well dressed. How many men did that describe in Hollywood?

"I think he's for me," Allona said.

"Nope, that boy's for me," Doug argued.

"How on earth can you tell?" Allona demanded.

"I know."

"I'll bet you're wrong. He's for me."

"Maybe," Serena pointed out, "he's married."

Doug stared at her. "I assure you, he's not married."

"Or," she added firmly, for Doug's benefit, "maybe he's already involved in a serious relationship with a male partner."

"Maybe," Doug argued, "but I don't think so."

They were on Sunset Boulevard, at a table out on the sidewalk. Tapping the table idly, Serena marveled that it could be such a beautiful winter's day. There was a tremendous bustle of people going by. At the House of Blues, just blocks down the street, a gospel group was performing. People were out in large numbers, headed for the show, out for brunch, or out just to cruise the many boutiques that lined the boulevard. Despite the beautiful day, she was distracted, uneasy. She had been since Jane's death, always having the eerie feeling that she was being watched.

Both Doug and Allona were still studying the man.

"Cute. Very cute," Allona said. "I'd like to write for him. In fact, I'd like to write myself right into the scene."

Serena groaned, stirring her coffee idly. She didn't know why she was stirring it; she drank her coffee black. "Why doesn't one of you just get up, go over to him, and ask him for a date?"

"You can't just walk up to someone like that," Doug said.

"Why not? Neither of you is *overly* shy," she said, her sarcasm subtle and teasing.

"Is she insinuating that we're *brash*?" Allona asked Doug.

"Oh, she wouldn't!" Doug said.

"Well, if you're that interested, just go talk to him."

Doug looked at her, a smile on his lips. "And what if he comes over here and realizes despite that schoolmarm's bun into which you've twisted all that glorious red hair of yours—and the deep, dark shades you're wearing—that you're *the* Verona Valentine of television's most popular soap?" Doug demanded.

"What if handsome over there—ordering an iced cappuccino, skim milk, please—is a reporter?" Serena inquired. Maybe that was why he was familiar to her.

"He'll pin you to the chair. Maybe he's just a fan, and he'll scream your name, and all these people will come running over?" Doug taunted in return.

Serena pulled her glasses down, eyeing him coolly. "If Clark Gable arose and came walking down the street, people would come running over. I just saw the kid from that new teen band that's got the entire country in his hands walk on by, and no one screamed and came running over. I think a soap actress is fairly safe in a city of hundreds of top box office per-formers, don't you?"

"You never know," Allona said. "One-hit wonders and instant stars shine and fade—a soap star lives in the heart of the American household forever."

"Or at least while the show is on top," Doug said cheerfully.

"If he's a reporter, he'll pin the both of you to chairs as well," Serena said.

"I doubt it. You're the performer. We

merely put our words of incredible depth and wit into your mouth," Allona said. She waved a hand in the air. "Writers. We're a dime a dozen."

Serena pointed past him. "Your golden boy is about to tip the waiter and leave."

"Do something, Doug!" Allona demanded. "He is about to get away. At the least, we have to know if he was my prospective date—or yours."

Doug started to rise.

"Wait just one second," Serena said. She touched Doug's arm. "Is he familiar to either of you? I could swear I've seen him before."

They both sat still, watching the man again. Then Serena shrugged. "Maybe, but..."

The man took his coffee from the waiter at the counter, and turned toward them. "Doug!" he called, walking their way.

"I don't believe he's yours," Serena murmured to Allona, still confused as to who the man was as he came toward their table, smiling now.

"Kyle!" Doug stood, ready to greet him.

The man reached the table and shook Doug's hand, and Doug looked down at Allona and Serena, smiling. "Girls, it's Kyle Amesbury, with Haines/Clark."

"Oh, of course!" Serena said. Kyle Amesbury—how could she have *not* known? She hadn't seen him in some time, perhaps, and he had changed quite a bit. He was in the publicity department at the company that was the main sponsor of *Valentine Valley*.

Haines/Clark produced soap products; just as it had been at the very beginning of soap opera days, they were sponsored by a soap company. Haines/Clark made products that cleaned just about everything, from the human body to clothing, floors, appliances, rugs, drapes, and furniture.

The last time Serena had seen Kyle, his hair had been much longer, and his clothing hadn't had such an expensive cut. He'd rubbed her the wrong way then, she suddenly remembered. He didn't like her, and she knew it, though she wasn't sure why. The one time she'd been at his place, he'd wanted to show her all the bedrooms, and he'd suggested that Andy come along. She felt he was always up to something. What, she wasn't sure.

But he had cleaned himself up since she'd seen him last. He'd acquired an air of sophistication since the party when the *Valentine Valley* cast and crew had gotten together with Haines/Clark employees.

"Kyle...Amesbury!" Allona said. She meant to sound pleased, but there was just a slight edge to her voice, and her smile appeared to be a little pained.

"Join us," Doug suggested.

"Sure, I'd love to. Let me grab a chair."

There had only been three chairs at their table. As Doug and Kyle both looked about for a seat, Allona leaned forward to whisper quickly to Serena. "Didn't you hear? He's gotten promoted—he is in *charge* of their ad budget now."

No, she hadn't heard. Joe Penny and Andy Larkin were always worried about their position in the ratings. Every weird, foolish, or eccentric thing they ever did was aimed toward staying on top. There was always the threat that if the show didn't do well enough, their sponsors would pull out.

Doug found the first available chair, and both he and Kyle sat.

Kyle immediately looked at Serena. "Thank God you're all right."

"Of course I'm all right, but thank you."

"Serena, it's been in all the papers—it might have been you the other day."

She smiled grimly. "Right. Yes, I am grateful, and so incredibly sorry about Jane."

"We're all sorry," he said very seriously. "There's talk that..." His voice trailed off as the three of them stared at him. He shrugged. "There's talk that the show is jinxed."

"We've definitely had some terrible things happening around us," Allona murmured.

"Serena, if it had been *you*..." Kyle said. She wondered if his tone of regret was sincere.

"What? Haines/Clark would have pulled out?" Doug demanded.

Kyle leaned forward slightly. "I guess I should tell you—we're getting worried as it is. Bad press, you know. One of our biggest new products is a baby shampoo, friendly to tiny scalps."

"So?" Doug said.

"New moms get queasy about bad things happening."

"That's true," Kyle admitted.

"Then..." Allona prompted.

"There's just talk at Haines/Clark. About being associated with *Valentine Valley*."

"Kyle," Doug said, sitting back, a rueful grin curling his lip, "at this particular minute, as far as we're concerned, you *are* Haines/Clark."

"And you *are Valentine Valley*," he returned to Doug. "*The* writer."

"Hey!" Allona protested.

"Sorry, Allona," Kyle said. "Doug is the head writer for the show."

"Yeah, and that gives me a pile of headaches, arguing with the producers for days on end, arguing with the actors, and telling my very talented associates that we have to write plots and dialogue that are totally outlandish and at the moment..."

"In totally bad taste," Allona finished for him.

Doug shot her a warning glance. Allona shrugged.

"Last time we had an...*incident* at *Valentine Valley*," Doug said, "Sherry Marlborough was the senior exec in publicity and marketing at your company, and she said that all the press was great."

"Um. But Sherry is gone," Kyle said, and something in his voice warned him that he was, indeed, the top gun now. "And last time, the show itself wasn't at fault."

"Are you telling us that you're pulling out?" Serena demanded. She thought about the screen test she had done for the movie, now suddenly wishing more than ever that she would get the role, but she was incredibly defensive about her soap as well. She did love *Valentine Valley*, and her associates.

Kyle smiled at her. *Very cute, and sharp as a razor,* she thought. His looks would disarm people. She didn't know why she didn't like him—there was just something slimy about him.

"No. We're not planning on pulling out—now." The "we're not" really meant "I'm not," she thought. And the "now" had definitely been stressed.

"Gosh oh golly," Doug murmured, a trace of sarcasm in his voice. "We're going to have to make more of an effort to stop terrible tragedies and accidents, girls," he said.

"Of course," Kyle said placatingly. He stared at Doug then, abruptly changing the subject. "I'm having a small get-together at the house tonight. Why not stop by?"

Allona glanced at Serena with a small shrug that said, *"Okay, so it turns out that we know this guy—and he's definitely for Doug. The head writer wins out."*

Kyle looked at the two women. "You're invited, too, of course."

"Thanks," Allona murmured politely. Certainly, they could come; Doug was the one who was really wanted.

"That's very nice of you," Serena said. "I'm still a bit shaken by events. I think I'm going to spend my evening curled up in bed, probably watching Nick-at-Nite reruns. I'd love a rain check, though."

"Sure. You're always a delight, Serena," Kyle said, smiling. "How about you, Doug?"

Serena was certain that Allona kicked Doug under the table, warning him he definitely should go.

"I'll be there," Doug agreed pleasantly, shooting Allona a quick—but totally filthy— look.

Kyle Amesbury rose then. "It is a great soap. And we've always been glad to be a sponsor. Keep yourselves safe, huh?" he said, looking at Serena again.

She didn't know why she shivered. *Because of that feeling she'd had. That strange sensation of being watched. A silly hunch. Caused by things—like this—that people kept saying to her. Caused by the fact that Kyle Amesbury was slimy.*

By Sunday night, Liam was wishing that he had said no. He'd trailed Serena, but learned precious little for his effort. All he'd really been doing was watching her. Yesterday at the cafe, smiling, laughing, sipping coffee, easy and at home with her coworkers—and all of them studying the guy at the window.

Today he'd resorted to climbing a tree to make sure she was all right with her sister and brother-in-law in attendance. No other way to keep an eye on her out on the patio. And still no way to hear what was being said. He watched Jeff and Melinda, heads together frequently whenever Serena disappeared into the house.

Melinda seemed tense. Though older, she sometimes appeared to be a slightly faded copy of her sister. Serena was taller, her hair was redder. Her every movement was vibrant. They were both slim, striking women. Serena had a few more curves. Obvious now, as she walked around the barbecue in a bathing suit.

He'd talked to Conar last night, and Conar had told him about the way the entire cast had suddenly grown still when Serena had mentioned that Jane Dunne had been smoking in Jennifer's dressing room.

Little fool! he'd thought angrily. *You set yourself right up!*

Today had bothered him. He'd seen Melinda, her eyes concerned when she watched her sister, anxious, as if she wanted to say something. And once, when Serena had gone inside, she had turned on her husband.

"Tell her!" Melinda said to Jeff so emphatically that Liam actually heard the words.

Then Jeff bent low to her, speaking intensely, and when Serena appeared again, they were both smiling.

Tell her *what*?

Jeff was behaving damned suspiciously. He was among the suspects. And they included anyone who might have been in the building between seven-fifteen and nine.

That meant most of the cast and crew. Including Joe Penny, Andy Larkin, a slew of secretaries and assistants and makeup people.

Later, from his cell phone in the car, he put in a call to Bill Hutchens.

85

"Liam, you know what time it is?" Bill asked.

"Sorry. You put me on this one, remember?"

"Olsen put you on it. Where are you? You're starting to crack up on me."

"In my car," he said briefly.

"Have you met with Serena yet?" Bill asked.

"No," Liam said briefly. "I need to know exactly who was in the building the morning Jane died. Have you got a list?"

"Yes, of course, I have a list!" Bill said, his tone somewhat defensive.

"Sorry. You think you could let me see it?"

"Yeah, of course. I'll fax it over to your house. Even if it is near midnight. Hey, you know, I am the lead investigator. If you get anything..."

"You know I'll work with you."

He heard a deep sigh from the other end of the line. "Sorry. I'm frustrated. I hate to say it, but I think this whole thing was an accident. Somebody got sloppy."

"Dayton and Garcia deny that emphatically."

Bill snorted. "Of course they do! Their jobs are on the line."

"Sure. But fax me the list anyway, huh?"

"You got it. Right away."

"Thanks."

"No, I'm not such an egotist that I'm not glad for any help you can give. Just try not to make me look like an ass."

"Are all the forensics reports in yet?"

"No, but I should have something more

definite soon. And when I do, I'll let you know."

Liam rang off.

He stared at her house once again, gritted his teeth, and sank back in the car seat.

Damn, but the nights could be long.

Chapter 7

Monday, back on the set, Serena was early. Her weekend had been restless, to say the least. She had thought that getting to work as early as possible and getting on with her usual routine would be a good idea.

She was so early that only Clancy, glumly on duty on the ground floor, was there to greet her. Heading up to her dressing room, she passed the standing show sets—still dark, except for the emergency lighting.

On the board by the stairs she saw huge shoot notices posted for the day: "Meeting! All cast and crew, no exceptions! 9:00 A.M. sharp. SHARP!"

Beneath that order was a call notice: "Serena McCormack, Conar Markham, extras—Egyptian set, 10:00."

There had been some rewrites for the day, that was certain. Extras? What extras? What were they shooting?

She looked around the big room with its many sets on either side of the central aisle where the cameras moved. Crime tape still surrounded the restaurant set where the light had fallen. That must not be making Joe and Andy very happy, she thought. Of all the sets, the restaurant one was used most frequently.

She heard a noise on the set and froze for a moment. Turning around, she saw only a shadowy figure at first, coming from the area of the crime scene. As he moved toward her, she saw it was a man, very tall and broad shouldered.

A murderer! she thought, the unease of the last few days setting in.

No, she told herself logically. He must be an extra. Maybe he didn't know where to go.

She started toward him. "Excuse me. You must be lost. I don't think you should be wandering around on the set alone. The police still have that area roped off. If you go up two floors, you'll find costuming and makeup for the extras."

She was stunned by the answer she received.

"I'm not a damned extra, and I don't need a costume or makeup, Serena."

The man stepped into a pool of light. His dark hair was rumpled and slashing across his forehead, and an annoyed scowl tightened his rugged features.

Liam.

Her first thought was that she was a total disaster. Here she was, not a speck of makeup, hair barely brushed, in leggings and an oversized T-shirt.

She'd heard from Conar, who was one of

Liam's best friends, that he was dating an archaeologist, or a paleontologist, or something like that—a young blonde who for some reason dug holes in the earth and loved the outdoors. A woman with a *real* purpose in life. Probably all legs and tan and...

"Hello, Serena."

"Liam," she murmured. She wondered what emotion her voice registered.

"Yeah. Sorry," he said curtly, and she realized that she had sounded displeased.

Well, she was displeased. It was much better when she didn't see him. But there he was, in the flesh. Or rather, in a casual beige jacket, khakis, and a dark blue tailored shirt that worked especially well with his coloring. His hair was very dark, as close as possible to black, and his eyes were nearly the same shade. He had classically defined features, like a carved Roman statue, yet he still managed to have a rugged air, very masculine and decidedly sexy. His hair was damp from a recent shower, and he wore an aftershave that instantly made her think of...

She harnessed her thoughts. "What are you doing here?" she asked politely. "Conar said that you had left the police force and were working for yourself."

"I am," he said. Hands casually shoved in his pockets, he looked at her. "You mean that neither Joe nor Andy has spoken with you *yet*?"

She frowned. He was very familiar with the cast and crew of *Valentine Valley,* having

89

been on the force during a series of murders involving the show. That was when she had met him, of course, when she had trusted in his steadfast concern for her safety.

"No one has spoken with me about anything," she said sharply. "What's going on?"

"I've been hired by the soap," he said.

"Hired by the soap?" she inquired. Her voice, she thought, was growing shrill. She had to stop that. She had to appear calm and reasonable. She was an actress. Surely she could manage so simple a feat. "You're going to be an actor?"

"Not in this lifetime," he assured her. "I was hired by the producers, because of the recent death," he told her.

"You're investigating Jane's death?" she said. "But Bill Hutchens is going to be in charge, I believe, under that George Olsen fellow. I don't understand—"

"I've been hired to protect you, Serena."

She stared at him, openmouthed, horrified.

She wasn't sure how long she stood there looking like an idiot. He just stared back at her. She didn't like what she saw in his eyes. He thought that she was a prima donna, about to go have a fit about something she didn't like.

She fought for a semblance of control. Desperate to speak rationally, she knotted her hands into tight fists at her side. "I really don't think that would be a good idea. To begin with, I don't even believe that I'm in danger. A light fell. To the best of my knowledge, no one has proved anything else as yet."

"I hope you're not in danger. It will make my job easy."

She remained dead still and said very softly, "I don't think that you have a job."

He shrugged as if he couldn't care less. "Fine. Go to the producers. I'm here sort of as a favor to a few people. You want to go have a tantrum about it, go right ahead."

"I don't have tantrums."

He shrugged again, totally indifferent, those ink-dark eyes conveying definite contempt. "You do whatever it is you feel you need to, Serena. I'll be around. I'm sure someone will let me know the outcome."

He was about to turn around and walk away. Just as he had walked away before.

She didn't think she was up to this a second time. She spoke quickly. "I don't need a guard, but thanks to whomever you owed that favor to."

He paused, glancing at her, and she took that opportunity to walk away herself, striding to the elevator. She nearly short-circuited the button, she was certain, she jabbed it so hard.

Naturally, the elevator didn't come. And she was very aware of him, standing right behind her.

"We had an accident on the set!" she hissed, spinning toward him.

"I don't have the forensic information, so I can't agree with or dispute that statement," he told her.

The elevator opened. She stepped into it. He did too. In the small space she was all the more aware of him. She hit the button for Joe Penny's floor. He didn't touch a button; that was exactly where he was going.

She didn't want to have this out with Joe Penny with Liam in the room. But apparently, short of shooting him, there would be little to prevent him from following her.

The seconds in the elevator seemed interminable. She pounded the button, then stopped, realizing that he was watching her every move. Too bad she couldn't just stand back and carry on a pleasant conversation. *How is that blond bimbo you're dating? Not a bimbo, huh, she has college degrees up her butt, you say. Oh, well, are you sure she's old enough to be out nights with you?*

The elevator door opened.

"After you," he said politely. But he was right on her heels. They came to Joe's door, which stood ajar. Obviously, he had come in early that morning as well. She didn't knock but sailed on in. Pretending she hadn't the least idea Liam was so close behind her, she started to slam the door. He caught it neatly.

Joe Penny was behind his desk, studying scripts. He looked up when she entered. Hair perfectly in place, perfectly lifted face bronzed and handsome. "Serena, hey, I'm glad you're here. I needed to speak with you. Oh, Liam, you're here, too. That's perfect. Serena—"

"Joe, I don't need a bodyguard," she said.

"Serena, I hope not," he said, rising, crossing his arms over his chest and taking a seat on the edge of his desk. "But it's better to be safe than sorry."

"Have the police determined—"

"The police are concerned," Joe said patiently. "And Andy and I are concerned. Serena, do you know how important you are to this show?"

"Joe, it's nice, really nice, to be appreciated—"

"You're...you're just *wicked*," he said with real admiration. "And still loved. Serena, your character is the most popular on the show. We need you. And, of course, we all love you, too. We can't risk anything happening to you. The police have advised us that Liam would be the best man for the job. He knows most of us—hell, he's *questioned* most of us. He knows the set already. He knows *you* already. The cops can't give us the kind of coverage they say you should have. Serena, I really need you to be an adult about this."

She felt as if she was being cornered. Liam seemed ready to leave, convinced that she would have a tantrum. Joe kept looking at her, entirely earnest.

"Serena, you know how I feel about you," Joe said.

"Um. How?"

"Like a father, just like a father. Then, of course, there's the show..."

"Yes, exactly. *Valentine Valley*. And you feel just like a father in regards to the show, too, right, Joe?" she asked softly.

"I did create it," he reminded her. "Serena, I know you're independent, but I also know that you're an intelligent woman who would never jeopardize her own safety."

"I don't ever jeopardize my own safety," she said. "That's why I don't need a bodyguard."

"Serena, would you put yourself at risk," Joe queried her, "when it's totally unnecessary? When we do have the ability to provide you with extra protection. Would you put us all at risk?"

Great. Now he was making her look really bad, like a sulky child, heedless of the concerns of others.

"All right, fine," she heard herself saying. Calmly, maturely. "You want me to have a bodyguard. I want a normal life." She spun around, staring at Liam. "I need some distance," she told him. She wasn't referring just to work.

"Don't worry," he said laconically. "I'm not moving in." He seemed amused, as if the thought that he might get a bit too close was ludicrous. "You haven't noticed me yet, have you?"

Noticed him yet? This time she felt an incredible sense of righteous outrage.

"Yet?" she snapped, turning on Joe. "You hired him already—what? *days ago?*—and he's been *watching me,* and no one informed me?"

"We didn't want you to be upset, Serena," Joe said.

Liam stepped forward, placed a hand on her arm, and turned her around. "Don't get all crazy. I haven't been peeking in your windows or anything." Staring at him, she wanted to scream. It was there again, that something in his voice that made her want to leap out a window. Disdain. As if he wouldn't *bother* to peep in her window. He'd seen it all. Not worth it.

She looked from his eyes to his hand and back to his eyes. "Don't touch me," she said softly.

He moved his hand, not a flicker of emotion touching the ebony of his eyes. "I've trailed your car," he continued flatly, "and watched your house, just making sure no one followed you or accosted you."

She turned to Joe. "How could you do this to me?" she demanded.

Joe lifted his hands helplessly. "Serena, we *love* you."

She was going to explode. She had to get out of there—away from Liam. "Keep your distance!" she snapped.

Ink-dark lashes fell over his eyes. "Your every command is...my *pleasure,* Serena," he assured her.

She put her hands on his chest and shoved past him—but certainly didn't move him an inch. She started out the door, started to slam it again. She was behaving very badly. She wanted to be poised and calm. She *would* be poised and calm, if it killed her.

He caught the door before it could close and followed her, at a distance. They went to the elevator and up to the dressing rooms. She barged into her room, slamming the door after her.

He didn't try to follow.

"Damn him!" she swore.

Then she nearly jumped a mile as a scream

erupted from the corner of her dressing room. Spinning around, she saw that Jennifer was there, sitting in the plush rocker with her baby, who had been frightened by the violence of Serena's entrance.

Jen gave Serena a look of dismay. "You woke him!"

"Oh, God," Serena exclaimed. She walked over to Jennifer, who looked tired, and reached for the baby. "May I, please? I'm sorry, Jen, but—what are you doing here, in my dressing room? I didn't see you there, I didn't know—"

She plucked the wailing baby from his mother's arms and smoothed his little head, crooning to him, as Jennifer explained, "We were all called in for the big meeting. My dressing room is still off-limits—I don't know what they're looking for, but it's taped off. I came here, knowing that you, my dear friend, would welcome the baby and me with open arms. I could have gone to Conar's room, of course, but I do get to see my husband with wonderful regularity, while I don't see you all that often now while I'm off the set."

"Oh, Jen, I really am sorry. You are always welcome here, you know that. I just didn't see you, or this precious little bumpkin. Hey, sweetheart, it's okay, see, you're getting quiet now, I didn't mean to make that big, big noise."

The baby gulped, stared at her, waved a tiny fist her way, then smiled and leaned against her shoulder, at peace again. His body gave a little shudder as he quieted down.

"Thank God he loves you," Jen murmured.

"Thank God he's totally reasonable, merely indignant at his life being interrupted, but more than willing to accept an apology."

"Oh, Lord, what's up?" Jennifer asked, coming to claim the baby. She took him carefully from Serena and gently put him in his car seat carrier. He gave another little shake, waved his arms, and sighed into stillness.

Serena sat down hard on the chair in front of her dressing table.

"I can't believe I'm saying this—I need a drink. No, total anesthesia. Oh, hell, maybe someone could just shoot me."

"Serena, what in the world is the matter?" Jennifer asked.

Serena raised her arms and let them fall, then said indignantly, "They've hired a bodyguard for me." Then her eyes narrowed. "But come to think of it, you probably know, don't you?" she demanded.

Jennifer was quiet, but she looked guilty as all hell. Serena stared at her, shaking her head. "You did know all about it?"

Jennifer's continued silence assured Serena that her suspicions were true.

"Of course. Naturally, you knew that they had hired Liam. Conar would have known, and Conar would have told you," Serena said accusingly.

Jennifer cleared her throat. "I only found out yesterday. And I've been distracted because of the baby's ear infection. But I really didn't think you'd be that upset. You told me that the...thing

97

between you and Liam was over. A long time ago. You didn't behave as if it had been a horrible breakup. You were cool about it, as if it was a decision you had made. And before, when you and Andy were divorced, you came to work more cheerfully than ever before, and you were as kind as humanly possible to Andy, and you even did love scenes with him."

"Because I was desperate to divorce Andy."

"Well, think about the things you said when you split with Liam. You said that it just wasn't working out; you were into breakfast in bed and he wanted to cook snakes on rocks in the desert, or something like that."

"Did I say that, really? That he wanted to cook snakes on rocks?" Serena murmured. She should have been honest about it all—to Jennifer, at least. Ah, but there had been the matter of her pride. To Liam Murphy, she just hadn't been worth the effort.

"Yes, actually. Those were almost the exact words you gave me."

"I lied," Serena murmured.

"Great. To me. Your best friend. You lied."

"You're *his* best friend's wife."

"And I'm still your friend!"

Serena was silent for a moment. "He walked out on me," she said after a moment.

Jennifer gasped, instantly indignant on Serena's behalf, even if Liam was one of her husband's best friends. "He just walked out on you? No explanation, no—"

"No," Serena admitted, "he didn't *just* walk out quite that simply."

"Well, then..."

"He yelled a lot first."

"And I take it you're trying to tell me that you didn't say anything back?" Jennifer asked dryly.

"Oh, yeah. I had a lot to say."

Serena exhaled, remembering. And oddly enough, she could remember Liam exactly as he had been that day. They had been at his house. They'd both been off; they'd planned to spend the day together. And the phone had rung—her cell phone. It had been Joe Penny about the plot line and a private meeting he wanted to have with her and Andy before starting out. Liam had seemed amused and tolerant when she'd first answered the phone, though he reminded her that he'd actually told his boss he was out of town for the weekend, just so that they could have time without a phone ringing. They'd had conversations before about her being off the schedule, then running in at a moment's notice. She said that he did the same thing, but he had told her he was a cop. He didn't seem to realize how many times he *had* run out on her. But that was different in his eyes. His work was serious. That was the point. He was a cop. She was an *actress*. According to his way of thinking, *his* job gave him the right to break dates, fail to show up, and depart at a moment's notice.

She'd definitely resented his assumption, though she'd tried for a long time to understand. He hadn't returned the effort. Like

Jeff and Melinda, he didn't take her work seriously.

She could remember the casual way Liam had been sprawled on the bed, shoulders, legs, and chest very bronze beneath the white flat of a sheet thrown over his middle, his elbows folded behind his head on the pillow. When she hung up, he told her that it wasn't necessary for her to go right then—she could arrange a meeting with Joe the next day.

But Joe had sounded angry, and *she* felt she couldn't put the meeting off. She was still feeling a bit irritated as well over a flare-up she'd had with Liam about a few pictures that had made their way into the papers. So, after the phone call, she walked over, kissed his forehead, then headed for the bathroom and the shower, explaining, "I've got to go."

She'd barely been in the shower a minute before the curtain opened and he was standing there, naked head to toe, gorgeous.

"I've never seen anything more tempting in my life," she had teased, "but I've got to go. It's important." His cold, hard expression made her heart falter a little.

She remembered taking her hand, could even remember the way the water dripped from it as she placed it on his chest. "All right, well, maybe I could be a little late..." she'd told him in her sexiest voice, the one that supposedly made half the red-blooded American males who ever flicked a channel changer want to go to bed with her.

Not Liam. He took her hand, dropped it, and

stared into her eyes. "No, Serena. I'm worth more than a few minutes. We're worth more than a few minutes. I've gone along with all the hoopla, the papers, the guys at the station asking me about you in all these places with your arms around all these other guys, and I haven't flown off the handle once."

"What a liar! You fly off the handle all the time. You nearly broke my arm dragging me away from the newsstand the other day when that silly gossip rag printed that shot of Manny Martinez kissing my cheek—"

"He wasn't kissing your cheek, and you were naked."

"I wasn't naked! I don't know how they got that shot. It was taken on the set somehow when he was guest-starring as the Italian music craze at Prima Piatti—"

"Yeah, right, everything with you is a pub shot, and I'm supposed to look the other way."

"It was on the set—"

"Yeah, it was on the set, and then there was the article about you and Manny Martinez doing a lot more than steaming up the set, and you went right along with that."

"I didn't go along with it. It's not that easy to sue—"

"Forget it, Serena, forget it."

"I will not forget it!"

The water was hot, streaming down around them. He was getting soaked, and so was she, and steam was rising. "You take off all the time—because you're a cop. Cop! I think the word means *God* to you. Sometimes, instead of being so superior, you could try being supportive."

"A cop is different!" he flared.

She was mad already. That made her madder. And the madder she got, the more she wanted to hit him. So she did hit him. With both wet fists, right on the chest, and she stepped out of the shower still hitting him. "You know what I do for a living, you've always known what I do for a living, and you've no right to think you're better—"

"I never said *better*!"

"And as to the stupid pictures, you know the magazines will print anything, and—"

"And I know that you can correct people, and that you can stop some of it. Then, if you're not sleeping with every male who does a guest appearance on the show, you should—"

"You bastard! What a horrible thing to say!"

"Yeah, it is, right? But the magazines write it all up, and you don't change any of it!"

She faltered slightly. Joe had suggested that she let the last article, implying a lot, saying nothing, slide. So she'd done so.

"If you believe any of the rot you read, if you have any doubts about me, go—just go!"

"I'm going!" But he'd been backing away while she'd pounded his chest, and he suddenly caught her hands, and she came against him, and in all her life, she'd never needed anything more than to feel the pressure of his body against hers. She wasn't sure who started it, but he was kissing her, or she was kissing him and they were both soaked and burning and it wasn't just her, because when she ran her hands down the length of his body, he was aroused, really aroused, and that aroused her, and she couldn't have pulled away from him if the "big one" had struck California. And the way he made love, getting every little lick of water off her body, merging with her as if they were one, she felt as if she exploded into a physical rapture that surely brought them into a new place of being, and with something so wonderful, he had to understand; they'd talk calmly, and rationally, and...

It was his house, but he was up before she was breathing normally.

He could dress with the speed of lightning. While she was still there, stupidly staring at him, thinking she had just been to heaven and back.

"I can't do it, Serena. I can't."

"What—"

"If you can't see that you need a private and personal life, I can't do it. Your minutes are great, but I don't want a few minutes."

"You've lost me completely—"

"No, I never had you."

"Liam, this is crazy. You leave all the damned time."

"I'm a cop. And even being a cop, I don't have a quarter of the 'emergencies' that you do."

"Liam, that's a lie. You're behaving like a jealous idiot."

"Serena, I can tolerate a lot. But you're not even playing the same game."

He was reaching for his jacket.

"You're walking out on me—*now*? After—"

"Seems as good a time as any."

"This is your house!"

"Yes. Lock the door when you leave, please."

She wasn't even sure what she called him then. A number of things. She wasn't sure what he said back to her—he was already on his way out.

"Serena," Jennifer said. "Serena!" she persisted, jolting her back to the present. "Talk to me. Tell me what happened. I'm your best friend and you lied to me."

"I didn't lie to you—it wasn't working."

"Why?"

"He didn't like my schedule."

"Really?" Jennifer said skeptically. "It was that simple?" Then her eyes opened even more widely. "Serena, you didn't...you didn't go running out on him in...in the middle of something?"

Serena was appalled that she could flush so easily. "No."

She had left Liam's house in tears, still believing he would call, apologize.

He didn't.

And she had never picked up the phone to call him. He had meant what he had said. He was out of her life. She'd left a few things at his place. A robe, a few shirts, jeans, makeup. He'd packed them all up neatly—and used Fed Ex to get them back to her. She'd left one message on his machine, informing him that he was a rude, unreasonable ass-hole and she never wanted to see him again. He left her a message in return, telling her he'd do his best to oblige.

She'd never felt so lost and alone in her life.

He had hurt her ego. She hadn't been so rudely dumped in—forever. But it wasn't her pride that hurt so badly. She had fallen in love with him. She hadn't really wanted to go tramping in the Southwest wilderness, but she had loved the idea of diving trips to out islands, of simple days of just being with him. She had loved the sound of his voice, his laughter, his touch, the way he looked sleeping, and awake. The feel of his arms...

But she hadn't been wrong; she was certain of that. She was an actress, and she had a right to be an actress. She felt strongly that every woman had a right to a career, just as every woman had the right *not* to have a career if she chose to stay home and manage a household and raise her children.

"I think he wounded your ego," Jennifer said.

"Hey, this is Hollywood, remember? I know the ropes—it's like majoring in rejection. You know that." Her friend was still staring at her. "Jen, it just wasn't working. He was always a cop first."

"He's not a cop anymore."

"Private investigator. The same, but worse. It's not just that. I don't like the things he does in his free time. Camping. Yuck. Bugs and smelly sleeping bags. And besides, he's seeing someone. And I..."

The thought trailed off. *I'll never set myself up for a fall like that again.*

There was a tap on her door. Jennifer leaped to her feet, ready to shush anyone coming in loudly. Serena walked to the door, ready to throw it open and accost Liam.

But it wasn't Liam. Doug was standing there, well dressed and handsome as usual, but wearing his sunglasses. Inside.

"Doug! Hey, come in."

"Quietly," Jennifer warned.

He stepped in, closed the door, and headed right for the sofa. He sat. They both stared at him. "Well, aren't you going to ask me how my night at Kyle's place went?"

"Oh! Yes, of course," Serena said. She'd forgotten that he'd gone to Kyle Amesbury's place.

"Kyle's place?" Jennifer said suspiciously.

"We ran into Kyle Amesbury—now in charge of whether or not his company continues to give us our advertising dollars," Serena explained.

Doug leaned his head on Jennifer's shoulder. "They sent me off like a virgin lamb to slaughter," he said.

"Yeah, right, virgin lamb," Serena murmured. Her hands were still shaking. She had to get a grip on everything going on here.

"She can be cruel," he whined to Jennifer.

"Doug, how did your night go?" She pressed.

"Great. I had a wonderful time. And I wasn't compromised in any way, although, of course," he said in an aside to Jennifer, "they gave me instructions to sacrifice my honor if need be, for the benefit of the show."

"You told him to do that?" Jennifer asked Serena.

"Never," Serena assured her.

"Liar," Jennifer told Doug.

"Well, he is very good looking these days, smooth, suave, entirely sophisticated. He had out the best caviar I've tasted in ages."

Yeah, sucker Doug in for the kill! Serena thought, then winced at the very idea. She had no right to impose her own dislike of Kyle on Doug.

"And guess what I got this morning in my dressing room?" Doug continued.

"Candy?" Jennifer asked.

"Very, very expensive champagne. With a note saying that we should keep up the excellent work."

"Where's Allona when we need her?" Serena said. "She'd be asking if he meant the writing on the show or ridding the world of Jane Dunne."

"Hey, Serena, look," Doug said. "You've got an admirer, too."

She glanced over at her dressing table. There was no large display of flowers. Only a single rose, lying there right in front of her makeup station.

"A single rose," Jennifer mused. "How sweet. Hey, maybe Liam left it—a peace offering."

"If so, he can take it right back." She hesitated, then looked at Doug. "Was he still lurking outside when you came in just now?"

"Who?"

"Liam."

"Liam? Liam Murphy? Tall, dark, macho, used to be a cop?" Doug queried, studying her.

"Yes, Liam," she said impatiently.

"Nope. Can't say that I've seen him." His brows shot up. "Should I have seen him? Ohmigod! You two made up—"

"Not in this lifetime," Serena murmured.

"Then—"

"He's her bodyguard," Jennifer said.

"Hmmmmmm..."

"No 'hm,'" Serena said firmly. "Maybe he quit."

"I doubt that," Jennifer said.

Serena looked at her. "He doesn't quit," she said with a shrug. "Not until the bitter end."

"I think we'd better get going; nearly time for that mandatory meeting," Doug said, his eyes rolling. "Ah, but this is rich. I like it. You have the falling-out of your life with a cop who comes back as your bodyguard. It's so...Hollywood."

"Doug," Serena warned, "I didn't have a falling-out—it wasn't working. I've dated before. I'll date again."

He'd been heading toward the door. He turned to pat her cheek. "Sure you will, sweetie."

"Doug—"

"Both of you hush. I'm going to try not to wake the baby," Jennifer said, going for the carrier.

"Go on. I'll be along in just a minute," Serena said.

"We're not allowed to be late," Doug warned.

"I'm coming. In two seconds. I promise," she said.

When they had both exited her dressing room, she stepped over to her phone and dialed Jinx's extension. When her assistant picked up, she asked first how she was.

"Still scared," Jinx told her.

"There's nothing to be afraid of," Serena said.

"I've been nervous since this all started."

"It will get better," Serena lied. Then she asked, "There's a rose in my room. Who sent it?"

"A rose?"

"Rose, Jinx. Long-stemmed red flower. Do you know who sent it?"

"Gosh, no, I'm sorry. I haven't been in your dressing room this morning. Serena, do you think I have to go to that meeting?"

"Mandatory for everyone, I'm afraid," Serena told her. "Jennifer even came back from maternity leave with the baby."

On the other end, Jinx sighed. "All right."

Serena hung up. She hesitated, looking at herself in the dressing table mirror. She still looked like hell. She should have come in and fixed that.

Her eye fell on the flower. Just a single rose. Was it a peace offering?

There could be no peace.

She'd tell Liam what he could do with it.

Chapter 8

Serena wasn't looking forward to the meeting herself, but she exited her dressing room quickly and headed upstairs to the conference hall. All of the full-time cast members were there, and many of the crew. Vera Houseman, the slight, silver-haired, blue-eyed matron of *Valentine Valley*, Marina Valentine, was seated near the head of the table, deep in conversation with Hank Newton, who played the baritone-voiced patriarch of the show, Vittorio Valentine. Kelly and Jennifer and Conar were next to them; they had saved her a seat. Andy Larkin, here both as the actor playing Dale Donovan and as the producer, was at the head of the table with Joe Penny. Jim Novac, the director, was between the two producers. Jay Braden was at the end of what seemed to be the actors' side of the table; across from them were Doug and Allona. Emilio Garcia and Dayton Riley from lighting were standing along the wall, with the other backstage personnel.

Liam Murphy walked in, and Serena, taking her seat, ignored him. Vera and a number of the others who had met Liam before jumped up. Vera walked around the table, eager to greet him. "Lieutenant Murphy! How wonderful to see you, we've had strangers among us, so dreadful, you know."

"Sorry, Vera," Liam told her. "I'm afraid I'm not a cop anymore."

"He's a P.I."

"A private investigator? Just like on *Magnum* or the *Rockford Files*?" Vera asked.

"No, Vera," Hank sighed. "Just like real life."

"Oh, dear, who hired you?" Vera asked, frowning. She was easily flustered.

"The show," he said briefly, squeezing her hands in a reassuring manner. "Why don't you let Joe and Andy do some talking?"

Silently, so no one would notice him, Bill Hutchens slipped into the room. He must have decided to come this first day back on the set, Serena thought.

Joe Penny stood then, clearing his throat. "Well, it's been a long time since we've all been together like this. And I'm afraid that it's a sad occasion that has brought about this meeting. But that's why it's important that we get together. We're like a real family here at *Valentine Valley*, and I want to assure you all first that we'll never let such a tragedy occur again. Every light on every set has been gone over, every camera has had a thorough check, and our set designers have gone over everything, absolutely everything, to make sure that we now provide a totally safe environment in which to work. This has been a shattering blow to all of us. Andy and I feel the sorrow and the significance of what has happened more than you can imagine. But we don't intend to give up on *Valentine Valley*, and we hope you all feel the same."

"But," Vera said, "you've hired a—a private investigator." She paused to smile at Liam.

"Don't you have faith in the regular police?" Jay Braden asked. He was leaning back, frowning. He seemed agitated.

"Of course we have faith in the police," Joe said.

"So, if this was an accident, why do we need a P.I. on the set? No offense, Liam."

"None taken," Liam said.

Joe sighed. "We just want to do everything right on this. We've had a terrible tragedy. We hired Liam as protection. But we want to get back to normal, too. Get working again, move on with our lives, and our professional obligations."

Listening to the words being spoken, Serena almost forgot that Liam was in the room. She couldn't keep still any longer. "Wait, wait, wait!" she exclaimed, standing and facing Joe and Andy. "I was questioned by the police, like all of you. Why are we pretending that we *know* this was an accident? We don't know what happened!"

"Is this over that silly note you think you saw in that ashtray?" Andy demanded, staring at her with narrowed eyes, as if she were attacking him personally.

"What note in an ashtray?" Emilio demanded. She didn't realize until he spoke then that he and Dayton must have been through hell, riddled with guilt about what happened.

The police had told her not to say anything. She had slipped at the funeral.

"It wasn't an ashtray; it was a saucer. And I noticed it because Jennifer doesn't smoke,

112

and there aren't any ashtrays in her dressing room," Serena said.

"So what the heck does a note in an ashtray mean, anyway?" Jay demanded.

"There was no note in an ashtray," Joe said gruffly.

"When the police went back to look, there was no note and no saucer," Serena corrected. "That's the point. I saw it, and it disappeared, so maybe it meant something."

"And maybe somebody just hid it so that Jane wouldn't look bad...since she was dead, and couldn't defend herself," Andy said.

"All right, great," Conar said, standing as well. "Who hid the saucer with the note?"

The room was silent.

"This meeting was supposed to get us working together again peacefully," Andy reminded Serena.

"Yes, and I hope we all do work peacefully. As long as we don't forget that whether we did or didn't like Jane, she still deserves that the truth be discovered."

"We checked that equipment," Emilio said. His voice sounded like a growl. "We always make sure the clamps are secure."

"So you're accusing someone of intentionally making the light fall?" Kelly asked indignantly.

"You know what?" Jay said, "I know lighting as well. I spent a few seasons of summer stock helping out on the lights. A clamp must have been loose."

"Bull!" Emilio roared.

"Oh, great," Joe muttered. "We're going to have a riot." He stared at Serena.

She stared back at him, then swung around to look at Liam. He'd taken a seat in the rear and was remaining totally silent. He was listening, she realized. To every word said, every nuance spoken.

Joe spoke again. "Listen, all of you. This soap opera is my life. You all know that. I want a safe working environment, and I care about every single one of you. Now...we are getting back to work today. Andy and I want to assure you that we're interested in all your feelings and comments. If you need help coping, please come to us. We can arrange for counselors and therapy, if necessary. Don't be afraid to come to us with anything. We are family. Is there anything else?"

The room was silent.

"And now that we're functioning as a family again," he said, "I'll let you all go and get on with your day. Meeting adjourned!"

As she had expected, it was a long day.

The extras had been hired to bring in the latest "finds" that she was somehow managing to get spirited out of Egypt. Jeff was on the set all day, arguing over the fact that it wasn't easy to take historic treasures out of the country in which they were found. A sarcophagus couldn't be hidden in one's luggage. They went back and forth over several fine points, the writers were called in, some

114

changes were made, all dealing with private planes, bribed officials, and the great wealth of the Valentine family. The scene was an argument she was having with Conar over his character's pursuit of her youngest sister, who was infatuated with him, while he was simply after the Valentine vineyard. He'd already had an affair with Natalie Valentine, Jennifer's character, and his determination to seduce Marla and extract secrets from her had now been going on well over a year. As David DeVille, son of a neighboring wine patriarch, he was accosting her because she kept telling Marla, her soap sister, to stay away from him, and she was ready to light into him because she was the oldest sister, the toughest, ready to do battle.

She was ready for the scene in which she attacked him with a canopic jar—one of her rare, smuggled items from the tomb of Hathesput Amen, a fictional pharaoh. Naturally, invading his tomb carried a terrible curse.

Most of the rest of the cast had been given revised scripts and dismissed until the next day. Serena had no difficulty in working with Conar; he was wonderfully professional. He could be given a new page of lines and repeat them perfectly in a matter of seconds. They worked well together.

The extras had been called in as employees. The casting director had asked for Hispanic types, since they were supposed to be Mexicans who were in the States illegally, and therefore not about to ask Verona Valentine the source of her treasures.

The men brought in were great. Despite the fact that the sarcophagus had been crafted out of soft pine and Styrofoam, it was heavy, bulky. Jeff had painstakingly detailed the set piece himself. He had been practically neurotic, giving directions to the stage carpenters so that it was just right, making Jim crazy. Because it was so awkward to carry, they had done four takes already. Jim sounded as if he were at his wits' end.

"We're not shooting *Land of the Pharaohs* here!" he complained to Andy. "This is a showdown! The damned coffin thing is too heavy. Let's start off with it in place already and the men just leaving."

"Fine, fine!" Andy said impatiently.

As the sarcophagus was rearranged, Conar stood with Liam. Serena felt ridiculous, standing around alone. She turned to one of the extras, determined that she was going to be as charming as she could. The man could only stutter and stumble in reply.

"We're on in five, four, three..." Jim commanded, then he went silent and used a finger count for the last two numbers.

In the changed scene, she thanked the men as they supposedly set down the heavy sarcophagus, taken from its packing crate and set in the cottage by the pool where she worked and often slept. She paid them, thanking them again in Spanish, and putting her fingers to her lips. They did the same.

116

They disappeared from the set. She started talking to herself, pleased as she unwrapped the canopic jars from another crate. Then she heard Conar enter, and she spun around.

She berated him for coming in, telling him he was not invited anywhere on Valentine property. She was going to call the police and have him arrested for breaking and entering. He told her he had an open invitation from Marla to come at any time. And while she was reporting him to the police, she could explain all the treasures in her cottage.

With that, she informed him he was to stay away from her sister.

He told her she'd have to make him.

She swore again that she would find a way to do so.

He accused her of being jealous, of wanting him herself. She was indignant. He was seductive, getting close to her...too close...too intimate, moving the hair at her nape, pressing his lips there...then whispering again that she was jealous, that she wanted what her sister had. And if she kept him from Marla, she'd better be willing to give something herself.

That was when she hit him with the canopic jar. She grabbed it in the midst of his coercion, and cracked him over the head. Naturally, it was made to break apart on impact. He grabbed his head and stumbled back, falling to the floor. She knelt down beside him, afraid that she had killed him, only to find him seizing her.

The scene ended there, with David DeVille telling Verona Valentine that she didn't know what she wanted herself, but that he was going to see that she got it.

Jim was pleased. "There you go! The scene—the actual scene—in one take! Oh, my God, there's hope for the world—and this soap. Serena, what anger, what passion! I loved it! You are so wonderfully self-righteous but really mean and egotistical! I love it!"

"Thanks, Jim," she murmured as Conar helped her to her feet.

He was grinning. "You bitch, you," he teased.

She managed to smile in return. Conar, she knew, was joking. "Thanks."

"Don't mention it. Hey, it looks like we're out of here," Conar told her.

"Watch the camera!" Jim called absently. Serena noted that the second camera, and a number of wires, were in the way.

"We'll back out," Conar said. "Want to go have a drink?"

She eyed him skeptically. "You and me? Are we meeting Jen somewhere?"

"Jen will be happy to come if I call her. Maybe we can make it dinner."

"Ah, except that we both know I'm being tailed."

"Hey, Serena! Watch it!" Jim called suddenly, the tone of his voice frantic.

What was she about to step on now? she wondered. She didn't get to think long. A blur suddenly came leaping over equipment and sets.

She was shoved into Conar, and together they were thrown to the ground with a force that sent the air rushing from her lungs. She felt herself crying out.

Conar took the brunt of the fall. Someone was on top of her. *Liam.*

She heard a thunderous clanging. The sound sent panic pulsing through her veins.

Close to her. So close...

The floor reverberated. Dust swirled around her. She lay stunned, her heart thundering. Afraid to move...

Chapter 9

Liam rolled off her, not helping her up, but heading for the huge A-frame ladder used to set the lights in the overhead grids. The heavy piece of equipment had fallen from there. It had barely missed the scenery that represented the wall of her room.

Serena scrambled to her feet, reaching down for Conar. She forced herself not to shake.

Conar rose with swift agility, taking her by the shoulders. "You all right?"

She nodded. "Fine."

Conar was looking behind her. Liam was hunched down on the ground by the fallen ladder, giving it a thorough inspection. Emilio Garcia rushed onto the stage. "I left the damn thing on the safety hooks. I swear it!" he cried. He pointed at the building wall beyond the set. "There—see, those hooks hold the ladder in place."

Serena walked over to the fallen piece of equipment. Bill Hutchens was among the crowd gathering around it. While they stared at it, as if a whale had beached in the middle of their studio, the detective knelt down beside Liam.

"Hey!" Serena protested. "A ladder fell!" she said quietly. She touched Emilio on the shoulder. She liked him a lot, and his dark eyes were so troubled. "Emilio, it's all right, honestly!"

He looked at her, his eyes curiously guarded. "A big ladder, Serena. Someone could have been hurt badly."

He was shaken himself, she could see. Scared.

"Don't anyone else touch it," Bill said firmly. He was staring at Emilio.

"Look! I'm telling you, I left that ladder secured to its safety hooks!" Emilio insisted.

"Maybe someone wants to ruin the show," Jim observed glumly.

"And maybe the ladder just fell!" Serena said. "Maybe it was an accident."

"That's the second 'accident' in a week," Conar said doubtfully.

"You should call forensics," Liam said flatly. "That ladder should be dusted for prints."

"Yeah, and you know what?" Emilio said.

"You'll find my prints—and Dayton's. Whoever is doing all this is smart. You won't find any prints other than ours."

"We'll take every precaution anyway." Liam was gazing at Emilio as if the "whoever" had to be him. Finally he broke off the stare and looked around at the others. "Anyone see someone hanging around that wall where the ladder was?" Liam asked.

"Jeff was over there, after all the sarcophagus moving around," Joe Penny said.

Serena instantly felt herself go on the defensive. "Jeff left a while ago."

"Right. No one walked up to the ladder in front of all of us to unhook the hold pin," Bill said quietly.

Serena thought desperately for a minute. "This is all ridiculous. Jay Braden was behind the camera with Vera and Hank, too, when we were setting up." She winced inwardly. Here she was, trying to accuse Jay, just to divert suspicion from her brother-in-law. But they had all been on the floor for a while, watching the filming.

"So you think Vera might have fixed a ladder?" Liam asked politely. She didn't like the way he was staring at her. As if she was speaking like a total fool.

"It's not difficult to slip a hook," she replied. "And yes, once again, it could have just fallen! If you all will excuse me, I really need to change," she finished, determined.

"Serena—" Liam began, frowning.

"I'll be very careful."

She walked away, starting for the elevator. She thought that Liam was following her, and she turned around quickly. It was Conar. He looked grave.

"You're really okay?"

"I'm absolutely fine. How about you? You hit the floor—and made a nice cushion for me."

He smiled, for the first time since the ladder had fallen. He looked very earnest. "I'm fine. In fact, I was thinking about dinner. Together. It's been a long day."

"Dinner?" she said, frowning. "Tonight? Oh, you're just trying to watch out for me."

"The four of us. I'll call Jennifer, you, me—and Liam."

The four of them. Once upon a time it had been easy, doing anything together. Now, she was still completely off guard, with Liam back in her life again. On top of all that, she was scared. She was going to be walking around, looking over her shoulder all the time. It would be a good night to go home, close the doors, lock up. "Look, Conar, it's really sweet of you to be concerned. But, you know, I'm really tired—"

His frown deepened; he seemed concerned. "Hey, Serena, I think it's good for you to be with friends—"

"Conar, I want to live my life normally."

"Be with friends while living your life normally. I'm shaken right now, aren't you? Is there a problem? I thought you and Liam broke it off because you just had such different interests—"

"Oh, that's true," she murmured.

"I was trying to talk her into dinner," Conar said. She realized he was talking to someone standing behind her just off the set.

Liam.

"Serena won't want to go to dinner," he said. He was distant. Tall, hard, remote. Black eyes not betraying a single emotion.

Guilt stirred within her. Liam's quick action had saved both her and Conar from a nasty accident—no matter how the ladder had fallen. She would never admit it aloud, but she was definitely feeling a growing sense of unease. No, she should admit it to herself, at least. What she was feeling was fear.

"Don't be silly. I'd love dinner," she said. "And definitely on me. I mean, as long as you're willing to have dinner with us. Thank you, Liam. Sincerely. I don't believe I said that yet. Your quick thinking saved us." She realized that she was sounding incredibly patronizing, but her words just weren't coming out right. She turned from Liam to Conar and offered him her most brilliant smile. "Should I call Jen, or will you?"

"I'll give her a ring; make sure it's okay. Abby doesn't have anything this week, so she'll be happy to take Ian."

"Great," she murmured, and turned again to hurry to her dressing room.

She didn't hear Liam behind her until he followed her onto the elevator. She hated being in the small, confined space with him.

"I don't think that they mean you have to stick to me like glue," she murmured.

"Yeah, well, at the moment it seems like the right thing to do," he replied, watching the lights above the elevator door.

"That's ridiculous. I thought you were investigating the ladder—"

His ebony eyes flashed to hers. "The police can investigate the ladder. And you know, you're making my job hard for me, running off your mouth about that saucer."

Her jaw dropped. Then her teeth clenched. "Running off my mouth—"

"Let's just say that it wasn't an accident, that someone wanted Jane—or you—dead. We're talking about someone on this set, with a big grudge. Now what if that killer thinks that you are on to him because you told everybody in that meeting about finding that burned note in the saucer. Now the killer will really, truly want you dead. You opened your mouth and put your life at greater risk!"

She was going to defend herself, but the elevator door had opened. Jinx was standing just outside with a pile of scripts.

"Oh! I'm so sorry," she exclaimed, turning bright red. "Excuse me, I didn't mean to...to intrude."

"You're not intruding," Serena shoved Liam's shoulder. He backed away.

"Jinx, this is the ex-cop who's watching over us all," Serena said irritably.

"I—I—know," Jinx stuttered. She struggled to balance her scripts and stretch out a hand to shake Liam's.

"How do you do, Jinx?" Liam murmured politely.

Jinx turned a shade redder, but she smiled. "Better now. It's great to have you here. I've heard such wonderful things about you... I feel so much safer. And less worried about Miss McCormack."

"Thank you, Jinx," Liam said.

"Yes, thanks, Jinx. We'll just all sleep so much better, knowing that Liam Murphy is on the job."

Serena knew she was a good actress, for the words had come popping out with enthusiasm. She smiled warmly at Jinx and passed on by her, hurrying down the hall. This was amazing. She hadn't seen Liam in months, and it suddenly seemed that they had never been apart. They had split up arguing; and now they were arguing again.

She opened her dressing room and stepped in. The door didn't close when she pushed it. Liam was behind her, coming in. She backed away from him uneasily.

"Look, thank you again for pushing me away from the ladder. But if you'll excuse me, I think that I need some privacy—"

"You could have had a lot more privacy if you'd learn to use some good sense." He was sounding really angry.

Gruff. The way he did when he was worried or concerned and determined not to show it.

"Look, Liam, I am aware of danger. But I didn't hire you to be my keeper."

"Right. You didn't. The producers did. If you weren't in danger before, you are now. Two coincidences are one too many, in my book. I took this job, and I'm going to do it. So you can be as unpleasant as you want, we can skip dinner if you want, but I will be on your tail, day and night, until this is solved, one way or another. Do you understand?"

From the corner of her eye, she saw the single rose that still lay on the counter. She picked it up, waving the flower at him.

"Fine!" Her temper soared, despite her resolve. "You'll stick to me, because that's your job. But you know what? Don't throw any courtesy into the mix, and don't drop off ridiculous peace presents."

She was surprised by the dark scowl that tensed his features.

"I didn't give you any presents. What are you talking about?"

"This rose," she snapped.

"I didn't leave you a rose. I promise I didn't," he said.

She felt her cheeks flame. "It—wasn't you?" Her voice faltered. The deep sense of unease filled her again.

"No, certainly not," he said. "Give it to me."

"It's just a flower," she faltered. "A flower. Not an attack on me. Are you really going to follow me—constantly?" she demanded, backing away to avoid his possible touch.

"For the most part, yes."

"Great. Well, for your information, I don't believe that my friends and coworkers are homicidal." Was that the truth? What was the matter with her? She was afraid, and here was protection. But she was too unnerved to calm down enough to be reasonable. "And I have a life to lead," she informed him. "I don't intend to change a thing for your benefit."

"Really?" he queried, crossing his arms over his chest. "Well, you needn't worry. I wasn't asking to get into bed with you."

"I wasn't suggesting you were."

"Are you afraid I'm going to interrupt something?" he demanded. His eyes narrowed. "Have you asked the Hispanic types over already?"

"You asshole," she spat at him.

"All right. Sorry, that was uncalled for," he said softly. "But I want the rose."

His hand wound around her wrist. The very simple touch of his fingers on her seemed like fire. She was going to start shaking and beg him to get away from her.

"Let go, please."

He did so instantly. She meant to step back, to behave, but the crack he had made still hurt. "Don't touch me again." She hauled off and slapped him.

She stepped back quickly, horrified by what she had done. "Sorry—really. That was uncalled for," she told him.

The bronze of his cheek was turning white, and the imprints of her fingers were very visible. She held her breath, praying that he didn't come back at her.

"Serena, I will definitely follow that order." The cold tone of his voice seemed far worse than a physical comeback. "Conar wants to go to dinner. If you really can't handle it, go home. I'll be in a car outside."

"I said I'm sorry. I can handle dinner."

"All right. You call the shots. All of them. I'll do my best to oblige."

He stepped out of the dressing room. Shaking and disconcerted, Serena nearly ripped her costume, Verona Valentine's smock, pulling it over her head.

She saw something on the floor. The rose. She had dropped it; he had forgotten it. Clutching the cotton garment to her breasts, she bent to retrieve it just as the door opened again.

Liam. Startled this time as he looked at her. "Sorry, I just—the rose."

She straightened. They stared at one another. Her lips were painfully dry; she couldn't have spoken if she'd wanted to.

Black eyes hard and fathomless, he took the rose. "Lock yourself in," he told her. "I'll be back for you in about fifteen minutes." He started to depart but turned, speaking again. "Don't open your door until you hear me."

"Liam, really—"

"Do it!"

Liam returned to the set, bearing the rose. Bill was standing in the center of the studio, while lab techs dusted the ladder for prints.

Liam approached Bill with the rose. "This

was in Serena's dressing room. Apparently no one knows where it came from."

"From Serena's dressing room?" Bill pulled an evidence bag from the pocket of his jacket. "Sure. Thanks," he said gravely.

"It's probably nothing," Liam said, "but..."

"Hey, we have to follow up on all angles," Bill agreed.

"Thanks," Liam said.

He returned to the elevators, rising to the dressing room level. He glanced at his watch. He still had a few minutes. He followed the stars on the doors, finding the wooden astral design with the name Jay Braden. He tapped on the door, wondering if the actor would still be in.

"Yo!" Jay called. In another moment, he opened the door. Seeing Liam, his features tightened.

"Come in," he said with a shrug, opening the door farther for Liam to enter.

The dressing rooms were a lot alike. Dressing tables with bright lighting. Sofas for relaxing. Small refrigerators for the actors to bring in their own food and drink. The coffee table in front of Jay's sofa was piled with magazines.

He took a seat on the sofa. "You heard about the ladder?"

"Yep," Jay said, pulling out the chair at his dressing table.

"Mind telling me what you did after the meeting?"

"I came back here. Ask Doug—he brought in a script change for me."

"You watched some of the taping today."

"I did. I came out to watch for a while. Why are you asking?"

"A ladder—just fell."

"Oh. So you think someone pushed over the ladder?"

"Yeah," Liam said.

"I was nowhere near the ladder," Jay said.

"You know a lot about stagecraft and lighting."

"I've never denied it."

"What about your relationship with Jane Dunne?"

"I hated her guts," Jay said cheerfully. He leaned closer to Liam suddenly. "But I think the world of Serena. You can ask anyone. You will, of course, right?"

Liam nodded. "What about Jeff?" he asked.

"Jeffrey Guelph?" Jay asked. Liam thought he looked a little uneasy.

"Yeah."

"I like him okay. He's not really one of us. But the advice he's given has been helpful. I guess."

"What about Jeff and Jane Dunne?"

Jay shrugged. "I can't tell you anything about that."

He was lying, Liam thought. Or being evasive. Had something happened between the two of them?

"You need to ask Jeff about his life," Jay suggested, unnerved by Liam's silence.

"Yep, thanks, I should."

"You're worried about Serena, right?"

"That appears to be a sensible concern," Liam said.

"I guess. She was there when Jane...and then, now, the ladder..."

"Who do you think might dislike Serena?"

"No one," Jay said flatly. "Except maybe some deranged fan. But a deranged fan couldn't be on the set." He was quiet for a minute, thinking. "Everyone disliked Jane. Maybe the ladder did just fall."

"Maybe." Liam stood and walked toward the door.

"Hey, Liam," Jay said softly.

Liam paused.

"I did sleep with her."

Liam turned, frowning, wondering at the tension in his grip on the door. "Pardon?"

"Jane Dunne. She was very friendly when she first got here. It wasn't an affair. Just a few quickies. She just liked to prove she could suck people in and then...well, then spit them back out, I guess."

"Thanks for the information."

"You'll be asking for more, right?"

"Yep."

"I'm telling you, Serena has no enemies. Not in the cast. Of course she was married to Andy...but Andy wants to remarry her—not kill her. He thinks it would be great if their characters remarried to coincide with a real remarriage. Now, there's a soap plot for you."

"Think Serena would agree to it?" Liam asked.

Jay laughed, honestly amused. "Not in this lifetime!"

Liam smiled tightly and left.

Gut feeling, no proof. The lighting guys were innocent, though. They were truly horrified by what had happened.

Was it someone obvious, or something he was missing entirely?

He had a feeling they'd only begun to scratch the surface.

Chapter 10

A tap came on Serena's door almost fifteen minutes to the second after Liam had left her.

"Serena?"

At the sound of his voice, she turned to exit her dressing room quickly, having changed to her street clothing and scrubbed away all stage makeup.

"Are the sunglasses really necessary?" Liam asked when she emerged out into the hallway.

She inched the glasses down her nose, staring at him over the rims. "We're going out to eat. I'd just as soon do so privately."

"Do people fall all over you every time you go somewhere?" he queried.

She counted to five, still staring at him. "No, they don't. But I know how irritated you become every time a soap fan does come up."

"No, I don't find that irritating," he replied, definitely irritated.

"Look, this is insane if we're going to fight through the meal—"

"I wasn't fighting; I was asking."

"In a very negative tone of voice."

"Sorry. I just find sunglasses ridiculous inside."

"Then you shouldn't wear them inside."

"Let's forget this. We'll get Conar and go."

There was a crowd at the restaurant, but no one approached them as they met Jennifer, who kissed Conar and told him that the baby was happy with Abby, her mother, and then told them that the host inside had assured her he would seat them as soon as her whole party arrived. She was anxious about the ladder, another accident on the set. They made light of it in front of Jennifer.

The young man was true to his word, seating them quickly at a back booth. There was low lighting in the room.

"You'll trip with those shades," Liam told Serena as she groped for the back of the booth while entering. She cast him an evil glare. Once seated, she removed her glasses.

Within a few minutes, they'd made a choice from the wine list. Serena had moved over so far she was practically hugging the wall. She was certain that Liam was aware of her discomfort. She studied the menu while he and Conar talked about a dive trip a group of friends had planned for the next month.

"I've decided to go too," Jennifer told Liam, "but I don't dive. I know that Conar really hopes you'll go. We're going down to Baja."

133

"You're going on a dive trip?" Serena said to Jennifer. "What about the baby?"

"Well, he is nursing. Where I go, he goes."

"Brent MacVie just bought a real beauty of a boat; it sleeps eight with four separate cabins. Brent isn't seeing anyone at the moment, so he's offered us the master's cabin. Plenty of room for the three of us," Conar assured Liam. "You can have the aft cabin, bring Sharon if you want, and he and Dave Marshall will take the two side cabins."

"Sounds good. I'd like to go. If time allows."

"You should definitely go," Serena told him. She hated herself for the jealousy she felt. Sharon. Blond hole-digging degree-laden bimbo.

Their wine had arrived; Liam sipped his. "If time allows," he repeated.

"Time will allow," she assured him pleasantly. "This is your only case at the moment, I take it, since you're trailing me like toilet paper glued to a shoe."

"Oh, look at this, will you?" Jennifer said. "They have a great-looking mushroom soufflé."

Serena didn't think Jennifer was particularly fond of mushrooms. She cleared her throat and looked over at Liam. "Seriously, if you're looking forward to a dive trip, you should plan on going. I can promise you I'll hang around with Bill Hutchens while you're gone."

He gave a noncommittal shrug, looking across the table again. "You know, you have the most stubborn producers in town. You'd think they'd be willing to make serious changes

134

to the plot line. All that stuff about 'dead by Valentine's Day.' It's not just bad taste—it may be dangerous."

Conar agreed. "I've talked to both Joe and Andy on a daily basis. They keep pointing out the fact that the 'bible,' or plan for the season, has included this suspense angle all along. There have been accidents on other sets; and most of the time the show or the movie has still been made."

Right then Serena was nearly blinded as a flash went off. At first she was simply stunned and couldn't see. Then she realized that, of course, it was a photographer.

If she had ever wanted to have a tantrum in her life, it was then. She wanted to leap up and sock the stringy-haired busybody in the jaw. Of course, she didn't.

Leave it to Liam. He almost lunged from the table. Conar, opposite him, half stood quickly, placing a restraining hand on his shoulder. Liam seemed to accept instantly that he couldn't deck the guy—or break the camera, which seemed to be his desire as well.

"Thanks, Miss McCormack. He's a good-looking hunk," the young man said, indicating Liam.

The restaurant's smooth host was rapidly moving toward their table. "There's no harassing folks who are peacefully eating in a restaurant, buddy. Come on, move along."

"Sure," the photographer told him. "I got what I need. Come on, Dara."

Serena saw with dismay that he hadn't been

alone. A slim girl with a notepad went hurrying out after him.

"I'm so sorry for the disturbance," the host told them.

"It's all right," Conar told him.

The host smiled and excused himself.

"That's going to be all over the papers tomorrow," Serena said.

"Well, hey, that's what happens when you're a star, eh?" Liam muttered, his tone annoyed.

He had once made a big deal out of pictures of her that had appeared in papers. Now he would find out what freedom of the press meant. He'd be the one she was supposedly madly in love with.

"Maybe the photo won't come out," Jennifer suggested cheerfully.

Liam apparently shook off his tension and spoke to Jennifer. "How's your mom doing?"

Jennifer plunged in quickly, telling them that Abby was doing great. From there they went on talking casually until the food came.

When it was time to leave, Serena remembered that her car was at the studio. Liam told her to forget it; he'd just drive her in the next morning. Almost immediately, Jennifer and Conar departed in Jennifer's car, and she was ashamed to realize that they were getting away before she could persist in an argument.

"You're going to drive me home, watch me lock up, and come back in the morning?" she asked.

"Something like that."

"You're going to sleep in your car," she accused him.

"It's where I've been sleeping."

The valet arrived with his car; Liam tipped the man, who then ushered Serena in. As they started down the street, she turned on him. "Just how long have you been following me around?"

He was quiet so long she thought that he hadn't heard. "Just how—"

"Since the night Jane Dunne died," he said.

She sucked in a breath. "Since she died?"

"Yes."

"You've been spying on me all that time?"

"I've been tracking your movements."

"You were spying on me."

She was startled when he suddenly swerved the car off the road. He twisted in the seat to face her. "No, I haven't been *spying* on you. I was hired to make sure you didn't go the same way as Jane Dunne. It's a job, Serena, one I've been hired to do, and whether you like it or not, I'm going to do it. So go ahead, let's have it out now."

She stared at him for several seconds, furious. "What did you discover, spying on my house? Have you been peeping in my windows, too?"

"No."

"And why would I believe that?"

"Why would I want to peep in your windows? I know everything in that house—including you—inside and out."

"Did Joe say you should spy on me?"

"Dammit, I'm not spying on you."

"We have different definitions of the word."

"If you're upset, I'm sorry. Take it up with Joe."

"I intend to."

He reached into the glove compartment and produced a phone. "Go ahead."

She shoved the phone back at him. "On my own."

"May I drive without you leaping to your death on the pavement?"

"I wasn't about to leap to my death on the pavement!"

He turned away from her, revving the engine, guiding the car back onto the road. They drove in tense silence for several miles. When they reached her house, she got out of the car and slammed the door as hard as she could.

He followed. She didn't stop him. When she entered, she made no attempt to close the door behind her. Instead she stepped aside. "I assume you're going to check out the place?" she inquired.

"Yes."

He walked through the house while she stood by the patio doors, waiting. No wonder she had felt as if she were being watched—she was. He reappeared in the living room.

"You keep wearing different clothing," she told him. "Are you changing in the car, too? Giving the neighbors a chance to peep back?"

"Your neighbors are at quite a distance, but no, I haven't been changing in the car.

138

There's been a black-and-white watching your house at times."

"Great. I feel all warm and cuddly."

"Yes, well, you should appreciate the fact that both the police and your employers are interested in keeping you alive. Excuse me, will you? I'd like to get some sleep."

He waved a hand in the air and started for the front door. "Lock it and set the alarm," he told her.

Then he went out, closing the door tightly behind him. She stood by the plate-glass windows and the door to the patio, staring after him, still frustrated, at a loss. If he wasn't being such a jerk, she'd have suggested he sleep on the sofa in the den, or even in the spare bedroom.

She picked up a pillow from the sofa in the living room and threw it against the door as hard as she could. Oddly enough, it did make her feel better. She walked to the door, picked up the pillow, and started beating it against the door.

The door suddenly opened, and the pillow hit Liam right in the face. A lock of dark hair fell in dishevelment over his forehead.

Gasping, she stepped back.

He just stared at her, then at the pillow in her hand, then into her eyes. She thought that the smallest twist of a smile tugged at his lips.

"You didn't lock the door or set the alarm," he said quietly.

"I—will," she said.

"Beat up the door often?" he inquired.

"Only when you've just departed through it," she admitted. "That means you shouldn't just open my door like that." She smiled, hugged the pillow to her. "Good night," she said, and closed the door firmly. She immediately locked it and set the alarm.

"Good for me," she said softly, but her hands were shaking.

She forced herself to go through the motions, shower, teeth, face, and bed, with the remote control in her hand. She turned to the news.

Surely, shattering events were taking place in the world somewhere. But that night they had on a "Hollywood reporter," a woman with a lot of hair and makeup and twitchy eyes, and she spoke with one of the anchors, giving "gossip" from around town. Naturally, she brought up *Valentine Valley,* and the still mysterious accident that had caused Jane Dunne's death.

"*This* reporter has it from the inside, however, that this accident was no accident! Further details," she promised with a wink, "when we have them. In the meantime, keep an eye on *Valentine Valley,* where the trailers are now advertising on-screen murder and mayhem! Bad taste, ladies and gentlemen? Yes, but what the heck, this *is* Hollywood, and I'm your one and only Hollywood busybody, bringing you the *reel* scoop."

Serena flicked off the television.

And lay awake for a very long time, staring into the darkness.

Melinda Guelph pretended to be intensely interested in the magazine article she was reading on skeletons recently exhumed from the Sahara.

Over the edge of the magazine, she watched Jeffrey.

Same old routine, as it had been for all of her adult life. In the bedroom, he removed his watch, set it on the dresser, and unbuttoned his shirt. The shirt fell in the laundry hamper. His shoes were not tossed off, but removed and placed in the closet. He stripped off his socks, but no more. They'd been accustomed to having the twins in the house, so to peel away any more clothing, he went on into the bathroom.

She heard the shower a few minutes later. She laid the magazine on her lap, telling herself that either she had to believe him—or not. She couldn't go on torturing herself this way.

They had a good marriage. Every relationship suffered a setback somewhere along the line. They had everything in common. They had two beautiful children.

The shower stopped. She picked up the magazine again. A few minutes later, he came to his side of the bed, a towel wrapped around his middle as he put a comb through his damp hair.

"Melinda?" he said after a moment.

"Hm?" She didn't look up from her magazine.

"Melinda, talk to me."

"Sorry, I was just trying to get to the end of this article—"

He reached over and took the magazine from her. She looked at him. He stretched across the bed, meeting her eyes. "No, you're not. You're trying to avoid me. God, I've said I'm sorry. I've begged your forgiveness. You're my wife, and I love you."

"I have never said that I didn't love you," she responded quietly.

"No, but you've been as far away as the moon."

"I've been right here."

"Melinda, if you'd been sleeping any closer to the edge of the bed, you'd be on the floor."

"This isn't easy, Jeff—"

"It doesn't get better with you pushing me away all the time."

"I'm sorry."

"Melinda, I want my *wife*. I want to make love."

"Like I said, I'm sorry. I don't intentionally feel this way."

"Want to give me a chance?"

She hesitated. He had fine eyes and a gaunt but distinguished face. There were a number of gray strands in his hair now—more than just a month ago, she thought. But she reached out and touched his hair. He rose slightly, letting the towel slide away, and pulling the cumbersome sheets and comforter from her length.

He paused, watching her, then slipped a hand beneath the hem of her gown, brushing his fingers up her thigh, directly between her legs. She caught her breath.

She thought some of her feeling for him had died. It had not.

He was slim and tight, and had always been a good lover. She had wondered once if he hadn't researched sex and the female body as carefully as he studied any other interest. He knew not just where to touch, but exactly what created instant arousal *for her*. He was still just as able. Her fingers fluttered to his chest. He stroked her; she opened her mouth, ready to protest again, but he kissed her. And this was her *marriage*. She kept letting him touch her, aware that every second she was giving away more, and that it didn't matter. A moment later, her nightgown was gone completely.

He was trying to make amends.

He did.

Foreplay was forever.

She wondered if the words whispered so intimately against her flesh were true.

It didn't matter. She didn't really care at that moment. Making love was good. An instinct, something needed. She was glad of his flesh, next to hers, the hairy feel of his legs, the panting, the perspiration, the whispers, grunts and groans. She climaxed violently, then felt limp and drained. Usually, she curled next to him and slept that way.

It had been all there but not quite.

She twisted, her back to him. *Let it lie,* she

thought. *Let tonight be the start of healing.* But she couldn't quite let it lie.

"Melinda?" he inquired gruffly.

Her back to him, facing the dresser where his watch lay, where it had lain all the many nights she could remember, she couldn't help but ask:

"What was *she* like?"

Chapter 11

Joe Penny loved a good party. He loved well-cut clothing, fine dining, and an excellent vodka martini. All were offered that evening at the home of Eddie Wok, up-and-coming Hollywood director and movie mogul.

Actually, he knew Eddie through Serena. She had met him while giving a class at the film institute years ago, and believing in his passion and ardor for his subject, she had introduced him to a number of friends and gotten him his first job as a production assistant.

Eddie had gone far. Not yet thirty, he had directed two of the biggest box office hits of the last two years. He was young, down-to-earth, a Chinese Dominican with a mastery of four languages and a deep appreciation for the opportunities to be found in the United States. He now attracted beautiful people like flies, and his parties were the best.

Tonight Joe arrived very late, and Eddie said

hello with the warm pleasure that was natural with him. Joe saw that Doug was in attendance, as were Jay Braden and Allona Sainge. To his surprise, Jay was with Jinx, the timid young assistant they had recently hired. She looked good, though the party seemed to be overwhelming her a bit. Joe made a point of talking to Jay and Jinx. He tried to make her feel comfortable, and he was pleased, thinking she was glad of the recognition.

He noted then that Doug Henson and Allona Sainge seemed to be with Kyle Amesbury. Good or bad? He wasn't sure. He made a point of talking to them as well. Allona was trying to tell Doug the real lowdown about growing grapes for wine. He didn't really want to hang long with the three of them. He didn't want Amesbury to start his pretentious guff about Haines/Clark pulling out on the show. Amesbury would do it, too. He liked an audience.

Joe waited too long. In the middle of listening to Allona talk about types of red wine, Kyle suddenly turned to Joe. "So you're holding up?"

"Of course," Joe said. He really hated the little snot.

"Terribly tragic," Kyle said.

Joe saw Allona clench her teeth. Kyle couldn't see her. She caught Joe's eye, winked, and put her finger to her head as if it were a gun, then blew the tip of her finger as if clearing smoke. He concealed a smile.

"The company is terribly nervous," Kyle continued.

"Hey, Doug, Allona, can a company be nervous? I mean, does that work, grammatically?"

"A death on the set," Kyle said with a tinge of anger. "Then your reigning queen in all the newspapers, tête-à-tête with her old flame, the cop."

"Maybe it's love," Joe said flatly.

"Maybe. But the headlines suggest that *Valentine Valley* is a dangerous place to be, in truth. I think the article read, 'Miss McCormack may be looking to new associates to guard her against very real danger.'"

"No one has ever been able to control the papers," Allona injected. "There's freedom of speech here, you know?"

"Well, you all could be more careful."

"Yeah," Jay Braden said, joining the group. He wore a pleasant smile. Joe knew that smile too well. "We could all watch out who we hang around with. Guys known to offer pleasure palaces in their own homes. Oops...that could be you, couldn't it, Kyle?"

Kyle stared at him. "Why, really? What have you been up to at my place, Jay?"

Joe looked at his head writer. Doug wasn't happy. Joe wasn't sure why, but he had a feeling Amesbury was pressuring him and he didn't want to be pressured.

"Right. I'm damned sorry. Damned sorry. But I can't turn back time. But I'll tell you what, Kyle. If Haines/Clark wants to pull out, hell, what can we do? They'll have to go. *Valentine Valley* is on top of the ratings, and we will stay there. If you all leave, I've got a gut feeling there will be other sponsors out there. Didn't mean to dampen the party here. I'll move on." Jinx was staring at him with her eyes really wide. "Honey, you look like a million bucks tonight," he told her.

She beamed at him.

"Pretty as a picture," Kyle Amesbury agreed, as if Joe's comeback hadn't meant a thing to him. Maybe it hadn't. But then he stood, his jaw locked. "Excuse me, Joe, will you? There are some people I have to see."

He was really angry. Joe wondered if he had just blown his financing.

"Asshole!" Allona whispered when he was gone. She moved closer to Joe. "Weird asshole at that! He wants both Doug and me to have dinner at his place."

"Just dinner," Doug said.

"Watch out for him," Jinx warned. Startled, Joe looked at her. "He has no right to egg you on, Mr. Penny. You're too decent to everyone."

Decent? When she said that, he suddenly felt like a dirty old man.

"I wish I were that decent, Jinxy." He touched her cheek, smiled, and left them. Jay had his hands on her shoulders. Was there something going on there? Jay liked to play the field. Jinx was an innocent in Hollywood. Maybe Jay was just playing big brother.

Joe swept a martini glass from the tray of a passing waiter and moved on.

Around three, the crowd started to die down. By then he'd had more than one very good vodka martini. He'd had...

He knew he'd lost count of his drinks when he realized that he was in the hot tub. A couple of young hopefuls—one blond, one brunette—were with him. Their clothing lay in a disheveled heap. He'd managed to neatly fold his own. Strange that he could drink enough to peel it all off and still fold it so neatly. He had a martini in his hand. He didn't remember getting that martini either. He closed his eyes and concentrated. Yeah, he could dimly recall laughing, flirting, crawling in. The hot tub was in a little enclave just outside one of the guest rooms. It had been the blonde's idea. She had started asking him what they were doing on the set now that Jane Dunne was gone. She was subtle. She had suggested the hot tub rather than asking outright for a job. The brunette had supplied the martini he now had. So this was the "casting hot tub," he thought wryly. So much for hopefuls being lured to the couch.

The blonde was across from him. He felt her toe sliding along his inner thigh. She had talented toes, he thought as she moved them higher. Still, he'd been seduced before. He eyed her over the martini glass and smiled. "What was your name?"

She pouted. "Glenda. Glenda Richie."

She moved across the tub. Positioning herself before him, she took the glass from him and set it aside, then maneuvered him so that she was in front, the brunette was in back. Her fingers took over for her toes. Her lips were close to his. "You can't let that show fall apart. Jennifer Connolly is out of it, and no Jane Dunne."

"Jennifer is coming back," he said huskily. The brunette was moving too. Interesting. How many friends would help seduce a guy for the other's benefit? He wondered what their work might have been before they'd come to Hollywood.

"But Jane is gone, and...well, you know, of course, that Serena McCormack did a screen test for Eddie."

Serena? His Serena, his star? And she hadn't told him?

He was about to go dead limp in the blonde's hands. He had to get out of this situation quickly. His head was suddenly pounding.

And he had just defended her right to do as she pleased!

He slid from between the two women quickly and determinedly. His future reputation was at stake. As he moved, their well-endowed chests fit together like bricks in a wall.

"Joe!" the blonde cried, upset.

"Sorry, girls, we don't cast the show this way. You'll have to call your agents, and they'll get hold of our casting director. Good night, now. Besides, what's the matter with you girls? We're into the twenty-first century here. Use some sense. You're supposed to be practicing *safe* sex. Go buy some condoms!"

He grabbed his clothing and dressed quickly in the room. The thought of Serena made him sick with fury. And though he suddenly felt stone-cold sober, he knew he'd had more than a little to drink that night. That made it all the worse.

Overkill. Maybe the whole thing was ridiculous.

Liam closed his eyes, thinking about the days—and nights—gone past. So he was making a lot of money. He was still sleeping in his car.

But the A-frame falling today had shaken him. Again, Serena had been too close.

He glanced at his watch. Four A.M. Ricardo Carillo, twenty-five, good motorcycle cop with a new wife and baby, was due to show soon. Black-and-white patrol cars had steadfastly watched her neighborhood since Jane's death; now Liam wanted more. He trusted Ricardo, and Ricardo wasn't working for the department when he spelled Liam, he was working for Liam. Hell, they'd paid him enough to bring in his own help, and Ricardo needed the money.

He eased back in his seat again, wishing he was sleeping on her sofa.

No. The sofa was too close to the bedroom. He was too smart to go that route again.

No, he wasn't. Smart had nothing to do with it.

He groaned aloud and looked at his watch. He was an asshole, that's all there was to it. He ought to be out in the wilderness with Sharon.

He shook his head, looked at his watch again. Rick was due any minute.

He frowned, seeing lights coming around the corner. A car just passing by? He straightened in his seat, instantly alert.

The driver must not have noticed Liam's car discreetly parked at the corner of the yard. He pulled his BMW right up behind him and exited his car hurriedly. He didn't, however, head for the front door; he started around the back.

Toward Serena's bedroom?

Serena wasn't sure why she awoke; there was a noise. When she had finally fallen asleep, she had slept deeply, and coming out of it left her feeling alarmed and confused.

Oh, God, there was someone out there, someone thrashing through the leaves. She leaped up in a panic. The fear that had first risen within her when the ladder had fallen swelled to a full-blown panic. *Yes, someone was after her, someone was outside.*

Liam was out there, Liam was out there! she told herself.

But the rustling was coming closer and closer...

She flattened herself against the wall, her heart pounding a ferocious beat.

Liam was out of his car in a flash, racing after the man. He'd headed exactly where Liam had thought; directly toward Serena's bedroom window.

He never reached it.

Liam tackled him about ten feet from the window. The fellow let out a howl like a wounded buffalo, fighting at first, shouting, cursing, but then going still when Liam rose and rolled him over.

Joe Penny.

"What the hell are you doing, Joe?" Liam demanded gruffly. He was surprised at the way his heart was pounding. Joe Penny? Why the hell would he want to hurt Serena?

"Liam! Dammit, let me up."

He'd been drinking.

"What the hell are you doing here, Joe?"

"I have to see her! I'd like to throttle her," Joe moaned.

Liam should have had some sympathy. He'd been feeling that way himself. "Why?" he demanded.

"She'll understand."

"You have to see her at four in the morning?" Liam demanded curtly.

"I don't know what time it is," Joe said. He touched his dirt-stained face. "You bruised me!" he added in horror.

Joe was usually so impeccable and calm. Liam studied him. He had been drinking, yes. But he wasn't that loaded. He really was angry with Serena. How angry? Enough to want to kill? Was it possible that the man who had hired him was out to injure his own star?

"I have to see Serena."

"Why didn't you knock at her door?" Liam asked harshly.

"She'd have to wake up if I pounded at the window," Joe said.

The lights flashed on in Serena's bedroom. A second later, she came out the patio doors, racing across the lawn to them. She was wearing some kind of a silk nightgown. It hugged her every curve. Her hair was wild and mussed, her eyes were wide and bright. No makeup. He liked her that way, though she'd never know it. She was raw and exciting when she was a tousled mess, and he felt his tension increasing a dozenfold.

"What are you doing, running out here like that?" he yelled at her.

Outraged, she came to a standstill, shoulders squared, tall, straight—and bathed in the glow of the patio lights. She might as well have been naked, the way the illumination backlit the silk.

"I heard the shouting—"

"Which means you should have stayed the hell inside!" he told her.

"It's Joe!" she said indignantly.

Liam stepped back. "You were expecting him?"

"No, of course not, but if you'll excuse me, he is a friend," she told him.

She started for Joe, still prone on the ground. But Joe chose that moment to find the strength to stumble to his feet. Then he let out a cry of fury; Liam thought he was lunging for her. Once again instinct leaped to the fore, and he

153

charged Joe. Serena stepped back just in time.

"Hey, I only stumbled," Joe cried. Then he fell face forward at Serena's feet, Liam on top of him. But Joe managed to catch the hem of the nightgown and Serena went down as well with a gasp of surprise, caught off balance.

"I'm going to throttle you!" Joe raged.

Serena scrambled away on her haunches, staring at Joe in amazement.

"Liam, now you're breaking my leg. Let me at her. You must want to kill her, too."

Serena shook her head with real confusion, eyes wide. She was pale, shaken, and not afraid at all, but amazed and disturbed.

"Joe, what is the matter with you?" she asked softly.

"You're screwing us all," Joe raged.

Liam, one knee wedged in Joe's back, stared at Serena and arched a brow. The look she gave him in return was truly scathing.

"Joe, I swear to God, I don't know what you're talking about."

"Eddie Wok!" Joe spit out.

"You're screwing Eddie Wok?" Liam couldn't help but ask politely, feeling like ice.

She stood with tremendous dignity. "You should both go dunk yourselves in the pool, gentlemen!" she said coolly.

"Serena!" Joe cried.

"Joe, calm down, and I'll talk to you," she said.

"Are you calm?" Liam asked.

Below him, Joe nodded. "Yeah, I'm calm. I need a Tylenol. A drink."

"You surely don't need a drink," Serena said firmly. "I'll make coffee."

"Why don't you put some clothes on, and we'll all talk?" Liam said.

"You're not a part of this conversation," she said smoothly.

"I'm making myself a part of this conversation," he told her. She must have known that he would absolutely not back off on this one. She didn't respond. She turned and headed toward the house.

Joe had managed to get to his feet by then. "Now there, she does walk in beauty," he murmured. "Nice as—backside," he amended, seeing Liam's face.

"Joe—" Liam began. The name sounded like a growl.

"Sorry. But she works for me, you know. You work for me too."

Liam gave him a shove on the back. "That's right. And I'm working, and you're going to get your money's worth. Get on in there. I want to know what's going on."

"Why not?" Joe said. "You know, I was in a hot tub with two buxom beauties...and now here I am, at her doorstep," he said with self-disgust.

"Get in. And explain why."

Serena had donned a velvet robe. It didn't seem to help Liam's restless irritation much. There was a wide satin lapel to the robe, and it created a great V. She had already started the coffee, and was standing in the kitchen when he entered with a sheepish Joe.

She didn't even seem to notice Liam. She glared at Joe with real fury. "What in God's name is going on with you?"

"You!" He waggled a finger at her.

"What?" she demanded.

He said two words. "Eddie Wok."

She shook her head. "I take it you went to Eddie's party?"

"Yes."

"And Eddie told you about the screen test."

"You didn't. And you're under contract."

"My contract is up for renegotiation in five months, Joe."

"So! You were about to walk, without a word, without a warning—"

"No, Joe. I never intended to walk. Eddie asked me if I'd just test for the role, no obligation. I haven't been offered anything. And Eddie is an old friend."

"Eddie owes you! He'll give you the role."

"If Eddie did make me an offer, I would consider it, yes, Joe. But I never intended to walk. I would have asked for a leave. They won't start filming until Jennifer is back, anyway. I'd never have left the show in a bind."

Joe seemed somewhat mollified, but he was still staring at her with narrowed eyes. He pointed his finger at her angrily again. "You're supposed to be my friend, too. We're a family. And you didn't say anything."

"I didn't say anything to anyone," Serena insisted. "Joe, it was my business. I didn't make any commitments. I didn't do anything illegal or unethical. I went and did a screen test. I don't even know now if the role is something that I want. Would you please calm down about it? And sit—right there at the table. I don't trust you standing with a coffee cup right now."

Joe sat, still staring at her as if she had sent an arrow straight into his heart.

The coffee had perked. Serena poured him a cup and set it before him. "Joe, please, drink that."

"I told you, I'm not plastered."

"It will be good for you anyway."

He picked up the cup and sipped the coffee. He waved a hand in her direction.

"Joe, I didn't set out to do anything to anyone, or upset you! You and Andy have always said that you want your actors to take on extra projects. It gives the show more exposure."

"The show has plenty of exposure now," Joe said and then shook his head. He swallowed more coffee. "I'm going to have a long talk with Andy about this, you know," he told her.

"Well, of course, talk to Andy. I didn't mean to make it a deep dark secret," Serena said with a sigh.

Liam had stood at the back of the room, watching the exchange. Joe was still staring at Serena as if she had slid a knife into his back. Serena was merely impatient. He thought she had forgotten that he was there, but then her eyes met his.

"Joe, I know you're not loaded, but you were drinking at that party, and you are upset. Liam, I think you should drive him home."

"There will be a cop outside in a few minutes. He'll take him home."

"A cop?" Joe said with a growl. "Cops, cops! They're crawling all over us! They dissected our set, and they haven't found out a damned thing. They're worthless!"

"I beg to differ," Liam told him.

"Yes, you would. I hired you—at great cost!—and I'm the one you're tackling to the ground."

"You hired me to guard Serena. You were a threat to her."

"There's the point. I've hired you. I can fire you," Joe said sternly.

"Go ahead, fire me."

Joe stared at him. "You know damned well I'm not going to fire you. I'm praying that you will find out what's going on before I start tearing my hair out."

"Joe, don't do that," Serena said, amused. "You paid a lot for that great transplant. You don't want to mess with it."

He glared at her. "I can fire you, too."

She shrugged, still smiling slightly.

"Yeah, yeah, yeah, you'd have job offers all over the place. I just wish that you had talked to me."

"Joe, honestly, I'm sorry."

"Yeah, well, I guess I was out of line, the way I came over here. But after everything that's been going on...and then hearing this..."

"It's all right, Joe."

"Try knocking at the front door next time," Liam suggested.

He left Joe and Serena in the kitchen and strode to the front door, having heard the arrival of Ricardo's car. Out the window he saw Ricardo was approaching the house.

"Everything all right?" Ricardo asked when the door opened and he saw Liam. "I saw the lights and your car—"

"Yeah. I'm going to stay on here. I need you to run a man home."

Ricardo arched a brow. "He isn't going to puke on me or anything, is he? Not that I wouldn't do anything for you, Liam, but I've got the new car—"

"This guy got mad, upset, and had a few drinks. He's not going to throw up."

"Who is it?" Ricardo asked.

"A man named Joe Penny."

"Joe Penny, producer of *Valentine Valley*?" Ricardo inquired.

"Yep. Get him on home, if you will. Take his car—the BMW there—then call a buddy on patrol to pick you up at his place."

"Great!" Ricardo agreed. "That's a good-looking car."

Liam opened the door wider, and Ricardo walked on in. Liam followed him into the kitchen. Serena had taken the chair next to Joe's. Her head was close to his. She had been whispering to him vehemently.

She started when she saw Ricardo, then stood quickly, and offered her hand. "Hi. I know you from somewhere—"

"Grainger House, a while back, Miss McCormack. I was working for Conar Markham."

"Yes, of course. Would you like some coffee?"

"No, thanks. Come on, Mr. Penny," he said to Joe. "I'm going to get you home."

"Serena—" Joe began, pointing at her.

"Joe, if you wag that finger at me again, I'm going to break it off," Serena told him firmly.

Joe turned, winking at Liam. "She's a tough one, isn't she?" He looked at her again. "Good night, Serena. You know I do love you. You just wounded me. To the quick."

Liam followed Joe and Ricardo to the front door, running his fingers through his hair, then over his cheeks. He needed to shave. He needed to sleep.

He needed to get the hell out of this house.

He was startled to see that Serena had followed him out to the living room, and he was alarmed to realize that he hadn't heard her. His senses weren't as sharp as they should be.

Her eyes were very wide, as teal as the Caribbean Sea. That V on her robe was falling over the contour of her breast.

"What time is it?" she asked him.

"Four-fifteen."

"If you need to go home, I'll be all right," she told him. The words were supposed to be strong and sure. They fell a little short.

She lifted a hand and let it fall. "I was scared to death when I heard all the thrashing out there, but it was just Joe."

"Yeah, just Joe. And I'm going to start wagging a finger at you in about half a second. I don't care who it was or is—don't come running out until you're absolutely certain that the situation is under control."

He crossed the room to her, pausing in front of her to press a point.

Big mistake. He forgot his point.

She smelled wonderful, like the scent of the stuff she bathed in. Clean, sweet, fresh, feminine...and sensual.

He set his hands on her shoulders, drawing her undivided attention. "Whoever pushed over that ladder was someone at *Valentine Valley*. Which *could* mean Joe. Serena, you don't want it to be anyone you know. You don't want to believe that behind the facades that are the day-to-day faces of your friends, a killer may lurk. Right now you can't trust anyone."

"But I'm supposed to trust you," she reminded him.

He pulled his hands away. "Yeah, don't trust me. Don't trust anyone."

She stepped away from him. "There are still a few hours to catch some sleep," she said.

He rubbed his chin, wincing. Dumb what he was about to say. "I need a shower and shave. May I use your guest room?"

She shrugged, as if it didn't matter in the least. "Sure."

He turned and walked to the door, locking it. He looked back at her. "Is the alarm code the same?"

"Yes."

He keyed in the alarm. He stared at her from a distance. Damn that robe.

"Can I borrow a razor?"

"I still have one of yours. You, uh, have some shirts, socks, and underwear here, too, I think."

"You didn't burn them?"

"Too busy," she said. "Help yourself, your things are...where they were."

That surprised him. He walked past her into her bedroom. Nothing had changed. At that moment, he would have given anything to forget the past months and belong here again. She had a great bedroom. Designer sheets that were sensible rather than frilly, in sea patterns. The drapes were aqua, like her eyes. The carpet was rich; the furniture was antique.

The sheets were rumpled—she had been in bed.

He walked into the bathroom, found his razor in the cabinet. Back in the bedroom, he hesitated, then opened her closet door. Two shirts were still hanging to the right of her extensive wardrobe. In a small chest of drawers just inside the closet were some socks and underwear. He took both and stepped out of the closet.

She hadn't followed him. He walked back across the living room. "Guess I've got everything. Go get some sleep."

"Fine. The coffee is still on if you want some. Good night."

She turned and started for her bedroom herself. The door closed.

He watched after her, hoping against hope that the door would open again. It didn't.

He berated himself for being a fool, then helped himself to a cup of black coffee and brought it with him into the guest room.

He left the bedroom and bathroom doors ajar.

This room was done in wicker. Cute, welcoming. The bathroom sported a big tub and a separate shower enclosed on three sides by glass.

He shaved first, then cast off his clothing and stepped into the shower. He ran the water cold at first. Icy. Then he ran it hot.

A second later, he heard a tapping. "Liam... sorry, I forgot. There are hand towels in here but no bath towels. I'll just throw one in the door for you."

Standing in the steaming spray, he looked down at his body in dismay. Here he was trying to be sane and responsible, and the sound of her voice was like an instant call to duty.

"Yeah, thanks," he said hoarsely.

He realized through the mist that she had entered quickly to throw in the towel, but then she hesitated. An irrational anger seized him.

He threw open the door. Steam rushed out like a silver-gray cloud; water sprayed everywhere. She had obviously gone back to bed—the robe was gone and she was only in that wisp of silk that gave away far more than it concealed.

"Look, sorry," she murmured, as if she were about to flee.

But he stepped out of the shower stall and grabbed her arm. "I'm sorry, too," he told her.

She was there, in his arms. Arms that instantly dampened the silk and made it adhere to her flesh. She felt fire, she smelled like something wonderfully wild, sweet, and exotic, and he was certain that she hadn't seen but she could now *feel* the extent of his arousal. His palms, wet, traced her cheek. He held her jaw and found her lips, telling himself that if she protested in the least, he'd be back in icy water. Her lips parted to his with the slightest little moue. He remembered the way she kissed, openmouthed, tongue dueling, sliding, teasing, tasting of sweet mint. Before he knew what he was doing, he had her off her feet. The spread on the wicker bed, he noted, was a white knit. He eased her down on it, tongue tracing the pattern of the wet silk over her body. His hand cupped a breast, he laved it through the silk with his tongue, rounding the taut peak of her nipple. She arched against him, gasping something incoherent, her fingers in his hair, on his shoulders. His fingers ran down the wet silk, finding the hem of the gown, stripping it upward so that he touched bare flesh. His trembling fingers raked the length of her and gloried in it, peeling the silk higher and higher, as far as her hip. Her pelvic bone created a dip and a shadow; he pressed his lips to the hollow there, spreading his liquid caress to the point of her navel, back to her hip, stroking her inner thigh, then pressing it wide. He could drink in the scent of her, the taste of her. He seemed wrapped in an essence, his own heart pulsing like thunder, creating a throbbing and pounding that seemed to fill him. He stroked between her thighs, lowered his head, and reveled in sensation. She arched and writhed against him like a wild thing, an angel gone mad. Her fingers tore into his hair, her nails scraped his shoulders, and she cried out, ecstatic, embarrassed, consumed, and reaching a volatile peak in a matter of seconds. He rose above her, seeking her eyes. They opened, a dazed aqua pool; her lashes shuttered. He caught her lips again, bringing her into the fervent desperation now riding him. A second later, he sank into her, encased in the sheath of her sex and moved with an urgent beat that seemed ready to snap him in two. Her arms were around him, fingers touched, brushed, stroked. So easy...she was lithe, agile, erotic in her own movements to meet his, writhing, reaching. The scent of her, taste of her, drove him to a frenzy. He knew her, God yes, he knew her, the way she could close around him, move instinctively to bring him to an explosive and shattering climax. His body locked in muscled tension, he thrust deeply into her again and felt the sexual tension in him burst like a fireworks display. He shuddered into her again, and again, and again, and still it seemed that the force of his climax swept from him. It was several long moments before he lifted his weight from hers, falling to the bed at her side.

He meant to take her into his arms. From there...where? He wasn't certain.

She didn't give him time. She sprang up,

trying to adjust the remnants of silk back around herself as she headed for the door.

"Serena!" he said, half rising.

"Good night!" she said firmly.

"Wait!" he was up, naked, striding after her. "Wait, dammit, I'm sorry—!"

She spun around in the living room. "I know you're sorry, I know you've got a life, and I'm sorry, too, and we'll just forget it. You don't have to worry about your hole-digging blonde; she need never know this happened. Good night—get some sleep, I know I need some."

"Dammit, Serena," he said again. "Look, I didn't mean to—"

"Great. You didn't mean to!" she said angrily. "Well, actually, I didn't mean to, either. Or maybe I did. It was wrong. I'm sorry. Good night!"

"Serena, wait—"

"Wait? Why? You just walked away. Allow me the return courtesy and allow me to just walk away this time."

He still followed her across the room. But she slipped inside her door.

It closed with a heavy slam.

He stood outside it, hands clenched at his sides, jaw locked, his teeth biting his lower lip.

He stalked back into her living room. The lights were dim, but on. The drapes to the patio were wide open, as they had been. So he was standing there, naked, blowing in the breeze, as if he were on a giant TV screen.

If there was anyone watching...

He was suddenly certain that there *was* someone out there.

Trees were rustling, a shrub wafted in the breeze.

He hurried back into the guest room, slipping into his pants only. He returned to the living room, keyed in the alarm, and opened the patio doors. He stepped out into the yard.

He was as certain then, as certain as he had been that there had been someone, that now the someone was gone.

Still, he walked across the yard. It was enclosed by a privacy fence, but it was at least an acre of lawn and shrub and ivy. He passed an oak and saw that the bark had been skimmed. There were branches down by a small fig tree farther back.

He eyed the length of the wall in self-disgust.

He had lost his quarry.

He swore, then headed back into the house, carefully keying in the alarm entry once again. *What the hell was going on here?*

He finished dressing, poured himself coffee, and sat down in front of her door. He dozed now and then.

When he heard the rustle of her first movements in the morning, he rose again, swearing as he tried to stretch out the cricks in his neck and back.

He made fresh coffee. Then he left her a note saying that he was waiting in the front yard, and he'd be there, whenever she was ready.

He stepped out on the front porch. There, right on the doorstep, lay a rose.

A single bloodred rose.

They had definitely been visited in the night.

Chapter 12

Joe Penny got up ridiculously early and went to the studio. He sat in his office, reading the new scripts the writers had given him for the next week's filming. He nodded now and then, or pursed his lips with displeasure, and even spoke aloud at times. "No, no, no. That won't work. They'll have to go back on this... that's good, um, that will work, yes, I think..."

The interoffice phone buzzed. He looked at his watch; it was still very early. He hesitated, then picked up the line. "What is it?"

"Joe. It's Bill Hutchens here. Down in the studio. Can I talk to you?"

"Be right down."

Hutchens was standing by the set where the ladder had fallen. The ladder was gone.

"Did you get anything?" Joe asked him.

"We lifted some prints, and we asked both Emilio Garcia and Dayton Riley down to the station for theirs. Olsen wanted the ladder dusted," he explained with a shrug. "That's one of the things I wanted to ask you about. Whose prints should be on the ladder? I mean, who touches the equipment, other than the lighting technicians?"

Joe grimaced. "Lots of people. Set design, cameramen, production assistants—actors, if they're walking around the ladder."

"That's what I thought. We'll pursue the process, though. Any little thing might mean something."

"Just what do you think it all means?" Joe asked.

"To be honest, I thought you all had an accident on your hands. Tragic, but no menace intended. Now...well, again, ladders have fallen before. Is Liam in yet?"

Joe shook his head. "Not that I've seen."

"When you do see him, tell him that his rose was a rose was a rose."

"What's that supposed to mean?"

"He'll know. Just tell him for me."

"Sure. Can I do anything else for you?"

Hutchens shook his head. "No, not for the moment. I wanted to know about the ladder. Call me if anything comes to you, anything at all."

Joe nodded and watched him walk away. A second later, he jumped when Andy clapped him on the shoulder. "Bad morning already?" Andy asked.

At that moment, Joe wished he had his partner's youth and looks. He felt a hundred years old that morning. Andy liked to say that he was getting old and stressed and whine about the pressures of acting and producing. If Joe looked like Andy, he'd say the hell with producing and spend his days acting—and leaving the set at night without the headaches of producing! No, that wasn't true. He liked power. Liked it a lot.

"The morning is all right. Last night sucked."

"What happened last night?"

"I went to Eddie Wok's party."

"Eddie Wok gives great parties."

"I wish you'd been there. Kyle Amesbury was acting like an ass."

"Kyle Amesbury *is* an ass. What was he saying?"

"Oh, talking about pulling out."

"Let him."

"That's what I told him." Joe grinned. "There was a picture of Serena with Liam in the paper. He didn't like that, either."

"The fans love to see us in the newspapers—Serena was *with* Liam?"

"Andy, quit acting like a jealous fool."

"I'm not. I just thought—I thought she really disliked him. I thought the... I thought that the affair thing between them was really over." Andy was tense. He had never quite gotten over his divorce from Serena. He'd never accepted the fact that any woman would willingly divorce him.

"I think the picture was taken when they were at dinner, Andy. They weren't caught at the dollar-an-hour motel or anything."

"Still, I didn't think that she'd sit down and *eat* with him."

"Dinner is not a commitment, Andy."

"We shouldn't have hired him."

"The cops said we should. Besides, her picture in the paper is nothing. She's done dozens of photos with near strangers because we've asked her. We do have another worry on our hands."

"What?"

"Serena screen-tested for a part in the new Eddie Wok movie."

"What!"

That made Andy as tense as a bowstring. "She—she's under contract!"

"For how long?" Joe reminded him glumly. "She's only got another few months on this contract. And she's friends with Eddie Wok—she met him years ago when he first came to Hollywood. She brought him to some parties...he likes her...he's grateful to her."

Andy pondered that, shaking his head. "She wouldn't just...leave."

"No, I don't believe she would. But I thought you should know." He sighed, feeling very old again.

"Serena," Andy said very softly, "stabbing us in the back."

"She won't."

"Really? Well, she's cut me to the quick once. What's to say she won't do it again?"

Joe was surprised at the sound of anger in Andy's voice. Their divorce was long, long over.

"I've talked to her," Joe said. "If she accepted the role, she would take a leave of absence. She wouldn't just leave the show."

Andy turned and walked away. "I'll be talking to her," he said.

171

Even when Serena finally got to sleep, she slept badly. The alarm sounded like an air raid warning, brutally loud and cruel. She pounded it, and it turned off. She lay there several minutes, wondering if she had completely lost her sanity, or what. She had let Liam into the house. Well, that had been Joe's fault.

Joe didn't matter. His learning about the screen test didn't matter either. It had been due to come out sooner or later, and she hadn't done anything wrong. What had happened after...mattered.

Like an idiot, she was still in love with him. She'd known that. Staying away from him had been sane. Last night had been...insane.

She could have dropped the towel and left. But she had stood there, watching him through the steam, and all she had remembered was what it had been like to be with him.

Great. She had refreshed her memory.

She forced herself to crawl out of bed. In the kitchen, she found fresh coffee already made. And a note. Liam was waiting outside. Liam, who was making her crazy. She crumpled the note into a ball and tossed it into the wastebasket.

She inhaled the first cup and poured another, wishing she could just drink a gallon of wine and find a hole somewhere to crawl into. She couldn't do that. She stepped into the shower instead and stood under the pouring water without moving. It was going to be a hell of a day; she could tell already.

Out of the shower, she slipped into her robe, went back to the kitchen for still more coffee, and walked into her bedroom to dress. But when she set her coffee down, she found she was just staring at her closet. Liam. Last night had made her forget everything he had been saying.

She turned around, went to her bedside phone, and dialed her sister's number, suddenly worried and hoping to talk to her.

When Jeff answered the phone, she was silent for a moment, not exactly sure what she was going to say. "Jeff, it's me, Serena."

"Oh, hey. Melinda just left—"

"Oh," Serena said, disappointed.

"You can talk to me, you know," he said.

"I—I've been worried about you two," she stammered.

"Really?" His tone was cool.

She had gone this far. "Jeff, what's going on?"

"I don't know. What's going on?" He sounded breezy, casual. No—he was *trying* to sound breezy and casual. There was tenseness in his voice. He had taken a beat to think out his reply.

"Jeff, something is going on. You and Melinda are whispering all the time."

"We're thinking about a trip to New York," he said.

"Jeff, I've had people comment on..."

"On what?" he demanded.

"On your whispering. Look, I'm just concerned, and I don't mean to intrude, but—"

"Then don't."

"What?"

"Don't intrude, Serena. Worry about your own life. Mine is in better shape."

To her astonishment, the line clicked. He had hung up on her.

She stared at it. "Well," she murmured aloud, "that surely didn't make me feel any better."

She went to get her coffee. Was she being a busybody? No, she was just worried.

The phone rang. She jumped. She walked across the room and answered it. "Hey, kid, I was way out of line. I'm really sorry." It was Jeff.

"It's all right. Your life is none of my business. And it probably is in much better shape than my own."

"I'm going to make it up to you. I promise. I'm going to send you a great gift."

"Look, I don't need a gift, Jeff. You don't have to—"

"No, I've been meaning to do this anyway. Forgive me?"

She was silent for a moment. "*Is* everything all right?"

"Yeah. We're like all married couples. Hills and valleys. But we're on the right track. We're okay. I love your sister. And I love you too, okay, kid?"

"Sure, Jeff. I love you both."

"Well, get to work. Go knock 'em dead. Oh,

sorry, I guess that's a bad expression these days."

"It's all right."

"Want me to tell Melinda you called?"

"Sure."

They rang off again. As she thoughtfully set the receiver down, the doorbell rang. Still thinking about Jeff, she wandered to it. She gazed out the peephole.

Liam was standing there impatiently. His hair was sleek, ebony, combed back from his forehead. Somehow, he managed to be both casual and all pulled together in his sports jacket.

Here she was, with a worn robe, towel around wet hair, no makeup. The hell with it. She opened the door.

He looked her up and down. "Running late, are we?"

"One of us is. You'll have to excuse me. I had a rough night. Would you like some coffee?"

"No. I'll be waiting. I just wanted to make sure you were awake."

"Great."

He turned.

She should have let him go.

"You are allowed to wait indoors, and the coffee in the pot is fresh. Of course, you know that. You made it."

Liam turned back, arching a dark brow. "You're not going to throw it at me or anything, are you?"

"Not at the moment."

She left the door open and strode off to her bedroom. She slipped into a knit sweater and jeans, and halfheartedly dried her hair. She could finish at the studio. She really was running late.

She was still brushing her hair when she walked back into the living room. Liam was standing at the pine counter between the kitchen and living room, so deeply engrossed in the paper he was reading that he didn't even look up. But he knew she was there.

"Well, you were right," he said softly.

"What?" Her stupidity of the previous evening, and then being worried about her sister and brother-in-law, had consumed her thoughts that morning.

He turned the paper toward her. The photograph was in a gossip column, rife with speculation about danger to be found on the set of *Valentine Valley*. The photographer had gotten her leaning toward Liam. It didn't look like she was arguing with him. It looked as if she was getting as close as she possibly could.

She swore.

"Hey, you said it would happen."

"Yes, but..."

"I can see where this sort of thing gets very annoying."

She opened her mouth, about to tell him that she wasn't seeing anyone at the moment, it wasn't really going to hurt her, but what about his blond bombshell? She didn't say that. She didn't want to admit that she wasn't dating.

"Sorry," she said simply.

"Yeah."

"What is what's-her-name going to think?"

"Sharon?" he inquired.

"What's she going to think?"

"Nothing," he said. "She knew I was taking this job."

"Hard job, isn't it?" she inquired bitterly. "And that's what it is—a job."

"You know, I tried to talk to you last night—"

"I don't want to talk. If Sharon isn't going to be upset, hey, great. Are you ready?"

"Whenever you are."

She preceded him out the door, but turned back to lock it when they were out. When they reached his car, he had the passenger door open for her. She slid in. They started driving.

"Sharon is all right with all this?" she asked after several minutes of silence. She didn't want to talk, she reminded herself. She didn't seem able to help herself.

"Sharon isn't your concern."

Great, involved answers, she thought.

"Is she the free-spirit type?" she asked, then answered herself, "No, I guess not. You wouldn't like that."

He glanced her way at last. "Why? Do you consider yourself a free spirit?"

"Actually, no. And come to think of it, you didn't consider me a free spirit, either. I think it was something much worse."

"Not worse. Just something I couldn't handle," he said flatly.

"Something…" she murmured.

"Very, very busy. Always," he said.

"There's an implication there," she said lightly. "But let's see…here we are all this time later, and you're the one involved already."

He arched a brow in the mirror, his lip curling slightly. There she went again. Provoking him, saying things she didn't mean to say, giving away too much of her own life.

"Ah. I'm involved. And you're just flirting with handsome 'Hispanic types' and 'rock star' types, or the newest, 'Latin lover' types?"

"Hey, I just carry on friendly conversations."

"Yeah. And you don't notice the tongues lying on the floor that you trip over on your way out."

"I'm always very polite," she told him. "So…I hear that Sharon likes to dig holes in the ground."

"She does."

"That must make you very happy. You're so fond of…nature."

"She can survive a weekend without room service bringing coffee, yes."

Serena fell silent. She should have just kept her mouth shut. It hurt to hear that they went off on weekends. She wasn't taunting him anyway; she was merely torturing herself.

"Great. I'm glad you found what you were looking for. Even if she is a little young for you."

He looked at her, then back at the road. "She's not that young. Twenty-eight."

"Still young."

"How old do you think I am?" he asked her.

She was startled, realizing that she'd never asked him just how old he was.

They hadn't made it to a birthday for either one of them. Somehow, the subject of age had never come up.

"Forty?" she suggested. He could have been anywhere from thirty to forty.

"Thirty-six. Eight years. So she's eight years younger than me. That's not exactly an eon."

"Well, I guess it isn't exactly child seduction, then. Well, listen, please, don't take last night to mean anything—"

"What does mean anything to you, Serena?" he queried. She didn't like the harshness of his tone, or the ice in his dark eyes as they met hers.

"Last night you—"

"Wait a minute! Last night *I*?"

"Yes, *you*—"

"Hey, I was in the guest room, minding my own business."

"You didn't have to hop out of the shower."

"You didn't have to bring the towel and stand there staring at me."

"I wasn't!"

"You were! I merely thought I'd give you a better view."

"A view? That was a view?"

"Serena, I'm not sure what it was. And you won't talk seriously—"

"I can't. Here we are, tha—" She broke off before she could complete "*Thank God!*" She had put herself into this misery; she would be glad to be out of it. "I'm sure you could drop me in the front," she amended coolly.

"No, I have a place in the garage, right by the elevator."

"That's Joe's place."

"He insisted I take it."

He parked. She didn't wait for him to come around. The second the car stopped, she hopped out. She slung her bag over her shoulder and hurried past him. "I think I'm late," she murmured.

She knew he was close behind her, though. Into the elevator, out of the elevator. Well, hell. She was his job. He was good at his job. They had almost reached her dressing room when she turned to him. "Don't you think that this is overkill?" She winced at her choice of words.

"Don't worry, I'm not following you into the dressing room."

She shook her head and went on in, allowing the door to close behind her. A second later she heard a tap, and Thorne came in quickly. "You're late."

"I know. Sorry."

"Sit still."

He started quickly in with base and a sponge. "See the paper?" he asked her.

"Yes."

"You two back together?"

"No. Emphatically, no!"

"Looked like it."

"Thank you, Thorne."

"You're tense. Stop wrinkling up your forehead."

Serena sat still while he worked on her face. "I didn't even look at the schedule; nothing changed, did it?"

"No. You're due on your Egyptian set in...three minutes," he told her, running a brush over her lips. "Blot, blot!" He held a tissue to her mouth. She blotted obediently. He stepped back. "You look great. Oh, honey, you are a truly beautiful evil woman. Even when you don't sleep. You've got a few bags under those eyes. In fact, like a whole day's shopping worth of bags."

"Thank you so much for noticing."

"Oh, they're gone completely now. I do good work."

"Thanks. You're right, you do do good work," she told him, rising.

"Your costume is there...can you imagine anyone working with Egyptian treasures in those pants? They'd be dusty in two seconds. Of course, your fakes aren't actually dusty, thank God! Could you imagine old mummy wrappings on that gorgeous silk? Ugh!"

With that, Thorne departed.

Serena dressed quickly. When she stepped out of her dressing room she was startled to see that Liam wasn't alone in the hallway.

There was a woman with him. He was leaning against the wall, head slightly bowed to her height. The woman was very close. She appeared to be upset, but she quickly masked her expression when Serena appeared.

She was tall, naturally very blond, slim and tan in a simple white sheath that enhanced every one of her good qualities. She really was gorgeous. And young. Serena felt her stomach pitching and twisting into terrible knots.

They both turned to Serena as she exited her dressing room. "Good morning," she said, for lack of anything better to say.

"Sharon, Serena McCormack. Serena, Sharon Miller," Liam murmured politely.

"Serena McCormack," the blonde said, smiling.

Serena had known, without Liam's introduction, that this was, of course, the hole digger. "Sharon? Hi, nice to meet you." She stepped forward, offering a hand and the blond girl shook weakly. It was good that she had decided on the sciences; she wasn't much of an actress.

"What a pleasure to meet you, Serena. My brush with fame," Sharon said. Her words were too pronounced.

"It's a pleasure to meet you, too, Sharon."

The girl had very blue eyes. She studied Serena meticulously. "This is a closed set, I heard," Sharon said. "They didn't want to let me on it. I feel very privileged."

"The producers like to keep their plots a secret," Serena explained. It was torture, standing here, trying to be casual. "And of course, given our recent tragedy we're all a little edgy. I hope it wasn't that difficult getting in."

"No, not really," Sharon told her. "Not when I explained that I wasn't out to steal plot secrets, that I only needed a few moments."

182

For the first time Serena noticed that Sharon had the daily paper folded under her arm. "The paper," she murmured. "I'm sorry. In fact, we were having an argument."

"Don't worry. I wasn't bothered," Sharon told her.

"Good," Serena said. Her stomach continued knotting in a vicious manner. She wouldn't be able to keep the smile going much longer. "Well, if you both will excuse me, I'm due on the set."

She started down the hallway. When someone slid up beside her, she thought at first that it was Liam, doggedly doing his job no matter what. But it was Doug.

"The plot thickens," he whispered.

"What are you talking about?" she asked with annoyance, far more shaken than she wanted to admit.

"Ruggedly handsome bodyguard, a new love, an old flame—"

"Don't you dare call me old this morning," she hissed to him, causing Doug to laugh.

"Think about it, Serena. There you have her—the young, beautiful new girlfriend. Innocent in appearance, far removed from the day-to-day action! But underneath it all, she's desperately in love with her new guy and knows that somewhere inside him, his heart is still beating—thump-thump, thump-thump— for the exotically glamorous star of daytime. The gorgeous, athletic blonde isn't as sweet and naive as she appears. Beneath the casual exterior, she is seething. She wants her man, so she plots, she plans, she bribes someone on the set—"

"And kills Jane Dunne?" Serena murmured, looking back. Liam was following behind her, still talking with the blonde.

"She didn't intend to kill Jane Dunne. She meant to kill you."

"Great planning. She commits a murder, and the killing sends the macho bodyguard here, hired to guard her intended victim."

"I love it!" Doug said.

"Doug, even for a soap that's reaching."

"I think it's a wonderful plot twist."

"I think you're cruel."

"I think you're jealous."

"I probably am."

They had reached the elevator.

"Push the button, quick," Serena told him.

He smiled, folded his arms over his chest, and waited for Liam and Sharon. Liam introduced Doug and Sharon. As the two made small talk, Serena realized she was acquiring a tremendous headache.

She stepped off the elevator and almost walked right into Joe Penny. He pointed a finger at her. "You. Andy wants to talk to you."

"I can't talk now. I'm due on set," she said. She realized that Joe was looking past her to see the newcomer.

Usually, Joe was irritated to have anyone else around. Today he smiled. "Good morning, Liam. And hello, Miss…"

"Sharon Miller, one of our producers, Joe Penny," Serena said.

"Hello," Sharon said. "How very nice to meet you."

Joe hated people on his set, but he liked attractive women. He smiled at her. "A pleasure to meet you. You're a friend of Liam's?"

"Yes, and don't worry, your security is safe. I had to talk for twenty minutes to get escorted up by an armed guard."

"We're terribly sorry to have put you through so much," Joe said.

"It wasn't that bad. To be honest, I think I have an old friend who works on this set. I would have pulled some favors if I had needed to."

"Who's the old friend?" Joe asked.

"I'm not divulging any secrets. I may need help in the future," Sharon said.

Joe didn't press the point. He seemed impressed by Sharon, and he looked at Liam. "Bill Hutchens was here earlier. He said to tell you that the rose was a rose was a rose. Whatever that means."

"Thanks," was all Liam said. Serena stared at him. He looked her way, but added no more. Sharon was watching them both. Serena found herself very anxious to get away.

She escaped them all, striding across the floor to Jim Novac, who was setting up on the Egyptian set. "Morning, Jim."

"Hey, Serena, barely on time."

She smiled. "Sorry."

"We rehearsed this several times, but that was before...before we lost so much time. Think we should go over it again?"

"I'm fine with the scene. Is Kelly here?"

"Right here!"

Kelly came around the side of a huge, standing sarcophagus. "Ready to tear your hair out. Come on up."

"You know what to do with this one," Jim said.

Jim called for quiet on the set, and started his countdown: "And we're on in five, four, three..."

"How dare you—how *dare* you—presume to get involved in my life, Verona!" Kelly charged. She walked around the set, furious. "You're just trying to ruin my life because your own is a miserable mess. You stay away from David DeVille, do you hear me?"

"Marla!" Serena said, taking her stage sister by the shoulders and shaking her. "He's bad news, don't you understand that? He uses everyone, everyone!"

"So that's it, is it?" Kelly demanded, shaking off her touch. "He uses everyone. Well, according to the gardener, he used *you*!"

Serena gasped, and gave Kelly a stage slap.

Kelly backed away, near tears.

"You don't understand! I love him. You don't love anyone. You're all rolled up in yourself. Go back to Egypt, stay in Egypt, maybe the sands will bury you forever—"

"Marla, I've tried to protect you—"

"Your way of protecting me is to take your clothes off for David. No, thanks!"

"Marla, please—"

"You slept with him."

"Marla—"

"If you go near him again, Verona..."

"Marla, you're being far too dramatic."

"This isn't drama at all, Verona. If you go near him again, I'll kill you."

"I'm your sister, Marla—"

"I'll kill you, do you understand that? I don't know how, or when, but I'll do it! I will kill you. And trust me, I'm not so frail, or innocent, or so *naive* that it won't happen. I'm warning you, *you will be dead*!"

Kelly slammed her way off the set.

"Cut! Terrific!" Jim cried out.

Kelly was already laughing at something the cameraman was saying. Serena walked off the set more slowly.

The lights were in her eyes. The rest of the room seemed very dark, and the other sets created vast shadows. Where people stood here and there about the cavernous floor, they, too, seemed all shadow.

She shivered, suddenly afraid. She wanted to get off the set.

A hand suddenly landed on her shoulder.

"You! I am going to kill you! How could you, Serena, how could you? Without a word?"

Chapter 13

Sharon Miller stood at the elevator, praying that it would come quickly. She should have never come here. She was about to burst into tears, and all she wanted to do was get away.

From the moment Liam had said that he was taking a job at *Valentine Valley*, she had known it was over. He'd never lied to her; he'd never said that he loved her. She'd known about Serena, and she *should* have realized from the way he acted far too often that there was still someone else in his heart.

She pressed the elevator button again. "Come, come, come, *please*!"

It hadn't helped that she'd seemed to be so cordial, so reassuring, and so *decent* when Liam had said that they were worlds apart. His relationship with her just wasn't fair because he couldn't be what she wanted. She'd tried to tell him that she didn't want a commitment if it made him uncomfortable. He had told her gently that she deserved a lot more. Every time a guy said that a woman deserved a lot more, you just knew you were screwed. He did care about her, she knew that, just not the way she wanted, not the way she had hoped.

"Sharon?"

"Hey!" she said happily. She did have a friend on the set.

"You're leaving?"

Sharon nodded. "I've got to get out of here,

fast." She wiped below her eyes. "I've just been given the kindly brush-off."

"It's Serena, right? Serena McCormack?"

"Not her fault; he just isn't...he isn't in love with me."

"Still..."

"Hey, if any more lights or pieces of scenery fall, try to push her in the way, hm?"

"Sharon, I'm so sorry—"

"Don't be. I didn't mean it."

"It is too bad because Serena probably is the most decent person here. Too bad she's just so..."

"So *Serena*?" Sharon said with a laugh. "Can you imagine this whole thing, the way that it's happened? Oh, God, there's the elevator. Listen, call me at home, please. We can talk then. Really talk. It's great to see you— I just have to pull myself together!"

The elevator arrived. Sharon slipped in and waved good-bye to her friend.

"Serena, I just don't believe this," Andy said. He clapped his hand to his heart. "You've wounded me. Deeply."

"Andy, you know, you are one hell of an actor."

"There you go, striking into my heart again."

"Andy, I didn't do anything evil. I did a screen test. I have not been offered a role. If I am offered a role, I will discuss it with you anyway."

"Why the screen test if you—"

"Andy, you know that I met Eddie at film school. He asked me to do a screen test. So I've been his friend, and I thought, hey, why not? And why didn't I tell anyone? Frankly, I'm not so sure that he will offer me the part, and you know what, Andy? I still have something of a delicate ego. I don't like the whole world to know when I've been rejected."

Andy understood that.

"You rejected me."

"Oh, Andy!"

"I still love you, Serena. I remain crushed."

"Right. So crushed that you run into the arms of every woman in town."

"Ouch!" he said. "You rejected me, remember? I have an image to uphold. And speaking of parties, we've been invited to one tonight."

"Oh?"

"And I wish you'd come."

"Who's having the party?"

"Kyle Amesbury."

Serena stiffened. "Andy, I'm sorry—"

"He and Joe apparently had words last night. He wants to have a small dinner."

"Good for him. I don't like him, Andy."

"I'll watch out for you."

"Andy, I just—" She paused. He wasn't paying attention to her; he was looking over her shoulder. She spun around, frowning. Liam was just behind her.

"I think *we* should definitely attend that party."

"See, there you have it," Andy murmured. "Even Liam thinks you should go."

"Where? When?" Liam asked.

"Kyle's place, in West Hollywood. Eight o'clock cocktails and a dinner buffet."

"We'll definitely be there," Liam said.

"Great," Andy replied stiffly. "I—uh—I think he meant just the cast and some of the crew—"

"Where Serena goes, I follow," Liam said. "That's pretty much what you hired me to do, right?"

"Yes, I guess so. Well, then, I'll see you both tonight. No, wait, Serena, I'll see you later on the set. We're scheduled in a scene together at four o'clock."

"I'll be there."

Andy nodded and strolled on over to Jim Novac, who was on the *Valentine* family living room set, talking to Hank and Vera, who were about to have a huge row over their children.

Serena turned and headed toward the elevators, aware that Liam was following her. She was ready to throttle him for saying they'd go to the party.

She wasn't going.

At the elevator, fully aware that he was behind her, she spun around. "Liam, there aren't many people I really dislike, but Kyle Amesbury is one of them. He watches people, assesses them as if he's the devil and he's wondering what price he's going to pay for a soul."

"It's still important to go to this party."

"Why?"

"I want to watch him."

"Liam, he wasn't on the set when anything happened!"

"I want to see what his relationships with other people are like."

"Question him."

"I intend to."

"Liam—"

"Please, Miss McCormack," he said politely, with a slight smile. "Think of it this way. If you want me out of your life, helping me to find out what is going on will move things along."

If she wanted him out of her life? Or if he was in a hurry to get out of it?

"Where's Miss Miller?" she asked him.

"Gone."

"Gone where?"

"She's gone, Serena, I don't know where."

A wave of guilt suddenly came over her. "Oh, God, the picture in the paper did cause you problems. I am really sorry—"

"It wasn't the picture in the paper, Serena, so don't worry about it." His voice was harsh.

"Liam, honest to God, maybe I can do something—"

"I don't want you to do anything, Serena. My life is my concern, all right?"

"Exactly."

She realized that the elevator door had been open for some time. She hurried into it, and he followed. It felt warm in the elevator, too close.

"Liam, I'm on break. I'll lock myself in. You

can go..." She paused, because what she really wanted him to do with himself threatened to trip off her tongue. "You can go have lunch. Or shoot the bull or whatever it is you do with Conar. I'll be all right alone."

"You make sure you lock yourself in."

"I will."

He walked her to the door of her dressing room. She closed and locked it.

With a real headache now, she flopped down on her sofa and closed her eyes.

Liam found Andy back on the set, watching the scene between Vera and Hank as the two veterans rehearsed, and then tapcd it. Andy looked glum. The glance he gave Liam was somewhat hostile. "So...have you got anything?"

"Joe Penny was ready to do violence last night," Liam said.

Andy let out a snort. "In a thousand years, Joe would never hurt Serena." IIc shrugged. "She's the strength of the show. His prize."

"Yep. But his prize misbehaved, in his eyes."

Andy looked at him. "You're crazy if you suspect Joe."

"Actually, I don't."

"Who do you suspect?" Andy demanded.

"Almost everyone else."

"Me?"

"You're still in love with her. She divorced you."

Andy smiled, looking toward the stage. "No, actually, she had me file the papers. She made me look good all the way through the divorce. Better than I deserved, probably."

"But you are still in love with her."

Andy, still smiling, glanced his way. "You're the one who's still in love with her. You slept with my ex-wife. You'd lie down and die yourself before letting anyone get to her, so therefore you're the last person I'd want to have around." Andy hesitated. "You know, I've talked to the police, and I've tried to remember every moment of the morning Jane Dunne died. I was never on the set that morning; I was still up in my office when the lights crashed down. But"—he hesitated—"I know that Jeff Guelph was on the set, and he said he hated her. I also know that Jay Braden had a few words with Jane, because he came up and told me that if Jane stayed on the show, there would be a good chance he'd be leaving."

"When Olsen interviewed you, did you tell him all this?"

"More or less. But there were lots of people in the studio that day, and everyone hated Jane. Allona loathed her. Doug said he couldn't stand writing for her. Even Jinxy had a bad time with her. She started out as charming as could be and in three short weeks turned from the beautiful queen to the wicked witch." Andy eyed Liam for a moment. "You know, Detective Hutchens still thinks the lights were an accident."

"A loose clamp isn't an accident. It's either negligence or premeditation."

"And you think—"

"What I don't think is that your lighting guys are negligent," Liam said. "Anyway, thanks for the help. See you tonight."

Serena couldn't believe that she'd let Liam bully her into coming to the party.

Liam had been withdrawn all afternoon, leaving her alone but never being too far away. He'd come in at her house, showered and changed in the guest room in record time, keeping his distance, and watched the evening news while waiting for her to finish dressing.

They'd barely spoken on the way to the party, traveling the short distance from Glenwood to West Hollywood. A number of the cast and crew were already there—the driveway was filled with cars. She saw Joe's BMW, Andy's new Jag convertible, and Doug's car as well. The red Fiat was Jay's.

"I hope this accomplishes something for you," she said to Liam as they rang the doorbell.

The door was opened by Kyle Amesbury himself. His hair was clean and slicked back, and he was casually dressed in Versace jeans and a silk V-neck shirt. He smiled broadly at the sight of Serena. "Hi! Welcome! Thanks so much for coming!" He reached out, took her hand, and kissed it. She tried not to squirm. His words were ingratiating. His eyes gloated. He was probably sure she had been forced to come.

"Thanks for having us. Kyle, this is Liam Murphy."

Liam stretched out a hand. "Hi."

"Welcome. You're the hunk who was in the paper, aren't you?"

"That's me," Liam said.

After a pause, Kyle realized he wasn't getting any more than that. He threw out his arm, indicating that they should enter. "Most everyone is here. Drinks are at the bar, buffet is there in the dining room."

"Thanks," Serena said, moving on in.

She saw Doug, standing by the bar with Allona, and hurried over to greet both writers with a kiss on the cheek.

"Why *are* we here?" Serena murmured, accepting a glass of wine from Allona. She made a face at Doug. "Sorry. I guess you like him."

"I'll say I'm reserving my opinion," Doug said, looking across the room to where Kyle had settled himself on a handsome leather sofa with Joe and Andy in chairs across from him. He shrugged at Serena. "The wine is safe—I've been drinking it for a while now."

"Good to hear," she said, lifting her glass to him.

"Good. I'll have wine too, then."

She turned. Doug was grinning at Liam, ready to pour another glass of wine. "Welcome there, Mr. Murphy. What a surprise to see you both. Andy said you were coming, but I didn't believe him until I saw the whites of your eyes."

"Where she goes, I follow," Liam murmured, leaning against the bar and eyeing his surroundings.

"I don't want to be here," Serena said.

"Why are any of us here?" Allona snapped. She raised her arm. "He's a show-off. He just wants to make sure that we know he's gotten rich and has a big house, great pool and patio, and a Dalí and a Picasso." She gestured toward the walls.

"It is a great house," Doug said, "and he likes to show it off. Conar and Jennifer are here, Serena. They're upstairs taking a tour right now with Hank, who happened to know the previous owner."

"Conar and Jennifer are here?" Serena said, surprised. So they had been coerced as well. "Who else?"

"Jay, Thorne, and Jinx are by the pool," Allona told her, pointing out the sliding glass doors.

"It is a great pool," Doug said. "Like something out of a travel brochure for Hawaii. There are little rock cliffs, waterfalls, flowers... we should go out."

The pool area was spectacular. The free-form shape was surrounded by stonework caves and grottos, with waterfalls all around. There was a cabana to the rear, in the midst of palms and shrubs. It had the look of an Old Hollywood bungalow itself, a small-scale Garden of Allah out of an old movie-time past. Jinx and Jay were sitting in patio chairs near the cabana, deep in conversation.

Jay rose, greeting Serena with a kiss. "You are here. It's a miracle. Hey, Liam."

Jinx stood as well. She looked very pretty in a short blue halter dress, but she seemed uncomfortable. "Hi," she told Serena. "Joe told me I should come tonight."

"Sorry. This isn't part of your job description."

"Oh, no. I like dinner parties. It's just, I'm not really cast or crew—"

"You're as much a part of the show as anyone else, Jinx," Serena assured her.

She smiled. "Thanks. I'm running in for a drink, then."

She left them.

Joe appeared at the open French doors. "Hey, Liam, can I see you for a minute?"

"Sure," he said. His dark eyes touched Serena's. "Be right back. More wine?"

"Sure."

"Me, too," Allona said quickly. She rose. "I'll help. Hey, here's another good thing about Kyle, Serena. He knows good wine."

She gave a thumbs-up sign to Allona.

"So, Jay," Doug said flatly, when the other two had disappeared, "are you dating Jinx?"

Serena gazed at Jay, a smile curling her lips. She'd been curious herself, but hadn't thought to be quite so direct.

Jay shook his head. "No...not dating. It's a big brother kind of thing, I think. The kid is cute as can be, but she reminds me of a deer trapped in someone's headlights."

"You should watch it, though, Jay," Doug warned. "She may not see you as a big brother.

She may be falling in love. You know, you're the devastating leading man type."

"Am I that devastating?" Jay said lightly. "Conar seems to be the one they're all fighting over. That's brutal on the old ego, you know."

"It's a soap opera," Doug said. "I'm supposed to keep you all sleeping with one another, procreating in secret, losing babies all over the place, and constantly plotting the downfall of one another."

Laughter suddenly erupted from the house. Jay rose, looking through the French doors. "I'll think I'll see what's going on," he said, and started in.

Doug shook his head as Jay left. "I think he's in for trouble."

"I think he's trying to be nice."

"That's because you wouldn't fall for a Jay Braden."

"No, I *married* an Andy Larkin."

"Yep," Doug said, grinning. "Know what he told me once?"

"What?"

"You were his punishment from God for all the mean and careless things he had done to other women."

"Great."

Again, laughter rose from the house.

"All right, now I've got to see what's going on," Doug told her. "You coming?"

Serena shook her head. She hated to admit it, but it felt good to sit by Kyle's pool. The dim lighting cast a blue tint, and as Allona had said, the wine was very good.

"I'm just going to sit here," she said.

Doug shrugged and went on in.

Serena stared out at the water, sipping her wine. She half closed her eyes. The breeze drifted by her, just lifting her hair.

Her eyes suddenly flew open. The breeze had slammed one of the French doors shut. She sat up in her chair. A maid came and shut the other door.

Serena sat back again.

The wind and the maid had only closed the doors. Liam was inside, close by. Conar was there, Jennifer. All her friends.

The lights began to dim, until the patio was bathed in a twilight blue. The once benign hedges and foliage now seemed like dark screens behind which someone could hide.

She should just get up and go inside.

"I'm sorry. Did I make it too dark?"

The question came from behind her. She almost jumped out of her skin as she spun around. Kyle Amesbury, in his perfect clothing, with his perfect hair, stood behind her.

"God, I'm really sorry. I didn't mean to scare you."

"You didn't," she lied.

"This is my favorite part of the house, though it's a great house all over. It once belonged to a guy named Ray Lawson, in the early forties. He was an early special effects wizard. They say he had great parties here. Gable and Lombard supposedly stayed in the cabana. Ray died young—he was a drug addict, but a brilliant man."

"It is a great house," Serena said.

"Hey, you know, I'm sorry," Kyle said.

"For what?"

"For whatever I've said or done to offend you so much."

He was just talking, casually, trying to make amends, or so it seemed. She shook her head. "There's nothing to be sorry about," she told him.

Where was everyone?

"Want to see the cabana?" he asked with a childlike excitement.

"Oh, well..."

"It's great! Come on. I promise, you've never seen anything like it before."

He turned and started toward the cabana. It wasn't thirty feet from where they stood, no more than fifty from the back of the house.

Serena followed him. He pushed open the slatted wood doors to the cabana house, flicking on a light as they entered.

Turning on the light didn't do much. The room was arranged like a pleasure palace always in readiness. The bed was huge, covered in pillows, with a rich medieval tapestry with winged cupids, flowers, stars, and naked cherubs. There was a beveled-glass mirror set into the arched canopy above the bed, which looked onto a dark wood entertainment center. The draperies around the windows and bed had a Middle Eastern flavor. Large doors opened to the cabana bath, which offered a huge Jacuzzi, glassed-in shower, thick throw rugs, and a cooler with clear glass doors that displayed a bottle of champagne and two elegant flutes.

"Isn't it beautiful?" Kyle asked with pleasure. He touched her on the shoulder, leading her in so that she could get a full view of the bathroom. "Can you imagine Gable and Lombard? If the stories are all true, of course..."

His touch had her skin crawling. She was about to slide away when he turned. He ran his hand over the tapestried bed, with his little-boy enthusiasm intact. She thought there was something else in his eyes, though. A lasciviousness that didn't quite go with the naive excitement.

"You've got to try the bed!" he told her.

"I wouldn't want to just lie down and fall asleep."

"No, no, you should just lie on it for a minute, see how great it is. I won't let you fall asleep."

She wasn't quite sure how he had done it, but he was standing between her and the doors, and she found herself backing toward the bed.

"I think I hear Liam calling me," she said.

"Want me to go get him for you?" he asked.

"I can just go on out," she said.

"Serena, you know, I'm trying hard to be friends with you."

He was almost on top of her. With another step he *would* be on top of her, and she'd be falling back on the bed to avoid him. "Serena, do you know how important you are to the show, to all of us? If you'd only ease up a little bit—"

In two seconds she was going to scream. Every nerve ending in her body was shouting. She was trying to tell herself that she was in no danger, but her imagination was running rampant. His eyes weren't just lascivious, they were evil.

"Serena..." His voice was a whisper now, a hiss. He had something in his hand, she saw. A handkerchief...a cloth?...he'd drawn from his pocket. Every crime show she'd ever seen flashed through her mind. He was about to cover her nose with a cloth soaked with chloroform. He was too close; the way he said her name made chills snake through her.

She'd had enough. She started past him.

"Oh, no!" he said softly, catching her by both arms.

Joe had called Liam in because Conar had been asking for him.

At first, in front of the others milling around, Conar was casual. "Hey, it's great that you're here. You got Serena to come, eh? She's the original recluse of the group. There's a room upstairs I wanted to show you. I'm thinking of some redecorating."

Conar had never mentioned redecorating before in his life.

"Great. Let's see it."

They excused themselves to Joe and those around them and started up the stairs. "A room?" Liam said. "You're going into design?"

"You'll see." Conar flashed him a smile. They walked down the long hall.

"Master bedroom," Conar said briefly, pushing open a door.

The room was huge, including a sitting area and double closets that led to a bathroom the size of a small country. Liam briefly noted the size and decor, but he had discovered what Conar had wanted him to see immediately.

The large entertainment cabinet in front of the bed was open. He saw the configuration of television, VCR, and stereo, and the tiny circular lens in the center of the controls.

He nodded to Conar. "Yeah, sure, you want to do something just like this. Jennifer would love it."

He walked over to the entertainment cabinet. Amesbury had a large collection of DVDs and a larger collection of tapes. Liam selected one. *Blue Velvet*. He pulled the tape out of its box; the packaging again announced *Blue Velvet*.

He put it back and selected a tape from a row of classics. *Jamaica Inn*.

Again, the inside packaging was the same.

There was a row of tapes from *Valentine Valley*. They were numbered by episode. There were also notations on them. *Featuring David's Return. Featuring Marla Valentine, Featuring...*

Verona Valentine. Serena McCormack.

At least ten of the episodes in the row of fifteen or so featured Serena.

He didn't want to look further at the moment. The camera lens was above him.

"The guy has some great films," he said briefly. "There are guest rooms on this floor, too, right?"

"Yeah, want to take a look?"

"Sure. Kyle doesn't mind?"

"Not at all," Conar said clearly. "He's proud of the house."

He made a quick perusal of the three other bedrooms on the floor. All were lavishly appointed, with special attention paid to the bedding and entertainment systems.

When they started down the stairs, Conar asked softly, "What do you think?"

"I think he has a serious case of voyeurism."

"Illegal?"

"This is private property," Liam said. "Depends on what he's doing."

"That's his security system?" Conar said doubtfully.

Liam barely heard him. Looking downstairs, he saw that Doug, Allona, and Jinx had come inside and stood by the buffet talking to Jennifer. Serena was nowhere in sight.

"Serena," he said softly and hurried ahead.

Chapter 14

Kyle's hands were on Serena, his breath hot against her cheeks. "Serena, you don't understand, I'm trying—"

"There you are, Serena!"

Kyle's hands fell from her shoulders. He spun toward the door.

To Serena's surprise, it was Jay who entered, and Jay's flat, cheerful tone that dispelled the demons in her mind.

"Jay!" She slipped around Kyle, anxious to reach Jay's side.

Before she could do so, Liam appeared behind him. He put an arm around her shoulders, pulling her protectively against him as he looked at Kyle. "It's a really great house, Amesbury," he said. His tone was light, complimentary. His eyes were not. Kyle didn't notice, nor did Jay. But when Liam's gaze fell on Serena, she knew that he was thinking she was an idiot and that she never should have gone into the cabana.

"Thanks," Kyle said, recovering quickly. "I am really in love with the place. Big mortgage, though, you know. That's why I'm so anxious about the show."

Liam left Serena's side, walking into the cabana, looking around with appreciation.

"If you ever want to stay for the night, this is the main guest room," Kyle told him.

"Hey, I may take you up on that," Liam said. "It would be my big chance at a night like the rich and famous. Cops and P.I.'s don't do as well as business moguls, you know."

"Cops do all right in this town," Kyle said with a shrug. "And now that you're on your own... I hear that on this case, you're just about worth your weight in gold."

"I don't come cheap," Liam said.

"Try the bed," Kyle told him.

To Serena's astonishment, Liam grinned and did just that, falling onto the mattress under the canopy and lacing his fingers behind his head. "A great entertainment center here, too. You have one hell of a movie collection."

"Everything you can think of," Kyle agreed. "Everything."

Serena detected something in his tone. A guy's way of telling another guy that he was loaded with the best in pornography as well?

Despite Liam's return and Jay's being with them as well, Serena was anxious to escape. "I think I'll grab something to eat." She was sure that Liam would come with her.

"I'm hungry, too," Jay said.

Liam didn't rise. Serena turned and headed out, Jay at her heels. Liam stayed behind.

She nearly screamed when Jay put his hand on her shoulder as they started back across the pool area. "You okay?" he asked her.

"Yeah, sure. He just makes me nervous." She looked at Jay, who was studying her with a concerned gaze. "You came to rescue me, didn't you?"

"I—I don't really trust the guy either," he said briefly.

"Thanks."

"You'd have been okay. Your bodyguard was behind me, flying across the patio like a linebacker."

She arched a brow. Liam had entered the cabana as casually as if he were sightseeing.

"Well, thanks. You got there first."

Jay grinned at her, but she found herself frowning. "Jay, Kyle knew Jane, right?"

"Oh, yeah."

"They had a thing?"

"Serena, what do I really know about other people?" His voice had a bitter tone. "She came on like a blockbuster, bigger than life, nicer than pie. And yes, she had an interest in Kyle. He was with the money people, you know."

"I know you know more than you're saying."

"Okay. I'm sure she slept with him. Probably back there on that nice big bed he asks everyone to try out."

"Everything okay?"

Serena started. The French doors were open again. Jinx was standing there, looking out anxiously.

"Right as rain," Jay said as they both joined her. Serena gave Jinx a reassuring smile, and they walked in to the buffet table.

Doug and Allona were deep in conversation with Jennifer. Joe and Andy were talking. Conar was standing with Dayton Riley, who was chewing on a chicken wing. Conar had been watching the door, and he noted her return.

Serena helped herself to another glass of wine. She wasn't hungry at all.

A minute later, she saw that Kyle had returned and joined in the conversation with Joe and Andy. She didn't see Liam again, not for a few minutes.

By the time he finally reappeared, she'd had it. She set her wine down, approached Kyle, and thanked him for the get-together. She was afraid that Liam was going to say something about having a great time, they should stay longer, but he thanked Kyle as well, complimented the house again, and said his good-byes to the others.

They walked out. He opened the passenger door for her silently and didn't speak when they started down the street. Then his words were like a whiplash.

"Don't ever go anywhere alone with that man again."

"Excuse me, I didn't even want to go to that party," she told him angrily. "I didn't mean to wind up alone with him. You know my opinion of him—"

"So, great. Wander off into a cabana alone with the guy then."

"You're the bodyguard. You should have been there."

"I'll remember that."

"You spent the whole party nearly kissing his butt," she snapped.

He didn't reply to that. He kept driving in silence. By the time they reached her house, she was seething. She slammed the door of the car on her way out. She could barely twist her key in the lock, and tap in the code correctly for her alarm. Inside, she walked straight into her bedroom and closed the door. She sat on the bed, still unnerved.

She sat there for a long time. Waiting. Thinking he would come. Like a dictator, of course. He would tell her more about what she had done wrong. Warn her to watch out. Give her a hard time about something.

But he didn't. After a few minutes had passed, she was pretty sure he wasn't coming. Maybe he was on the phone with Sharon, patching things up. She looked at the phone. *You will not pick it up and listen!* she told herself. *You are not that type of person; you are better than that.*

Despite herself, she picked up her bedroom extension, then felt like a fool. A dial tone greeted her ear. Still, she was restless. Tired, but not at all able to settle down.

She exited her room quietly. He was not in the living room. She ventured down the hall. The door to the guest room was closed. She was tempted to test it—see if it was locked or not.

She put her hand on the knob and twisted it silently. He couldn't possibly hear her. There were sounds coming from the guest room. He was watching television or...something.

She stood very still outside the door. She could hear...moaning? And panting.

For one horrible second, she thought that he had invited his girlfriend to her house, and that he was with another woman in *her* guest room. But the dim light visible beneath the door assured her that he was watching television. Or a tape. A tape with...

Moaning. Heavy breathing. Some shrieking...some screaming.

The door suddenly flew open. And there she was, just standing there. And there he was, down to a pair of black Calvin Klein boxers.

"Yes?" he asked politely.

I was just passing by? No. *What could she say?*

He leaned against the doorjamb, arms crossed over his chest, waiting.

"I was going to make tca," she lied. "I just wanted to see if you wanted any."

He shook his head in disappointment. "You can do better than that."

"All right. What are you watching?"

He arched a brow. "You can hear the tape down by your room? You came to check out what I was doing? Lord—you thought I'd brought someone into your house?"

"No!"

He caught her arm and pulled her into the room.

"Wait! I do not want to watch a...a...porno flick with you!" she protested, her cheeks red as a lobster.

"Maybe you'll recognize the people in it."

"What?"

He had pulled her in front of the television. To her astonishment, she immediately recognized the room. She had recently been in it. The setting for the tape in the VCR was Kyle Amesbury's cabana.

Her jaw dropped. There were two people on the bed. The lighting was very low. The female's body was fully exposed. The man's head was bent over, dark in the shadows.

"It's Jane!" she whispered.

"Different camera angles, even," Liam commented. "I saw the lens set in the middle of the controls. The other one is situated in the bed frame."

Suddenly the tape went to fizz. Serena stared at Liam. "Where did you get that?"

"Where else?" he asked with a shrug. "The cabana."

"That's why you stayed behind."

"There are cameras all over the house."

"That must be illegal!"

"It's private property. He owns the place."

"Still, it's an invasion of privacy—"

"He can call them security cameras."

"In a bed?"

"Trust me, they'd never get anything against a guy for cameras in his own house."

"But this tape... Jane wouldn't have allowed it. She was incredibly aware of her value, and she—"

"She's dead. And I can't figure out who the guy is. Can you?"

She shook her head. "I just saw the head—"

"Yeah, strategically positioned. That's all there was."

"You stole this tape?"

"Yeah, I did."

"That's illegal."

"I'm trying to find a killer."

"Kyle was never at the studio—"

"Maybe he used these tapes to blackmail people. Or maybe he's just close to someone. This was the only tape I could slip out easily."

"You could get a search warrant."

"I'm not a cop."

"But Bill Hutchens or George Olsen could."

"Not yet."

"But Kyle's a slimy rat."

"You can't arrest people for that, especially not in Hollywood."

"I'm confused. We should do something. We—"

"*We* shouldn't do anything. *I* am doing something. I'm investigating. You're an actress. Act. Go to work—do your job."

"But...Kyle has to be stopped."

"How do we know Jane wasn't willingly being taped?"

"Because I know Jane!"

"Serena, you have to pretend you haven't seen this."

"But—but I have friends who go over there. I can't let them... I can't let them wind up on tape without having a clue!"

"Serena, I need to find some things out. Without people knowing that I'm on to them. Understand?"

"So what? You're going to break into Kyle's place and steal all his tapes? Without him noticing? He has a tape of Jane. Give it to Olsen."

"To prove what? That she slept with people?"

Serena spun around and left the bedroom.

She walked into the kitchen, straight to the bar, and poured a shot of whiskey. She hated whiskey, but she kept a tight grip on the bottle anyway, glad of the stinging warmth of it as she downed the shot.

She jumped when she realized he was right behind her. "I thought you were making tea."

"I was. Things change."

He came up to her, took the whiskey bottle from her and set it on the counter, pushing it back.

"Hey, this is my house, my whiskey—"

"Yeah, but you're just trying to hide behind it."

"Excuse me—"

"You didn't hear that video from down the hall."

She was an actress; she could keep her jaw from dropping. She turned away and started back toward her own bedroom.

"Serena."

She stopped.

"If you want something that you know you can have, why don't you just take it?"

She turned back around slowly. "How do I know I can have it?"

"Uncertainty? That's not like you," he said, leaning against the counter.

"All we ever do is fight."

"Not in bed. We're very good together in bed."

"Is that enough?"

"For tonight? It would be enough for me."

*The night. Oh, sure, the night. It wasn't
enough for her.*

But she didn't want to be alone. She had gone
to find him.

She looked him up and down without
replying. He wore boxers very well. She turned
again, slipping off a shoe as she did so, taking
a step, shedding the other shoe. He hadn't
moved, hadn't taken a step to follow her.
Dangling both heels from her fingers, she
told him, "If you want something you know
you can have, why don't you just take it?"

This time he followed her.

And later, when they were quiet, and it
was the dead of night, she heard the leaves
rustling outside her windows, and she was glad.
She fell into a peaceful sleep.

Toward daybreak, she awoke to find him
standing by the bedside window, looking out
into the yard. She came up on her elbows, rubbing her eyes. "Liam?"

"It's all right. Go back to sleep." He let the
drape fall. "Really, go back to sleep."

She was so tired that she closed her eyes. Half
asleep again, she realized that he hadn't
crawled back in beside her. But she was too
close to sleep to gather the energy to wake up
and find out where he was.

She dreamed. Dreamed she woke up and
started looking for him. He wasn't in the
house. The doors to the patio were open.
She walked out, feeling the breeze. But in
the breeze she heard a rustling, coming closer,
moving toward her. She spun around and

around, trying to find the direction of the danger. *Serena...!* Her name was hissed with the wind that stroked her ears. She was inside the cabana, and she could hear the whir and roll of a camera, and someone was behind her, reaching out. She could almost feel the touch of fingers against her nape...

She woke with a start, bathed in a cold sweat. She was alone. She almost leaped up in a panic. She took a deep breath. From the kitchen, she could hear the reassuring sound of Liam's voice. Then a clattering noise alerted her to the fact that he was making coffee.

She showered and dressed, then went to the living room.

She found him dressed in a suede jacket and Dockers, dark hair freshly washed and combed back. "You're late," he told her, pouring her a cup of coffee. "You'll have to take this in the car." His manner was all business.

He was quiet on the drive. She shook her head, watching him. "I still think I should tell people about that tape."

He glared at her before giving his full attention to the winding road down to the valley from Glenwood. "Serena, you announced to everyone that you'd seen something in Jane's room, a saucer used as an ashtray and a half-burned note."

"Yes?"

"What do you make of it?"

"That she was nervous and smoking, and pissed off about something someone wrote to her."

"Right. And then she was dead. And you started getting warnings."

"What warnings?"

"The roses. The one you got at the cemetery. Then there was the rose in your dressing room, the one you thought I gave you." He hesitated. "Then there was another rose, on your doorstep yesterday morning."

She stared at him. "There was a rose on my doorstep yesterday?"

"Yes."

"But you were protecting me. And the house."

"I'm good—not perfect," he told her.

She didn't reply.

"Serena, someone is possibly trying to kill you."

"We still don't know that."

"What the hell do you want? Me to find your body and say, 'See there, I was right'?"

"Doug has been over to Kyle's a few times. And he's been kind of quiet about it. For Doug."

"That wasn't Doug in the video."

"No. It was someone with dark hair."

"Jay," he said. After a moment he added, "Or Jeff Guelph."

She flared at that. "If we're going by dark hair, it could have been you or Conar."

The look he gave her might have frozen fire. He didn't respond. He didn't talk to her again until they pulled into Joe Penny's space at the studio. "Serena, leave it alone for a while. That's why I didn't tell you about the tape right away. I want to do a little further investigating on my own, without anyone knowing about it. All right?"

"He had dozens of tapes," she told him.

"Yes, I know," he said quietly.

She exited the car, and he followed. They walked through the downstairs entry, waved to the guard, and headed up the elevators, straight to the dressing rooms. Serena opened her door. There was a box of candy on her dressing table.

Liam started walking on by her, ready to take it.

"No, it's all right."

He gave a questioning look.

She smiled. "I know the brand. And when I talked to Jeff the other day, he said he was sending me something."

He kept waiting for more.

"Liam, I had a little argument on the phone with Jeff the other day. He called back, upset, apologizing. He said he's been meaning to send this and that it would come soon."

"Throw it out. If Jeffrey wants to give you something, let him hand it to you in person. Let's see where he bought it." He picked up the candy.

She snatched it from him. "I know where he bought it. It's my favorite kind of candy. Every time I celebrate something, he and Melinda send this particular candy. I know this is from my brother-in-law. He's not a killer!"

She made a point of opening the candy.

Then she stuck a piece defiantly in her mouth.

"You idiot! Spit that out."

She bit into it, and was surprised to find it was a chocolate-covered cherry. She hated cherries.

"Now! Spit it out. I mean it!"

To her amazement, he wrenched her around by the arm, ready to pry open her jaws.

"All right, all right!"

She took a tissue from the box on the dressing table and spat the candy into it. She lifted her chin. "I hate chocolate-covered cherries anyway."

"Don't touch that candy. You should have more sense than to touch anything that comes in from a fan, even at the best of times."

"I don't eat things that come in the mail from strangers. This is from my brother-in-law," she said indignantly.

"We'll give it to Hutchens."

She decided not to argue. "All right, all right, but hold off for just a minute. Please, just let me call the store first and find out if Jeffrey did order the candy for me. I won't eat any; I promise. And I swear I'll tell you what the shop says."

Liam backed away. "All right, here's the deal. You don't eat that candy—no matter what. Call the shop. I'll wait outside and let you get dressed."

"I think I can resist," she said.

"No thinking about anything. If you want me out of this room so that you can get ready, swear you won't touch anything that comes in here through an unknown source. And don't leave this room alone."

"I won't leave the room alone."

Liam headed straight down the hallway to Serena's assistant's room. He knocked on the door, then opened it. Jinx was behind her desk, working away at her computer. She hadn't heard his knock, apparently, nor did she hear him enter.

"Jinx?"

The girl jumped out of her chair.

"Hey, I'm sorry, I didn't mean to startle you."

She smiled at him, her hand against her chest. "No, I'm sorry I jumped, like a goose."

"You're scared around here lately, huh?"

"Well, a little nervous, I guess. But I always startle easily. What can I do for you, Mr. Murphy?"

"Liam, if you don't mind. Do you know about the box of chocolates in Serena's room?"

"Of course. They arrived a while ago—with a zillion other things. Serena receives all kinds of gifts in the mail. I censor it all." She smiled. "But the chocolates are from Jeff and Melinda."

"You know that for certain?"

"Well, no," Jinx said, frowning, "but they always send her candy on special occasions."

"What's the occasion?"

"I don't know," Jinx said. "You'll have to ask Serena about that."

"Thanks. Do you have a phone number for Jeff?"

"Sure. There in my Rolodex."

"Thanks."

"Help yourself to the phone, too."

"Thanks. I will."

He dialed the number to the Guelph home. An answering machine picked up. He didn't leave a message.

"Thanks," he told Jinx. "I didn't mean to interrupt you."

"Mail," she said with a grimace. "Tons and tons of it."

"You know to watch for—"

"Anything remotely threatening," she finished for him. "I do. I pull it all out. I was told from the beginning that anything ugly or mean goes to Joe first."

"There's a lot that's ugly and threatening?"

Jinx laughed. "This is a soap, and Serena plays a manipulative woman. She gets mostly adoring stuff, but hey, you know. Some people don't seem to have anything better to do than write nasty letters. There aren't many in comparison to the great stuff, but hey, like I said, it's a soap."

Liam suddenly wished that he was still a cop. He'd like to be reviewing the mail first. Hutchens would share anything he found suspicious, he was certain.

"Well, thanks again. If I need anything, I'll try not to scare you next time."

"You didn't scare me. You just startled me. And it's okay, really. Please, I'd just die if anything happened to Miss McCormack."

"Don't worry. Nothing will happen to her."

Serena tried calling the candy store when Liam left, but she couldn't get through. The line continued to be busy. Valentine's Day was coming up.

At the sound of a tap on her door, she jerked around. Then she shook her head with disgust, telling herself that if there was a murderer out there he wasn't going to knock first.

She walked to the door, still hesitating. "Serena, it's me," Allona announced.

Serena opened the door.

"Mind if I come in?" Allona seemed agitated.

"No, of course not."

Allona walked into the room and plopped on the sofa. "They're making me crazy."

"Who?"

"Joe and Andy."

"Oh?"

"This should happen, that should happen, this is a great scene, this is too...too tame! We can't be so tame all of a sudden!"

Serena smiled at her. "So, what's so different?"

"Well, you've got a point there. But I don't know how you guys are going to deal with all this. You get your scripts, you read, you learn, you rehearse...and two minutes later it's all been rewritten four times."

"It isn't easy, that's for sure. But I know they're trying—"

"They're trying to stay with the original bible for the season; with Jane gone, everything has to be reworked. Even Doug is going nuts. Although," she said, smiling, "he's been rewriting one scene for you over and over again. He's all excited. He says everyone loves a good dirty love scene."

"Dirty? You don't mean too sexually explicit, do you? I mean, we already go too far for daytime—"

"I didn't mean explicit, I meant...dirty. He wants you rolling in the field, or something like that. Personally, I think he's been watching too much mud wrestling on cable, but hey...who am I to judge?"

"Great. A day in the mud," Serena murmured. "Oh, well, I guess sex is better than murder and mayhem."

"Most people would probably think so. I mean, would I rather have my day filled with great sex, or murder and mayhem? Sex, I think. Oh, well. I've bitched long enough. Back to the grind, I guess." She stood up and stretched.

"Try to rein Doug in, okay?" Serena said, and picked up a mascara wand to touch up her lashes. She paused, looking up to see that Allona had opened the box of candy and popped a piece in her mouth.

"Don't!" she cried.

Startled, Allona swallowed the candy whole, then coughed.

"Water, hang on, I'll get water—"

Allona lifted a hand. "No," she gasped.

"I'm all right. It's just that—when did you get so stingy with your candy?"

"I'm not being stingy, I'm just being careful."

"Of candy?" Allona asked incredulously.

"Well, I'm not positive it came from Jeff."

"That stuff always comes from Jeff. Wow. And I got a chocolate-covered cherry. Really delicious. If you don't want me eating the cherries—"

"I hate the cherries; you're welcome to them, except that—"

"I thought you loved cherries."

"I'd be delighted if you'd eat them all, except that, with everything going on around here...just don't eat any more, okay?"

"It's creepy," Allona said, nearly shuddering. "It's like having...eyes, eyes crawling over us all the time. Oh, you know what I forgot to tell you?"

"What?"

"*He* was sniffing around here again this morning."

"*He* who?"

"Kyle."

"Kyle Amesbury was on the set?"

"He pretended he came to see Doug when I ran into him in the hall, but you know what?"

"I haven't a clue. What?"

"I asked Doug, and Doug said that he hadn't seen him."

"Maybe he didn't get to Doug's office yet."

Allona shook her head. "He left. I saw him go down on the elevator before I came in here."

"Maybe he came to threaten Joe again."

"Maybe," Allona agreed with a shrug. She made a face, pointing at Serena. "You know, you're the one he seems most interested in."

"I don't like him, and he knows it. He makes my skin crawl. I wish I could make Doug stay away from him."

Allona stretched and yawned, then said, "I think Doug is watching his step. You know, Serena, I ate that candy and I haven't dropped dead yet."

"Don't even say that!"

"Can I have another?"

"Allona, let me find out first—"

"Fine. Keep your old candy," Allona said. "This whole place is going nuts!"

She left, slamming the door.

Chapter 15

George Olsen was up in Joe's office, telling him they hadn't gotten anywhere. The ladder had so many prints on it that there was no way to discover who had pushed it over.

Joe sat glumly in front of him. Jinx had just brought in a box filled with fan mail, most of it telling Serena how wonderful she was, a strong woman, and even if Verona Valentine wasn't always entirely ethical, she did take responsibility for her own actions. Most wrote that she was a wonderful actress, that she entertained them tremendously, and that they got through mounds of housework, pet messes, laundry, baby care, and cooking—because of her.

Not all the mail, however, was positive. Of course they all knew that. Sometimes they would laugh over a fan taking the soap too seriously.

Some of it was mail telling Verona Valentine that she was a monster and that she needed to stay away from her sisters' husbands and lovers. A few notes were worse, telling her that she should be shot, horsewhipped, and sunk to the bottom of the sea. Usually they found such passionate hatred, which was actually necessary to the longevity of a soap, to be amusing.

None of it was funny now.

Joe had told Jinx to make sure that he saw anything threatening before Serena did. There were a few letters that the police had seen and dismissed; letters that dealt with the nastiness of her character, warning that she had to be very careful because there was such a thing as karma and something terrible could happen to her, too.

One of them read, "Verona! You love Egypt so much, you should sink into the desert sand and mummify yourself!"

Joe had gotten a big kick out of that letter. He wondered if it might be used for a scene. Maybe a dream sequence, in which Verona imagined herself a queen of Egypt, falling in love with the wrong man and earning the vengeance of the pharaoh. She could wake up, smothering in the covers, and find herself saved by...oh, well, that one would have to be figured out. Verona Valentine wasn't saving herself for anyone special.

"Mr. Penny," Olsen said, "have you been listening to me?"

"Of course. I always listen to you, Lieutenant," Joe said politely. "I just had a thought. A creative idea, you know."

"I said, I would like to see Serena."

"I'll call her up."

Joe buzzed through to Serena's dressing room, telling her that Olsen was there, and would she mind terribly coming up?

A few minutes later, she walked in, followed by Liam Murphy.

"Serena, have a seat," Olsen invited, nodding to Liam.

Serena sat across the desk from Joe. Liam Murphy remained standing, but he immediately said, "Serena received a box of candy this morning. It should be checked out."

"Oh?" Olsen looked at Serena. She pursed her lips. "Miss McCormack? Do you know who sent you the candy?"

Serena hesitated, glancing at Liam. "I can't be certain."

"Who do you think sent it?"

"It's the kind of candy my brother-in-law and sister send me on occasion."

"But you're not certain it's from them?"

"I couldn't get hold of the shop where they buy it, and no one answered their home phone."

Olsen nodded and picked up a radio. "Hutchens, you there? Good. Go to Miss McCormack's room and pick up the box of candy you'll find there. Yeah, for testing."

Liam was satisfied, but Serena was still nettled.

"Serena," Olsen said. "Sorry about your candy, but we're trying to be very careful here. Now, I understand a man gave you a rose at the cemetery, following Jane Dunne's funeral. Then you found a rose in your dressing room? And you're aware that Liam found another rose yesterday, in front of your house."

"So he told me."

"What do you think these roses mean?"

"I think they're from a soap fan. I've gotten flowers before."

"These flowers may be a warning. Jane Dunne died with a single rose in her hand. We tested one of the flowers sent to you, and nothing came up."

"Well, that proves they're just roses."

"The one in front of your house didn't bother you at all? Knowing someone was actually *in your yard* didn't frighten you?"

She shot a long glance at Liam. "I have an alarm—and protection."

Olsen sighed. "Miss McCormack, you have to be careful."

"Lieutenant, I don't think that I can be much more careful."

"We're trying to protect you, Miss McCormack. You can't trust anyone."

He was interrupted by the intercom on

Joe's desk as it buzzed loudly. Joe pressed the button. "We're in a meeting here."

"I know." The voice that came over the intercom was Thorne McKay's. "We've got a problem here, a serious one," he said breathlessly.

"What's happened?" Joe demanded with a frown.

"We've just called the paramedics. Jinx has been taken ill. The paramedics are on their way, ready to rush her to the hospital."

The killer stood on the set.

So distant. Watching.

Jinx had come down here, trying to find help. She had stumbled in, nearly walked in circles, fallen, crying out for help.

Thorne was the one who discovered her. He screamed and fled the stage.

Serena stayed with Jinx, holding her hand, reassuring her. Poor little Jinx. A scared little rabbit. Thin as a rail. She was screaming with the pain that was wracking her.

"Appendicitis?" Serena suggested, so concerned, that perfect face knotted in worry.

"I don't think so. It looks like...poisoning of some sort," Liam Murphy told her.

"Poison!" Serena cried with alarm. And naturally, the cry became a murmur that spread about the cast and crew gathered now at Jinx's side. They could hear the ambulance's siren.

"Food poisoning. Maybe she ate something that was really bad," Liam said firmly.

"Jinx, just hold on, hold on. The ambulance is nearly here," Serena told the girl.

Then the paramedics rushed in, and the others moved back, and Jinx's vital signs were relayed to some great medical voice that came through the radios. An IV was begun, and she was carefully rolled onto a gurney. She was still holding Serena's hand.

How touching.

How ironic.

Jinx was nearly to the elevators, stretched out on the gurney, pushing aside the oxygen they were trying to give her.

"It hurts," she managed to whisper, through white, foaming lips. "It hurts, and I feel so weak...I'm sorry..."

"Jinx, whatever are you sorry about? The ambulance is here, and we'll get you well!" Jinx had her hand. She was jerked into movement; they rushed alongside the girl, ready to go to the hospital with her.

The chocolates, the chocolates, the killer thought.

"Ate..." Jinx began.

She didn't finish. She had another spasm of pain.

Olsen reached them, and he looked grim.

"Jeffrey Guelph. Get the man and bring him downtown," Olsen ordered. "Get an APB out on him now, just in case you can't get him at his house."

"Wait—" Serena cried.

The elevator door closed.

Ah, well...

It could have been Serena. And she could have eaten more than one chocolate; she loved the *brand. Her family always sent her that particular chocolate. The killer had made a point of knowing that.*

Jeffrey Guelph sat in the police station. He'd been picked up by two cop cars—one heading him off, one blocking his rear, their sirens blaring. He thought at first he'd been speeding, but then he'd realized that the way they'd hauled him in was overkill for speeding.

He hadn't had a cigarette in ten years. When the uniformed cop who had brought him into the interrogation room offered him one, he took it. He coughed like a fifteen-year-old at the first drag. Opposite him was Bill Hutchens, who was looking at him with sympathy and trying to make things easier for him. Either that, or he was trying to disarm him, make him feel all comfortable so that he'd be willing to say more.

"Coffee is coming," Bill told him.

"Great."

"You could use some coffee, huh?"

"Yeah. Bill," he said, then added pleadingly, "Why was I brought down here?"

Bill leaned forward on his elbows, watching him intently, frowning. "You really don't know?"

Jeff felt a flicker of fear. *Just what did* they *know?*

"I don't know why, no."

Bill sat back, sighing. "Jeff, the chocolates."

"What chocolates?"

"The candy you sent Serena."

"I didn't send Serena any candy."

Bill sighed deeply. "Oh, come on, Jeff. The candy, it's the same candy you and Melinda send her all the time. The same brand. From the same store."

Jeff shook his head, bewildered.

At that moment the door opened and George Olsen stepped in. He already knew Olsen; he'd been questioned by him the day Jane Dunne had died.

"Hello, Mr. Guelph."

So polite. That was really scary. He crushed the cigarette out. He rubbed his forehead hard, wondering what Melinda was going to think. God, this was horrible. The humiliation.

Worse... *What if they did pin something on him?*

"We need to hear about the chocolates," Olsen told him.

Jeff sat back, bewildered. "I didn't send Serena any chocolates, not lately," he said.

Bill Hutchens rose, still looking at him sorrowfully. Olsen sat. "Jeff, you told Serena you were sending her something. She received a box of candy. Her favorite kind. The kind of chocolates you send her every so often on special occasions."

Jeff stared at him blankly. "I told Serena I was sending her something. It was a necklace I had made for her. It had her name...in Egyptian hieroglyphics. The kind they sell at museums. I had sent to the Museum of Natural History for it, ordered it from the catalog. It was just something that we'd gotten to say thanks for having gotten me work on the show."

"And you sent it today?"

"I was going to have a messenger service pick it up and bring it over, but I started reading a new journal...and I forgot," Jeff said.

"But the chocolates did arrive."

"I didn't send them."

Olsen tapped the table impatiently, as if this was wasting his time.

"Look," Jeff said. "I know you guys can pull phone records. I'll sign whatever you need to get my records right away—"

"We've already done that, Jeff," Olsen said quietly.

"Then you know!"

"We know that you didn't send the order in from your house."

"I didn't send the order in at all!" Jeff said, pleased at last and seeing a ray of freedom. "If you've checked, you know—"

"Oh, yeah. We checked. We checked everything, you see. The order came in from a pay phone at the convenience store near the studio."

"So there you have it—"

Olsen interrupted him with a deep sigh. "Jeff, the order was called in from a pay phone, but..." He paused, shrugging, then leaning toward Jeff. "But the order was charged to your Visa card."

It had been a long and truly terrible day. The only bright spot was because the paramedics had acted so quickly, Jinx's stomach had been pumped out in time. She had ingested arsenic, as it turned out. That was what had caused such terrible pain.

Arsenic was not that difficult to obtain. It was an ingredient in many rat poisons.

After the first few hours they knew that Jinx was going to be okay. She would have to stay in the hospital for a night or two, but she would pull through fine. She still hadn't spoken much; she'd been too out of it. The doctors had tried really hard to get her to tell them what she had eaten, but she hadn't been able to answer. With or without her help, they would know soon, though.

They had taken all kinds of samples. The contents of her stomach had included an onion bagel, cream cheese, egg, chocolate, cherry, and the arsenic.

Serena stayed through the day in the hospital waiting room along with Joe Penny, Andy Larkin, Thorne McKay, and, of course, Liam. Olsen had remained at the hospital for a while, then a uniformed cop had replaced him, and a few hours later Bill Hutchens had replaced him. When he learned that Jinx wouldn't be able to speak with the police for some time, Bill sat and quizzed Serena, asking her about the candy. She didn't need to tell him too much; Liam was there, answering most of the questions with terse, concise statements. She had to explain that she had believed Jeff had sent the chocolates only because he had told her he was sending something.

"Do we know that the arsenic was in the chocolate?" she asked Bill.

"Looks that way," he told her.

"What about the piece of chocolate Serena spat out?" Liam asked Bill.

"It's being tested. You all right, Serena?"

"I'm fine. I hardly got the candy in my mouth before Liam took it away from me," she assured them, but then she remembered that someone else had eaten a piece of chocolate. "Allona!" Serena cried. "Allona ate one of the chocolates."

Allona was brought in during the early afternoon.

She came with a police escort, and was already greatly agitated when she reached the hospital. "I'm fine!" she insisted. "Not sick, not a cramp—nothing. They are not pumping my stomach. Dammit, Serena, why are you making me go through this?"

"Allona, Jinx could have died. You're better safe than sorry."

"Serena, I would know if I was sick," Allona ranted.

"Please, Allona," Doug said to her quietly.

She exhaled on a long sigh. "All right— fine!"

So Allona had her stomach pumped. There

was no trace of arsenic found in the candy she had eaten. Even weak and sedated, Allona remained furious. "I told you I was fine," she charged Serena when Serena tried to comfort her in outpatient recovery. "Look what you've done to me. Do you all think I'm an idiot, that I couldn't tell if I had been *poisoned*?"

"Allona, people don't always know—"

"Serena, I'm uncomfortable, and I'm miserable, and I'd like to be left alone."

"Sorry," Serena said simply, and left her.

The tests on the candies remaining in the box turned up no more arsenic. Apparently, only the chocolate Jinx had eaten had been poisoned.

Out in the hallway with Bill and Liam again, Serena suddenly had a flash: "Cherry!" she exclaimed.

They both stared at her.

"Don't you see?" she explained. "Whatever is going on, Jeff didn't do it. He wouldn't have put cherry chocolates in an order for me. He knows I hate them. And you're all being far too certain. Everything you have against Jeff is entirely circumstantial," she told Bill.

He and Liam both looked at her as if she had seen one cop movie too many.

"It's all right, Serena. You hadn't done anything wrong to anyone. The truth always comes out," Bill told her. "Listen, I have to get back to the station. It sounds like Jinx is going to be just fine."

Right after Bill left, Jay Braden, who hadn't

been scheduled on the set until the late afternoon and had apparently just discovered what had happened, arrived.

He stormed down the hallway, blond hair uncharacteristically mussed. He stopped abruptly in front of Joe and instantly began shouting. "She's alive, thank God she's alive, if she were to have any recurring problems...she should sue the shit out of you, Joe. She should sue the show for every penny that it's worth!"

"Dammit, Jay!" Joe thundered in response. "This isn't my fault!"

"You're supposed to be watching the set. There's a maniac in our midst—"

"I have someone watching the set!"

"Hey! This is a hospital!" Liam reminded them sternly, just as an irate nurse appeared and glared at them.

"Take it outside, gentlemen, if you must shout like children," she commanded.

But Jay wasn't going anywhere. "Jinx is a friend of mine. A good friend. I'm going to sit with her," he told the nurse.

The woman, tall and stout, with matronly gray hair, wagged a finger at him. "She's resting quietly. No one is to disturb her. She has a nurse around the clock—and a cop at her door, I might add."

The last was said in warning. Jay scowled and took a seat in the waiting room, crossing his arms over his chest. He looked at Serena. "If she were to die...that chocolate was intended for you!"

"That's enough, Jay," Liam grated harshly.

"Who the hell do you think you are, Murphy?" Jay demanded.

"I'm calling the cops," the nurse announced.

"No, we'll take it outside," Liam said.

Jay shook his head at that, looking down at his hands. They were shaking, Serena noted. "No, it's all right," she said. "We're all just upset here."

"That's better," the nurse muttered.

As the nurse left, a doctor appeared. "The young lady really is going to be all right," he told them. His manner was Hollywood pleasant. "Your friend is resting quietly; she's sedated, but she's going to be just fine. You should all go home now."

"Good enough for me," Jay muttered. He walked past the others, hesitating briefly as he looked at Serena. Then he hurried on out.

"I guess we can go now, too," Andy said.

They trudged toward the emergency exit from the hospital as if they were all half dead themselves.

"I may never sleep again," Joe Penny said wearily. He shook his head. "Where did we go so wrong?" he asked helplessly. "What do we do now? Where do we go from here?"

"We should plan on closing down—before they close us down," Andy said despondently.

Joe shook his head. "We didn't do this, Andy, don't you see? We were never careless or negligent on our set."

"Maybe you should get Serena off the set," Liam suggested.

"Wait! Don't talk about me as if I'm not here."

"I'm not suggesting you should be taken off the show," Liam said. "Just off the set—for a while."

"Maybe the cops will figure out who pulled this candy bit right away," Andy argued. "I mean..." He looked at Serena with an unhappy shrug. "You even think that your brother-in-law sent you the candy."

"It's what I had thought—"

She never finished the sentence. She broke off because she saw that her sister was coming down the hallway of the hospital exit, striding along with tremendous agitation.

She didn't seem to see anyone but Serena, passing by the others without a glance.

"Melinda—" she began.

She never finished that sentence either.

Melinda stepped right up to her, in tears, threw her arms around her, and nearly fell. "Do you know what they've done?" she cried, near hysteria.

"Melinda—"

"Oh, my God, Serena! They hauled my husband in for attempted murder! They've pulled him in for trying to kill *you*!"

Chapter 16

Feeling helpless, Serena smoothed back her sister's hair.

"Melinda, I knew that they were going to talk

to him, but as for arresting him..." Serena looked at Liam accusingly. "Did they *arrest* him? Did you know about this?"

"No." His eyes fell on Melinda. "But I'm afraid it isn't surprising that they brought him in for questioning."

"Bill Hutchens didn't tell you about bringing Jeffrey down to the station, and anything he might have said?" Serena demanded.

"No," he repeated irritably. "You know everything I know." He turned away from her and spoke to Melinda. "I'm sorry, but as I said, it's not surprising. And it may not be that serious. Has Jeff called his attorney?"

Melinda didn't answer right away. She was now sobbing in Serena's arms, great gulping tears.

"Melinda, did Jeff call an attorney?" she persisted quietly.

Melinda regained some calm, straightening. "I...yes, he's gotten an attorney."

"Melinda," Liam said evenly, "I don't think you need to be so upset, honestly. They didn't tell me they were arresting Jeff, but Hutchens did tell me that they traced the candy and that it had been charged to Jeff's card."

"You might have told me that!" Serena said angrily.

Melinda let out a shuddering sigh, getting angry. "And did he order *poisoned* candy?" she demanded.

"Melinda," Joe Penny said, stepping forward, "of course he didn't. He ordered the candy and then..."

"Someone injected a piece with rat poison," Andy said wearily.

"Jeff didn't even go in today," Melinda said.

"That's right. He wasn't in," Serena said.

"That's funny—" Andy began.

"What's funny?" Melinda asked sharply.

"Oh, nothing. I was just thinking out loud," he said.

"About what?" Joe demanded.

"Nothing, nothing. Melinda, if Jeff has called his lawyer, he'll be out in no time."

"All they have against him is circumstantial," Liam explained quietly to Melinda. "You're right—it's unlikely that the candy came from the store poisoned."

Melinda's cell phone started ringing. She dug in her oversized bag for it, couldn't find it, and cried out with frustration.

"Let me help you," Serena told her, but before she could, Melinda dumped the bag on the hallway floor. Her wallet, change, phone book, checkbook, lipsticks, compact, tissues, gum, mints, and calendar fell to the floor along with the phone. Melinda grabbed the phone, and the men politely stooped and helped Serena to put all her sister's belongings back in the bag.

"Hello?" Melinda said. "Yes, yes, yes, of course! I'll be right there."

She flipped the phone closed and looked at Liam. "He's out. They interviewed him, but he hasn't actually been charged yet, just told not to leave town. His lawyer took care of things.

They've warned him he might well be charged with attempted murder, and that he'll definitely be needed again for questioning. But he can come home, and I'm going over."

"Melinda, you're upset. Let me drive you," Serena said.

Melinda smiled, shaking her head. "I'm okay, now that he's been released. But you can walk me to the car."

"We should drive you—" Liam agreed.

"Liam, honest to God, I'm fine to drive," Melinda said. She looked at Serena. "Walk me to my car," she said, then paused, staring at them all with stricken eyes. "Jinx! Is Jinx...oh, my God, I didn't even..."

"Jinx is going to be all right," Serena assured her quickly.

Melinda lowered her head and nodded. Then she stared at Serena, her eyes widening. "Oh, Serena! Someone *is* out to get you. You've got to hide, go somewhere—"

"Melinda, I'm all right, I'm not alone, I...I have Liam."

"Jeff would never hurt you," Melinda whispered. She looked as if she was about to burst into tears again.

"We really should drive you home," Liam insisted.

Melinda straightened her shoulders and wiped her face. "No, honestly. I'm all right, Liam. You just watch out for my sister. Serena...walk with me for a minute."

"Go ahead," Liam said softly, and he smiled at the skeptical glance she gave him. "Yes, I'm going to follow you, but I'll stay at a decent distance. How's that?"

Serena put an arm around her sister's shoulders, and they started across the parking lot. "Serena," she whispered softly, "I need to talk to you. Really talk to you."

"Melinda, don't you worry, I know that Jeff wouldn't hurt me, and we'll find a way to prove it, I swear—"

"No! No!" Melinda glanced over her shoulder. Liam was a good distance away, true to his word.

"Serena, I don't know what's going on. I was nervous before...but not scared for you. I was worried about what had happened because... Jeff slept with her."

"What?" Serena said, completely lost.

"He slept with Jane Dunne. Oh, it was terrible when I found out!"

"You should have told me."

"I was humiliated! And it ended before she died, and then I was afraid to tell you, and now—now I'm so afraid that the police will find out, and use it against him."

"Melinda, apparently many men slept with Jane Dunne."

"Oh, Serena, I was so upset, and I couldn't even tell you, and now...I love my husband. I really have forgiven him, and he's been in such agony over this, he's paying in an awful way for what he did to me. But he would never, never hurt you. Please, please, you can't tell anyone."

"But, Melinda, it's better to admit the truth."

"No! Especially not now. Swear to me,

swear! Don't say anything, especially to Liam. I had to tell you because I couldn't stand it. He said that you had called the other day, that you were worried, and oh, God! Serena, I was even afraid myself for a while, but you know, if you love someone, you believe in him. He fell prey to temptation, but not to the point of murder."

They'd reached the car. Melinda whispered, "I had to tell you, but please, keep this secret."

Serena hugged her sister tightly. "I won't say anything to anyone. I love you, Melinda."

"I love you, too. So much."

"I'd feel better if I drove you."

"Jeff will be home when I get there. I just want to be with him. I'm all right now. And I want you home. Locked in. Safe. With Liam watching over you."

Serena nodded. "Call me, and if you don't get me, leave a message on my machine saying that you got home okay."

Melinda nodded and slipped behind the steering wheel. Serena stepped back, waving as she drove away.

Liam came up behind her. "You sure she's going to be all right? Maybe we should follow her."

"No, I know my sister. She's all right."

"Did she confess to you that Jeff was sleeping with Jane Dunne?" he asked, nearly catching her off guard.

She didn't look at him. "Don't be ridiculous," she murmured.

He shrugged. "The thing is, the police will find out."

"She was just upset because someone stole his credit card number and used it to order the chocolates."

He didn't say anything more before they rejoined the others at the hospital exit.

"Don't look so glum," Joe told Serena. "Even if Jeff ordered the candy, it came to the studio. Anyone could have tampered with it there. And Jeff didn't even come in."

Andy shuffled his feet uncomfortably. "Jeff did come in this morning. Jim Novac said he saw him leaving the studio very early, right when the writers were arriving."

"You're sure?" Serena demanded.

"No, I'm not sure. Jim is the one who saw him. He asked me if there was anything wrong with the Egyptian set. I guess that's where Jeff was. If there was anything wrong with the set, I didn't know about it; they never told me. Oh, well. There's nothing more to do here. I'm calling it a night." Andy waved and started for his car.

"I'm going for a drink," Joe told them. "Maybe I'll go see Kyle Amesbury. Tell him what's happened before he reads it in the papers. He's always got plenty of alcohol on hand. I might as well go get numbed while he threatens to swing the axe on me."

Serena put a hand on his arm. "Joe, it will work out. Hey—there are lots of other sponsors—"

"Yeah. And they'll all want to take on a show with poison on the set. Sure."

"Joe, go home. We'll talk tomorrow."

He sighed, opened his mouth as if he wanted to say more, then shook his head and walked away. Liam looked at Serena.

"Let me take you home," he said.

When they reached the house, he opened the door and went through the routine of checking the house.

Serena sat on the sofa in her living room. A minute later, Liam came back and sat on the richly upholstered chair opposite her. "Everything seems to be all right."

She stared ahead, biting her lower lip. "You're staying here, right?" she asked softly. "You're not going to decide to leave me now, are you?"

"Why would I leave you now?" he asked.

"I don't know. Would you?"

He smiled at last. "Come over here."

She stood up and walked hesitantly over to him. He reached up, and before she knew it, she was sitting in his lap, leaning against him, and he was smoothing her hair back.

"Never," he said softly. "I swear to you, whatever the future might bring, I'd never leave you in danger."

"I don't know how it happened," she murmured. "My life is suddenly such a mess. The cops are after my brother-in-law, Allona is pissed at me, Jay is losing it, and Jinx. Poor Jinx! I always think that I'm standing up for her, protecting her...and she's in the hospital because she ate my candy."

"Jinx is going to be fine."

"She could have died because of me. I could have died! And you know, it's my fault they called Jeff in. I said he had sent it."

"Serena, they would have found out, and they would have brought him in, no matter what you said. Trust me."

She nodded, feeling somewhat better. Then a burst of fear swept through her. "And now I guess I have to face the facts. Someone is trying to kill me," she whispered. "Jane Dunne...Jane Dunne probably died because of me."

"You're not to blame for someone else's criminal acts," Liam said. Then, to her surprise, he suddenly rose, setting her on her feet and lifting her chin. "Go take a hot bath. I'm going to fix you a drink. A strong one. Then you can get some sleep."

She nodded, determined then that she wasn't going to be weak. She wasn't going to cry on his shoulder.

She started for her bedroom and then paused. "Liam?" she said.

"Yeah?"

"I was just thinking. I'm sorry for messing up your life—"

"Serena, you didn't mess up my life."

"Sharon—"

"Don't worry about Sharon."

"But that photo must have upset her. She came down to the studio because of it."

"I asked her to go."

"But Liam, that's my fault."

"Serena, stop it. I make my own choices about things, and things—"

"Just weren't working out?" she supplied dryly.

"Serena, let's forget about it, all right?"

She nodded.

"Go. I'll make you a drink. You really do have to get some sleep."

Serena went into her bathroom, ran a hot bath with lots of oil and bubbles, and sank into it. She made the water very hot, and it felt good. Yet she couldn't relax. She kept thinking of Melinda, Jeff, the poisoned candy, all in a chaotic whirl.

She closed her eyes, trying to let the water work its magic.

"Serena?" Liam was calling her from the bedroom door. She hadn't closed it, or the door to the bathroom.

"Yes?" She hesitated. She had enough bubbles to form a blanket of white foam all over her, but what did that matter? "Come in."

He walked into the bedroom, then paused at the bathroom door. He had a tall glass in his hand.

"Want this in here?" he asked.

"Sure. What is it?"

"Bourbon and coke. Very strong."

"Good. Thanks."

He walked to the tub, sitting back on her oak laundry hamper to hand it to her.

"Thanks very much."

"My pleasure. I sipped it first, by the way, to test it."

She couldn't tell if he was joking, some

dark cop humor. "Do you think that...that someone got in *here*?"

He shook his head, smiling. "No. The doors and windows were all secure; the alarm hasn't been tampered with in any way. I called the company and checked. Anyone else have a key to the place?"

She nodded. "Jennifer."

"Not your sister?"

"No. Actually, you know, she did have one. But she lost her key chain ages ago."

"She lost it?" he said sharply.

"Out in the desert somewhere. They were on vacation a few months ago. No one could have found it, and known it was mine."

He didn't reply. She knew he was thinking she needed to have her locks changed anyway.

"Liam, I really don't believe that my brother-in-law would hurt me."

"Drink that."

She took a long swallow. It burned from her throat to her stomach, and it felt good.

The phone started ringing.

"I'll get it," he told her.

"There's a machine—"

"That's all right. I'll get it."

He left the bedroom. A moment later, she heard the deep drone of his voice. He reappeared, a drink in hand himself.

"Who was it?"

"Jeff."

"Jeff? You should have called me."

"He just called to say that he and Melinda were both home and together and Melinda was fine, and that he would never hurt you, and he wanted you to know that."

"I should have told him that I know that."

"It's all right. I said it for you."

"But you're the one warning me...the one who thinks that he's guilty!"

"Guilty of something. That affair you won't admit your sister told you about. It would be better if he admitted to the police that he did have a relationship with Jane Dunne."

"He's not angry with me at all?"

"No. Definitely not. Jeff was fine, very calm. He doesn't really blame the police. He denies that he bought the candy. And you know, it is possible to steal a credit card number. Jeff will talk to you tomorrow, okay?"

She bit her lower lip and nodded.

He was still staring at her.

"What?" she asked softly.

"Nothing. I'm just thinking of how much I want to sleep with you."

She smiled and gripped the edge of the tub to stand. He grabbed a towel for her, and she stepped into it. He wrapped it around her, pulling her tightly against him. Then he caught her chin, lifted it, and kissed her lips.

She felt as if she were melting...

He had that effect on her. He kissed her with a passion that was consuming, lips and tongue instantly creating a molten heat that fired straight through her limbs. She was glad he was holding her. Her knees were weak, as if they would give way any minute and refuse to hold her up. She felt the restriction of the towel, anxious to slip her arms around him, hold to the power of his shoulders, feel the length of his hair beneath her fingers. He smelled wonderful, delicious, and tasted like the rich, amber-toned bourbon they'd been drinking. She could have stood there forever, feeling the force and hunger of his lips, the simple pressure of his body against hers, but she wanted more. Her hands slid between them, fingers deftly, eagerly working at the buttons of his shirt. A minute later he was struggling out of it, his tongue still entwined with hers. Then she was crushed to him again, her towel fallen, his shirt gone, and the naked expanse of his chest hard against her breasts. At last they broke the kiss, gazing at each other. Serena gasped in a long breath, then moved against him again, the top of her head against his chin as she splayed her fingers over his chest, feeling the rough texture of the crisp dark hair, then brushing the tips of her fingers down his ribs to rest on the band of his Dockers and slip beneath it. She pressed her mouth to his chest, running her tongue against it, then rose on her toes to meet his lips again. He swept her up, and they moved to her bed. But when she fell against it, she sat up, aware of the pounding of her heart as he shed his pants and briefs and came toward her. She rose to her knees on the mattress before he could come down. She laid her cheek against his chest again, holding him there, reveling in the sheer pleasure of touching him again. She loved everything about him; the feel and texture and movement of him, the color of his flesh, his hair, the ripple when she touched him, the tension, the heat. Her lips fell against him in erratic little movements, evocative, wet, fulfilling. His fingers tangled into her hair, and a groan escaped him. She loved the sound of it, deep and throaty, reverberating through the length of him. She drew her hands down his back, around his buttocks. Then she stroked his thighs with the backs of her fingers, his abdomen with the lure of her tongue, and brought both closer and closer to the center until she slipped her fingers around the hardness of his arousal, worked them, found the intimacy so arousing that she could not bear it. He savored her aggression for so long, then shuddered, hoarsely groaning, whispering, lifting her head, finding her lips with his own again, and pressing her back with passionate force that brought her beneath him, gasping, trembling with the sudden power of his thrust into her, a movement that sent streaks of lightning throughout her, shattering in its initial moment, building with each subsequent rugged thrust, drawing her into a desperate frenzy to reach a culmination. She clung to him, heart racing, thundering...and then it seemed that the heavens opened, and stars rained down upon her, and she couldn't breathe at all, but she could hear herself, and she couldn't stand to let him go, to withdraw from her, until a wave of shocks swept through her, and she felt as if she were a lava bed, filled with liquid fire that was awesome, and yet cooling, so slowly, so slowly...

How had she ever lived without him?

But that wasn't the question.

How had he walked away so easily?

She wouldn't ask him that, and she wouldn't whisper that she had been in love with him, that she loved the way that he made love, that nothing in her life had ever been so good before. She wouldn't pressure him in any way, and she'd keep her mouth shut about Sharon, even if it killed her to think that he had been this way with another woman, that he was here with her now because she was in danger, because...the sex was so good.

She eased her arms from around him, allowing him to fall to one side. He pulled her against him, holding her, his thumb stroking the line of her jaw. After a moment he asked her, "What are you thinking?"

She tried to be light. "I'm thinking that if I'm going to die, this is the way to go."

He didn't laugh, or even smile, but rolled back over. His features were hard and strong and tense when he said, "I'm not going to let that happen."

She smiled, touching the rugged contour of his cheek. "Thank you."

He watched her so closely that she began to feel uneasy, afraid that she would burst into tears again, say things that she shouldn't say, that would only bring further hurt to her later.

"I guess I really do need some sleep."

"Want me in the guest room?"

She shook her head. "No, I want you right here."

"Let me look around the house one more time."

"You really think there's any danger?"

"No, but I know someone has been out there at times."

He rose, crawled quickly into his Dockers, and disappeared. Serena got up as well, ripping the comforter down and sliding beneath the coolness of the sheets. She was amazed at how easy it was to close her eyes. Soon he was back, and he slid in beside her. Naked, warm. An arm curled around her. She set her hand upon his, where it lay at her waist.

"Thank you," she said softly.

"No problem."

She smiled. "Honestly, I never would be able to sleep without you here tonight."

"I take my work very seriously," he teased.

She didn't respond to that. She did sleep.

Sometime in the night, she awakened, feeling something pressing against her. Liam. She turned into his arms.

Sex with him was delicious even when she was half asleep.

After that she slept deeply.

That was good, because from the moment they reached the studio, the day promised to be long.

The cops were everywhere once again.

Bill Hutchens was in charge. He was polite, courteous, treating them all with respect and consideration. He made use of Joe Penny's office, going through another round of questioning with everyone regarding the box of candy. Serena, with Liam at her side, told him everything she knew—which wasn't much. Why she'd thought Jeff had sent it—the brand—and why she was certain after she opened it that Jeff hadn't sent it—he knew she hated chocolate-covered cherries.

Hutchens didn't press her as hard as she had expected. He leaned forward, eyes grave and serious. "Stick with Liam. Or me. Or another cop. Don't be alone with anyone who might remotely be a suspect. Watch every move you make. Don't trust friends, or family."

"Yes, Bill, I promise," she told him.

When they went down to the studio, Joe Penny was glum, sitting on the edge of the cottage set, one leg crossed over the other, leafing through one of the soap magazines.

Liam stopped just off the set to talk to Conar. Serena, in jeans and a T-shirt, sat on the floor near Joe, looking up at him.

"Hey, Joe, we're going to make it through this."

Joe shook his head. "Serena, I'm really worried about you."

She waved a hand in the air, determined not to tell him that she was becoming afraid herself. "We are having some bad days here, aren't we? Did you get your drink last night?"

"Oh, yeah. I stopped by Amesbury's." He slapped the magazine down in sudden anger. "The guy is a true little prick. He was nice as could be, but then he starts telling me he's a voyeur. Of life, and human foibles, so he says. Men...women too, though they're not his preference. He says that life is one great journey to be explored."

She didn't comment. Joe himself loved to party, and he loved to date. The more women he had around him, the happier he was. She wondered if he had any clue that Kyle Amesbury videotaped his guests. Liam was still keeping quiet about the tape he had stolen that featured Jane.

"Joe, you probably shouldn't have gone over there."

"You're right." He shook his head again. "Such a pathetic little upstart. I ought to tell him to take Haines/Clark and stick the whole shebang where the sun don't shine. But do I dare do that now?"

"Joe, money rules Hollywood. And this show brings in many, many viewers. Yes, this is horrible, but we'll survive it."

He didn't even seem to hear her.

"We're going to, yes. I'm going to make sure that *you* survive. You're going to take some time off," he said with conviction.

"Joe, we have to keep going."

"Not if something might happen to you. Take some time, Serena. Investigations can't be done in a day. The cops need time."

"All right, agreed. I'll take a break. But before I do..."

"What?"

"Let's double up on my scenes. Get the

tape in the can, and then we'll be ahead of the game. What do you think about that?"

He smiled slowly. "I guess we could do that. We'll shoot like wildfire. Then you'll take a break."

"We'll do it," she said.

He was looking over her head. "Looks like it's my turn with Bill Hutchens. Like he didn't talk to me long enough, all those hours at the hospital yesterday."

"Bill is pretty gentle," Serena said.

He rose. "Here I go."

She gave him a thumbs-up sign. "Oh, I called the hospital. Jinx is fine. She's insisting on leaving the hospital this afternoon."

"I know. I called too."

Jim called her onto the set. Before she even set foot beneath the lights, Liam walked over and talked with Emilio Garcia. Everything seemed to be fine. Her scene with Conar went like clockwork. They barely took a break; then she filmed a second confrontation scene with Kelly.

Verona was seriously into conflict these days.

Conar remained with Liam, watching the taping as she worked with Kelly. He smiled at her as she stepped off the set platform and came up to them. "We've got to get together soon. Jennifer has been going crazy over this. She isn't going to be sane again until she sees you."

She lifted her hands. "It looks like I'll be available a lot after the next few days."

257

"Oh?" Liam said.

"We're going to double up shooting on my scenes, then I'll take a few days off. Joe and I just discussed the idea."

"That might be a really good thing," Conar said.

"I think I'm going to try calling Melinda," Serena said. "Just make sure that she's doing all right."

She started past them, then paused and turned back. They were both following her.

"You know I'm going where you go," Liam said.

"And I haven't anything better to do at the moment," Conar said.

Serena left the door open, letting them both follow her into her dressing room. "There are Cokes, water, and juice in the little fridge," she told them, then paused. "Oh, I guess no one wants anything from this room."

"We probably should clean it out—and you should bring in only what you're going to use during the day."

"Or buy a beagle and make him sniff all my food?" she suggested.

"He might slobber on it a lot," Conar said, taking a seat on her sofa and picking up a magazine from the coffee table.

She dialed her sister's number. While the phone was ringing, she glanced at a box of mail that had been left on her dressing table. She noted the envelopes, then saw there was a piece of paper wedged among them.

The paper was a huge heart, the kind found

in many a box of children's valentines. The message, however, had not been handwritten. It was from a typewriter, or a printer.

Serena picked up the paper, still listening to the ringing tone on the other end of the phone.

A gasp escaped her. She dropped the phone as she reread the paper.

Roses are red.
Soon you'll be dead.
Violets are blue.
I'm coming for you.

Chapter 17

Bill Hutchens was upset. When he heard about it, he rushed into the dressing room and slipped the valentine into a plastic evidence bag. He promised to have it tested for prints immediately.

"This has to be taken very seriously. Serena needs to get out of here," Liam said firmly.

"But that's your job, isn't it? To watch her?" Andy demanded.

"I can watch her, but when you see a twister coming, you move out of the way," Liam replied evenly.

"We've all agreed. We double up on the scenes, and then Serena takes some time off."

"That's fine," Serena said. "Joe and I discussed it before I found the note."

"I told Doug that working on your scenes, all rewrites, everything, was a top priority. I'm working on a new schedule now. You'll go from eight to six for the next several days, Serena, but then you can take the break you need. Only..."

"Only what happens when she comes back?" Liam asked quietly.

"We'll hope to have something by then," Bill said, tapping the evidence bag.

"Serena, we'll get in another scene today," Joe told her. "I'll call Doug, and get a revised draft down to you right away. You have more scenes with Conar, Kelly, Jay...and Hank. They're easy scenes; you'll handle them one, two, three." Joe paused as his intercom rang. He pressed the button. "Yes?"

"Someone to see you," came the voice of his assistant.

"I'm busy—"

"You'll want to see her."

There was a tap on the door, then Jinx stuck her head in. Serena jumped up. "Jinx!"

Her assistant smiled. "Yep."

"Young lady, you should still be in the hospital," Joe said firmly.

"I couldn't stay there any longer. I'm fine now, really fine."

"What are you doing at work?" Serena asked her incredulously.

"Well, if you fall off a horse, you get back on, right?"

"But, Jinx, you ought to be in bed," Serena told her.

"Honestly, in the middle of the night last night, when all the sedation wore off, I felt fine. Tired, and then this morning—hungry. I want to be here. Please?" she asked a little anxiously. "The mail piles up quickly, you know."

"Speaking of mail..." Bill Hutchens said, walking over to her. "You take care of Serena's mail, right?"

"And Jennifer's."

"Have you ever seen anything like this before?"

He showed her the note.

Jinx read the words through the plastic, paling slightly as she did so.

"Well?"

"No." She flashed a glance at Serena. "Well, I mean, we do get threats against Serena, or Verona Valentine, but...that's a valentine."

"And you haven't seen anything like it before?"

"No." Her eyes widened. "This is terrible, Serena."

She sighed. "Jinx, you were the one something horrible happened to."

Jinx smiled just slightly. "And Allona. I heard that they pumped her stomach, too. And that she's still hopping mad."

"We have insurance," Joe said simply. "And you'll receive compensation, Jinx," he said.

The door to Joe's office suddenly burst open. Jay Braden came striding in, ignoring everyone there and heading straight for Jinx. "What are you doing here, you little idiot? You should still be in the hospital. You shouldn't

261

be here!" He glared at Joe, as if the producer had ordered her in.

"Jay!" Jinx protested. "I came because I wanted to—honestly. This place is like home to me. I need to be here, believe me. I didn't want to stay in the hospital. And I didn't want to go home alone...please! I want to be here."

Jay glared at Joe and Andy and even Bill Hutchens. "She really should sue the show. There's poison in a box of chocolates right on the set."

Joe looked irritated, as if Jay was really on thin ice.

"Jay, please!" Jinx put a hand on his chest. She smiled brightly at him, then at the others. "Please, don't you all keep staring at me like that," she said. "Jay, I'm okay, honestly. I just won't eat on the set for a while."

No one, Serena thought, would be doing much eating on the set in the near future. "You were in terrible shape yesterday," Serena reminded Jinx.

"But I'm fine *now*."

"Just crazy," Andy said.

"I'm fine, I want to work. I don't need to be compensated," Jinx said.

"Jinx—" Serena began. "Never mind. We'll talk."

Late that afternoon, when she had finished her final scene for the day, Serena found Conar, Liam, and Bill Hutchens waiting for her just off the set. Her last scene had been with Hank. An argument about what she was doing, and what was her sister doing, and a warning that they had better both stay away from David DeVille. All he wanted was their wine. Naturally, she fought her father, telling him people were worth more than wine.

When Jim called cut and told them that the scene was in the can, she walked over to the three men.

"Serena, Conar's taking you to their place for a while this evening."

"That's really nice, Conar, and you know I love to see Jennifer and the baby, but I'd like to get home."

"I have some things to do," Liam said. "You need to go with Conar."

Serena was alarmed by the instant squeeze that seemed to wrap around her heart.

Jealousy.

He had *things* to do. Naturally. People did.

She had forgotten that despite how well they were managing to get along, she was still a job for him. Naturally, it was difficult for him to be with her every minute.

She wasn't going to allow herself to wonder what "things" he had to do. But she didn't want to be out tonight. She wanted to go to her own home where she could simply get some rest. She'd turn on the alarm and close all the drapes.

"Conar, thanks," she said. "But I'm sure that Bill can see me home, and then I'll lock myself in."

"Jen would really like to have you," Conar said.

Liam was staring at her. He was irritated.

"Look, I'll lock the door, I'll put on the alarm. I'm going to make a salad, and go to bed. I'm tired. Really tired."

She stared back at Liam.

"Bill has worked hours, nonstop," Liam said.

"Hey...it's all right, honest. A cop is never off, you know that, Liam. I'll get Serena home. I'll wait around a while...is Ricardo coming on tonight?"

"Yes. I'll see that he does," Liam said.

He turned and left. His shoulders were squared, his back was straight. He was angry, Serena thought. He had wanted her with Conar and Jennifer so that he could feel secure about her himself. In his eyes, she was certain, she had behaved like a prima donna.

Well, he tended to act like a dictator.

"Are you ready? I imagine you must be anxious to leave this set these days," Bill told her.

She shook her head, smiling. "I love the set. I love the show. Except that...why would somebody be doing all these things, Bill?"

"Motive? Come on, I'll walk you to your dressing room, drive you home, and along the way, I'll get started!"

Captain D. J. Rigger was sixty, with short-cropped silver-white hair and steel-blue eyes.

264

He was the father of five, grandfather of sixteen, tall, spare, deceptively powerful, and a good judge of character. Liam had made arrangements to see his old captain because he wanted to look over some of his own old files, and he didn't want to go through a truckload of red tape to get his hands on them.

He asked to use Rigger's phone first and called Ricardo. When Ricardo picked up, Liam asked him to go on early. "Serena is with Bill Hutchens right now, but I don't know how long Bill can stay around. She'll be inside, locked up in bed, but I'd feel better if you can pull the hours."

"Will do," Ricardo assured him. "My wife is out right now. The minute she gets in, I'll head on over."

Liam thanked him and rang off.

"You're using Ricardo again?" Rigger said, referring to the occasion when Liam had suggested Ricardo to Conar Markham at the time of the Hitchcock killings. "I'm glad. He needs the extra income—kids are expensive these days."

Rigger lit a cigarette. There was supposed to be no smoking, but Rigger had pulled out his air filter and closed the door.

"So, you think you can find something new in the files we gathered when you were investigating the Hitchcock killings?" Rigger asked him. "I'm sure you have your suspects."

Liam shrugged. "Someone on the set has to be involved. I'm inclined to look toward Jay

Braden, who has behaved very erratically lately."

"What about the brother-in-law?"

Liam hesitated. "I can see Jeff maybe coming close to blows with someone because of an argument over an Egyptian deity, but attempting to murder a woman he's known since she was a kid...it doesn't gel."

"So you're looking at Braden."

Liam shrugged. "I found some things in here." Liam picked up Jay Braden's file. "Went to Harvard," he murmured. "Started off in law, as his folks wanted. Left after his second year to join the chorus of a Broadway show. He started doing underwear commercials... Here it is. He was arrested once for battery. I think I'll make a point of seeing him, and asking about that situation."

"If you're looking for arrest records," Rigger said, tapping the pile of files, "check out Allona Sainge. Rich—and outspoken. And arrested numerous times. She was involved with actors marching for the ethical treatment of animals. Black Power. Gay rights. Women's rights. You name it—she's ready to jump right in. By the way, I checked on arrest records for the lighting guys and the assistants. Nothing on any of them. And I pulled out one more for you. The man you mentioned when you called. Amesbury. Their current liaison with Haines/Clark."

"He does have an arrest record?"

"He was taken in at a drug bust."

"What a surprise. Drugs at a Hollywood party."

"It was a regular cornucopia of drugs. Heroin, LSD, crack, cocaine—uppers, downers, your drug of choice."

"Was Amesbury convicted of anything?"

"No—a good lawyer gave him back to society."

Amesbury. Liam wanted to see the man again. He wanted to get into the house. He remembered he had something more to do that night.

He stood up suddenly. "Thanks, Captain. I can keep these?"

"They're copies. I've made sure Hutchens has the originals."

"They may not give me anything at all," Liam said.

"Maybe not. Maybe we're looking too hard at what seems to be obvious. Anyway, if I can help again in any way... I think you need to move as quickly as possible."

Liam arched a brow.

"The light was well planned," Rigger pointed out. "But the candy—it was stupid. A dead give-away. Your killer is getting either more care-less or..."

"Or?"

"More desperate."

"You know," Bill warned, glancing her way as he drove, "this is really serious. You can't be careless in any way at all, Serena."

She nodded glumly. "I know," she said softly. "I just can't figure out *why* anyone would hate me enough to want to kill me."

"Trust me, I've seen a lot," Bill said. "Men have shot their wives for changing the TV station in the middle of a football game."

"I don't think that's what we're looking at here, Bill," Serena said.

"People kill for revenge. And then there's money. Greed. Jealousy." He was quiet for a minute. "You know, Serena, it is looking bad for your brother-in-law."

"You're full of it!" she said angrily. "My brother-in-law is a decent—"

"There were those who would have sworn that Ted Bundy was one of the nicest young gentlemen they had ever met."

"You have nothing on Jeff," she said. "Nothing solid."

He didn't reply to that. He looked at her with a concerned smile. "You know, you have to eat. Want some pizza before I bring you home?"

"Sure."

They stopped for pizza at a chain near Serena's house. Bill offered to take a bite of Serena's first, and she smiled, shaking her head, telling him she really didn't think that anyone had managed to get to a pizza house they hadn't known they were going to.

As they ate, Bill said, "Serena, we will solve this. It may take time, but we will find this person."

She gave him a grim smile. "No leads, no clues. It's frightening."

He shook his head and admitted, "I'm sorry to say there are cases that are never solved. But this won't be one of them. There are clues—we just haven't worked them out yet. You know, I did think that Lieutenant Olsen was being overly cautious at first, but now…well, it's obvious that you're in danger. I wish…"

"What?"

"Well, I wish now that we had moved faster. That we had found that note you saw burned in Jane's dressing room. It might have been the clue we really needed. I know that it didn't strike me as terribly important at first, but…you're sure you didn't read it, any part of it, that you've no idea what became of it?"

"Bill, I just stopped by her dressing room. I'm not even sure it was a note. If so, it was only the remnants of a note. Whatever it said must have made Jane mad. She tried to burn it; it just didn't burn."

"This has got to be one of the strangest cases I've ever had. And I've had strange cases in Hollywood."

"Like what?"

"All right, let me think…there was the actor who murdered a set designer for creating a scene all in wicker. And the woman who killed a costume designer because she freaked when she saw that her entire wardrobe for a movie was in pink. There was the director who killed three women because he liked the way they looked at his house and he wanted to keep their bodies sitting properly in the chairs at one time."

"Okay, those are pretty weird. But you found the culprit right away. Murder with a spotlight. Who would think?"

"We can't think. We have to keep working," he said. "Come on. I guess I'd better get you home."

"Hey, thanks for doing this."

"My pleasure. It's fun to be with you, even for pizza."

"Thanks."

A few minutes later they came to her house. Bill followed her to the door, waited while she opened it, and stood patiently while she keyed in the alarm. Then, as Liam did, he went through the house.

He returned to the living room. "Lock me out—"

"And key in the alarm again. I know. Thanks, Bill."

"You're sure you're going to be okay?" He touched her cheek. "Silly question. I guess you're back with Liam now."

"We're not exactly back," she murmured. "But it is great not to be alone right now."

"So he is...staying with you."

She felt her cheeks burn. The first time she'd had coffee with Bill, she'd barely refrained from crying on his shoulder. He was good to be with—a friend. Rock-steady, reassuring, strong, and brave. She had known that he'd wanted to take the relationship farther, and it was one of the reasons she had cut it off so quickly. The way he touched her cheek and looked into her eyes now, she knew that he was really concerned for her; he cared for her.

"Hey," she said, taking his hand from her

cheek and squeezing it warmly with her own, "he's definitely a great bodyguard. And yes, whatever comes in the future—assuming I have a future—I'm grateful not to be alone now."

"Serena, you will have a future. Passionate, dramatic—you've only just begun. We'll see to it!"

Passionate and dramatic himself, he held her by the shoulders and kissed her on the forehead. "Lock up—"

"Immediately. I know."

Liam arrived at Jeff and Melinda's house at about eight-thirty. As he stood on the front porch he could hear sounds from inside. A fight. The two were arguing.

He rang the bell and waited. A moment later Melinda opened the door. "Liam," she said, without pleasure.

"May I come in?"

"Are you going to get a warrant if I don't let you in?"

"I'm not a cop anymore, Melinda."

"That's right. You're a private investigator. Well, we've answered enough questions, I think. And since you're not a cop—"

"Let him in, Melinda," Jeff said.

Melinda pursed her lips. She and Serena looked very much alike; Liam even recognized the expression. She was a very attractive woman, but signs of the stress she was feeling were evident in the gaunt look of her features.

She backed away from the door.

"Come in, Liam," Jeff said. "Can I get you something to drink?"

"No, I'm fine, thanks."

"Have a seat."

Liam took a chair in the living room. Jeff sat across from him. Melinda stood behind her husband's chair.

"I didn't send the candy," Jeff said flatly. "That's why you're here, isn't it? I have nothing against my sister-in-law. Hell, I've known Serena since she was a kid. Melinda and I went to her every silly high school and college play. My kids are in a great college because of her help. I don't know what else to say. I have no reason on earth to want to harm Serena."

"Does my sister know you're here?" Melinda demanded sharply.

"No. No, she doesn't know I'm here."

"Aren't you supposed to be guarding her? Isn't that your job? If you're not a cop anymore, you're not supposed to be harassing us."

"Melinda, I'm not harassing you. I came here to find out what *is* going on between the two of you. And to ask you if you know any reason someone on that set may have killed Jane— and if anyone there has access to your credit cards."

Jeff inhaled on a deep breath. "Jane was a bitch. She came on set yelling at everyone," he said. "This wasn't right, that wasn't right. There was this party when we all met her...and she was charming. Then she changed. Once she'd finished negotiating, she had something to say to everyone. She really thought that she ruled the world. So...who can say who hated her the most? She got a little power, or so she thought, and went mad. And as to my credit card..." He hesitated, looking at Melinda. Then he shrugged. "We use credit cards all the time."

"We're careless," Melinda said.

"And broke, too often," Jeff said. He lifted a hand. "There you have it. My sister-in-law bails us out of trouble with embarrassing frequency. Why on earth would I want anything to happen to her?"

"Why are you two always arguing?"

Jeff opened his mouth.

Liam was very sure Melinda pinched him on the back of the neck.

"We're married," he said dryly. "What more do you want?"

The truth, Liam thought. He decided not to push it for the moment. He needed to talk to Jeff alone. That was something he'd have to arrange, making sure Melinda wasn't with him.

"Well, thanks for seeing me," Liam said.

Melinda didn't answer. She stared at him, her face set in stone.

He had risen; Jeff did the same. "I'll walk you to the door."

When they reached it, Jeff told him, "It seems really strange to me that Allona ate those chocolates and was just fine. Almost as if she knew which ones to eat and which ones not to eat. That is, if the arsenic was really in the chocolates."

"Very strange—or incredibly lucky. Apparently, according to the lab tests, only one of the chocolates had poison in it."

"Are you planning on talking to Allona, too?"

"I'm planning on talking to everyone," Liam told him pleasantly.

"Well, you'll have to talk to me here. I'm not going on that set anymore. Everything in that place winds up being blamed on me."

Liam looked at him. "You were on the set the day the chocolates arrived."

"Of course I was. Serena had a scene coming up in which she gets caught in a booby-trapped sarcophagus. It's my job—was my job—to see that it was all done right."

"It's not a real sarcophagus?" Liam queried.

Jeff gave him the look a real academic could give when the lesser world didn't seem to understand something that everyone should know. "Of course not. Such a piece would be prohibitively expensive, if it was even possible to obtain. We bought it at an auction—it had belonged to a magician. Good piece, though. Great hieroglyphics. Very real looking, and I had them add more."

"No one has suggested that you leave the show."

"No, they just think that I'm guilty of murder. And I've been warned that I could be arrested at any time."

"Someone did kill Jane Dunne. Maybe by accident, in an attempt to get to Serena."

274

"Well, Jane was pretty well hated all around."

"The chocolates came after she died," Liam reminded him.

Jeff looked a little pale at that. "I've said it a million times. I'd never hurt Serena."

"I believe you."

"Do you?"

"Yeah, I do," Liam said, and added bluntly, "But you're covering something up."

"I've got to go back in. Melinda is jumpy and bitter these days."

"Sure. Although it might be better if you just tell me what's going on."

Jeff looked at him blandly. "We're married. We fight."

"Yeah. Sure. And the fighting has nothing to do with Jane Dunne. Good night."

"Liam, I..." Jeff looked over his shoulder, back toward the house. "Liam, you know, you don't always have a good comprehension of women. I've got to get back in."

"Good night." He turned toward his car.

"Hey, wait," Jeff said. Liam paused. "Keep her safe, huh? I mean it. I love my sister-in-law. So does Melinda. And we both like you, too. It's just...Melinda is a little weird right now."

"I understand."

Liam had planned on heading straight to an office just off Sunset Boulevard, but before he could reach his destination, he slowed his car as he passed a trendy cafe on the boulevard, not far from the House of Blues. At an outside table for four, he saw Allona Sainge sitting with Doug Henson and Jay Braden. Seeing a parking spot, he slipped into it.

As he walked down the street, Allona hailed him. "Hey, Liam!"

She seemed genuinely pleased to see him. Doug greeted him warmly as well. Jay Braden offered a semi-smile, moving the free chair out so that he could take a seat.

"You've left my baby all alone?" Doug asked.

"Locked in at home."

"Safe and sound?" Allona asked wryly.

"Bill Hutchens took her home," he said, assuring himself that they were all left aware that she was protected by a police detective. He smiled at the group. He needed to talk to them all one by one, get them to say things they might not say in front of one another. But sometimes, he had learned, it was just as interesting to see what people did say in front of one another.

Jay Braden leaned forward. "So what the hell is going on here, Liam? Whatever it is, it's going to wreck all our lives." His behavior was more subdued than Liam had seen lately. "You must have some kind of an idea," he said. He was not as hostile as he had been at the hospital, but he was still agitated.

"As of yet, we don't have much," Liam said, watching Jay. He wondered if the man didn't look just a little relieved when he heard that.

"Something will break," Liam continued. "Something usually does."

"That's not true at all," Allona argued. "Police files are filled with unsolved cases."

"True."

"Way back to Jack the Ripper," Doug said.

"Well, if they'd had today's science when Jack the Ripper was busy, the case wouldn't have been unsolved—they would have prints, blood, DNA. They could have, at the very least, disproved a lot of theories," Liam said. He sat back, observing them all. "Where's Jinx? Isn't she usually out with you all?"

Allona looked surprised. "Not *usually*," she said.

"Jay plays big brother a lot," Doug said easily. "But he has an image, a career to maintain. We can't let it appear that he's getting too serious."

Jay lifted his hands. "She's like this sweet, scared little rabbit. And she's a pretty girl. I'd just like to see her have a life."

Liam nodded, then smiled across the table at Allona. "So what are you up to, outside of work? Any new organizations, save-the-harried-writer societies, or anything of that sort?"

Allona stiffened, her eyes narrowing. "You've been going through our records, haven't you, Mr. Murphy?"

"What we do know is that someone on the set is guilty of tampering with lighting, equipment, and chocolates. Therefore, everyone on the set has to be considered a suspect."

Allona had built a wall around herself. Her body language shrieked smoldering anger.

"Hey," Doug said, "poisoning...isn't that typically a *woman's* tool?"

"Yes, actually, poisoning is frequently a woman's method of dispatching her enemies. Definitely a thought-out and premeditated act."

Allona's expression was so icy it appeared that she might crack if touched. She leaned forward, her voice full of venom. "Yes, Mr. Murphy, I've been arrested in protests. Because I always speak my mind, and I speak the truth. But don't forget, I had to have my stomach pumped. For nothing, as it turns out."

He leaned forward as well, challenging her. "But you ate the candy while you were with Serena. Maybe trying to get her to eat along with you. And if you had poisoned only the one candy, you would have known which one it was, right?"

She had been holding a swizzle stick. It suddenly cracked in her hand.

"Serena is as much a part of my livelihood as that of anyone else. I also like her; she's a friend. Why would I want to get rid of her?"

Liam shrugged. "Good point. I haven't a motive for you."

"Well, great," Doug said. "It's hard to find someone who doesn't like Serena. Except for maybe..."

As his voice trailed off, they all stared at him. "Who?" Allona demanded sharply.

He shrugged unhappily. "Kyle Amesbury." He hesitated, then continued, since everyone was staring at him. "I think that...well, other people kind of play a game. They may think he's an asshole...or come to realize he's an asshole...but they still play the game. They talk to him at parties, they invite him places, they go to his house. Serena manages to evade him all the time."

"I thought he was a friend of yours," Liam said.

"He's a damned scary friend," Doug said simply.

"In what way?"

"Oh, nothing illegal. I don't think so, anyway. He wants people to stay all the time. Sleep at his place. Bring friends."

Yes, stay at my place, I'll make you a star! Liam thought.

"Kyle wasn't on the set at the time of any of the incidents," Liam pointed out.

"Maybe he's working in collusion with someone else," Allona said, and staring hard at Liam she added, "And it isn't me!"

"Today's science...lot of good it's doing," Jay said with disgust. "They've taken fingerprints, they've talked to us all—you've gone through police records, and all the king's men—Olsen's men, that is—can't seem to find a damned thing. Our jobs and our lives are all going down the tubes."

"If it weren't for the candy..." Allona began, then looked at them all. "Well, the killer should have been after Jane. That made sense. She was wicked. And the guys...she tried to seduce everyone."

"She didn't try to seduce me," Doug said.

Allona stared at him, then shook her head.

"Jay, was she like that?" Liam asked.

"Yeah. Yeah, she was," Jay agreed. "Where is the waiter? It's chilly tonight. I think I'll have coffee instead of beer. Hey, yeah, you want something, Liam?"

"Sure, I'll take a beer."

"And I'll take another," Allona said. "It's not that chilly. And life is going to hell in a bucket. I'll definitely have another beer. Doug, what about you?"

"I got to go," said Doug.

"Oh, yeah?"

"Plans this evening," he said with a wave of his hand.

"You're going out with *Amesbury* again?" Allona asked.

"No. He's gotten a little too...strange."

"He's a sick-o," Allona said.

"Are you going to his party Thursday night?" Doug asked.

"Wouldn't miss it," Allona assured him. She made a face. "Joe seems to think we should be sociable—until this is all over."

"You going to let Serena go?" Jay asked Liam, watching him sharply.

"I'm not her parent. I can't tell her what she can and can't do," he replied.

They were all silent for a minute, as if they didn't believe him.

"If she wants to go, we'll go," he said.

"He throws an interesting party," Allona murmured. "Filled with interesting people."

The drinks had arrived. Jay asked for the check. Liam thanked him for the beer. "Hey, are you guys a duo again?"

"Right now, we're just trying to get at the truth of whatever is going on here."

"You don't believe Jeff did send that candy, do you?" Allona asked.

"No."

"Then who did?"

"Someone who knew she liked that kind of candy," Liam said.

"That would be anyone involved with the show," Allona said. "Back to square one."

Liam shrugged, watching them all. "Not necessarily. It would have to be someone who didn't know that she doesn't like chocolate-covered cherries."

"Well, that leaves me out," Doug said, pleased. "I knew she hated them."

Allona was silent, then said, "Well, I didn't know, but I ate the damned things."

"The *right* damned things," Doug pointed out.

"Hey, boss man, watch it!" Allona told him.

"That was close to an accusation, Doug," Jay Braden pointed out politely. "Coming from Liam...it's his job. Coming from you...it's close to an accusation."

"It was not. And you be careful what you say to me—I'm the head writer. I'll shut you up in an Egyptian tomb for the next two weeks."

"And I'll have a fit, naturally, about not being on set often enough," Jay said pleasantly. "I

281

am, after all, Verona Valentine's latest ex. She's probably carrying my child."

"I'll lock you both in a tomb," Doug said. He glanced at his watch. "I have to go."

"Yeah, I guess we'd all better get going. Places to be, people to see," Allona said.

"You've got a date?" Doug asked her.

"Yeah. Me and my pillow," she said.

"What about you, Jay?" Doug asked.

"I, unlike the rest of you exhibitionists, keep my private life private."

"Are you heading over to see our little Jinx by any chance?" Allona asked.

"Why did you say that?" Jay asked quickly.

"As our good ex-cop pointed out, you are with the sweet thing a lot."

Jay shrugged. "I'm trying to be a friend."

"She can look darned good," Doug said.

"Cute little figure," Allona agreed.

"Yeah, she washes up nice," Jay said. "But my every evening is not spent as a charity event. In fact, I'm out of here now." He rose, waved a goodbye.

Liam waited, watching him, finishing his beer.

"Jay is a good-looking guy," Doug pointed out to Allona. "The two of you—"

"It would be like dating my brother!" Allona said in horror.

"Well, I guess," Doug said with a shrug. "Don't worry, though, the right guy is out there, somewhere. Of course..."

"Of course, what?" Allona demanded.

"Maybe you shouldn't be quite so opinionated."

"The right guy would appreciate a woman with opinions. And by the way, I didn't ask for yours."

"I'm always willing to give it—without being asked. And I'm right, don't you think, Liam? Especially when it comes to the way you felt about Jane Dunne."

"I'm honest!" Allona argued.

"What do you say, Liam?" Doug demanded.

"I say it's time I leave," Liam said, rising.

"Cop-out!" Doug accused him.

Liam grinned. "Thanks for the company."

"You off to watch over Serena?"

"Something like that," he said vaguely. "Good night."

Liam started to his car. As he neared it, he heard footsteps behind him. He turned quickly as he reached the vehicle.

Jay Braden had followed him. "You mentioned Allona's arrests. You didn't mention my record," Jay said flatly.

Liam leaned against his car, ready to listen. "I thought I'd bring it up privately," he said.

"Good of you."

"Battery, Jay. Against a woman."

"In my wild younger days. We were both struggling. She was a bit older, sophisticated, living off my rent, and sleeping with a cinematographer. She threw a drink in my face. We'd both had a few too many. I slapped her, and she called the cops. I was hauled in. There was nothing vicious or dangerous about it—except, perhaps, the woman involved. Look, I've been as honest with you as I can be.

I'm telling you I'd never hurt Serena. I'll answer any question I can about anything."

Jay was speaking earnestly, but Liam found himself staring at the guy's head of thick dark hair.

There was somewhere else he still had to go, and he was anxious to get back to Serena.

"Thanks. I appreciate that," Liam told him.

The phone rang. Serena let the machine pick up.

Silence played over the line, then a tiny click.

She had left the drapes over the patio windows and sliding doors closed. She walked over to them now, pulling the drapes just enough to see out in the darkness.

One of the pool lights had burned out. The area seemed very shadowy. Serena saw tree limbs dip and wave, creating more shadows. Shapes seemed to dance between the shadows.

She let the draperies fall closed, and walked around the house, turning on every light. She was fine, she told herself. She had locked herself in, and the alarm was on. There was nothing to worry about.

Liam had things to do.

She had lived here alone for many years. She had never been afraid before. That wasn't entirely true, but she had trusted in her own intelligence—and in her alarm. She hadn't wanted anyone guarding her every second.

She'd been brought home by a cop. A homicide detective, who had checked her house with the same thoroughness as Liam did. She had grown too dependent on Liam.

She was safe in here. It was ridiculous, absolutely ridiculous, to have someone watching out for her every minute of her life.

The phone started to ring once more, causing her to jump.

It's the telephone, for God's sake, she told herself.

The answering machine would kick in.

Again she waited, with growing tension.

The machine picked up. Silence from the other end, then...a click.

"I hate people who do that!" she said aloud. "Just say something, anything!"

She clenched her teeth as she heard a thud against the rear of the house.

"Branches," she murmured. "Branches hit the house all the time."

Tonight he'd had *things to do.*

He had broken it off with Sharon, or so it appeared. Maybe he had needed to talk to her. Maybe she was waiting for a man who was never coming back, not even for the time it would take to get through all this. What if they never got through all this? What if threats just kept coming, and people started dropping like flies all around her, and they never found out what was going on? She had to learn to live with this again, to trust her alarm system, and her house.

She walked into the kitchen, and poured herself a glass of white wine. The label on the bottle said VALENTINE VALLEY, SPECIAL VINTAGE, SAINGE VINEYARD. Allona's family had bottled the limited-quantity white Bordeaux especially for the show's five-year anniversary. It really was excellent wine. Each cast member had received a half case. It seemed an ironically good time to crack open a bottle of it.

She sipped the wine. She'd been tired; she'd wanted to come home. Now she wished she'd gone home with Conar. She could be talking to Jennifer, playing with the baby.

Thinking, of course, that her own life was a disaster compared to her friend's, and that was before strange warning flowers, Valentine's threats, and poisoned chocolates. Jennifer had Conar, a fellow actor, for a husband, a man who knew the pressures of the business. She had her mom and her baby.

While she herself had a failed marriage—whatever had induced her to marry *Andy?*—no children, a career on the rocks with all the strange things happening, and an infatuation with a man who had walked out on her.

"Here's looking at you, kid," she told herself softly, lifting her glass. Then she was angry with herself for the fear and the pity. "You do have a life!" she reminded herself. "And a career, and a home, and a sister who loves you in spite of everything, two great nephews, and really fine friends."

Again, the phone began to ring.

This time she didn't hear silence or a click. She heard a voice, husky, strange, saying her name. "Serena, Serena, Serena..." There seemed to be no gender to the voice. "I can see you, Serena, I know that you're there. I watch you, Serena. Take care. *Roses are red, soon you'll be dead, violets are blue, I'm coming for you.*"

She stood frozen for a moment. The voice had been eerie. Purposely so, she told herself. Someone was trying to scare her.

Someone was doing a good job.

She squared her shoulders, then went striding from the kitchen out to the living room. Standing by the machine, she took another sip of wine—meant to be small, but it was half the glass—and reached for the call return button on the phone.

Before she could hit it, the telephone started to ring again.

She hesitated. The machine picked up.

"Serena, Serena, Serena, I see you...the cops are not so good after all, are they? 'Cause you're trying to find out who I am, where I am. Well, you're about to find out, Serena. The cat is away, and so the mice will play. I'm inside the house, Serena. Inside the house.

"Have you got that. I'm *inside* the house."

Chapter 18

Kyle Amesbury, perfectly polished, as usual, opened the door himself. He didn't invite Liam in; in fact, he stood blocking the doorway. He was wearing dress trousers and a short-sleeved shirt, unbuttoned. His chest was well muscled and clean as a whistle. Totally devoid of hair.

"Well, hell. You're Liam Murphy, aren't you?" Tonight, Amesbury was smoothly hostile. "What can I do for you? I'd invite you in, but..." He shrugged. "You see, I'm in the midst of a private party."

"Who are you 'starring' tonight?" Liam asked him.

Amesbury gave him a rueful smile. "None of your business."

"You know, secretly taping people is illegal," Liam informed him.

Amesbury waved a dismissive hand in the air. "Secretly? My cameras are all obvious. I have a right to protect my property. There are priceless antiques in every room of this place."

"You're pushing a fine line there."

"I have excellent attorneys."

"Amesbury, you're throwing threats at *Valentine Valley* about pulling out when they're doing their best to uncover a crime. What does your company think of your lifestyle?"

"Hey, Murphy, my lifestyle is private. And you're infringing on my personal free time right now. Do you think you have something on me?

Have you come over here to try to blackmail me in some way?" Amesbury seemed amused by the thought.

Liam forced an easy smile. "No, I'm simply warning you that I'll be watching."

He laughed. "You think *I'm* after Serena. Sorry, buddy, not my type. All I ever try to do is make amends with our soap queen."

"You're involved with this somehow, Amesbury. You suck people in—"

"I'm a player. And yes, bless the Lord! I attract people here."

"What people, Amesbury? And what are you trying to get out of them?"

"Murphy, the people are my friends. I protect them. I let them play, indulge in their fantasies. What I know about anyone stays secret with me."

"You're involved, and I will find out how and why."

"You're going to get me arrested—for being kinky perhaps? In Hollywood? I don't think so, Murphy."

Liam shifted his weight from foot to foot. Obviously, Amesbury wasn't as confident as he pretended, for he jumped backward in the doorway. "Hey, you touch me, Murphy, and I will have you arrested. I have friends at the station, too, you know."

Liam smiled. "I don't think I'd dirty a knuckle on you, Amesbury. Just remember, I will be watching you." He took a step toward the man. "But if I ever catch you—"

"Catch me what? Turning your precious little

girlfriend into a porn star?" Amesbury whispered.

Liam caught him by the collar of his designer shirt, coming nose to nose with him. "I catch you threatening a hair on her head, and you're a dead man." Amesbury went pale. Liam turned and started down the walkway. Amesbury slammed the front door. Liam paused for a moment. The front draperies were open.

Kyle Amesbury flipped a minute phone from the pocket of his perfectly pressed trousers and spoke angrily into it. He looked up the stairs. Someone had called him. He started up the steps.

Liam returned to his car, headed for his next stop. Amesbury had dark hair. Thick, wavy, dark hair.

"In your house, close, in your house with you, coming closer..." the husky, rasping voice continued in Serena's ear.

Serena didn't think; she bolted.

She raced to the door, throwing it open. It occurred to her, even in her panic, that by running out without keying her pad, she would set off the alarm.

She burst out of the house and across the yard, heading for the street. But as she did so, a huge shadow swayed before her from the front. In the darkness of the night, she could make out nothing at all about the form; all she saw was a shape.

Dark and menacing. She was blocked from reaching the street.

Now the door to the house stood open. Someone waited within.

Someone...something...waited outside as well.

She flew around the side of the house, not looking for the gate, but reaching for the top of the privacy fence and leaping over it into the backyard. She heard her heart racing, and the sound was so loud it drowned out all others. She didn't know if she was being pursued or not. In the backyard, she raced for the huge old oak, stretching to the darkness of the sky. She reached the tree, slipped around it, leaned against it, and breathed shallowly, so as not to make a sound. She waited. How much time had passed? Seconds...minutes?

The alarm had not gone off.

She hugged the oak, trying to remember that she could hide in its dark shadow. She needed to still the racing of her heart, be silent, and listen, not give away her position with the ragged storm of her breathing.

Time passed...

She turned, staring around the yard. There was the pool, the swaying palms around it. The barbecue, the lounge chairs. The foliage that made the yard so beautiful...

And so dangerous now.

Then, at the corner of the house, by the bushes at the wall, she saw movement.

Was it just the breeze? Branches everywhere were dipping and swaying.

A twig snapped.

She nearly screamed aloud. Then she saw a squirrel racing pell-mell from the oak. She had scared the creature as much as it had scared her. The sound of her heart was growing louder once again.

The backyard held nothing, she thought.

Nothing but shadows...

Trying to breathe very deeply and slowly, she realized that dashing into the backyard was the worst mistake she could have made. Here she was trapped. A killer could do anything, protected by the wooden privacy fence. She needed to make her way back to the front, somehow, keeping to the shadows herself.

She stared at the next large tree, to the right of the pool.

She began thinking about all she had learned from movies.

Scream.

The killer calls the house and unnerves the victim. The victim searches for the killer, the source of danger, and runs right into...

Death.

Fool! she chastised herself.

The phone call had come. She had panicked and fled. Her house had been sealed. Now the door lay wide open. And she was in the darkness and shadows, and every tree was moving and whispering in the darkness, seeming to chant her name.

She waited, tense as a bowstring.

At last she made a move.

She sprinted to the next tree, sliding against

the bark. She watched and waited again. Now her backyard seemed silent.

Then...

A thump. Not a rustle. A *thump*!

Somewhere on the other side of the yard.

She was just fifty feet from the wooden wall to the front of the yard. She held her breath, realized she was doing so, expelled it, and breathed deeply.

She broke from the tree, rushing for the fence. She jumped over it. Even as she did so, she heard rustling again, running, someone coming after her. In the seconds it took her to skim the wall, she was thinking. *Don't return to the house. Run like hell. Get to a neighbor's house, beat on the door, scream loud enough to wake the dead.*

She slipped over the side of the fence, hit the earth with her knees bent, ready to run again. She started tearing across the lawn.

Her heart slammed hard against her chest. Headlights beamed on the street. A car was coming. All she had to do was reach the road, scream, shriek, stop the driver...

A shadow stepped out from one of the huge hibiscus bushes that flanked the walkway, directly in her path.

She turned and ran again, into the darkness of the rear of the yard.

Shadows in front, shadows to the rear. She had trapped herself.

She inched into the darkness, hit brick with her back.

Trapped!

Idiot!

The night was alive with rustling, sounds... whispers.

And shadows that moved.

The room was dark except for the glow of light that streamed from the computer screen. Liam stood behind Oz Davis, the wiz kid of his senior year in high school, a man who had gone on to become a technical master of film and video in every variety, and computers. He'd taken the tape, honed in, enlarged, and defined the picture to every length possible by science.

But staring at the man with Jane Dunne— honed, defined, and enlarged as he might be—Liam was still frustrated.

"It was almost as if this man knew there were cameras in the room," Oz said with disgust, shaking his head. He pointed to the screen. "I've gone through the entire tape, over and over. I've digitized and asked the computer for help. But you can never get a clear picture of even an angle of the face; the best you'll get is here—if you can recognize a man by his shoulders. Maybe I can give you something—the guy doesn't have a wisp of hair on his shoulders or back. That suggests an actor, body-builder— or just a guy who's had a great laser removal done because he was embarrassed by the hair on his back."

"Maybe that is something," Liam said. He

remembered the shiny smooth line of Kyle Amesbury's hairless chest. Grabbing his collar, he had touched his nape and back.

Smooth.

He glanced at his watch, then stared at the screen again. The man in the tape maintained the same basic position throughout. No matter how the footage was segregated and enlarged, there was nothing to be seen but the top of a dark-haired head, and a view of the shoulders and back. But Oz was damned right about one thing—the guy hadn't so much as the stubble of a single hair on his shoulders or back. "Thanks, Oz," he said.

"I'll keep playing with it," Oz assured him. "I'm not sure where I can go with it, but I will keep trying."

Liam left the studio and drove for Serena's house, disappointed that he hadn't found out more, yet hopeful that he might have gained something. The man in the film might have been Jay Braden. Or Kyle Amesbury.

Or Jeff Guelph?

As he headed from the city and back up to the hills, he took a sudden, unplanned turn. Might as well check out one thing right now. He was close enough.

He drove back to Guelph's house.

Jeff must have heard his car as he pulled into the drive. Before he reached the front door, Jeff had opened it. He stared at Liam quizzically. "Am I about to be arrested—"

"No."

"Are you coming back in?" Jeff asked.

"No. I want you to take your shirt off for me, please?"

Jeff looked at him with astonishment. He didn't even ask why. He was wearing a polo shirt, and he pulled it over his head and shoulders.

"Turn around."

Jeff did so.

The man was a veritable grizzly bear.

"Thanks," Liam said.

"Don't mention it," Jeff murmured. "Are you going to tell me why you just had me do that?"

"Yeah, sometime," Liam said.

Melinda suddenly called to him from the house. "Jeff? Is anything wrong? Is someone there?"

Liam shook his head. "I'm leaving," he told Jeff. "Tell her that everything is all right. I think that it is. You slept with Jane Dunne, at least once. Where? Not at Kyle Amesbury's, right?"

"At Amesbury's?" Jeff said, sounding baffled again. His face reddened. "It was only once," he said, his voice pained. He took a deep breath. "In her dressing room."

"Thanks," Liam said, and headed back to his car.

Serena thought she knew now what it felt like to be a hunted animal.

She leaped back over the privacy fence to

the rear with the simple thought that there had definitely been something in front of her. But when her feet hit the ground in the rear, she could see someone on the other side of the pool. Not clearly. The form was close to the foliage, masked by the deep shadows from the illuminated pool.

She headed toward the bushes and the large palm to her right. They would give her a little cover.

The figure by the pool was moving. She needed a running start to scale the wooden fence. Her heart was beating like a wounded hare's. Her every breath was beginning to sound like the storm of the century. She sprang from the bushes and started running.

"Serena!" she heard her name called as she ran. Was it the voice from the phone? She didn't know. It was blocked by the wind in her ears, the rustle of foliage. She leaped the fence and started for the road again.

Once again, a shadow loomed before her.

She zigged and zagged, and the shadow before her danced and did the same. She screamed in desperation, trying to make a mad dash for the road.

She flew straight into the shadow...

A deep sense of alarm filled Liam the minute he came around the bend and neared Serena's house. Light was pouring from the front of the house; the door was gaping open. Cars were drawn up on the yard.

He hit the gas hard, speeding to the embankment in front of her house, then slamming on the brakes. He leaped out of the car just as he heard a scream loud enough to shatter glass.

Serena.

He raced across the yard, bursting through side hedges. There was Serena, and someone else. He moved so fast he practically flew, throwing himself at the form in front of Serena. A huge fellow, a man. He wrestled him to the ground. Serena fell and rolled, shrieking again. "No, no, Liam—!"

The man beneath him was powerful. Liam rolled him over.

Bill Hutchens.

"Jesus Christ, Liam, it's me!" Bill complained.

Liam rose, staring down at the cop and friend he had just flattened. He stood back, ready to reach for the gun beneath his jacket as he heard a rustling and a thump at the privacy fence. He nearly drew his weapon.

Then Ricardo appeared, coming over the fence and running toward them. Serena was still on the ground, looking dazed. Liam walked to her, grasped her hand, and pulled her to her feet.

"What the hell is going on here?"

"I drove back by to see if you were here yet, and if not, to make sure Serena was okay," Bill told him disgustedly. "I saw the door wide open, and heard a commotion, and started around the back."

By then Ricardo, winded and panting, had reached them. He had apparently heard some of what Bill had said.

He put his hands on his knees, gasping for breath. "I got here—saw the door open, saw the light, called Serena's name, got no answer..." He inhaled deeply. "Heard something in the back, jumped the fence, saw a figure, and came racing after it. The figure disappeared, then came flying over the fence again, and I came at it again, calling out, pretty sure then that it was Serena, and trying to tell her it was me, but...she was already over the fence."

Serena, next to him, was shaking.

Liam stared at her. "What were you doing out of the house? What happened? What started this?"

"I got a call. A bunch of calls. Then someone reciting the valentine I had been sent...and saying that they were in the house."

"So you ran out?" He stared at her incredulously.

Hostility touched her eyes. "The caller said that he or she was *in the house!*"

"Has anyone searched the house?"

"I searched the house the minute I brought her home," Bill told him indignantly, straightening his shirt and trying to dust the grass from it. "It was clean. I'd bet my life on it."

Liam realized that they were all staring at Serena. So far Bill and Ricardo had refrained from calling the stupidity of her act to her attention. He was too shaken to be so tolerant.

"You're an idiot!" he blurted out harshly. "You knew that the house was clean—"

"I was frightened!"

"Great, so run out into the arms of death!" He turned his back on her, afraid that she would see how badly he was shaking. "Has anyone searched the house again yet?"

"Liam, we must have both gotten here right before you drove up," Bill said. "We haven't searched anything." He shook his head. Then he remembered that he was in charge; Liam was hired help. "We'll take the house. Ricardo, search the yard."

"Yes, Lieutenant."

Liam stared at Serena, who was panting, hair wild, eyes wild—and still narrowed with fury at him. He gritted his teeth. He needed to shut up. He wanted to shake her. She had been tricked, surely, and she had fallen as easily as a ripe apple from a tree.

He walked ahead. Bill Hutchens put an arm around Serena, coming toward the house with her.

"You all right?"

"Yes, thank you, I'm fine."

His reproach was gentle. "Serena, you know I checked out your house."

"Bill, I heard the voice, and I panicked."

"Maybe this is good. Maybe we can trace the call. We'll hear the voice. We can have it analyzed. Of course, maybe it was just a trickster—"

"A trickster who knew about that valentine's message, and quoted it word for word?" she said.

"We'll search the house; then we'll hear the message."

Liam reached the house ahead of them. Maybe that was why he'd finally left the police force. Public relations. Once upon a time, he'd been good with victims of crime. Tonight...he was seriously on edge himself, angry, afraid.

He started with Serena's bedroom, searching everywhere, under the bed, through the closet, the bath, behind the curtain. Her bedroom took up most of the right side of the house; opposite it, across the hall, was a library. No bath, no closet, nowhere for anyone to hide. It was empty.

Back in the living room, it was easy to see as well that no one could hide there. He went to the back family area where the plate-glass windows and sliding doors led to the pool area.

Bill appeared from the other side of the house, where he had searched the two guest rooms. Staring at Liam, he shook his head.

Serena was standing in the entry.

"Let's hear this message," Liam said.

She walked to the answering machine and hit the Play button. A mechanical voice came on. *"One new message."*

The voice that came on was Melinda Guelph's. "Serena, Serena, pick up. It's me, your sister. I know you're there, screening your calls." There was a silence. "All right, fine. Don't speak to me."

There was a click.

The mechanical voice came on again. *"End of final message."*

She stared at the machine incredulously. "I swear to you that there were messages. The caller phoned a few times, breathed without speaking, and hung up. And the voice came on, repeating the valentine and saying that the killer was in the house!"

Ricardo appeared at the still open front door, winded. He shook his head. "Nothing in the yard."

"I'm telling you—" Serena began.

"Can these messages be canceled from somewhere else?" Bill asked gently.

"Sure. You can erase the whole thing if you call in from anywhere else with the code."

"Well, then, we'll trace the calls to your house," he told her. "We'll get in some fingerprint people and make sure that no one did slip in here. And we'll pull phone records. We'll get on it right away."

"Do you need Serena?" Liam asked.

"Sure. She's going to have to file a complaint, make a statement—"

"All right. Let's get to it all fast. I'm going to take her out of here tonight."

Serena stared at him. "You think that I'm going crazy, imagining things that didn't happen."

"I never said that," Liam told her curtly.

"No, you're saying that no one was ever really inside my house, but I should leave it?"

"Yes," he said firmly. "Bill, can you get started as quickly as possible?"

"Sure."

It was two hours before the paperwork had been filled out.

He chafed with impatience the entire time, even though he knew the procedure, knew the kind of time that it took.

The fingerprint experts arrived to check the phone, the doors, and other areas of the house. They would be there for some time. Liam doubted that they would find anything because he didn't think that anyone had been in the house. The call had been made either to scare Serena or to lure her outside.

There was no sign of forced entry, of course. Serena had left the door wide open. There was no sign of anything. Just Serena's statement about what had occurred.

The tape was pulled from her machine to be analyzed. Perhaps something could still be drawn from it by the experts. Her incoming calls would be traced.

When she had signed the last sheet of paper, Liam told Serena, "Go get your things."

"There can't be anyone here now. The place is crawling with cops," she told him stiffly.

"We're getting out of here tonight," he told her.

"That doesn't make any sense—"

"I don't want an argument. I want to get you out of here."

"Liam—"

"You do what I say, or I walk," he told her.

"What?" she said incredulously. She tried to smooth back a lock of tousled hair, raising her chin.

"I believe that you were hired to follow me."

"You do what I say, or I walk," he repeated.

He could hear her teeth grinding. All right, so he probably hadn't handled the situation really well.

"Walk. You're good at that, aren't you?" she snapped.

They were in the hallway, away from the others. "Don't be a little fool," he told her. "We're talking about your life here. I'm doing my damned best to preserve it."

"Liam—"

"Do you really want to be alone? Or take a chance with some other hired asshole who doesn't know squat?"

She could be regal when she wanted. She drew herself up to a great height. "I'll get some things together," she said smoothly. "Where are we going?"

"You'll know once we're there."

"But I need to go to work tomorrow—"

"You'll go to work."

"I don't understand why you can't tell me."

"I don't want anyone to know. Anyone."

"I'm going to have to call my sister back. I don't want her to think that I'm ignoring her—"

"We'll call your sister. We won't tell her where you are. Get your stuff."

Ten minutes later they were in his car, driving.

"We're going to your place?"

He nodded. "Any objections?"

"No...I guess not."

She remained silent as they drove. He tried to keep his mouth shut. He couldn't.

"Serena, dammit, that was an incredibly stupid thing to do."

"You've told me that."

"There might have been someone out there, waiting."

"There might have been someone in the house."

"Bill checked out the house."

"He might have missed a closet—"

"He wouldn't have."

"All right, fine. Will you quit telling me how stupid I was if I admit it?"

"There could have been someone in the yard. The call could have been a ruse, just to get you outside."

"I know."

"You went tearing out into the darkness—"

"I know, dammit. I was scared!"

He fell silent. Again, he tried to stay that way.

"If you're locked in again somewhere, you have to stay locked in, do you hear me?"

"Yes. I can't possibly miss hearing you!" she retorted angrily. Then she added, "I don't think a bodyguard is hired to scream at the body he's supposed to be guarding."

"Like I said, hired help can quit."

"I don't want you to quit. I do want you to stop behaving like a dictator. I'll try never to be so stupid again in the future, but then, I'm an actress, and I know your opinion of that."

"I don't have a bad opinion of actors and actresses," he said. "Just the way they run their lives at times. As if the real world is never as important as what's written in the press, or shown on tape and celluloid." He cut himself off; he had yelled a lot and had behaved badly. He was angry. Still tense, still wound up.

And still afraid.

They reached his house. His front yard was totally illuminated. No one could hide near the front door, or on the tiled entry porch.

He exited the car, coming around for her. She was already out of the vehicle. "May I take your bag, Miss McCormack?" he asked politely.

"I have it, thank you. We actresses are capable of carrying our own bags. And guess what? I've even made coffee over an open fire. I simply don't like sleeping with bugs and dirt. Okay?"

She preceded him to the house, then realized that he had the key. He opened the door, ushered her in, and keyed his alarm.

She stood in the living room for a moment.

He wondered if she was thinking about the last time she'd been here. He was thinking about that day himself.

He'd left...

He'd been far too involved with her. In love. Hell, he'd found himself stopping at jewelry store windows, staring at the diamonds, wondering if he could afford a stone that would be right for her, wondering if she would even consider marriage, and if they could make it, him a cop, her appearing frequently on magazine covers, in the news, here and there, with this guy, that guy...

Jealous?

Yeah, he supposed.

"Well, where do you want me?" she said at last.

"Take my room. I'll stay out here."

She walked away. He heard the door close.

The night was cool, and he decided to build a fire. Just when he really got the blaze going, Serena reappeared. She had showered; her face was scrubbed clean of makeup, her hair was brushed out, long, glistening, the red highlights enhanced by the glow of the fire.

"May I use your phone? I want to call my sister."

She expected his answer to be yes, and so she started for the phone by the sofa. "Wait," he told her. "Use my cellular."

The tight white line of her mouth informed him of what she thought about his doubts regarding her sister and brother-in-law.

She accepted the phone from him, her fingers brushing his. She was wearing that robe with the deep V again. He wondered if she had anything on beneath it.

She started dialing. "Don't tell anyone where you are. Anyone."

She didn't reply. She finished dialing and listened. He could hear her sister's answering machine picking up.

"Melinda, it's me. I really wasn't there. I—I'm not at home. I'll try to get you again in the morning. I'm going in to work, early."

She hung up and handed the phone back to him. "Thanks," she said, and turned around and started back for the bedroom.

"Hey," he said, calling after her.

"What?" she turned back.

"Can I get you anything? Of course, you know where everything is. If you want anything..."

"Thanks, I don't." She walked on into his room. Again he heard the door shut.

He sank down on the couch and watched the flames, determined to put his thoughts in order.

Eliminate the impossible...

Nothing was impossible with the phone calls. The way technology was these days, her number would have been easy to obtain. Anyone could have Serena's code to her phone. Anyone with the code could erase the messages from anywhere.

He heard the door open again. She appeared before him in the living room. Her eyes were wide, beautiful, truly amazing. Her hair was loose.

That V...

"Are you staying up all night? Don't you ever sleep?"

"I was going to take the couch," Liam told her. "It's a dictator's kind of bed. I didn't think that you were particularly fond of me this evening."

"You are a dictator."

"I'm not really a dictator."

She arched a brow.

"Dammit, Serena, I was scared."

"Don't you understand? I was scared as well."

"And you're scared now? Is that why you're asking me where I'm sleeping? Do you want me in there? Someone to hold while you're afraid?"

"Now you're being a stupid fool *and* a dictator," she told him.

"Oh, yeah?"

She kept staring at him.

"Do I always have to ask you?" she said quietly. "Would you consider...coming in? Never mind. Don't answer."

Sometime in the night, Serena heard a phone ringing. She struggled halfway up.

Liam, at her side, turned. "It's the cell. It's on the nightstand, next to you."

"Here," she murmured.

"Just answer it. Say hello."

She did.

Silence greeted her. Then a soft click.

Serena looked at Liam. "Someone knows where I am," she told Liam.

He took the phone from her, smoothed back her tousled hair. "Yeah, they know you're safe. With me." He pushed a button, showing the Caller I.D. Sharon's number appeared. "It was just a friend," he told Serena softly. He set the phone by his own side of the bed and put an arm around Serena, pulling her close.

"You are safe," he told her.

"With my richly paid bodyguard."

He ran his fingers through her hair, staring into the night. He had his .38 within arm's reach.

"Get some sleep," he told her.

Amesbury, taping people's secret fantasies and dirty little secrets. Things that happened on the set, and Amesbury was never on the set...

There was more than one person involved.

All he had to do was make *one* of them crack.

Chapter 19

*M*orning *came, another day.*

He came in, closing the door, startling the killer. "You idiot!" he said.

"Idiot?" The killer was dumbfounded. "But you said that you needed—"

"Idiot! You don't think when you do things. My God, if this can be traced—"

"I knew what I was doing. It was safe, trust me. You said you needed an opportunity—"

"Bullshit! You're scary, you're dangerous!"

He wanted to kill the killer. His own creation.

His fingers were twitching. He looked around the room, as if he were looking for...something. A weapon?

Then his name was called.

He wagged a finger. "We'll talk later!"

Talk...

The killer was afraid.

Serena's sound sleep was interrupted when Liam bolted straight up beside her. She tensed, instantly alarmed by the suddenness of his movement.

He stared at her. "The alarm on your house didn't go off."

"Pardon?"

"Your alarm didn't go off. Did you turn it on when you came home?"

The way he was staring at her, she was certain that he doubted she had.

"Yes, I turned the alarm on."

"You're certain—"

"You can ask Bill."

He sighed. "Serena, how could Bill know that you turned the alarm on? He had to have been on the outside."

"He told me to lock up and turn the alarm on. The same way that you do. He stepped out, and I did just that."

"Then why didn't it go off?"

"A malfunction?"

"We'll have to call the alarm company," he said. He swore. "I knew I should have had you change that lock when you told me your sister had lost the key."

"She was out in the wild when she lost the key!"

"If there was no malfunction in the alarm, and there was someone in your house, they must have entered with a key."

"Great. I'll change the locks," she said. "Will the police have finished with the house by now?"

"Yes."

She had the feeling that he didn't think the police had found anything and that even having them look for fingerprints and a possible entry had been an exercise in futility.

She was too tired to argue. She managed to squint at her watch. It wasn't yet six. She put her head back down on the pillow.

"What are you doing?"

"Going back to sleep."

"You have an early call, and now I have to see about this alarm business."

"Not this early," she murmured.

"I know how to wake you up."

She smiled into the pillow, thinking he would have something artfully romantic in mind. A second later, the sheets were gone. She felt the sharp clip of his hand against her backside, and turned, half rising in indignation.

"That's it. That's what you get from a macho ex-cop—"

But by the time she had gotten that far, he had crawled back into bed and silenced whatever other insults she had to hurl with his mouth. A moment later he murmured against her lips, "Now that I have your attention..."

It wasn't, however, a morning that offered time for endless ecstasy, whispered conversation, or repeat performances. Within an hour they were both out of the shower, he was on the phone, and she was inhaling her second cup of coffee. He'd called Conar, whom she would have met at the studio anyway, but he wanted Conar in early, with her every step of the way.

"You have things to do again?" she inquired politely.

"I'm meeting a man from your alarm company at your house," he told her. "Take your coffee in the car."

A minute later he was propelling her out the door, and soon they were halfway to the studio.

"Are you just dropping me off?" she asked him.

"No. I'll go in with you."

She decided not to argue.

He parked in Joe's spot, and they entered the studio. He walked with her to the elevator, and up to her dressing room. Conar was already in the hallway, leaning against the wall by her door, waiting. She arched a brow at him.

"You know," she told them both, "this is rather cruel to Conar. He doesn't have to be here until the Egyptian scene."

"Not true," Conar argued politely. "You have a scene with Kelly, ready to tape, set to go as previously written and rehearsed. You have a scene with Vera, who is going to tell you to quit sleeping with your sisters' lovers. Of course, good ol' mom doesn't know that you're sleeping with me, the horrendous, evil, and scheming David DeVille. If she did, she'd tell dad, and you'd both be horse-whipped—or thrown out of the old vineyard. We have a quick discussion about meeting later so that you can tell me off. Then you have a fight with Jay Braden, who is still married to your sister but has impregnated one of the illegal alien vineyard workers. Then, you have a discussion with the wine buyer from the very pricey new Euro-American restaurant. Then, my dear vixen, you have the scene with me, the fight with me, we roll around in the vineyard—they've brought in mud and vines just so we can do that convincingly, then I follow you to your workshop, you throw out more threats—and I lock you in the sarcophagus. Between scenes I pay a visit to your father so that he can be nasty and I can gloat about the fact that I'm sleeping with two of his daughters. Not at once, of course. We're not getting that kinky."

"It's a full day," Liam said dryly.

"Yes, all this sex," Conar said. "It's a bitch, you know, but someone has to do it."

"See you both later," Liam said. "I won't be gone any longer than I have to be."

"We should be okay. Olsen was in earlier, and Hutchens intends to stay for the taping today."

"Did Olsen say anything about tracing the phone calls, or if they were able to pull any fingerprints?"

"They got tons of fingerprints—probably yours, mine, Jennifer's, and so on. The last call to Serena's house came from her sister; those

314

made immediately before that came from a cellular phone belonging to a Harvey Moss, traveling salesman from Idaho, who reported the phone missing around midnight. He'd last used it to call his wife and child around six. You don't look surprised."

"I'm not. I was expecting something like that."

"Yeah. Everything around here seems to be like that."

Liam shrugged. "Stick close to her."

"Like glue. I won't leave her alone for a second."

"Conar," Serena said, "I'll need to change, you'll need to change——"

Conar grinned, waving a hand in the air. "Do you believe that? I've slept with this woman a dozen times onstage. I think we'll manage."

"Conar, that didn't sound quite right," she told him.

Liam lifted a finger beneath her nose. "Don't go off without him," he said.

"Yessir, just like American Express, I will not leave anywhere without him!"

Liam and Conar exchanged a last look, then Liam turned to leave.

"There is safety in numbers," Conar told Serena.

"He trusts you," she told him. "He doesn't seem to trust many people."

"He was a cop."

"Was a cop? He thinks he still is. Born and bred, so it seems. You know how pit bulls and Rottweilers are bred to attack?"

"Whoa," Conar said. "Are you telling me that you two argue now? Still? And it looked as if you were getting along."

"Oh, we *can* get along."

"Ah," he murmured knowingly.

"What is that 'ah' for?" she demanded.

"Nothing."

"Conar, dammit!"

"All right—I was thinking that you get along when you stay in bed."

"Conar Markham!"

"You insisted on knowing my thoughts."

"Remind me not to insist on it again."

She opened the door to her dressing room. Conar followed her, picking up a magazine, sitting on the couch. Jinx came in and went through Serena's wardrobe.

"Serena, I heard about those phone calls last night. Are you sure you're all right? Ready to do this today?" Jinx asked her. "I can go to Joe...well, *I* can't go to Joe, I'd stutter and be afraid, but someone could go to Joe—"

"I'm not giving up on the soap, Jinx. And I'm fine."

Conar looked up from his magazine. "You know Joe, Jinx. Acts like a tough guy, but he's a teddy bear. If Serena was afraid, she'd just go tell him, and that would be that."

Jinx nodded happily. "I'm glad. I love my job. I'd hate to see us give in and fall apart."

"We're not going to," Serena assured her.

When Jinx left, Thorne arrived with makeup. Conar offered her coffee from a large thermos he had brought from home. She thanked him for it, and sipped it as Thorne went to work.

"Hey, give me your pages. I'll prompt you while you run them."

Thorne touched up her eyes. Conar gave her lines; she answered them.

The day had begun, and for once it seemed normal.

The fellow from First and Foremost Alarm was tall and lanky, a man of fifty or so who had been working with alarms for nearly thirty years and who had been with First and Foremost for twenty of those. He hailed from Texas, he told Liam, but he loved California. Lots of rich folks, and lots of folks who really valued their privacy.

"I've changed the locks on the front and rear doors. If you want, you can come around with me, and I'll show you how her whole system works," Judd Baker told him. They walked around the house and checked windows, doors, wires, the keypad, the connection to the home base, and the phone wires.

"She's got her new locks, so you can rest assured. There wasn't a thing wrong, so who knows? Maybe someone did get lucky with a key," Judd told him. "Do you think she might have forgotten to key in the numbers on the pad? Or maybe she keyed them in wrong. That would fail to set up the system, and if she was distracted...well, she might not have noticed that the little light there didn't go on."

"You're sure that the system was in no way tampered with?" Liam pressed him.

"Well, as sure as I can be. There's nothing wrong with it today. No shorts anywhere. Phone system is working. Like I said, most probably she thought she keyed in the numbers but didn't, or she hit a digit wrong. If strange things are going on around here, then she needs to be extra careful with details like that. You'll tell her, won't you?"

"Yeah, I'll tell her," Liam assured him.

"It's a good system."

"I believe it's a good system," Liam said.

"The whole thing is numbers. Numbers are codes, and if a code isn't set properly, and if you don't make sure the little light is on..."

"I've got it. Thanks."

"The police didn't find anything?"

"Nope."

"Must have been prank calls, someone giving her a bad time. That's the trouble out here, you know. You have those who get ahead and those who get real angry at those who got ahead when they didn't. Someone jealous. But she's all right, isn't she?" Judd asked anxiously.

"Fine. In fact, I was just about ready to leave to make certain about that."

Judd nodded. "I'll let you get going, then."

"Thanks. Thanks for all your help."

Liam shook Judd's hand and turned toward the car. Glancing skyward, he saw that the sun was already high in the western sky. He drove quickly, anxious to reach the soundstage.

The day had gone really well.

The scenes had been rehearsed and then taped. Costume changes had gone smoothly.

Because Kelly was doing a scene with Jay, Jim got it into his head that they could also do the scene in which Verona came upon her sister and mother, insisting that they do something to hurry the divorce—even though Natalie (Jennifer's character) had gone to the islands to recover from the trauma of her affair with Dale Donovan (Andy's character) while her marriage to Randy Rock (Jay) was in the process of falling apart. The maid, Serafina, had come to her to tell her that she had been seduced one night when Randy Rock was on the property, trying to see his wife and angry because the family wouldn't let him near her.

Vera, who liked to study her lines, had only two of them in the scene, so she agreed to go with a quick rehearsal.

Amazingly, that, too, went well. Then Andy appeared and, exhilarated with the way the filming was going, he decided to do a scene with Serena that had been scheduled for the next day on her Egyptian set. He came to her, telling her that she was an idiot, she had loved him always, she needed to get away from Valentine Valley and come back to him. There was a killer on the loose. She took dangerous chances, working in her cottage alone at night, far from the main house. She told him she would never marry him again, or consider being with him again—he'd had an affair with her sister during their marriage. She threw him off the set, and he vowed that he'd come back and find a way to force her to listen to him.

She did the seduction-in-the-mud-and-grapevines scene with Conar; they were both laughing so hard that it had to be taped twice. Jim shook his head in dismay and disgust. His pros should have done better work.

Serena ignored Jim. It was all going too well.

Even the scene with the extra hired in to act as the sommelier went like clockwork. The extra's name was Julian Page. Jim spoke highly of him once he'd left the set, saying that he'd be happy to work with the guy again.

Bill Hutchens soon arrived with a uniformed officer. He spoke with Serena and Conar about their findings on what had happened at her house, but unfortunately, he told her, he had nothing else new to report.

"I really don't think anyone was out there last night, Serena," he told her unhappily. "I think the caller is causing trouble, a lot of work, and costing the taxpayers a lot of money."

"I think I'm glad."

"You still have to be careful."

"Of course."

"Liam back yet?"

"No."

"Well, he may be a while. There was a bad accident on the freeway."

"It's all right. Things are going great. You're here, Conar's here...and lots of others. Jennifer sent in coffee and sandwiches—and water bottles from their house. I'm on a roll. Things are going great."

"Fine. Get back to work."

Then it was time for the Egyptian sarcophagus scene.

Jim blocked the stage directions with Serena and Conar, showing him how the standing sarcophagus worked. He grew exasperated a few times, calling in someone from props when he couldn't get the lid to swing open properly.

"This is an old magician's trick," he said. "It works perfectly when Jeff is around. I wish your brother-in-law hadn't quit, Serena."

"I wish he hadn't either. I'm not sure what he said to Joe and Andy—he was under contract."

"I guess he wasn't too happy here. And I guess the thing with Jane upset him pretty badly. She was fighting with him before any of this started—"

"*Jeff* was fighting with Jane Dunne? I thought he hardly knew her."

"You didn't have to know her real well to fight with her," Jim said. "Hey, Conar, come closer. Here. The spring is here. I found it. This thing is great. When you open it, you see the huge spikes. When you close it, it looks like the spikes will pierce you. But there's a thin steel slide that goes across them, pushing

321

them back. Originally, it was a great Vegas showpiece. You know, the gorgeous assistant stepped in, the magician showed the spikes, they closed the lid...and the gorgeous assistant stepped out still gorgeous. Anyway, here's the catch. You got it, Conar?"

Conar looked over the sarcophagus and the lid, checking for the catch. "I got it. Where's the door thing that closes over?"

"It's automatic. When the hinges move in, they hit that button, and the button triggers the inner lid.

"We'll run the scene once. You don't have to shut Serena in for that—we'll just go with the lines until you get furious and start to throw her in. All right? Let's run the rehearsal."

The rehearsal went beautifully. She and Conar ranted and raved. It was convincing, and Jim applauded.

"One take, Serena, one take, and we're done, ahead of schedule."

"One take, *Serena*?" she protested, laughing.

"Excuse me. We don't want to be politically incorrect here," Jim said with a sigh. "One take, *Conar* and Serena. Okay?"

"Gotcha," Conar said.

She went to work in her "cottage," her private little domain with all her Egyptian treasures. Conar burst in, furious. They yelled at each other. She reminded him that he hadn't had these problems with her in the vineyard. He told her she was always a problem, and that he loved her sister, Marla Valentine, and that she had to stay out of their lives. She told him

322

he didn't love Marla, couldn't love Marla, if he could pursue her the way he did. Furious, he told her that she couldn't keep her hands off a man—any man, so it appeared. She told him that he was a low-down wine-robbing bastard with a failing vineyard, that he was desperate for help from the Valentines, and that he wasn't going to use her sister to get it; she was going straight to her father. He said no, she wasn't. She started to scream for help. He clamped a hand over her mouth and dragged her to the sarcophagus, telling her that he'd have her and her treasure moved to a real vineyard, and they'd talk there.

She tried to scream as she saw the spikes that David DeVille didn't seem to notice. She broke free, shrieking, fighting, as he pressed her into the stage piece.

Then the lid began to close.

It seemed as if it would all work just the way that Jim had said it would. She could see the inner shield beginning to slide over the spikes.

Then it jammed.

And the lid, on an automatic hinge, kept closing.

At first Conar didn't realize that she was screaming for real.

Then he saw.

He swore, diving for the sarcophagus, grabbing the lid.

The spikes kept coming, no matter how hard Conar strained to stop it. "Find something, anything, find a way to stop this!" he shouted.

Someone swore. The cops started to move. Andy cried out.

She never saw Liam. Not until he reached her, thrusting his own length into the upright coffin with the swinging door, pressing her back and using his own bulk to force the hinge to break. Emilio came up with a fire axe and started hacking at the piece.

Then, between Liam's bulk and the blows of the axe, the wood shattered, and the whole piece broke in two. The front of the sarcophagus fell forward.

The rear crashed to the floor behind Serena and Liam. He was standing in front of her, almost on top of her, sweat beaded on his brow.

She inhaled with a gasp.

"Jesus!" he breathed. She thought it was spoken as a prayer.

She hadn't started shaking yet. It had all happened so fast.

"God bless it! We're never buying anything from a magician again!" Jim swore.

Andy sank down to the edge of the set, shaking. "God!" he said.

"Are you all right?" Liam asked Serena, his black eyes searching her face.

She nodded. "Where's Jeff when you need him?" she tried to joke.

His eyes narrowed. "Jeff fixed this set piece?"

"Jeff wasn't here today," she said.

He took her hand, turning to lead her off the set.

"My Lord!" Jim exclaimed then, looking over the cameraman's shoulder. "This tape is terrific. You can't see Liam's face. He and Conar are both wearing dark jackets...they could be one and the same."

Liam walked past the camera and suddenly sent a fist smashing out. The camera went over.

"Hey!" Jim protested. "Look at this—"

"Fuck this," Liam said, leading Serena away.

"Liam, wait," Serena pleaded. "This really was an accident."

"Oh, yeah, sure. Don't you think that there are too many accidents on this set?"

"But they need that tape—"

"Tape is hardy. It will survive what I did."

"Liam—"

"What? What? You want me to go apologize to your director? You were nearly killed!"

"No, I don't want you to apologize. I—I wanted to thank you. You saved my life."

He exhaled. He looked back across the studio. Serena did the same. Bill Hutchens and his uniformed man were up on the Egyptian set, looking over the destroyed sarcophagus. Conar was with them, angry. Even Jim had realized that this was one incident too many. Jay Braden was there, too, swearing that something had to be done. Someone else was going to die.

Liam looked at Serena. "You know what? This has gone too far. We're going to leave now. Really leave. Take a vacation. Let this settle down. Do you understand?"

She nodded. "All right. I think they got enough tape."

"All right? Really?"

She nodded.

"Get your stuff. We're going. I'll call Hutchens and explain, and we'll call Andy or Joe too. You're gone for a week. A solid week, no matter what they want. Give them a little time to find out something, you understand? You're like a damned sitting duck here!"

She stared at him, biting her lip. She refrained from telling him that they were actually ahead on taping. The day had gone so well—until the sarcophagus scene.

"Let's get your things. We're leaving."

"All right."

It wasn't quite so simple. Hutchens came over just then to talk to Serena, as did Jim, and Conar joined them, and others came rushing over to make sure that Serena was all right.

Then they all wound up in Serena's dressing room. Joe Penny and Andy came in, grave, worried, and eager to smooth things over.

Once again Liam insisted they were leaving. Right then.

"I'm taking her out of here," he said firmly.

"You're taking her out of here?" Andy said, annoyed. "You know, Liam, on this one you're just the hired help."

"Shut up, Andy," Joe warned.

Andy cleared his throat. "Sorry. It's just that...hell, you're right. Joe said she needed to get away for a while."

Serena put a hand on his arm. "If they can

use this tape, I won't have to worry about scheduling until... I'll be able to take a week with no problem, right?"

"It'll give you some clear time right up until the seventh. That's when we're filming the show for the fourteenth. That's really tight; but we're doing it that way on purpose."

"Use the damned tape, then," Liam said. "But I'm taking her out of here, *now.*"

Liam started to walk out.

He had her hand; Serena pulled free from him, giving Kelly a kiss on the cheek, touching Jay's hand, and telling Conar thank you as well. She didn't take Liam's hand again. She was grateful, but she refused to look like a child being dragged out of school by an irate parent.

When they reached the car, he stared at her. "You've got a problem with this? Or with me?"

"Yes—and no," she told him curtly, sliding into the front seat of the car.

He joined her, slamming the door.

"Yes—and no?" he repeated, looking her way as he gunned the motor.

"No, I have no problem with leaving. And I'm grateful to you—of course. But you didn't have to be so rude."

"Excuse me? You were almost killed again, but I should worry about being rude?"

"Yes."

He let the motor die and leaned his head against the steering wheel.

"The show means everything to a lot of people."

"The show is going to cost you your life."

She sighed deeply. "Liam, they're all as baffled as we are."

"Not all of them. One of those people I shouldn't be rude to is a killer."

She kept silent, staring ahead.

"Isn't anything ever more important than the show?" he queried.

"Yes."

He didn't say any more. He gunned the car, and they roared out of the garage.

"Where are we going?" she demanded.

"Hawaii."

"Hawaii?" she said, stunned. Then she argued, "You can't go to Hawaii just like that. We need tickets, arrangements—"

"I have a friend who's a pilot."

"But...just like that? It's so far—"

"Yeah. I'm hoping that by putting a large piece of the Pacific Ocean between you and *Valentine Valley* I can buy a few days of peace."

"I have to call my sister before we go—" she began thoughtfully.

"No."

"I have to—"

"No. I'll call Olsen or Rigger when we get there, and Conar. No one else is to know."

She wanted to argue. She was leaving, as advised. But her sister should know where she was going, and someone on the show should know.

Maybe not. She had to admit...

She was scared, and no matter how Liam behaved, she needed him.

"Fine," she told him coolly.

He looked her way. "Okay, fine. Go ahead, be all pissed off at me. We can go to war again—but away from here. From your family, your friends, and your whole soap society. Your life and your pretense. I wonder sometimes if you know the difference."

Chapter 20

They did go to Hawaii—just like that. Serena watched skeptically as Martin Tyler conducted a maintenance check of his small plane in preparation for leaving. Liam had gone to make some last-minute purchases, and Martin talked freely. He had met Liam years ago, when they'd both been starting out in the LAPD. Martin had gone on to work for one of the major airlines for a number of years before starting his own charter service. He had remained friends with Liam, he said, because he owed Liam.

"Don't tell me. He saved your life?" Serena asked.

Martin, a tall, slim man with soulful eyes and thinning hair, told her, "Did me one better than that. My daughter got mixed up with the wrong crowd, and one real bad guy. He tried to take her down to Mexico. God knows where it would have gone from there. Liam got her back for me. Shook up, scared as the devil, and I never really knew what all else. It didn't matter; he got her back alive." He brought a finger to his lips. Liam was coming back with a plastic bag of purchases. They were heading for Hawaii with nothing but the clothes they were wearing, his quick purchases, and the meager contents of her purse.

"Everything all right?"

"We're ready to roll. The flight plan is filed, she's gassed and ready to go." He patted his plane fondly.

The journey was loud, and long. Liam sat up front with Martin. At first Serena thought she wasn't going to have to worry about the situation at *Valentine Valley* anymore—she was sure she was going to die when Martin's small plane went down in the Pacific. But then the droning of the plane's engines began to create a lulling effect, and she dozed, and then slept well, and when she woke up, Liam was shaking her because they were on the ground.

They were staying right on the island of Hawaii itself. Since she had feared they would be sleeping on a stretch of black sand beach somewhere, she was pleasantly surprised when the taxi Liam hailed drove up to a resort she knew. In fact, she had stayed there two years earlier when they had done some location shooting for the show. She decided not to mention that to Liam.

She wasn't surprised when they checked in as Mr. and Mrs. Lawrence Rydell of San Francisco. Or that Liam had identification to go with the name.

When they at long last reached their room—an elegant suite right on the ocean with doors that opened to the beach—she was still exhausted, despite the sleep she'd had on the plane. She fell onto the bed. She wanted a shower. She wanted room service. It was late, but earlier than it would have been in L.A. There must surely still be room service.

She fell asleep, fully clothed, that thought on her mind.

When she awoke, she was surprised to discover that she was alone. She stretched, remembering where she was and why. She was cramped and rumpled, and she wanted a shower. And coffee.

The second arrived just as she was beginning to think that her longing for the hot brew had made her imagine the scent of it. Liam came through the doors to the beach, carrying a cup.

"You've risen."

"Kind of. Is that for me?"

He handed her the coffee. She noted that he had bought swim trunks and that he had been in the water.

"You left me alone long enough to get wet?" she inquired.

"I could see the bungalow all the while," he assured her.

She just bet that he could. "Nice place," she told him.

"I'm glad you approve."

"I thought we'd be tenting."

"It might have been a better idea."

"Do you really think that whoever is doing all this can stretch out an arm to Hawaii and find us—when we came on a private plane and have registered under an alias?"

"No, it's unlikely. But not impossible."

"Liam, you know, the sarcophagus might have been…faulty equipment."

"Yes, it might have been." He obviously didn't believe that for a second.

She sighed and set the cup down. "I need a shower," she told him, heading for the bathroom. She paused. "Did you buy me a toothbrush yesterday?"

"It's in there."

"Soap, shampoo?"

"All in there."

"Thanks. You're efficient as well as courageous," she murmured, closing the bathroom door behind her. Then she popped her head back out. "I know you didn't purchase a full wardrobe for me and bring it to the plane in that plastic bag."

"I bought you a bathing suit and something that goes over it," he said. "There's a little island shop in the center of the hotel. We can get whatever else we need there."

"Ah, and you're going to let me use my credit card—a piece of plastic in my own name—to make purchases?"

"No. I have cash."

"A rich and famous actress like me allowing a poor ex-cop, now a struggling P.I., to buy my clothing? I don't think so," she told him.

"I'm not struggling," he replied.

"Still—"

"I'll put the receipts with my expense bill when I turn it over to the producers."

"Great," she said, and closed the door.

A few minutes later she was standing under the hot water spray, feeling the steam work into her body. She closed her eyes, wondering if he would follow her into the shower.

He didn't.

She emerged in twenty minutes, wrapped in two towels. He was reading the paper. He didn't look up. He knew she was out, of course.

"You should be well rested and ready to hit the beach now."

"Hit the beach?"

"Why not? We're in Hawaii."

"You mean...we're not going to stay locked in here together for the days of my break?"

"God, no. One of us would kill the other by then."

"Great. Where's your little bag with all my earthly possessions for the duration?"

He pointed across the room. "Take your time. I'll be just outside."

She changed from the towel to the bathing suit and wraparound. She wondered how he had managed to make such a great purchase in a matter of minutes at an airport. The suit was a blue-green sea pattern, the perfect size, nicely cut. The wraparound was beautiful, an enhancement of the sea colors.

She dug her sunglasses out of her purse. Barefoot—the only shoes she had were the pumps she'd been wearing—she walked out the beach-side doors. He was waiting.

"There are chairs down by the water," he told her.

"Lovely. Let's go and watch the surf."

They didn't just watch the surf. When he felt they had sat long enough, he suggested a swim. When she refused, he picked her up and started walking toward the water. When she shrieked and an older woman gave him a warning glare, he smiled at the woman charmingly. "Forgive us, we're honeymooners."

The woman beamed.

Then he threw Serena into the water. She rose, sputtering, ready to hit him. He backed away. She spun into the water again.

"You do swim?" he inquired skeptically.

"Yes, I can swim!" she told him, ready to strike out again.

This time he caught her arms, pinned them, and swung her around so that she was tightly bound to him, her back against his chest, her arms crossed over her own.

"Wait, wait!" he said, voice level, the warmth of his breath touching her nape and her earlobe.

"Wait, what?"

"I'm proposing a truce."

"Oh, a truce?"

"Yes, for the duration of our stay."

"You're in a better mood today, so I'm supposed to forget the way you yell at me, the client you're supposed to be protecting? I'm supposed to say, Oh, wonderful! Here we are in Hawaii. Let's just forget everything else, and play all day?"

"Yes, that's more or less it."

"You're crazy," she informed him.

"Probably."

"I don't know. You may feel free to buy me something islandy and fruity to drink, and then I'll tell you."

"Think we ought to have something to eat first?" he asked.

"Why bother? We're in Hawaii."

"Hey, it's up to you. I'll race you to shore. If you beat me, I'll keep the drinks off the bill I'm giving to the producers."

"You do that. How about giving me a head start?"

"Sure. Go ahead."

He beat her, but not by much. Her ability surprised him, she knew, and she was glad. Okay, so she didn't dig holes for a living, but she wasn't totally inept.

The drinks he ordered were definitely islandy and fruity. He had been right, though. She should have eaten first. He fixed that by ordering little cakes of lightly fried mahimahi—delicious. They wound up talking about the food, about the sand, the beach, the sky, and the incredible beauty of Hawaii.

"I'd love to see the volcano," she told him.

"I don't know. I mean, can you imagine? I bring you here to keep you safe—and there's an unexpected expulsion of lava. Soap actress charred to Pompeiian beauty, immortalized forever."

"I would assume they know what they're doing."

"You assume too much."

"Do I? Don't we all!" She smiled suddenly. "Did you really threaten Kyle Amesbury on my behalf?"

He shrugged. His eyes covered by shades, he looked away. "The man is total scum."

"Well, thanks, anyway. I hope he doesn't file charges."

They stayed on the beach, talking and swimming and, at the end, trekked the few feet back to their door, weary but at ease. Liam headed straight for the shower.

As he did so, she noticed his cellular phone on the table. She walked over to it, listening for the spray of the water. She picked up the phone and quickly dialed Melinda's number, praying her sister was home.

Melinda wasn't even screening her calls. She picked up right away.

"Melinda? It's me, Serena."

"Serena! Where are you?"

"You can't tell anyone—"

"Of course not!"

"I'm in Hawaii."

"Hawaii!" Her sister screamed the word so loudly, she was afraid Liam might hear it in the shower.

"Melinda, I'm not supposed to be calling anyone. I just had to talk to you. Melinda, you're my sister. I love you. So much. I'm so sorry—"

"Serena, I've been horrible. I love you. It's

336

just been so awful, and so scary, and the kids have been calling, all upset, and I don't even know what to tell them, how to explain..."

"Oh, Melinda!" Was that the water being shut off? "I can't talk any longer."

"It's okay. When are you coming back?"

"By the seventh."

"We'll talk then. Really talk. Call me the minute you're back, promise?"

"Promise."

"Love you, Sis."

"You too. 'Bye!"

She hit the End button, and then the Clear, making sure that his phone was really off. She set it back on the table, picked up the newspaper, and walked over to one of the wicker chairs with it. When he emerged, a towel wrapped around his middle, she pretended to be engrossed in the crossword puzzle.

"You're out," she said pleasantly, rising. She walked past him and entered the shower.

When she finished washing the salt water from her hair and sudsing the sea from her body, she wrapped herself in towels again and came out of the bathroom. He remained in one of the terry robes provided in the hotel closet.

She'd apparently been in the shower a while. He'd ordered dinner to the room.

Coconut shrimp, rice, baby ribs, all kinds of vegetables, and everything arranged artfully around a center coconut. He had a glass of white wine already. Seeing her, he poured another glass.

"We forgot to go shopping. I thought that

given our current attire we should probably eat in."

"Are you trying to impress me, to prove that you are capable of ordering room service?"

"Maybe I'm just trying to avoid putting you in clothing."

"Big talk," she murmured, sliding past him to accept the glass of wine and head for the table.

He caught her by the elbow. "Don't throw out challenges unless you're ready to accept the consequences."

"Did I throw out a challenge?"

"How hungry are you?"

"Ravenous."

"I'll take that to mean that you're ravenous for me," he said softly.

Maybe she was. Towels and robes gave far too easily. She could feel the island breeze on her flesh.

There was no hurry...

And nowhere to be.

Yet still Serena felt such a sense of urgency that it wasn't until they lay together, after, slowly breathing, that she noted the deep red marks on his back. She ran her fingers over them. "What...my God!" she whispered. "The sarcophagus!"

He stretched, trying to see over his shoulder, gave up.

"That must have hurt," she said softly.

"Yeah, it hurt like hell."

"You really risked your life for me."

"Just doin' my job, ma'am."

"You're not a cop anymore. You're self-employed."

"Well, being my own boss, you know, I have standards to live up to."

"Are you ever serious?"

"It's dangerous to be too serious with you. And when I am serious about very important issues, you have an excuse for everything."

"A real excuse," she said.

"Ever heard the word 'compromise'?"

"I'm familiar with it, yes. Are you?"

To her surprise, he smiled, and drew a line down her face, following the shape of her bones.

"Maybe I don't give a lot," he admitted, to her surprise.

"Maybe you don't give any," she told him, then rolled against him. "Thank you. That was above and beyond, taking spikes in the back for me."

"I have a tougher back."

"All flesh bleeds, and all bones break."

"The shrimp is getting very cold," he said uncomfortably.

"Liam."

"Hm."

"I'm sorry for being such a pain."

"Serena..." He shook his head, rolling over to stare down at her, about to say more, then not doing it. "I have other scars on my back too. Don't worry about it."

"Just another job," she murmured.

"May I say that this particular moment is one of the nicest I've ever had while working?" he queried.

"You may."

He smiled. "The shrimp is already cold. I guess it won't make any difference if it gets a little colder."

"Not in the least."

Naturally, by the time they got around to eating it, the coconut shrimp was very cold indeed. It didn't matter. It was delicious. They finished the wine and the pineapple pieces back in bed. Curled up, they found *Casablanca* on an oldies station, and they both commented and critiqued all the way through, then agreed that it was truly a classic, whatever the stories behind the filming.

When she awoke the next morning, Serena didn't think that she had slept so well in years. This was everything a vacation was supposed to be.

She realized that he was watching her when she opened her eyes. He was propped on an elbow, studying her, and making no pretense that he was doing anything other than that.

"Coffee?"

"You made coffee already?"

"I aim to please, being the hired help and all."

"You totally exceed your duties."

"I don't mind at all. I told you, I take my work very seriously."

"Do you sleep with all your clients?"

"Only when they look like you."

"How kind of you. It's wonderful to be included among the elite."

"I'd put you nowhere else."

"Thank God. Would you mind getting that coffee?"

He rose. He looked like an islander, bronzed—and then white. He poured her coffee from the machine provided on the wet bar near the dining area table. When he returned, she had slid up to a sitting position, pulled the covers to her chest, and was ready to take the cup.

"The hired help...reduced to room service," he told her.

"Cheer up. I'll make you coffee tomorrow," she told him. Then she asked, "Do you really hate room service?"

"No."

"Well, good."

"Do you really hate camping?" he asked her.

"Yes," she admitted. "But..."

"What?"

"Nothing. I mean... I'll try almost anything. You know. Wild, wicked woman that I am."

"You—or Verona Valentine?"

"I think you were the one who decided we were one and the same."

"Never."

"Well, anyway, Verona surely loves camping. She's into desert sands and all that. Rolling in the grapevines."

"Speaking of rolling in the grapevines—you've had scenes with Jay Braden shirtless, right?"

"Sure."

"Does he have a hairy back?"

"What?"

"Does he have a hairy back?"

She shook her head, her brow furrowed. "Not at all. He used to wax it—better hunk image, you know. I think he had laser hair removal last year. The guys were all talking about it. Why?"

He shrugged. "I'd just like to know who was in that tape with Jane Dunne."

Serena sighed. "If it was Jay, what does it prove?"

"I'm not certain. I still think Amesbury is somehow involved." He hesitated. "He made a phone call after I talked to him, the night you were scared out of your house."

"This has really consumed all your time—and your life."

"We need answers fast."

She hesitated, sipping her coffee. Then she said quietly, "Don't jump down my throat for this, but...I'm sorry. I really am sorry if I got in the way of a relationship that was going to be the right one for you."

"It wasn't."

"But she is beautiful, and young. And she does like digging."

"Camping," he corrected.

"Well...they are connected," she murmured. "I'm sorry."

He sighed deeply. "Don't be. It wasn't working out."

"You seem to have that problem a lot."

He cast her a dark, warning glare.

"Well, it's true. Somewhere along the line, if you want a relationship to work, you're going to have to quit expecting the other person to do everything your way all the time."

"Really? Is that it?"

"It's just an observation."

"From a relationship expert?" he queried.

She made a face. "I'm just trying—"

"I told you—it wasn't working."

"I was just saying—"

"*You* married Andy Larkin."

She sighed, needing another sip of coffee before she could answer that one.

"The soap was just beginning, and he was a producer, and an actor, and he can be very handsome, and very charming, and I was probably far more naive than I should have been at the time. In truth, I have no excuse. It was a terrible mistake. I couldn't take it. And I don't think Andy has ever forgiven me for the divorce, though we are friends, and we do manage to work together."

"How mad is he?" Liam asked.

"Mad enough to kill me? Never. He did love me—in his way. That didn't exactly include monogamy or the other things one expects in a marriage, but he did, in his way, love me."

He touched her cheek, drawing her face toward his. He kissed her lips. "Sorry, I didn't really want to get going on that right now."

"Oh?"

"Hired help, ma'am. Trying to do my duty."

"You can't possibly be receiving enough compensation for such prowess," she told him.

"Hell, I like to go the distance."

She started to laugh, giving up the coffee cup as he grabbed it. "It really is a shame that things 'just didn't work out' with us. You can be tremendously entertaining."

"Ah, well, that's what we're all about, isn't it? Entertainment," he said dryly.

"Hey, wait—" she started to protest.

But when he didn't intend to listen anymore, he didn't intend to listen. His touch was aggressive...

Angry, she thought.

But passionate, fierce, and seductive.

Later, she couldn't remember what she had intended to say.

That day, after shopping for a few items of clothing, they went fishing, taking out a private charter. She wasn't so sure about baiting her own hook. The shrimp they were using were spiny, wiggly, and had things sticking out of their heads. She told Liam she felt sorry for them. She wondered if she'd ever be able to eat shrimp again.

By the end of the day, however, she had decided not to feel sorry for the shrimp anymore. She learned how to throw her line. She caught the biggest fish. She forgot all about *Valentine Valley*. She didn't think about it again until later that night when she heard Liam on his cellular phone. She paused by the bathroom door, listening. He was talking to George Olsen, she realized.

She remained where she was as he told Olsen good-bye. She was about to step out when she realized he was dialing another number. Apparently no one answered. He didn't leave a message.

Later that night, she hit the button on his phone that brought up the last ten numbers dialed.

The number would have meant nothing to her, but there was an I.D. on it. The words next to his last call were "Sharon, Home."

Chapter 21

That afternoon Doug Henson called Joe and asked how he could reach Serena. Joe told him that he didn't know. Doug was certain he was lying and that he had Liam's cell phone number.

"She's on vacation. Leave her alone," Joe told Doug.

Doug was excited; he thought he had a great plot twist planned for her. "Sure. I'll leave her alone."

He hung up and called Jinx. "I need to reach Serena."

"Sorry. Liam dragged her out of here without a word after the incident with the sarcophagus."

"Yeah, but I thought for sure she would have contacted you."

"Doug, she's trying to get away from us."

"So she really hasn't called you?"

"Nope."

"Liar."

"Honest, Doug. I don't know where she is."

"You know that in a thousand years I'd never hurt Serena."

Jinx sighed. "Let me see if I can find out."

Jinx hung up and pondered the question. She called Melinda. Jeff answered the phone.

"I was just trying to reach Serena. Do you know where she is?"

"No," he said crossly, then she heard a pause on the end of the line. "Why?"

"Doug needs to reach her."

"I don't think we're supposed to know where she is."

"She must have called Melinda. Doug is one of her best friends."

She could hear Jeff pausing. "Yeah, well, thank God I wasn't on the set the other day. I'd be guilty of attempted murder—no, I wouldn't have been. I'd have made sure that box was working right before she ever got in it. Wait a minute. Maybe I do know where she is. Melinda was scribbling something on a paper here...yeah. Well, hell, nice vacation she's getting. She's in Hawaii, I think. Probably at that place where they filmed on location one time."

"Thanks, Jeff."

"Sure."

Jinx wrote down "Hawaii," then checked the Rolodex for the name and number of the hotel where the cast and crew had gone to tape their location scenes those few years back.

She called Doug. He scribbled down the number.

Doug tried the hotel, but neither Serena's name nor Liam's was listed.

He hung up in frustration. He left his office soon after, leaving the paper by his phone.

Kyle Amesbury's next big party was a complete success.

Naturally, he had all the right people from *Valentine Valley*—which had become the hottest thing going. People loved trouble. Since Jane Dunne's death, the soap had enjoyed higher ratings than ever before. People who had never watched a soap opera were tuning in. Now there would be no way Haines/Clark would ever pull their advertising.

Kyle had a huge screening room, where he ran episodes of the show and some outtakes during the party. His guests loved the outtakes. And thanks to the *Valentine Valley* guests, he had more beautiful people. Tonight he even had super-hot new director Eddie Wok. Because Eddie was there, he had a troop of beautiful blond hopefuls.

Sipping champagne and listening to the buzz going on around him, Kyle thought that it was good to be king.

Doug Henson seemed unhappy to be there, but he had come. Allona Sainge was with him. She didn't appear thrilled either, but she was there to support Doug. And the pretty little redhead, the youngest Valentine sister, Kelly Trent, was there as well. Joe and Andy, as usual, were attracting starlets. Serena McCormack was missing, though, and that was a pity, because she didn't attend many parties, so when she did, they became newsworthy.

By midnight, the initial tension that everyone felt at a party—who's here, how do I look, who is watching me, where should I be—had ebbed away. Jay Braden had jumped into the pool; then he'd thrown Kelly Trent in, and Vera Houseman, *Valentine Valley* matriarch, had promised to beat him black-and-blue in the toolshed if he even considered doing the same to her.

That was life, Kyle thought, except that he liked his own life now. He had come to Hollywood with high hopes. Although he'd done what his parents wanted and gone to Clark for an M.B.A., he'd always wanted to try the movies. He'd been told his looks made him perfect leading-man material, and he had gone to audition after audition.

Unlike other aspiring actors, he hadn't needed to get a job as a waiter or bartender. His degree had gotten him into advertising. Then he found out that advertising was powerful. He took things step by step. And while taking those steps, he learned that the stars attracted fans and money, but the producers and directors were the ones with the power and the real money.

He was learning to wield his power. And he was making big money. Pretty soon he was going to be a big-name producer.

He'd already formed his own company. And he told people about it—on the Q.T., of course. It was tremendously amusing. He had people here all the time now, performing for him.

It was amazing what people would do if they thought it would get them a part in a movie. Sick, surely, some of the executives at his company would think. But he really didn't care anymore. He was just about ready to quit anyway.

Doors throughout the house were already closed. What some of his high-flying guests didn't know about were the cameras throughout the place. He got some really great stuff on film. Married studio executives with girls younger than their daughters. Sports figures, writers—and a few big-name stars. Maybe he'd write a book one day about the corruptible. And maybe even those who couldn't be corrupted or compromised. They were actually more interesting. They presented a challenge.

He excused himself from a pretty young girl who had stopped him, and slipped into his control room, a full bottle of Puerto Rican rum in his hand. He hit the remote control, bringing up the hidden camera screens. Drinking deeply, he started watching what was going on in different rooms. Joe Penny, you bad boy! he thought, catching the first guest room.

"Ridiculous underwear, Joe," he said. He watched for a while, then grew impatient. In the upstairs garret, he honed in on two men. Stud types, tsk, tsk. Why didn't they just come out? The third room had a ménage à trois going on. The girls were pretty, and only performing because the old guy was a director, he thought. Hell, he was keeping these tapes! You never knew when something like this might come in handy.

He was startled when his door suddenly opened. He had thought that he'd locked it. Careless. Maybe he was getting a little too cocky.

He turned in his swivel chair. Then he smiled. It was Jay Braden.

"You asshole," Braden said.

"What? You're no fool. You've seen the cameras."

Braden shook his head, furious. "You know, it would be one thing if you preyed on those who were already corrupt. But you're real slime. And you know what? The cops will come after you one day."

Kyle shrugged. "The cops can't touch me."

"Then you know what?"

"No, what? Are you going to threaten me, big boy?"

"Someday, someone will kill you!" Jay said, and slammed the door on his way out.

Kyle took another long slug of rum and turned back to his screens. Finally he tired of watching and returned to the party. It was winding down. They had all either gotten what they had come for or decided that they weren't going to get it.

At three, he said good-bye to his last guest.

He went out to the pool and looked over the water and his beautiful cabana. He looked at the bottle of rum he was still carrying. He'd managed to go through most of it.

His butler came out, asking to be excused until the morning.

He waved a hand in the air. God, he was ready to pass out himself. He slid into a lawn chair. Only then did he realize he wasn't alone. There was someone standing by the shadow of a hibiscus.

"You? Why don't you go home."

"You made me promises, Kyle."

His face ticked with annoyance. "You didn't do anything you didn't want to do."

"Is everyone in Hollywood a prick?"

"No. And everyone doesn't put out and doesn't get pissed off and screw people because they're pissed off at someone else. Hey, you're a gnat. Go home."

"You're mistaken. I'm not a gnat. And you know what, Kyle? You could really hurt the wrong people."

"Someone you care about, huh? But you're a fool. Because no one really cares about you. You're a gnat."

"I'm not!"

Kyle got up, staggering toward the remaining guest. "You're a gnat. A roach. A pathetic little bug. Get out."

"I've entertained you."

"Yeah, but you know what? You're not good enough."

"You don't know how good I am."

A hand came out, whacking Kyle in the face. He'd had so much rum, he couldn't even feel the blow. He reflected on that for a moment, then realized that he couldn't really feel his feet either, but he was stumbling backward.

Then he was teetering on the brink of the pool. "Help me!" he cried.

His guest didn't make a move, just watched him coolly.

Kyle keeled over, into the pool. His hands wouldn't move right. His legs wouldn't kick.

"Hey—"

"I'm just a gnat, Kyle."

"You're not capable of this."

"Oh, you just don't know what I'm capable of."

He'd gone in at the deep end. The water came over his head. His limbs wouldn't move right. He struggled, growing desperate for breath. He managed to break the water once again and give out a pathetic cry for help.

"Damn you, help me—you'll never work in this town again, if you don't."

"Oh, Kyle, you are just full of Hollywood rhetoric, aren't you?"

"Help me! Damn you!"

The killer watched impassively as Kyle Amesbury drowned.

He struggled, gasped, turned blue, went down, came up...

Went down.

A fitting end to such a man.

The killer sipped Kyle's champagne. This had been incredibly easy. An accident, of course.

The killer smiled. Another one down. Death could be so easy...

The killer waited a few minutes, then went into the now quiet house. The cleaning staff had already picked up a lot. The killer headed straight for Kyle's video room. Never a fool, not when it came to being careful, the killer slipped on a pair of medical gloves.

It took a few minutes to find the right tape.

The killer took it.

It was so late then. The killer paused, then drove to see him.

He was furious.

"I told you never to come here!"

"But I have something for you." The killer produced the tape. He snatched it away. "What is this, where did you get this?"

"It's you— acting like an asshole."

"Amesbury gave you this?"

"I took it. Amesbury is dead."

He froze. "What? People know you, someone will begin to suspect you."

"He was drunk, and he drowned."

"Oh, God, now this will never end. I should..."

The killer was scared. Trying so hard to please, and yet scared.

"No, you shouldn't. Because if something happens to me, I'll see that you're found out."

"Oh, yeah? What if you are dead?"

"You have to keep me alive! I thought, I thought that you..."

"That I loved you?"
His face gave it all away.
The killer turned to leave.
"Wait!"
The killer started to run.

Sharon Miller woke to find that she had fallen asleep with her half-filled suitcase at her side. She glanced at her watch. Well, sleep early, rise early. She still had plenty of time to pack. The dig would be good for her. Get her away.

She showered, slipped into a robe, and headed for the kitchen. After making coffee, she paused again. She needed to leave, yes. She needed to get away from the city. She was hurting.

But she still needed to talk to Liam. She didn't know why she had hung up when the actress had answered the other night. Yeah, she had hung up because it had hurt. Dumb though. She should have talked to Liam then. It was early. Maybe she'd go ahead and call him now.

She hesitated, though, going out to her bookcase. It was handsome walnut, a center piece that—totally filled with volumes, as it was—created something of a wall between her entry and living room. From the living room side, she looked through the volumes until she found her college yearbook. As she took it down, her doorbell rang. She walked to the door. Without the least thought of danger in mind, she threw it open.

Her eyes widened; she nearly gaped when she saw her early-morning guest.

"Hi! Got some coffee for an old friend?"

Cheerfully, her unbidden guest swept on in past her.

"Sure, sure! Coffee," Sharon said, hurrying on in, her only thought now to rid herself of this person. The book, the yearbook... what had she done with it?

"Great place!"

"Thanks. I'll get the coffee."

Her guest followed her to the kitchen. Sharon poured coffee, nervously saying, "It's early for a drop by, huh?"

"Well, you know, we keep saying we're going to call, we're going to get together...and then, well, you know. We never do. And I'm working in such a crazy place now... I had hoped that you'd be up, and that you wouldn't mind."

"Mind, of course not."

Her guest started toward the living room. Sharon thought of dialing a quick 911. Her uninvited guest turned back to her, smiling, then exclaiming, "Oh, will you look at that! You've got the old yearbook out!"

Sharon followed her guest to the living room. She sat in the chair in front of the heavy wood bookcase. "Yeah, the good old days!" she murmured. Her guest was starting to pick up the book. "I—um—wow, it's great to see you, and I'd love to take time having coffee, but—I'm going on a dig in about an hour."

"Oh, sorry. It's...Murphy. And Serena, right?"

"Well, I do like to go on digs."

"Sure." Sharon's guest swilled the cup of coffee. "Call me when you get back. We'll really get together then." Sharon started to rise.

"No, no, I know where the door is! Sit, drink your coffee, have a great dig—and call me!"

"I will!"

Her guest went around the bookcase to depart.

Sharon sat still, ready to hop up and get a hold of Liam, one way or another, as soon as the door closed.

She heard the door close. She started to rise.

She heard a creaking.

Then she screamed.

She tried to leap away, but the chair was behind her. As the heavy mahogany came crashing on down toward her, she grabbed the yearbook as if she could use it as a wall of defense in front of her.

The bookcase came down upon her.

Volumes fell everywhere.

She was only dimly aware of pain before the shelf that caught her in the temple sent her into oblivion, sweeping away all anguish.

Chapter 22

They had taken to making morning coffee themselves, drinking it on the veranda that led to the beach, then, after a swim, a shower, and time together, wandering to the main house for breakfast, brunch, or lunch—whichever it happened to be.

That day they both woke early and decided to go to the main house to eat. But as they reached their table, Liam spotted a headline in the *L.A. Times* that provoked a frown.

"What is it?"

He pushed the paper toward her. She read: ADVERTISING EXECUTIVE DROWNS AFTER WILD PARTY.

She looked up at him, then read the article. Kyle Amesbury had drowned in his home swimming pool. His guests, when interviewed, said that he had been drinking heavily. His blood-alcohol level had been sky-high.

"My God," she breathed. She stared at Liam. "But that has to be a real accident. He drowned. Alone, at home, in his own swimming pool."

"Yeah, an accident, but he is—or was—the exec for *Valentine Valley*."

"But still..."

"I don't like it," Liam said. "Excuse me. I'm going out for a second to put a call through to Olsen. Find out if it really was an accident."

She nodded, sipping coffee, reading the article again. Most of the cast and crew of *Valen-*

357

tine Valley had been at Kyle Amesbury's home that night. She felt a gnawing in her stomach, a rumbling of unease. The last few days had been too perfect.

"Miss McCormack?"

She looked up. Their waiter was approaching her.

She stared at him, surprised that he had used her real name. He winced, showing that he hadn't meant to do so. He was a handsome young Polynesian, shy and eternally pleasant to them. They'd had him as their server every morning.

"I'm sorry, but...well, I know that you are Serena McCormack—Verona Valentine."

She flushed, wishing that Liam was in the dining room with her. "You watch the soap?"

"My wife tapes it. We watch it together at night."

"Thank you for watching."

"The hotel staff...well, a number of people have recognized you."

"So much for being anonymous."

"You stayed here before, with the cast and crew."

"Yes."

"We try to be discreet."

"That's very kind of you."

"You are really on your honeymoon?"

She shook her head. "No."

"Ah, well...there is a phone call for you." He had brought a portable phone with him. She stared at him a moment before taking it.

"Hello?" she murmured, afraid she would hear the husky, whispered voice that had sent her flying out of her house that night.

"Serena!"

It was her sister's voice. Melinda was upset.

"Hey—"

"Kyle Amesbury is dead. Serena, even *we* went to his house that night. Jeff was upset about the sarcophagus, and he insisted he was going to go back to work when you did, and so he decided we'd better show up and talk to a few people."

"Melinda, calm down. I saw the papers—it was an accident."

"He drowned!"

"Yes, he drowned. Please, don't worry. No one will accuse Jeff of anything just because he was there."

She didn't hear Liam when he returned until he pulled his chair out and sat. As soon as she looked up, she knew that something was wrong from his side as well. His expression was a dark scowl. His eyes were accusing.

"You took the phone and called your sister," he said.

She paled. A totally involuntary action. It hadn't been wrong to call her sister. "Yes." She made no attempt to lie or hedge.

"I told you not to."

She swallowed hard. "My sister is on the phone now."

He took the phone from her. "Hi, Melinda. How did you get this number?"

He nodded gravely at her reply. Then, to

Serena's astonishment, he began to reassure her sister. Apparently Melinda didn't even ask to say good-bye to her.

"I used your cell," she told him, dismayed to feel so defensive. "I didn't tell her where we were—"

"And you didn't tell me that *Valentine Valley* had used this hotel when filming in Hawaii on a location shoot."

"You should keep up with the soaps better," she murmured in an attempt to be light. She winced. Bad mistake.

"Serena, you compromised everything I was trying to do."

She didn't reply. She was afraid that she had done just that.

"What did Olsen say about Kyle Amesbury?"

"Definitely a drowning. And he was definitely drunk. He had consumed most of a bottle of 151-proof rum."

"So it was an accident," she said.

"Apparently." He nodded, stretched his hands before him, and said, "Serena, you weren't supposed to call your sister, because that's how word gets around."

"I'm sorry. Really sorry."

"It doesn't matter. Let's go back to the room and pack."

"Pack?"

"There's no reason to stay here any longer. The whole world knows you're here."

"Liam, we've got to go back anyway," she told him, suddenly earnest. "Running away isn't solving anything. Amesbury is dead.

You thought he was involved, but it must be someone else. Don't you see? I want my life back. If you were receiving threats, you wouldn't run from them. You'd be more determined than ever to find out the truth."

"Serena," he said, shaking his head, not rising yet. "I was trained to be a cop."

"I'm not hiding out any longer," she insisted. "I'm scared, and I never should have told Melinda where I was. But please, Liam, let's go back. We'll never—I'll never have a life, a real life, again, until this is solved."

"I was planning on going back," he said quietly.

"Oh?" she said, startled that he had agreed so easily.

"You're right. Another person has been killed. This person is not going to stop."

He wasn't just angry with her for what she had done; he was deeply upset about something else, she realized.

"What happened?"

"Sharon Miller was found in her house by a grad student from UCLA. She was supposed to have been joining them for a dig."

Serena inhaled a gasp. "What—what happened?" she asked.

He shook his head. "Apparently, a bookshelf fell on her."

"Is she...?"

"No. But she is in the hospital. In a coma."

"Liam, I am so, so sorry!" she whispered. "Of course, you want to get back. But—"

"But what?"

"How can that...possibly be related to... *Valentine Valley*?"

"I don't know. Maybe it's not. But she went down to the police station. And she tried to call me. I never reached her return. I just...I just have a sick feeling. One that I have to look into."

Serena nodded.

They packed; they made arrangements with their pilot to get back home. But long before they boarded the plane, Serena knew that they had left paradise.

As it happened, their return put her back at work only a day earlier than planned. Liam went in with her, talked to Joe, then departed. She found out, however, that he had brought in another off-duty cop to watch over her as well.

Everybody on the set itself was talking about Kyle Amesbury—and all the videotapes that had been found at his house.

"My God, what a scandal!" Kelly told Serena, curling up on her couch, delighted to have her back and eager to talk. "The police found tapes...so many tapes! He was a regular voyeur, tricking people into doing things...all kinds of things. I wondered if he planned on selling some of them in the porno market! Am I glad I'm basically your corn-fed Midwestern girl! The tapes haven't gone anywhere, of course, it's all under police investigation, but...there's rumor afloat. This is worse than any scandal that's come before. Kyle Amesbury seemed so quiet, so well dressed, so...regular when we first met him, remember? Becoming a big executive must have gone right to his head."

Serena kept silent about the one tape she had been aware of.

Allona joined them in Serena's dressing room, bearing sheets of script rewrites. She heard the last of what Kelly had to say.

"I told you he was a sicko," she announced.

Serena glanced at her with an arched brow. "He didn't have anything on you, did he?"

"Me, honey? I'm as sweet and pure as café au lait." She laughed. "I'll bet you a few people are going to be caught in some trouble on this one, though."

"Probably," Serena agreed.

"Hopefully no one who was too innocent. He kept inviting Jinx over, I know. She must be in complete shock," Kelly said, "though I can't imagine her having sex with someone— besides Jay." She looked up sharply at this idea. "You know, the cops questioned everyone again. That must have made her a nervous wreck. I'm surprised she's been making it in to work through all this."

"She loves her work," Allona said. "Wish I did."

"I wonder who is caught up in all those tapes Amesbury made?" Kelly mused.

Allona laughed delightedly. "I'm willing to bet that both our producers will be caught with their pants down."

"Joe hated Amesbury," Serena said.

"Yeah, but Joe loves a party, and he loves sweet young things," Allona said.

"Well, men thrive on their reputations, and Joe and Andy like to be known as studs," Serena said. "If their names get out, it will only enhance their reputations."

Kelly giggled. "What if they're on tape not being able to get it up?"

"That's about the only thing that would horrify the two of them," Serena said. "Well, and then, if they caught Andy's bad side. Or if his hair wasn't perfect. Oh, my God, look at the way we're talking," she added. "A man is dead." She shuddered. "I really didn't like him, but..."

"He was a sleazoid who fell drunk into his own pool." Allona sighed. "Serena, you can't save the world."

Serena didn't reply because someone knocked on the door. It was Thorne, coming to tell Kelly she was needed on the set. Kelly left, and Serena remembered her pages.

"Here," Allona said. "There's so much going on, I forgot to tell you. We're going to do location shooting for the next two days. I think the big guys want to get out of the studio, despite the fact that it's been gone over with a fine-tooth comb."

"Oh?"

"Not far from here. They found a location that looks like Egypt."

"I'm—I mean, Verona is going back to Egypt?"

"Yeah. The *Valentine* finale takes place there."

"And we still don't know what happens?"

"We've written a bunch of pages. They're not even telling the writers what they're using until the last day."

"Well, who may be getting it?"

"Everyone."

"Everyone?"

"From Mama and Papa Valentine to the waiter."

"The waiter?"

"I'm kidding. But every main cast member is up for grabs."

"Including me?"

"Hey, I hear you haven't got that much longer on your contract. And you did screen-test for Eddie's movie."

"With everything that's been going on, we should have a pleasant Valentine's Day episode."

"Oh, Doug and I wrote you back in for a scene today, too. I'd written you out, having Vera and Marla talk about you returning to Egypt, but since you're here, it will be a much better scene if you're in it, saying you have to go, you have to get away, after the incident with the sarcophagus and all. Hey, I saw the tape— it's great. Liam should be an actor."

"Don't tell him that. It just makes him mad."

Allona smiled. "I won't say a thing."

With that, she left. As the door opened and closed, Serena saw her young off-duty officer just outside. He smiled, assuring her of his constant presence.

She thought about calling Liam, who had gone home for a few hours.

He might not want to hear from her, she thought. She stared at the phone. She didn't pick it up. He didn't always have to be at her side.

Liam spent more than an hour at the hospital. He talked with Sharon's doctors, away from her parents, whom he'd never met. They were hugging one another outside the intensive unit. He wanted to speak with them, to do something, say something. Tell them she was a beautiful person, smart as a whip, wonderful. He almost approached them, then he saw that their priest was joining them.

He'd asked Olsen to have a man watch her bedside. Even Olsen had seemed to think that he was overboard, but he promised a department man for the next forty-eight hours.

Comas could still be a mystery, even to physicians who specialized in head trauma and neuroanatomy. They considered the next few days crucial, though people had been known to survive comas at many stages. So far, she was showing more than ample brain activity; there had been no suggestion about taking her off of life support.

Liam stared at Sharon, looking pale and pathetic, full of tubes and wires, and feeling tremendous sorrow and frustration. No one saw this as anything other than an accident. Olsen was humoring him, with his police guard.

Finally, realizing that he was doing no good, he determined to get into Sharon's house.

He sidestepped the police tape that still wafted forlornly around the front door of the house. He still had a key. He opened the door and went in.

He felt another surge of anguish as he entered the house. She was always so neat and organized. Her small house had always been spotlessly clean, but homey.

Little had been touched since the paramedics had been in. He looked at the smashed wood, the crushed furniture, and the multitude of volumes spilling around the floor. Most of them had to do with her love of the past. There were books on anthropology, archaeology, ancient man, Egyptology, Stonehenge, the Etruscans, Chinese civilization, Mayans, the study of bones, forensics in archaeology, and much more. He went through title after title, then fell against the chair, frustrated. Then he saw the volume that had fallen, its cover badly damaged, by the broken chair. He picked it up. It was a yearbook from Hollywood High.

Leaving the police tape still flapping around the house intact, he departed her house.

Serena was able to put the day to good use. Jim was delighted to reblock the scene and play it as originally intended. Everything went well.

When she finished, she was relieved to find that Liam had returned and replaced the off-duty officer, and was waiting for her in the hallway. As they walked together to her dressing room, she said, "How's Sharon?"

"Holding her own."

She nodded. "I'm sorry."

"I know. I'm sorry, too. How have things been here?"

"It was a good, uneventful day."

He arched a brow. "The Amesbury scandal is uneventful?"

"No, of course, it's all anyone is talking about. Makes me glad I kept my distance from him whenever I could."

"I guess a few people from here are worried about what might be found."

"Did you tell the police about the tape you have?"

"No," he said flatly.

"Perhaps—"

"I'm not ready to turn it over to them yet."

"Do you still think that he might have been in on what happened? That he called me to scare me out of my house?"

"I don't know."

They left the studio and drove to his house, stopping at the store to buy groceries. Serena insisted on choosing the food, telling him she was going to cook. He agreed, and, once back at the house, he didn't tease her about the fact that she actually knew what a kitchen was. He sat in the living room, going through a book on deepwater exploration.

He seemed to try to be cordial and light when she told him dinner was ready.

"Chicken cordon bleu? So, you do have hidden talents."

"I can actually make many meals. My hot dogs are to die for."

"Great. Chicken cordon bleu and hot dogs. Interesting combo."

"Verona cooked chicken cordon bleu for one of her husbands once—I forget which one."

They had wine with dinner, and afterward washed the dishes together. But later, Liam returned to the living room, built a fire, and immersed himself in the book again. Serena sat in the living room, watching the flames as well. After a while she grew sleepy, from all the flying, she guessed.

"What is that?"

"Sharon's yearbook."

"Is it relevant?"

"It may be," he answered curtly. Then he looked up at her. "I have to admit, I thought Amesbury was in on it somehow. Someone on the set—and Amesbury."

"Maybe he was. And he's dead now."

Liam nodded. "And now, I don't think it's Amesbury."

"He drowned."

"After a party, attended by many people from *Valentine Valley*. And now Sharon..."

"Sharon wasn't a part of *Valentine Valley*."

"I think her accident was."

Serena couldn't see the connection. She understood his feelings. She intended to leave him alone. As he read, she slipped silently into the bedroom.

She awoke later in the night. He was with her. He seemed asleep, and she was surprised when he rolled over and made love to her. He was tense and passionate, as if in a tumult, holding her to him afterward. He didn't speak. Neither did she.

The phone rang very early. It was Joe Penny. "Don't forget, we're on location."

Serena looked at Liam, who had awakened as well.

"It's Joe. He didn't want us to forget that we were on location."

Liam nodded. "Are the cops going to be there?"

"Are the cops going to be there?"

"Either Hutchens or Olsen himself."

She repeated the words again for Liam.

He nodded, then rose and padded into the bathroom.

"Liam has the address. It's up in the hills," Joe told her. "A construction site. You'll love it."

Indeed, they had managed to make a cleared construction site look like an excavated Egyptian tomb. David DeVille had followed Verona Valentine, unknown to her, of course. Serena found out that day that Verona was pregnant, and that, of course, was the main reason she had fled—to talk to herself in the tomb,

370

trying to figure out what to do. David was going to reach her, and Jay Braden, as Randy Rock, was going to follow as well, furious about the way she was trying to ruin his life. Then, of course, Kelly, or Marla, would follow, convinced that something was going on and determined to have a showdown with her sister over David.

The set decoration for the tomb was great. There was going to be a cave-in after David reached Verona, and the two would be stuck in the tomb.

Both Joe and Andy were on the set, as were Allona and Doug. Hutchens was there, keeping his distance from the actors, it seemed, but watching with interest. Liam left Serena to go and talk with him.

Doug seemed to be in bad shape, and Serena went over to talk to him. "Are you upset about Kyle?"

"That jerk?" Doug said. He shook his head. "Remind me to quit looking for beautiful people, huh?"

"Darn. No more lunches watching guys?"

"Serena, I don't think that you need to keep looking for guys. You've got a good one."

"Well, you see, I don't actually have him."

"You're crazy. He's in love with you."

"He cares about me. But I don't think he wants a life with me."

"He must."

"Doug, he never even suggests... I don't know."

"You want a ring, a wedding, a house, a home, kids, a dog—"

"Yeah. He's never mentioned those things."

"You should ask him to marry you."

"You're kidding."

"Dead serious."

"I can't."

"Why?"

"I'm afraid of rejection, and…oh, let's just get through all this, huh?"

Doug shrugged. "Well, maybe, if you ever do ask him and he says yes, he'll still let you do lunches. After all, we'll be looking only for a guy for me then, and it will be a different kind of man we're searching for."

She kissed him on the forehead. Thorne was standing impatiently by the makeup chair.

Set designers, actors, props, costumes, makeup—everyone was standing by. The assistants were on the set. Everything was ready to go. The set designers and the man sent over from the construction company that owned the machinery for the sand dump were showing Joe and Andy how it all worked, assuring them that there was a safety lever that stopped the machine should the main controls ever fail to work.

While she was still being made up, Serena saw Jeff arrive on the set. He had obviously discussed his return with the producers, because he waved to them both. He was adamant in saying that he was innocent of any wrongdoing, and he wasn't going to lose a job he loved over what was happening.

Serena made a point of jumping out of the chair to greet him, kissing him on the cheek. "Jeff, it's great that you're back."

"Yeah. I didn't want you working with any more Egyptian equipment if I wasn't around."

She smiled. "I'm glad you're here."

"Thanks."

"Serena, get back in this chair," Thorne called to her.

As she sat there, Serena could see that Liam was still talking to Bill Hutchens. When Thorne went back to the trailer for new sponges, Bill stopped by for a moment.

"How are you doing?"

"Good, thanks. Under the circumstances." She stared at him. "They're sure that Kyle Amesbury's death was an accident?"

"We're sure that he drowned and that there was no sign of foul play."

"Maybe his tapes will provide some kind of answer."

"I hope."

"Don't you think some people must have known?"

"Sure, and they're suffering right now, with all the tapes in police custody."

When Thorne finished with her, Jim Novac called her over and gave her directions for the first part of the scene. Serena rehearsed her monologue, walking among the various canopic jars and statuettes on the set. It went well. Jim called to the cameramen, telling them they were ready to tape. He gave her his "And we're on in five, four…three…" silent two, silent one cue.

Her monologue went perfectly. Everyone was pleased. Joe kissed her. "Honey, we do miss you when you're gone."

"Thanks, boss."

She rehearsed the scene with Conar, in which Verona confessed to David DeVille that she was pregnant, and David DeVille told her that he doubted the child was his.

Then they were off the set as Kelly and Jay rehearsed their scene outside the tomb and then ran tape.

Jinx stood next to Serena, watching with her as the other two worked. Serena noticed then that Jinx was pale and seemed ill. She felt guilty. She had been so self-involved, she hadn't paid enough attention to the young woman.

"Jinx, what's wrong?"

Jinx shook her head.

"What is it? Maybe I can help you."

Jinx shook her head again. Then she whispered. "The tape."

"What tape? The taping is going well."

Jinx was distracted. "The cops...after Amesbury died." She stared at Serena suddenly. "Serena...I've been at that house."

"Oh? But, Jinx..."

"I had this ridiculous moment when...oh, Serena, it was so dumb!"

"Jinx, you had an encounter with someone at Kyle's house?"

Jinx went even whiter.

"Jinx, the cops won't be showing those—"

"Names get out."

"Well, don't worry about your job."

"No, you don't understand…"

"Serena!" Jim called sharply. "We're ready for you."

"Don't worry about anything," Serena told Jinx firmly. "Trust me. One indiscretion in Hollywood isn't going to hurt you."

"You don't understand. The one really… never mind." She looked at her suddenly. "Serena, you've been great to work with. I really do think the world of you."

"Thank you. But, Jinx—"

"Serena!" Jim called.

"Hey, chin up," Serena told Jinx. "You're getting upset about something that doesn't matter. We'll talk more later."

Serena hurried onto the set. Conar was waiting. "Same thing—one rehearsal, we go to tape. Got it?"

"Yep!" Conar called.

They rehearsed, stopping at the point when the sand would fall.

Then everyone was called into place for the scene. Joe Penny stood with Niall Meyers, who would work the hydraulic dump that was set to deliver the cascading sand. There was a safety lever at the rear of the truck, he had explained, if anything should fail.

"I'm going to stand by the damned safety lever myself," Joe muttered.

"All right. Places, everyone. This has to be one take…or we're back here tomorrow after the sand is cleared."

Serena and Conar took their places on the set. The cameras rolled into place. Jim called out an order to wait; a paper had blown onto the set. One of the production assistants ran to snatch it away.

Jinx, clasping her notebook to her chest and looking forlorn, stood near Joe and the safety lever. Liam was pacing behind the cameras. Jeff was standing close to Jim Novac. Jay Braden and Kelly were just off the set, ready to run in after the sand had fallen, calling and screaming out to Serena and Conar.

"And we're on in five, four, three..."

She and Conar waited for the silent "two" and "one" signals. Conar had the first line. He started shouting at her. She shouted back, reminding him that no one had made him come near her, that he had used the family, used them all, and now he was going to pay. He told her that she had to abort the child. She told him it was her choice, and she hadn't made it yet. He replied that he was in love with her sister, really in love with her, didn't she understand that?

She could almost forget everything when she was on the set. It was fun working with Conar. He could take even a tired line and give it real meaning and emotion. And actually, though the scene was definitely melodramatic, it seemed real that he could be in love with the one sister and in lust with the other.

She told him that he could never, ever make her give up the child if she didn't want to do so. He argued that Marla Valentine would never forgive him. That might be so, but he should have thought of that before, she said.

They were nearing the finale. He raised his voice again, telling her that she had set out to seduce him. She responded, "Just as you set out to ruin Natalie in Paris, and then set out to seduce Marla, here in the States, when Natalie wanted no more of you? You don't love Marla. At least what you wanted with me was more honest. But at the bottom of it all, David DeVille, all you really ever meant to do was take everything that the Valentine vineyards had to offer. You meant to strip my father of years of work and effort. You wanted the glory—"

"Whatever I wanted at the beginning doesn't matter anymore!" he shouted at her.

"Stop yelling!" she warned him. "The sands above have shifted over the years. We've dug this out of the dunes—"

"You're excavating a tomb," he cut in. "You came here to rob the Egyptians, just as you rob and manipulate everyone else you come near."

"I do not!"

"Damn you, I won't let you do this. I won't let you have my child." He started across the floor to her.

Small drifts of sand began to fall. She stared upward.

"Stop it! Stop it!" she whispered to him huskily, fear tingeing her voice. "Look, look, what you're doing—"

"You stop it, Verona! You'll use anything, any trick at all to keep from admitting I'm right. The only reason you'd ever have this baby is to hurt everyone around you."

"Stop, for the love of God, stop! The sand is coming in—it's going to block the passage. We'll die here, smothered!"

"Verona—"

He came to a dead stop. Right on cue, the sand started pouring down hard, blocking the entrance to the "tomb."

Conar rushed to grab her, sweeping her away from the falling sand.

They were supposed to watch in horror as the sand filled the entrance.

Crushed in Conar's arms, Serena whispered. "Conar, it's too much...it's flowing too hard."

"Damned right." He started to move off the set with her.

The sand fell harder. "Back up," he said. "Under the ledge."

"Conar—Joe is coming toward us. He'll get caught under the flow!"

Suddenly they heard a hoarse shout. Then someone cried out, "Joe is down!"

"Cut the sand!" she heard Liam roaring.

Conar swore suddenly, caught in an avalanche of white sand. He cast his bulk over her.

For one split second Serena could see what was going on. The sand had hit Joe, knocking him down before he could grab the safety lever.

Jinx was standing next to Joe—within reach of the lever. But she wasn't moving. She was just standing there, staring, her eyes fixed, her mouth gaping.

It seemed an eternity...

It was really only seconds, yet every second mattered. She and Conar were trapped on the set, and they would all be suffocated within a matter of minutes if...

"Jinx!" Serena shouted.

But Jinx didn't move. Jay, who had been ready to come onto the set, was staring at Jinx.

"Jinx!" Jay shouted.

Jay rushed for the lever, knocking Jinx out of the way to reach it. By then, however, the man from the construction company had seen that the main lever had failed. He reached the safety and hit it immediately.

Then Serena saw no more. Even Conar, trying to protect her, was knocked over as the sand poured over them with a force that stole away all strength...

And all air.

Chapter 23

It was amazing how quickly things could go wrong. It was supposed to appear that the tomb was being buried by a shift in the dug-up sand above. In seconds, what had appeared to be a smoothly running piece of theater became a disaster.

Liam wasn't near the lever, but as the sand kept pouring down, he tore across the distance between the cameras and Serena. Ignoring the still-flowing sand, he plowed beneath it. Jeff was beside him, digging as frantically as he was. He had seen exactly where Conar and Serena had been. He reached Conar and dragged him up. At Liam's side, Jeff held Conar steady while Liam found Serena's hand, then the rest of her, and pulled her, gasping and coughing, out of the granular torrent.

At that moment the safety lever kicked in and the sand stopped falling. Liam was barely aware of it. He was dusting the sand from Serena's face. She was still coughing and trying to brush it from her eyes.

The truck operator was down, out of his chair. "Is everyone all right?"

Serena nodded, still unable to speak. Conar was busy dusting himself off.

"Hey, someone help me with Joe!" Jay Braden called out.

"You all right, *really*?" Liam asked Serena. Covered in sand, her eyelashes, cheeks, and even lips white with it, she nodded. Then he realized that she was smiling. "Yes, I'm fine, really fine. It's sand, Liam, just sand, and the safety lever worked."

Liam left her, heading for Joe. Bill was already on his way. By the time they reached him, Joe was already emerging.

"Maybe we should get an ambulance," Kelly suggested.

Joe panted and wheezed, and struggled to his feet. "No!" He had to take a second to get his breath. "Kelly Trent, no ambulance. I'm fine. What about Conar, Serena?"

"I'm all right," Conar said. "Serena?"

"Absolutely fine," she assured them all.

Applause went up around the set. "See, there should always be a safety," Joe said, sounding authoritative once again. "Here you have it, a working piece of show biz, with everyone on hand ready to pitch in."

"Well, we do need showers," Serena said dryly, provoking laughter around the set.

"You and Conar can head on out, Serena," Joe said. "Jay, Kelly, the sand is practically perfect for the next scene. You two both okay?"

"Well, of course, we're okay," Kelly said. "But, Joe, you need a shower."

"Let's get back to work," Joe insisted. "Do you know what it will take to set up all over again? I want to finish with Jay and Kelly outside the tomb today. Then we can clean up tonight and get back in the tomb with Serena and Conar tomorrow. Everybody got it?"

"Think we could take five?" Jim suggested. "You could at least wash your face, Joe."

Joe scowled at him, but his scowl only provoked more laughter. "Hey, seriously. I want to thank everyone. There's always a risk with any location work. Everyone pulled through just fine. Take five."

He walked over to Serena, taking her by the shoulders. "You're really okay?"

"Just very dirty," Serena said.

She looked very strange, covered in white. She saw Liam and smiled at him. "You know, you are an awfully good bodyguard. You manage to be there for every emergency. But as you saw, this was really an accident. The truck hydraulics got jammed. Poor Joe got knocked down before he could protect his investment."

It had to have been an accident, Liam thought. He had watched the entire thing.

Serena was looking around.

"What's the matter?" he asked her.

"Where's Jinx?" she asked.

Liam shook his head. "I don't know." He looked through the crowd of people milling around. His first thought had been Serena. Now he realized that although the place was filled with bustling activity, there was no sign of Serena's diminutive assistant anywhere.

"She panicked, Liam. When Joe went down, she didn't hit that lever. I'm worried about her. We've got to find her. She's going to feel responsible for this, and she's already upset about something."

He nodded. "All right."

He caught her hand. They moved through the crowd of soap people.

Jay came up behind the two of them.

"Do you see her?" he asked.

Serena swung around. "You mean Jinx?"

He nodded.

"No. Where might she have gone?"

"Back to the studio?" Jay suggested. "To her home?"

"We'll try the studio," Liam said.

"I'll check her house," Jay said distractedly.

But as he turned to head back, he heard Andy shouting at him. "Jay, where are you going? Joe said that we're going to finish this up."

Jay shook his head. He was obviously concerned about Jinx. Why? Conar wondered.

"Hey," Serena said, "don't worry, we'll find her."

"Yeah, all right," Jay said huskily. He turned and started walking back, shoulders squared, spine rigid. "One take, one damned take, and no rehearsals," Jay called out angrily.

"Hey, it was just a bunch of sand," Jim said.

Serena turned back to Liam. "Let's go. We have to find Jinx."

He nodded. "I'll go back to the studio, and then on to Jinx's house. If you walk around the city like that, I can guarantee you'll attract attention."

"Liam, I'm really worried—"

"Don't worry. I'll find Jinx. I'll ask Conar to stay with you—hey, there's a high point to it. You can get that stuff all over *his* car."

She smiled, but said, "Liam, I'm afraid for Jinx."

"We can have the cops put out an APB."

"No, that could put her into a hole for the next year."

"Then I'll find her. Somehow."

An hour later, Serena was at last drying her hair. Kelly called to her that they had finished the shoot. A reporter who happened to be in the vicinity had come to the set—even something like a little extra sand on the set of *Valentine Valley* drew attention these days. "You know Joe. He used it, he was charming. He went right out to talk to the reporter, who stood there, of course, accusing him of seeking publicity. 'Did I call you?' he asked the guy," Kelly said. "Then he went on, 'Sand. We had a little sand. Everyone is fine.' Naturally, he then went on to tell them, 'Wait until you see it! It's a spectacular scene. And there will be more from *Valentine Valley*.'"

"Never miss a photo op, and there's no such thing as bad publicity," Serena said.

"I guess. Oh, well, it is pretty great. We get the scripts for the Valentine's Day crescendo tomorrow. Rehearsals right off...and then we shoot. Everyone shows up in Egypt. How's that for a plot?"

"I suppose the Valentines are rich enough to hop on planes to faraway countries at the drop of a hat," Serena said. She hung up.

Conar was in the living room, watching a Discovery Channel program about Egypt. Serena came out and joined him, telling him what Kelly had told her.

"I've heard most of it. We're having a huge family scene at the tomb. We get dug out—then something happens."

"I know Joe is going for secrecy, but he sure is taking chances, giving us scripts to learn that quickly."

"Jim complained. It did him no good. Liam called, by the way, while you were still in the shower."

"And? Did he find Jinx."

"No, not yet. He went to the studio, to her

house, and he prowled the streets. No sign of her yet. Jay was worried about her, too. I imagine he's out looking for her now. Liam is going to try both places again, then stop by the hospital. He'll be here after that. And Jennifer is coming over with the baby."

"Great."

She was delighted to see Jennifer when she arrived with the baby. They talked about everything that had happened. "We haven't been at any parties lately," Jennifer told her. "I barely knew Amesbury."

"You mean you two aren't going to be caught on tape?" Serena teased.

"Never," Jennifer said with mock horror. "We have a child to think about now."

Conar came into the kitchen. "I'm starving," he said, opening the refrigerator. "What's he got in here?"

"I'm not sure at the moment," Serena said, coming over to check out the contents of the freezer.

"Steaks," Jennifer said from behind her.

"He's a meat man," Conar said.

"Steaks. Maybe he'll show up by the time we've cooked them."

They were ready with dinner by the time Liam arrived. He shook his head at Serena's anxious look. "I tried everywhere."

"Did you...try breaking into her apartment?"

"No," he said. "Serena, that's not legal."

"Oh, right, and that concerns you."

"I couldn't break in. I might have...except

that I was pretty convinced she wasn't there. She has a porch and windows. I could see most of the place. Trust me. I'm anxious to see her myself. If we don't hear from her soon, we'll break in. I promise. Hey, it smells great in here."

"And dinner is ready," Jennifer announced.

"How was Sharon?" Serena asked.

"She hasn't regained consciousness, but the doctors say her vitals are good, and her brain activity is excellent, under the circumstances." He hesitated, then shrugged. "The neurologist told me today that he can't make promises, but he thinks she's going to pull out."

"Thank God," Serena said.

He smiled at her. He still seemed thoughtful, but a lot better.

They ate. With Jennifer and Conar at the table, the evening seemed more natural. Serena was glad that Sharon seemed to be doing well, but she was deeply troubled about Jinx. She called the girl's apartment several times, but the answering machine came on each time she dialed the number.

Conar and Jennifer went home around ten. They were barely out of the house before Liam sat down with Sharon's yearbook again.

Serena hesitated before approaching him. "Liam, about Jinx—"

"Come here," he said.

She walked over to where he stood. He was looking down at a picture. He pointed to someone standing on a ladder, adjusting lighting on a stage.

"Recognize her?"

Serena frowned at the picture, studying it. Then she gasped. "Jinx!"

"And look...here. There's a paragraph on her. Jennifer Blase...belonged to this honor society and that, pulled equal time in stage-craft and performance. Why do you think she's working as an assistant?"

Serena shrugged. "Maybe because she's so shy."

He shook his head, staring at Serena. "I think she got knocked down a few times too many. I've managed to read a lot on her now. Here she is, all talent and genius, but apparently, according to these records, she left school for almost a half a year. She graduated with Sharon; she should have graduated the year before her."

"Lots of people take time off."

"I think that maybe she left because of a breakdown."

"What? How can you say such a thing?"

"Right now, I'm speculating. I think that Sharon was going for this book," he said softly. "I think the more things started happening on the set, the more she worried about her 'friend' who had a job at the studio. I think Sharon was looking for Bill Hutchens to warn him that Jinx might have a screw loose somewhere. Then she was afraid she was way off base and might hurt someone, and decided not to say anything. Then more stuff happened, and she didn't want to tell the cops, but she could tell me. Only...someone surprised her before she could tell me."

Serena bit her lower lip, staring at him. "You might be the one unhinged, you know!"

The phone started to ring. Serena jumped. "I'll get it."

He nodded.

Serena had thought that it was a futile hope, but she answered the phone, her fingers tensed around the cord.

"Serena?" Jinx whispered.

"Yes. Yes, it's me," Serena said, nodding as she stared at Liam. "Where are you? I've been worried sick about you."

"I'm so sorry. So sorry. I just... I had to call. I wanted you to know...you are a good person, Serena, really good—"

"Jinx, so are you."

Jinx started to laugh. "No. Are you alone?"

She glanced at Liam, who was staring at her. "No."

"I wish I could see you. Talk to you before..." She sounded despondent.

"Jinx, listen to me. Are you home now?"

"Yes."

"I'm coming over."

"No. No, I can't talk with anyone else there, and Liam won't let you come alone."

"Jinx, we can talk alone."

She glanced at Liam. He was scowling at her.

"Stay calm. I'll be right there."

She hung up the phone. Liam was already up. "You aren't going anywhere by yourself," Liam said firmly. "And you should tell me now what you know that I don't."

"She...she had an affair...or just sex or

whatever with someone at Kyle's house. I think she's all upset about the tapes. Liam, we won't get anything out of her if I can't have a chance to talk with her alone."

"You can talk alone. But rest assured, I'll be there."

They left the house. He drove to Jinx's, which was not far from Serena's. It was a tiny, freestanding house with a fair expanse of lawn. Liam walked Serena to the front door, silently pointing to the window he had mentioned earlier. "I'll be here. Right here."

She nodded and tapped on the door. "Jinx. It's me, Serena."

"Are you alone?"

She frowned at Liam. He flattened himself against the wall.

"Yes," Serena said.

Jinx opened the door and stepped back to let Serena enter. She walked into the living room. Serena looked around curiously. She'd picked Jinx up for work a few times, and dropped her off. She'd never come inside the house before. She was amazed by the movie posters lining the walls. There was paraphernalia around as well—cases with props used in various shows, ray guns from sci-fi movies, gloves, tags, all kinds of things.

"Jinx," Serena said, "what's going on?"

Jinx turned around and faced her. "I did it," she said softly.

"Did it?" Serena repeated, still worried about Jinx's state of mind. "Look, I'm telling you, whatever you did at Kyle's house isn't going to matter."

Jinx smiled painfully, shaking her head.

"Serena, I've been doing it all. I fixed the lights, I unhooked the ladder, and I poisoned the candy myself."

Serena stood dead still, incredulous. "Jinx... why?"

"Why? Well, I was in love, you see. But I never hated you. Everything I ever said...I meant. I like you. I'm sorry...it's just that...oh, well, I didn't like Jane. Jane was...horrible. You don't know all the things she did. You don't know how she used people."

"Jinx," Serena said slowly, "I don't believe this. You were trying to kill me?"

"Amazing, isn't it? I didn't think it would work. But hell, if it didn't...well, again, Jane was no great loss. I might not have managed any injury at all. I was taking a terrible chance. Then...well, you didn't die, and you saw the note in Jane's room, though I didn't write that one. But you insisted we find out what happened...so I had to lure you into danger. Into fear. I sent you the roses. I fixed the ladder. Then I had to appear innocent myself, so I ordered candy and poisoned the one piece, and I have to say, I put on the performance of a lifetime. The things we do for love! I even wedged the safety slide on that sarcophagus. Then for fear. I went to school with Liam's girlfriend, Sharon. I liked her a lot. But I had a breakdown, a time-out, before my senior year. I was afraid she might remember that—

and just how incredibly good I was at stage-craft and film design. And it was horrible, but recently, I began to see that I had been blinded, that I had been so wrong.... There are so many awful, horrible people out there. But you're not one of them. And now...well, it's over, and I'm scared—"

"Jinx, yes, this is scary," Serena said. Her mouth was dead dry. She had been just standing there, staring blankly at Jinx, her mouth open. Had Liam heard all this?

They needed more, she thought, reason breaking through the stunned ice in her mind.

"Jinx," she said, "you were influenced by the person you were in love with. You did terrible things. But we'll work it out."

"Serena, you know it can't be worked out. And I'm scared now...because I'm scared of how I'm going to die. I'm going to die anyway, don't you see? So it's easiest to do it my way."

"Jinx—" Serena began and started toward her. It never occurred to her to be afraid of Jinx then; she was tiny, barely ninety pounds.

But suddenly Jinx picked up something from the table. A gun.

"Is that a prop piece?" Serena asked, trying to stay sane and calm. She could scream; Liam would be there in an instant. She spoke loud to make sure he knew that Jinx had a gun.

Jinx was seriously agitated, but she smiled. "No, it's real."

"Jinx, if you're so fond of me, why would you—"

"I'm not going to shoot you," Jinx said.

"I'm going to shoot myself. I just wanted you to know that I was sorry, really sorry." She moved the muzzle of the gun toward her head. "And afraid. And you have to—"

Her voice broke off.

Serena realized that the door had opened quietly. Liam had come in, hands up in the air, showing that he was unarmed. "Jinx, put that down. There's no reason for you to kill yourself," he said calmly, striding across the room toward her. "We can get help. We know that you weren't in it alone. Talk to us. We'll help you, honest to God."

Jinx didn't release the gun, but huge tears formed in her eyes. "I should have known you were there. You love her, and you're not like the others."

"Jinx, please give me the gun."

"I wanted it all, too. I studied so hard. I couldn't seem to break in...except at *Valentine Valley*. And then..."

"Jinx." Liam took another step toward her. "Jinx, you've been living a nightmare. You need to talk to someone, really talk to someone, and believe me, that will make it better. We can straighten it all out."

Serena was so involved in what Liam was saying to Jinx, softly, soothingly, that she didn't hear the arrival of others at the door.

Jinx did. In panic, she aimed toward the door.

Bill Hutchens appeared with a uniformed officer. "Drop the weapon!" he ordered.

Jinx's face went white. She raised the gun higher, her finger tightening on the trigger.

"Jinx!" Liam said, diving for her gun.

"No!" Jinx cried.

Serena screamed at the sudden sound of gunfire. Liam had caught Jinx's arm, and her shot, aimed straight at Bill Hutchens, went thudding into the wall.

Bill's shot, aimed at Jinx, went straight into her chest. Serena screamed as she fell.

"Get an ambulance!" Liam cried, falling down by Jinx's side.

The uniformed cop spoke into his radio. Liam feverishly applied pressure to Jinx's chest, trying to stanch the gushing blood.

Bill was on his way to her side. Serena dropped down next to her as well. Her eyes were open, glazed. Her mouth was moving.

"Shush, now. We're getting help," Serena told her, tears spilling from her eyes. She was still stunned by what she had learned. Jinx, tiny, shy Jinx, was a cold-blooded murderess who had made several attempts on Serena's life. It was shocking. Serena didn't feel anger, or relief, just a terrible pain in her heart, because it had seemed that Jinx had been in so much anguish, and they hadn't seen it—none of them had.

"Serena..."

Serena moved closer to her.

"Paper, ref..."

"Don't try to talk, Jinx. Help is coming."

She looked at Jinx, wanting her to respond, but the girl had gone still.

"She can't talk anymore, Serena," Liam said quietly. "She's dead."

Chapter 24

Jinx's death unnerved even Joe Penny. He suspended taping while the police went through their paperwork, interviewing cast and crew members once again and anyone who might have been involved with Jinx.

They had long, serious discussions with Jay Braden, since he admitted escorting Jinx a number of places and trying to draw her out of her shell. He said he had worried about her because she had seemed unnerved about everything going on, and he had liked her. He had learned about just how much she knew about all aspects of film and tape, and had tried to encourage her to go further, to get out, to play a few of the Hollywood games and move forward with her career.

Jay seemed earnest.

Serena was so upset herself at first that she didn't realize how badly the death had affected Liam. He was quiet and brooding during the long night that immediately followed Jinx's death; he and Serena wound up being at the police station until very late. When they returned to his house, he stayed up by the fire in the living room. Serena stayed near him. She fell asleep while he remained awake, brooding. He was still there, staring at the fire hours later when the snap of a log woke Serena.

"Liam?" she said softly.

He looked at her at last.

"I know that she killed Jane and that she

threatened your life, and if she had come near to taking it, I could have probably strangled her myself. But she was...sick. I could have gotten that gun from her. I've worked hostage negotiations and attempted suicides. I know I could have talked her down. But I called Hutchens down once I heard her talking. I should have seen this a long time ago. Jinx had access to your private life. She had phone numbers, names. She knew your family, knew what you liked. It was easy for her to get far too close to you. Hell, her house isn't far from yours. It was easy for her to threaten you, to call your house...even to slip into your yard. To watch you."

"She kept saying something about being in love."

"Yeah. So that leads back to Jay.... What was she trying to tell you in those last few seconds?" he asked.

Serena shook her head. "She said the word 'paper.' And something else... I don't know what."

"Was she in love with Jay Braden?" Liam asked.

"She never said."

"If she was that in love with Jay," Liam said, "I don't think he knew it. I just wish that I hadn't called the police."

"She might have killed Bill Hutchens," Serena reminded him.

He nodded. "I could have talked her down," he repeated.

"You need some sleep," she told him.

"Yeah, I guess."

The next day, the phone didn't stop ringing.

Jinx had left nothing. She had spent all her money on her collection of theater memorabilia. When the M.E. finished with her remains, their disposal came up for question.

Serena insisted she would make the arrangements. Jinx had wanted to rise with the stars. She would be buried in the famous old cemetery where Jane Dunne had been laid to rest, and Serena would pay the costs. Joe offered to pitch in; he had, after all, been Jinx's employer. Serena declined, telling Joe that it was something she needed to do.

Serena arranged for a simple Christian ceremony, and three days after she'd been shot, Jinx was given her service and brought to the cemetery.

There were more reporters present than ever, it seemed. They managed to escape them, Jennifer's mother opening her house to the cast and crew of the soap as a place to go to be together and escape the crowds. Olsen and Hutchens were invited as well. Hutchens seemed as sick as Liam about having to kill Jinx, but he'd had little choice when she'd been firing at him. He had been given leave and was seeing the department therapist after what had happened.

The cast talked; they were sad, but they were relieved. Jinx had been crazy; she had admitted to doing everything. She had done horrible things. And now, poor creature, she was dead as well.

Joe asked to speak to them all, tapping a glass to gain their attention. "I had been thinking earlier that I was quite a failure—"

There was a murmur of protest.

"No, no, listen. I thought that my capabilities as a manager and a judge of people were so poor that I should down all my efforts. But then I look around here, and I see all of you. And I know that I have one of the finest ensembles of people ever put together. Talented, professional, caring. I'd like to keep *Valentine Valley* together."

Applause greeted his speech. He smiled with relief.

Hank Newton, the *Valentine Valley* patriarch, stood up.

"I think I should explain to you, too, why Joe was insisting that we'd have to have murder and mayhem on the set for Valentine's Day. I was the one who was going to be killed. I had wanted to retire. But...I think I've changed my mind."

Applause sounded again.

"Hey, what the heck! We'll rewrite again!" Allona said. "We'll bring a mummy back to life—and then murder it!"

Laughter sounded then. And soon after, they were milling among each other again, talking about Jinx, as was natural at a funeral. She had done terrible things.

Most of them had done something terrible, too: They had failed to notice her.

Abby's backyard looked out over the canyons. Serena had come out for a moment's quiet when

Liam approached her. She felt him behind her, though he didn't touch her.

"Well...it's really over now," she said softly. "Jinx is dead and buried." She turned to look at him. "You don't have to watch out for me anymore. Your job is done."

"No, it isn't," he told her.

"Joe isn't paying you anymore."

"I'm still on the job. I still believe Jinx was working with someone. I don't think that it was her idea to try to kill you."

"So...we're going to stay together for now."

"Yeah."

It wasn't quite what Serena had wanted. It would do. For then.

They stood out by the canyon, watching the sunset. When darkness fell, they returned to the house. Both being such close friends of Jennifer and Conar, they stayed until the others had left. Eventually, they stopped talking about death and *Valentine Valley*. The diving trip came up again. "Are you going to come?" Conar asked Serena.

"I haven't been invited," she said.

Liam looked at her. "You're invited. If your busy schedule will allow."

"I can make my busy schedule allow."

He seemed pleased.

That night, when they returned home, they received wonderful news. Sharon was conscious. She had asked that the hospital call Liam. She had read the papers, but she was anxious to see both Liam and Serena.

When they reached her, Sharon was sitting up in her hospital bed. Her hair was brushed, and someone had helped her with makeup. She looked beautiful. Serena waited while Liam went in and kissed her and told her sincerely how grateful he was that she was going to be okay.

"I might have prevented it all," she said, looking toward the door where Serena was still standing. "I—I called. I'd been thinking about Jinx. But you answered the phone and...I was a ninny. And here I am, so sorry about everything..."

"My God!" Serena said. "Don't be sorry! You couldn't have known how far she had gone!"

She had walked into the room. Sharon smiled at her. "We both might have died. I'm very grateful that neither of us did."

"Sharon," Liam asked, "did Jinx tell you about anyone she was seeing?"

Sharon shook her head. "No, I'm afraid not. But she did it all, didn't she? I thought she admitted to every act?"

"She did," Serena assured Sharon.

They sat with her until it was almost time to be on the set. When it was time to go, Liam kissed Sharon. Sharon reached out her arms to Serena, and Serena hugged her tightly as well.

When they left, Serena told Liam that he should reconsider. Sharon Miller was beautiful and far more.

Liam didn't argue.

He looked at her.

"Yeah. She just isn't you."

The next day's filming was great. The entire family appeared. The threat to the family came from a new addition to the cast: an Egyptian furious with Verona's insistence on stealing artifacts from his country. After Verona and David were dug from the tomb and the family had its huge row, they were all held hostage. And despite the protests of Randy Rock, Dale Donovan, and David De-Ville—Jay Braden, Andy Larkin, and Conar Markham—Hank Newton was dragged out by the fanatical patriots holding them all hostage. Originally, they were going to execute him.

Now they were going to beat him, and he was going to escape.

"So who's going to be murdered to live up to our promos?" Serena asked Allona after the third day's taping.

"Heck, I don't know. Maybe we will have to bring in the poor waiter and draw and quarter him in the Arabian desert," Allona said. "Or maybe they liked my idea about raising a mummy and then killing it over again. I don't know. We'll get to it."

Allona left her. Serena sat at her dressing table alone, trying to remember everything that Jinx had said before she died. Jinx had been in love. She had done it all for love....

She sat in front of her dressing table. "Paper," she murmured out loud. "Paper. What *paper* was she talking about. And ref... ref..."

She drew a scratch pad to herself and started writing. "Ref...referee...refuse...refute. Hm." She stared idly across the room. "Refer to..." She paused, frowning, staring at the little white cubicle in her dressing room where she could keep cold drinks. "Refrigerator?"

She jumped up, rushing over, throwing it open. Nothing. Bottles of water, juice, soda. She went down on her knees, placing her hand around the sides and then the roof of the little box. To her amazement, she touched something. She twisted around to look upward. A small scrap of charred paper had been taped there.

Shaking, she carefully pulled it free. It was badly charred, damp, barely legible. There were only pieces of words.

But it had been handwritten.

She glanced at her watch. It was nearly six, but Liam, who, still distrustful, had agreed to leave her at the studio because Olsen had called him down to the station, was coming for her at seven. She knew that Liam didn't think that the danger was over, that they could let up. Olsen, on the other hand, seemed to believe that if anyone had been pushing Jinx, it had been Kyle Amesbury. A man who was dead now as well.

Still, Liam had quit being so continually tense at every turn. And tonight, they were going to eat out. He had said he needed to talk to her, and he had booked a restaurant with quiet booths and low-key music.

She left her dressing room and took the

elevator down to the set. Lights were being switched off; they were done for the day. Jim Novac was walking away.

"Jim—hey! Where's Conar?"

"Gone home."

"Gone?"

"Yeah, he was looking for you, but someone told him that Liam had already picked you up because no one had seen you for a while."

"I was in my dressing room."

"Sorry. Wow. And Conar is kind of pissed off, too."

"Great," she murmured.

"Is anyone still here?"

"I'm here, but I've got to go. Hey, Jay and Jeff have gone over to the tomb set. Jeff wanted to check something out for tomorrow."

Serena thanked Jim, then hesitated a few minutes. She didn't want to be here alone. She went back to her dressing room and tried to call Liam. She didn't reach him. The sergeant on duty jotted down her message that she needed to see him as soon as possible about the "ref" and "paper" and that he should pick her up at the Egyptian set rather than at the studio. Then she ran downstairs, hoping to catch Jim.

She saw his car retreating around the corner. She stood on a street corner, flagging madly for a cab. None stopped. She decided to walk.

There were gates up around the set, but she knew where there was a loose section that she could slip beneath. She swore, dusting off dirt and sand as she crawled under the wire. Her heels were unsteady on the dry, rocky ground as she traveled down the drive to the setup. As she approached the stage tomb, she could hear Jeff talking.

Jay replied.

There were some safety lights on around the set, but it seemed that darkness had fallen, that shadows had followed her right through the fence.

The set appeared very real at night. The sand seemed to be a towering dune, rather than a thin layer thrown over the shell of an old office building about to be completely razed.

"Hey!" she called out.

Coming around the path, through the trailers and the set itself, she came to a sudden, startled halt.

Jay and Jeff were both there.

They both had rifles.

Pointed at her.

Chapter 25

You know, Liam, you're driving this thing into the ground," Olsen said. He sighed. "I wanted you on the case, because you're good. But you know, Kyle Amesbury taped *everything*. There was a camera at the door the night you 'talked' to him. You threatening to kill him is on tape. You could wind up in jail yourself. It's a damned good thing his death was definitely drowning."

"Did you call me down to arrest me? If so, do it quick. I'll get a lawyer and get out of here. I still don't think Serena should be alone."

"Jinx is dead and buried."

"She wasn't working alone."

"You suspected Amesbury yourself. He's dead now, too. Some things, we're getting from the tapes. Some things, we'll never know." He sighed. "Too bad we didn't get some of these earlier. You know, Jinx starred in several of them."

"Can I see a few? That is, if you're not arresting me right now," Liam asked.

Olsen shrugged, and pointed toward a conference room. "Just hit the buttons."

Liam glanced at his watch. He had time. He went into the conference room and started running tape. And there was Jinx.

First, alone, standing in a room. She'd been listening to a voice give her instructions. Amesbury's voice. He was talking like a director. She listened, she obeyed. She objected once, saying she didn't want to be a porn star. "Hey, kid, all the big shots have to do love scenes. If you're going to go this route..."

So she had postured and postulated, and then the tape ended, and another began. Jinx, with a dark-haired man. The man's back remained to the camera. His hairless back.

He heard a door open and close.

"Jay Braden, you think?" Olsen asked.

"I don't know. Sure, I've suspected him. His denials, though, have been fierce. He was protective as hell of her, though."

The door opened again. Liam didn't glance up. "Hey, Bill. I thought you were taking a few days," Olsen said, concern in his gruff voice.

Bill Hutchens was in the room. "Yeah, I'm taking time. You watching this trash again? We should just fast forward the stuff."

"That girl had something going with a man," Olsen said firmly. "I'd like to know who. And who knows if the love was all in her head or real, someone really jerking her chain."

"Your answer is on that tape. Look at her listen to every disgusting word Amesbury says!"

"Could be," Liam murmured.

That tape flickered to an end, another began.

Jinx again. She had really been Amesbury's starring innocent.

Again, the man's back was to them. The room was darker. It was impossible to see his hair color or even make out much about his build.

Or even if his head was completely clean of hair.

"I haven't even had the stomach to sit through all these yet," Olsen said. "There's the last one.... I think that's it. It's amazing she didn't kill Amesbury," Olsen murmured.

"Maybe she did," Liam said. "Look what's coming up."

There was a scene by a pool. Amesbury jeering at the girl, all dressed up in party clothes. Jinx hitting Amesbury.

Amesbury falling in the pool. Begging for his life...

Jinx, frozen, watching.

There was a tap on the door. An officer poked his head in. "Sorry, sir," he told Olsen. "I thought Lieutenant Mur—sorry, again—Mr. Murphy might be in here."

"Right here," Liam said.

"I thought you had gone. There's a guy on the phone for you. Says his name is Oz and that he has something for you."

Liam jumped up, looking at his watch. He had time to run by Oz's studio before picking Serena up from Conar's care at seven.

"Great, thanks."

"There are more tapes—" Olsen began.

"Thanks. I'll check into them later."

Liam departed swiftly, not hearing the sergeant at the desk, who stared at his back, then called his name.

Bill Hutchens, following behind Liam, told the sergeant that Liam was heading out.

"I had a couple of messages for him. Officer Perez just told me he was still here. Think you can catch him?"

"He lit out like a tornado. Maybe I can catch up with him. What have you got for him?"

The sergeant grinned. "Well, first, his buddy Conar said that if he saw him to tell him he was an asshole for not letting him know he'd picked up his girl. Then Miss McCormack called herself. She said to tell him something about having found the 'ref' and the 'paper'— whatever that means. And also, he's supposed to pick her up at the Egyptian set, and not the studio."

"Shit!" Bill said, running his hands through his hair. "Shit! I hope I can catch him."

"Serena! Hey, what's the matter with you?" Jeff called out.

What was the matter with her? *You're pointing a rifle at me—what do you think?* she thought. She held silent. After seeing them, she had turned and run. Thankfully, there were sand-piles everywhere. There were trucks here now as well, big, military vehicles in khaki and green. They stood just off the "tomb" set and were placed to be taped as the trucks that carried the nationalist fanatics who were holding the Valentines hostage. Near the tomb itself were water troughs made to look like outer sarcophagi and standing pieces that the set designers had created to look like the inner coffins. With the scattered props around, it would be a great place for children to play hide-and-seek.

Except that she wasn't a child, and if she were caught, the game would be a deadly one.

She stared at the two of them for a split second, adrenaline racing into her system along with a sense of raw panic.

Then she ran.

She swerved behind a big Styrofoam sar-cophagus, zigged, zagged, and kept running. At last, she flew behind one of the big green army trucks.

"Serena!" Jeff called.

"Where the hell is she?" Jay said.

"You go that way. I'll come around," Jeff said.

Crouched down by the truck, Serena heard Jeff's footsteps coming around toward her. She was shaking, locked into uncertainty. Two of them, one of her. The footsteps were coming closer and closer. Her mind raced. Jeff—had he had something going with *Jinx* that none of them had suspected? Jay—Liam had been wary of him all along.

There was another crunch on the ground, closer to her.

Self-preservation kicked in. She rolled under the truck. She thought that she would leap to her feet on the other side and run again, finding a path behind the prop pieces until...

Until she could reach the street.

Dirt filled her eyes and nostrils but she kept rolling, cleared the truck, and flew to her feet.

She came up right in front of Jay Braden. She couldn't run; he blocked her path. If she turned, he couldn't miss—a bullet would hit her back.

"You!" she accused him, shaking, pointing a finger at him. "You...you...Jinx..."

"Hold it, Serena. What's the matter with you?" Jay demanded, frowning. He slung the rifle over his shoulder and took her by the shoulders. She shook him off, backing away, never taking her eyes from his.

"If you're going to shoot me, do it!"

"Shoot you?" He seemed really incredulous.

"Serena, how long have you been doing this? These aren't real guns—they're props."

She arched a brow, staring at him. Her knees were giving, and at the same time, she felt like a fool.

"You were sleeping with Jane Dunne," she said, still unnerved. "Did you get pissed off at her and write a note about killing her and suggest to Jinx that she should die?"

"Hell, no!"

"Serena, I'm sorry. You've got it all wrong."

It was Jeff who spoke, coming around the side of the truck. He looked weary. "This is still crazy, all of us distrusting one another. Serena, I can tell you this because I've been around sometimes in the studio when you weren't. Jay was kind to Jinx. Yes, he slept with Jane Dunne, and God forgive all of us, but yes, we all hated her. You want to know who slept with her, Serena? Andy, Jay, Joe, half of Hollywood—and as you know, me."

Serena inhaled, caught between Jay and her brother-in-law. They had obviously talked about this before.

"Jane was almost...evil. She started by seducing people, Serena, and then ridiculing them," Jay said ruefully. "I wish I'd been a better man. Or even a smarter man. But I never wrote anything to her, and I sure as hell never plotted to kill anyone."

"I don't think she even wanted me," Jeff said, stuck back on his humiliation and ego. "She wanted to prove to herself that she could have any man—happily married or not."

She stared at Jay. They were both close, and despite their words, she still felt uneasy. Yet she had come this far. "You're still talking about Jane Dunne. *I* was meant to die. Because someone had seduced Jinx! And someone had talked her into murder. Jay..."

"Serena, dammit, I was her friend. I tried to be with her around Amesbury because—because I knew he was doing really bad things. I knew that Jinx was... I don't know, I thought she was delicate, nervous. She told me that there had been someone, but that he had betrayed her. I think that whoever it was also slept with Jane. But whoever it was she had been seeing hurt her badly. I swear, it had never occurred to me that *Jinx* could.... Anyway, this man had needed her, and he used her. She wouldn't tell me who it was, only that she still loved him. She told me that I didn't really know him and certainly not the way that she did. She talked me into taking her to Kyle Amesbury's several times, so I thought that it might have been Kyle Amesbury. Because she said that *he* was going to be there, and it was getting harder for her to see him because he had suddenly turned against her and never wanted to see her at all. I knew that she was hurt, and suffering. I never knew that she was...lethal."

Serena believed him. She turned to Jeff.

He lifted his hands. "Hey, don't look at me. I got caught up in Jane Dunne's web. I never had anything at all going with Jinx."

"Did you write Jane Dunne some kind of

threatening note that might have made her really mad?" Serena demanded.

"I didn't write her any kind of note at all!" Jeff said indignantly.

Headlights suddenly hit them, a car bursting straight through the gate.

"What the hell...?" Jeff said.

"Jesus, someone is coming after *us*!" Jay cried.

"It's Liam, just Liam," Serena murmured, but the way that the car was coming through...

"Bullshit! Liam or not, the driver is trying to hit us!" Jay stated.

"Get behind the truck, or you'll get run over!" Jeff warned, dragging her toward it. Jay lit out for the tomb. The car came to a halt.

It wasn't Liam who stepped from it.

Oz was a magician. He had finally managed to freeze a single frame of the film, and in it, he could see the angle of a man's face.

Liam stared at it for a long moment.

"Recognize anyone?" Oz asked. "I can make it just a shade bigger...."

"Jesus!" Liam breathed.

"You know the guy?" Oz asked.

Liam couldn't answer. He was already on the phone. Sergeant Clooney was on the desk at headquarters. "I need Olsen quickly."

"He's gone, Liam. Sorry. So is Hutchens. He picked up your messages from Conar Markham, and then the one from Serena McCormack, saying you should get her at the Egyptian set. She had found the 'paper' and

411

the 'ref' and something about Conar leaving and being with Jay and Jeff. It's all written down here. Hutchens was going to try to catch up with you, but you were gone so fast—"

Liam had already dropped the phone. "Hey, Liam!" Oz called.

"Call the station. Try again for Olsen," Liam told Oz. "Or Rigger." He was moving as he spoke, thinking quickly. "Have one of them tracked down, insist on one of them, and send them out to the *Valentine Valley* set. Fast."

"But, Liam—" Oz began.

Too late.

But by then, Liam was out the door.

The car came to a screeching halt.

The man who emerged from it was Bill Hutchens. He sounded upset, worried. His gun was already out of his holster, at the ready.

"Serena!" he called, sounding frantic.

"Bill! It's all right!" she called, letting out a sigh of relief and starting to emerge from the barrier of the truck. Jay was already walking out from the tomb, probably heedless of the fact that he was carrying the fake rifle. Bill aimed his gun at Jay.

"Hey!" Serena called. "Bill, no—Jay! Get the rifle down! He'll think—"

A shot rang out. Serena shrieked, certain Jay had been hit. But Jay had fallen to the ground and rolled, shouting out a protest. "Bill! It's a prop—it's gone! See, I've dropped it!"

The prop rifle was lying in the sand.

Bill didn't seem to hear.

"Hey, Bill, no!" Serena cried.

A second shot was fired. Jay rose, scurrying behind a sand dune next to the main set.

"Serena!" Jeff hissed. He grabbed her, dragging her back behind the truck. She couldn't see what was going on anymore.

"Stop! Stop! It's a prop!" she heard Jay shouting.

But another bullet rang out and another.

Jeff had Serena's arm in a death grip. "Jeff!" she protested. "We've got to stop him! He doesn't understand that Jay was just carrying a prop—"

"He's *firing*, Serena. Shit! Maybe the Jinx thing unnerved him completely. Maybe he's gone nuts! We've got to get out of here."

"And let him shoot Jay down?" she demanded.

Before he could answer, another set of headlights illuminated the eerie set. They heard the opening and slamming of a car door and then trampling over the sandy terrain. Scurrying. The sound seemed to come from everywhere.

People...running.

Jay?

Bill?

The headlights created huge, ominous shadows around the trucks and the set pieces. Some shadows tall and lean, some squat, like the trucks.

Footsteps, scurrying, seemed to echo from shadow to shadow.

There was a sudden burst of gunfire. It was returned. The sound seemed deafening.

"Serena!"

This time, it was Liam calling her. Desperately. She started to answer. Jeff clamped his hand over her mouth, shaking his head with panic. "We can't have anyone know where we are!" he whispered. "They're just firing and firing!"

Another shot rang out. Footsteps crunched the ground, coming their way. They froze together.

"Oh, Jesus! Oh, Jesus!" Jeff breathed, holding Serena close.

Suddenly, a figure loomed out of the shadows. Serena opened her mouth to scream; the sound died in her throat.

Liam appeared at the end of the truck.

He had a gun, and it was soundly in his grip, ready to fire.

"Liam!" was all she managed to whisper.

His hand shook for a moment. He came closer. She saw the relief in his eyes, though they seemed almost black in the darkness.

"Stay down!" he commanded softly.

"What the hell is going on?"

"It's Hutchens."

"What?" Serena whispered, incredulous.

"Hutchens, Serena. Hutchens is trying to kill you...all of us now."

"Bill Hutchens?" she repeated incredulously.

"I told you he was firing on purpose!" Jeff hissed. "Liam, he...he might have gotten Jay."

Liam nodded. "Just stay down, both of you!"

They heard another gunshot. Liam sidled around the end of the truck, disappearing from Serena's view. She was sure he hadn't gone far. Time seemed to stretch endlessly.

Only seconds were passing in the sudden dead silence.

"Hey!" Jay called out from the tomb. "Hey, what the hell is this? I didn't do anything! You can't just shoot me."

Liam called out then, distracting Bill, who must have found Jay.

"Bill!" Liam shouted. "What the hell is the matter with you? You can't just shoot him down in cold blood! You have witnesses."

"I'm not leaving any witnesses!" Bill Hutchens cried back.

There was an exchange of gunfire. Then...

Silence. Again, silence, stretching and stretching...

From somewhere out in the shadows and light, the sound of footsteps falling on the sand and gravel came to them again.

Eerie laughter echoed in the night.

"Did I get you, old buddy?"

Jeff stared at Serena with horror and started to move. Terrified that Liam had been hit, Serena clutched Jeff's arm to keep him still and brought a finger to her lips. Taking care to be as silent as possible, she tried rolling under the truck again. She wasn't going to be caught unaware again. She remained under the truck, just inching out, trying to look around as she did so.

A hand fell roughly upon her hair and nape

Her face hit the dirt, then she was dragged to her feet.

She knew before she saw his face that Bill Hutchens had her in his grip.

He pulled her up; then wrenched her back hard against his chest, keeping his fingers vised into her hair.

"Let me go, you asshole bastard!" she cried, tears stinging her eyes, fury mingling with her fear.

"Shut up!" he hissed against her ear. "Just shut up, you bitch. You're about to get your just deserts. The Emmy of all time!"

"Let me—"

She broke off with a cry as he jerked her hair so hard that strands tore from her head.

"Hey! Liam!" he shouted out loudly. "You know, Liam, you were a buddy. I never wanted you hurt. Hell, I meant to help you. Jane was just a bitch, seducing men and discarding them in a single night. If she had died in the accident I suggested to Jinx—well, no big deal. But this one...the queen! Miss Serena McCormack! She makes you fall in love. She makes you see all the promise in the future. She's kind, she's nice—she gets you jobs as an extra in the movies. But that's just it. You're always an extra in her life. A bit player. I was there when you walked away. I was ready to be everything that she ever wanted. Except that she didn't want me. You should have been grateful that I was getting her out of your world as well! And you!" He wrenched on Serena's hair again so hard that involuntary tears stung her eyes. "I might have had you that night at your house when Jinxy made all those phone calls, thinking she was doing me a favor. Stupid girl. Without her, I could have gone back in. I had your key. She'd copied it for me. Slipped it right out of your purse and copied it for me. I could have gotten into your house without a soul knowing...and ended it all right there. But there you were, screaming your head off, running around.... Jinx was stupid that night. I had such an opportunity. But then, Ricardo was there, and Liam. Damn you, Liam!" he shouted suddenly and loudly. "You left the force, but hell, you're just the conquering hero, huh? When the cops can't find the answer, bring back Murphy. Hell, he's the best we ever had! Well, now, you are leaving the force for good. Come out right now, or I swear, I'll blow her brains out!"

His gun was suddenly against Serena's temple. She could feel the cold steel. The circle of the muzzle, pressing into her flesh. Her mouth went dry. She could almost feel the heat of the bullet that could, at any second, tear through flesh and bone and end her life....

He was trying to make Liam come out in the open. He had to kill Liam, and the others, to get away with this.

Despite her fear, she bit the hand over her mouth.

"No, Liam—"

Bill howled, but clamped his hand over her

mouth again so swiftly he nearly smothered her then and there.

But Liam had already appeared. He came walking out from the tomb area—a casual stride, almost as if they were meeting for lunch.

"You missed Braden, Bill, you know. Jay is alive and well."

"I won't miss when I fire next time."

"Jeff is out here, too."

"He'll be like hunting down a wounded doe."

"How will you explain the fact that we're all dead?"

"Easy. Everyone will believe that Jay, not Kyle Amesbury, was the man who goaded Jinx into her evil deeds. It all blew up out here tonight. I was trying to save Serena. Sadly, I failed, and you all died in the cross fire. Naturally, I'll kill the others with your gun."

"Who's going to believe that kind of shit?"

"Hey, this is Hollywood. All kinds of shit happen here. But don't worry. You won't be around to find out if it did or didn't work. You know, though, actually, I never wanted you in on this. Olsen insisted."

"When the hell did you go so bad?"

"When? Gradually, Liam. Really gradually. A little money here for a little thing.... It's not easy watching a bunch of assholes get rich because they're pretty boys. Then, suddenly, you begin to realize just how much power you do have."

"You're a fool. Jinx was in love with you."

"Oh, yeah, really in love. So much so that she lured me into Kyle's great porno flicks! But I knew the cameras were there. He black-mailed me, of course, even though I didn't think the tapes were that dangerous. But you knew, huh? You just found out recently, I assume, or you'd have been to Olsen or Rigger in a flash."

"I'm here," Liam said. "And you have to take me first. You know I won't go down easy. Let Serena go."

"Not on your life. Serena, you found what was left of that valentine I had sent Jane, didn't you? That's what little Jinx was whispering when she died. Funny thing—we never meant to kill Jane. But what the hell? She deserved it. But now, the paper...it could make me look bad. You see, Jinx wasn't all there. Well, you all know that. She was so... desperate. I gave her the suggestion long before she carried it out. So I was just pissed as hell with Jane...and she winds up dead when it was Serena I wanted dead. Serena, who just wouldn't take me seriously. I had to show her just where the real power was. The stupid paper! Jinx told me she'd gotten rid of it. But she hid it. She was crazy as a loon, but not stupid. So...where is the paper now? Um. I'm willing to bet Serena has it on her. She would give it to you first, Liam. But now...I'll find it."

"Bill, I'll give you the paper," Serena said quietly, watching Liam and desperately trying to remain as calm as he appeared to be. "You are surely hidden in the tapes. And if no one has the paper, you're in the clear. You weren't involved—" Serena said.

"Oh, no, I need to clean it all up. Jinx never meant to go down without me. Such a little fool. Who would have ever thought *she'd* be the one to get obsessed with me? She thought I should be there, just for her. I guess Jinx and I were both obsessed. We loved the movies... TV...fame. Look what's it all come to? Well, I will be the only one around to watch the miniseries. No more explanations."

"Oh, yeah, there will be explanations. Oz Davis has cleaned up one of those tapes, Bill. And your back...your clean-shaven back is in those tapes. You thought looking like a movie star could make you into one."

"I'll get that damned tape!" Bill swore. "You think you can always come out heads up, eh, Liam. Not this time. Conquering-hero type, it's time to die."

Hutchens removed the gun from Serena's temple. He started to aim straight at Liam's heart.

In raw panic, Serena slammed her elbow against his ribs, sobs escaping her.

Little good this can do! Serena thought.

But God knew, maybe it did help. It threw Bill's aim off a hair.

Liam secured the gun he had tucked into the back of his waistband.

Both men fired simultaneously. Serena screamed.

Bill fell to the earth, the impetus of his

weight bearing her down with him. She struggled against him; he was no longer holding her.

She stared into his face. His eyes were open.

There was a bullet hole dead center in his forehead.

She gaped at it, smelling the powder, horrified, yet marveling at the precision. She had never known that Liam was such a perfect shot.

Bill was dead. He was still staring at her. She choked, gasping, still desperate to get away from the entangling limbs of the man who had meant to kill them all.

Liam was there then, beside her, pulling her from the dead man's hold and into his arms.

He had never held her more tightly—or thrust her away more quickly, black eyes searching her thoroughly. "Are you all right?"

"Yes, yes, and you—"

She was already crushed back against him. "Dammit, I love you, Serena," he said softly.

They could hear the sound of sirens in the night. Jeff, coming around the back of the truck, pale as the sand, said, "The cops are coming!" He cried, "The *good* cops, I think."

"Olsen or Rigger," Liam murmured, still staring at Serena. "It took them long enough. But I was afraid if Oz didn't reach one of them, Bill could have fooled the other officers." He touched Serena's cheek. "We have another night at the police station," Liam said softly. "And I know how you feel about cops, and after this..."

"I love cops," she said softly. "Especially the

good cops. The conquering-hero types." She tried to speak lightly. Her knees were buckling. Without his support, she would have fallen.

Many times, she realized.

Epilogue

The papers were once again full of news about *Valentine Valley*.

And the cop who had wanted to soar to the heavens with stars and fallen to the earth like Icarus instead.

Once again, Liam was deeply troubled, as were many people Serena had come to love and trust. Serena told Olsen over and over again that she felt with all her heart that most policemen were wonderful public servants, risking their lives for civilians. It was only every once in a while when you came upon a...

Bill Hutchens.

At one point, she couldn't help but tell Liam, "There are good people, and bad people, in every sex, race, religion—and every line of work out there. Bill doesn't give a bad name to every cop, any more than Jinx...than Jinx's life implies that every actor or movie worker is crazy."

"I know that," he told her. "It's just...God! I trusted him not only with my own life, but with yours. And I should have known, I should have seen some kind of sign...."

"You discovered the truth in time to save my life again," she told him softly.

And he smiled at last, looking at her. "And you might have saved mine. You acted quickly enough. How did you know I had a gun?"

"I didn't. I just knew that he was going to shoot you. And I love you."

He nodded.

It was dawn. They didn't talk any longer then. They went to his house, and showered, and made love, glad to be alive.

The next days were chaotic. Liam spent a number of them at the police station. So did Serena. Then she fielded a dozen calls and carefully granted interviews.

Days passed and Joe Penny rallied, and they filmed their Valentine's Day segment. Hank Newton, as the Valentine family patriarch, was nearly murdered—the terrorist extra was killed instead, and it was David DeVille who saved him, deflecting the bullet, adding a layer to the story line now that a Valentine owed his life to the son of his greatest rival.

Valentine's Day arrived for real.

The ratings had never been higher.

Liam told Serena that he wasn't buying her flowers. He left early, once again going to the police station, finishing up some business. Serena sat down and watched her own soap. She liked the way it played.

In the early afternoon, she met Liam. He was grim, but ready to go.

"Are we really done with this yet?" she asked him.

"I think so. Come on. We have a great dinner reservation for tonight. It's a very cozy little place. We can go and have some privacy in a dark booth."

"It sounds great, except..." Serena was surprised herself when she said, "Liam, stop by the cemetery please."

"The cemetery?"

"Yeah. I just want to see...Jinx."

He thought she was crazy, she knew, but he stopped for her to buy flowers, and when they came to the famous old place, he helped her hop the small wall, since the gates had been closed earlier.

"If we get arrested..." he said. "Oh, what the hell."

They came to Jinx's grave. Serena knelt and said her little prayer. When she rose, Liam, still looking somewhat weary, his black hair tousled and his jacket thrown over his shoulder, was watching her. She walked over to him.

"You know, I really do love you."

"I love you, too. You know that. I've always loved you."

"But you left me."

"I wanted to matter."

"You always mattered."

"Maybe I was a little jealous, too."

"Maybe I should think before I do things," she murmured. She touched his cheek with her knuckles.

"It is Valentine's Day."

"I know that. And I told you, I didn't think that it was the right year for flowers—"

"I don't want flowers. I...I don't understand why you just won't marry me," she told him.

He studied her gravely.

"I thought you'd never ask," he told her.

She frowned.

"Does that mean that you are asking me to marry you?" she inquired.

"I thought you just asked me?"

"You're supposed to do the asking."

"Oh. Well, then...will you marry me?"

"Since you're so eloquent..."

She was startled when he took her hand and fell on a knee, a wry smile on his features. "Miss McCormack, will you marry me? We're opposites in a hundred thousand ways, but I've discovered that what's good in life is only good when you're a part of it, and that what's difficult is easier just because you're beside me. I'd rather face any misery in life—"

"Are you calling me a misery?"

"Will you please shut up for just a moment? I'm doing my very best to be eloquent. Where was I? Yes, I'd rather face anything in life with you. I want to wake up every morning with you by my side, to see your face again and again—"

"That is eloquent," she said softly.

"Can I get off my knees now?"

"I don't know. I rather like you there."

He rose, smiling. He cupped her cheeks, kissed her lips. "It's a very beautiful face."

"I'm older than you, you know."

"Serena, if you were eighty, I'd love you."

"What a liar!"

"All right, well, eighty might be pushing it."

She smiled thoughtfully, feeling the sun and his touch upon her.

"You didn't answer me, you know," he told her.

"Well, I didn't know it was necessary, since I rather prodded you into asking the question."

"I asked the question. I had intended to talk seriously about our lives and ask you to marry me at dinner. We didn't make dinner. So now you're supposed to say 'Yes, oh yes, I'll marry you, Liam, because I can't live without you.'"

"Yes, I will marry you, because I can't imagine life without you again. I don't ever want to face life without you again. I love you with my whole heart. And besides, I want our child to have his father."

He paled at that. A little hopefully, she thought. "We're...having a child?"

"Well, not at this moment, no, but we can't mess around too long. You are marrying an older woman. I mean, you don't mind, do you? I rather got the impression you liked children—"

"Serena, we'll have a dozen if you want."

"Two was the actual number I had in mind."

"Two," he agreed. "We should go to the restaurant. I mean, I'd never actually envisioned proposing in a cemetery."

"We've let the past rest," she told him, "and made a new beginning."

He nodded. "But it's time to leave the dead and start with living. Let's go to dinner."

"Liam, tonight I'd rather go to your house.'

She smiled thoughtfully, feeling the sun and his touch upon her.

"You didn't answer me, you know," he told her.

"Well, I didn't know it was necessary, since I rather prodded you into asking the question."

"I asked the question. I had intended to talk seriously about our lives and ask you to marry me at dinner. We didn't make dinner. So now you're supposed to say 'Yes, oh yes, I'll marry you, Liam, because I can't live without you.'"

"Yes, I will marry you, because I can't imagine life without you again. I don't ever want to face life without you again. I love you with my whole heart. And besides, I want our child to have his father."

He paled at that. A little hopefully, she thought. "We're...having a child?"

"Well, not at this moment, no, but we can't mess around too long. You are marrying an older woman. I mean, you don't mind, do you? I rather got the impression you liked children—"

"Serena, we'll have a dozen if you want."

"Two was the actual number I had in mind."

"Two," he agreed. "We should go to the restaurant. I mean, I'd never actually envisioned proposing in a cemetery."

"We've let the past rest," she told him, "and made a new beginning."

He nodded. "But it's time to leave the dead and start with living. Let's go to dinner."

"Liam, tonight I'd rather go to your house."

"My house?"

"I was thinking about...well, if we're going to have two children, perhaps this might be the time to start practicing for the first..."

"Practicing?" he inquired politely.

"Well, you know, working toward such a goal."

"My house it is," he said softly.

"One moment," she murmured, and she paused, kneeling down to arrange the flowers she had stopped to buy on Jinx's grave.

None of them would live forever. Jinx had taught her to be grateful for every moment she had ahead.

The roses lay prettily arranged upon the earth. Oddly enough, Serena knew that Jinx would have liked them there.

Liam helped her to her feet.

And hand in hand, they walked from the graveyard and back to the streets of the city that was teeming with life.